D0035591

"THE KIND OF IMAGINATION THAT MAKES SCIENCE FICTION WORTH READING...

an effective, affecting story . . . a thrilling climax and a moving finale."

—*Galaxy Magazine*

"It's the Wild West in outer space, complete with a chase that will keep you awake. Slick science fiction."

—*Los Angeles Times*

"George R.R. Martin has the voice of the poet and a mind like a steel trap."

—*Algis Budrys*

"Even in the best science-fiction stories, it is rare to find a genuinely alien culture that is believable and self-consistent. George R.R. Martin's novel presents several such cultures, and forces them into conflicts that bring out the best—and the worst—in the human characters who make this story live, and breathe, and bleed."

—Ben Bova, editor of *Analog Magazine*

SELECTED BY
SCIENCE FICTION BOOK CLUB

More . . .

DYING OF THE LIGHT

by George R.R. Martin

PUBLISHED BY POCKET BOOKS NEW YORK

POCKET BOOKS, a Simon & Schuster division of
GULF & WESTERN CORPORATION
1230 Avenue of the Americas, New York, N.Y. 10020

ISBN: 0-671-81130-4

First Pocket Books printing October, 1978

Trademarks registered in the United States and other countries.

Printed in the U.S.A.

for Rachel,
who loved me once

DYING OF THE LIGHT

PROLOGUE

A rogue, an aimless wanderer, creation's castaway; this world was all those things.

For uncounted centuries it had been falling, alone, without purpose, falling through the cold lonely places between the suns. Generations of stars had succeeded each other in stately sweeps across its barren skies. It belonged to none of them. It was a world in and of itself, entire. In a sense it was not even part of the galaxy; its tumbling path cut through the galactic plane like a nail driven through a round wooden tabletop. It was part of nothing.

And *nothing* was very close at hand. In the dawn of human history, the rogue world pierced a curtain of interstellar dust that covered a trifling small area near the up-edge of the galaxy's great lens. A handful of stars lay beyond—thirty or so, a mere handful. Then emptiness, a night greater than any the wandering world had known.

There, falling through that shadowed border region, it met the shattered people.

The Earth Imperials found it first, at the height of their giddy, drunken expansion, when the Federal Empire of Old Earth was still trying to rule all the worlds of humanity across immense impossible gulfs. A warship named the *Mao Tse-tung,* crippled during a raid on the Hrangans, its crew dead at their stations, its engines alternately shifting into drive and out again, became the first ship of the manrealm to drift beyond the Tempter's Veil. The *Mao* was a derelict, airless and full of grotesque corpses that bobbed aimlessly through its corridors and brushed against its bulkheads every century or so; but its computers still functioned, cycling blindly through their rituals, scanning well enough to note the nameless rogue planet on their charts when the ghost ship emerged from drive within a few light-minutes of it. Almost seven centuries later a trader out of Tober stumbled on the *Mao Tse-tung,* and that notation.

By then it was no news; the world had been found again.

Celia Marcyan was the second discoverer. Her *Shadow Chaser* circled the dark planet for a standard day, during the generation of interregnum that followed the Collapse. But the rogue had nothing for Celia, only rock and ice and never-ending night, so it was not long until she went on her way. She was a namer, however, and before she left she gave the world a name. Worlorn she called it, and never said why or what it meant, and Worlorn it was. And Celia moved on to other worlds and other stories.

Kleronomas was the next visitor, in ai-46. His survey ship made a few brief passes and mapped the wastes. The planet yielded up its secrets to his sensors; it was larger and richer than most, he discovered, with frozen oceans and frozen atmosphere, waiting for release.

Some say that Tomo and Walberg were the first to land on Worlorn, in ai-97, on their madman's quest to cross the galaxy. True? Probably not. Every world in the manrealm has a story of Tomo and Walberg, but the *Dreaming Whore* never returned, so who can know where it landed?

The later sightings had more of fact about them and less of legend. Starless and useless and only marginally interesting, Worlorn became a common notation on the starcharts of the Fringe, that scattering of thinly settled worlds between the smoke-dark gases of the Tempter's Veil and the Great Black Sea itself.

Then, in ai-446, an astronomer on Wolfheim made Worlorn the subject of his studies, and for the very first time someone bothered to string all the coordinates together. That was when things changed. The name of the Wolfman astronomer was Ingo Haapala, and he emerged from his computer room wildly excited, the way Wolfmen often get. For Worlorn was to have a day—a long bright day.

The constellation called the Wheel of Fire burned in every outworld sky; the wonder of it was notorious as far inward as Old Earth. The center of the formation was the red supergiant, the Hub, the Helleye, Fat Satan—it had a dozen names. In orbit around it, equidistant, arrayed neatly like six marbles of yellow flame rolling around a single groove, were the others: the Trojan Suns, Satan's Children, the Hellcrown. The names did not matter. What mattered was the Wheel itself, six medium-sized yellow stars doing homage to their vast red master, at once the most unlikely and stable multiple-star system yet discovered. The Wheel was a seven-day sensation, a new mystery for a humanity jaded on the old mysteries. On the more civilized worlds, scientists put forth theories to explain it; beyond the Tempter's Veil, a cult grew up around it, and men and women spoke of a vanished race of stellar engineers who had moved whole suns to build themselves a monument. Scientific speculation and superstitious worship both waxed feverish for a few decades and then began to wane; very shortly the matter was forgotten.

The Wolfman Haapala announced that Worlorn would sweep around the Wheel of Fire once, in a wide slow hyperbola, never entering the system proper but coming close enough. Fifty standard years of sunlight; then out again into the darkness of the Fringe, past the

Last Stars, into the Great Black Sea of intergalactic emptiness.

Those were the restless centuries, when High Kavalaan and the other outworlds were tasting their first pride and growing anxious to find a place in the shattered histories of humanity. And everyone knows what happened. The Wheel of Fire had always been the glory of the outworlds, but it had been a planetless glory, until now.

There was a century of storms as Worlorn neared the light: years of melting ice and volcanic activity and earthquakes. A frozen atmosphere came, bit by bit, to life, and hideous winds howled like monster infants. All this the outworlders faced and fought.

The terraformers came from Tober-in-the-Veil, the weather wardens from Darkdawn, and there were other teams from Wolfheim and Kimdiss and ai-Emerel and the World of the Blackwine Ocean. The men of High Kavalaan supervised it all, since High Kavalaan claimed the rogue. The struggle took more than a century, and those who died are still half-myth to the children of the Fringe. But at last Worlorn was gentled. Then cities rose, and strange forests flowered beneath the light of the Wheel, and animals were set loose to give the planet life.

In ai-589 the Festival of the Fringe opened, with Fat Satan filling a quarter of the sky and his children bright around him. On that first day the Toberians let their stratoshield shimmer, so the clouds and the sunlight ran and swirled in kaleidoscope patterns. Other days followed, and the ships came. From all the outworlds, and from worlds beyond, from Tara and Daronne on the other side of the Veil, from Avalon and Jamison's World, from places as distant as Newholme and Old Poseidon and even Old Earth itself. For five standard years Worlorn moved toward perihelion; for five it moved away. In ai-599 the Festival closed.

Worlorn entered twilight, and fell toward night.

chapter 1

Beyond the window, water slapped against the pilings of the wooden sidewalk along the canal. Dirk t'Larien looked up and saw a low black barge drift slowly past in the moonlight. A solitary figure stood at the stern, leaning on a thin dark pole. Everything was etched quite clearly, for Braque's moon was riding overhead, big as a fist and very bright.

Behind it was a stillness and a smoky darkness, an unmoving curtain that hid the farther stars. A cloud of dust and gas, he thought. The Tempter's Veil.

The beginning came long after the end: a whisper-jewel.

It was wrapped in layers of silver foil and soft dark velvet, just as he had given it to her years before. He undid its package that night, sitting by the window of his room that overlooked the wide scummy canal where merchants poled fruit barges endlessly up and down. The gem was just as Dirk recalled it: a deep red, laced with thin black lines, shaped like a tear. He remembered the day the esper had cut it for them, back on Avalon.

After a long time he touched it.

It was smooth and very cold against the tip of his finger, and deep within his brain it whispered. Memories and promises that he had not forgotten.

He was here on Braque for no particular reason, and he never knew how they found him. But they did, and Dirk t'Larien got his jewel back.

"Gwen," he said quietly, all to himself, just to shape the word again and feel the familiar warmth on his tongue. His Jenny, his Guinevere, mistress of abandoned dreams.

It had been seven standard years, he thought, while his finger stroked the cold, cold jewel. But it felt like seven lifetimes. And everything was over. What could she want of him now? The man who had loved her, that *other* Dirk t'Larien, that maker-of-promises and giver-of-jewels was a dead man.

Dirk lifted his hand to brush a spray of gray-brown hair back out of his eyes. And suddenly, not meaning to, he remembered how Gwen would brush his hair away whenever she meant to kiss him.

He felt very tired then, and very lost. His carefully nurtured cynicism trembled, and a weight fell upon his shoulders, a ghost weight, the heaviness of the person he had been once and no longer was. He had indeed changed over the years, and he had called it growing wise, but now all that wisdom abruptly seemed to sour. His wandering thoughts lingered on all the promises he had broken, the dreams he had postponed and then mislaid, the ideals compromised, the shining future lost to tedium and rot.

Why did she make him remember? Too much time had passed, too much had happened to him—probably to both of them. Besides, he had never really meant for her to use the whisperjewel. It had been a stupid gesture, the adolescent posturing of a young romantic. No reasonable adult would hold him to such an absurd pledge. He could not go, of course. He had hardly had time to see Braque yet, he had his own life, he had important things to do. After all this time,

Gwen could not possibly expect him to ship off to the outworlds.

Resentful, he reached out and took the jewel in his palm, and his fist closed hard around the smallness of it. He would toss it through the window, he decided, out into the dark waters of the canal, out and away with everything that it meant. But once within his fist, the gem was an ice inferno, and the memories were knives.

. . . *because she needs you,* the jewel whispered. *Because you promised.*

His hand did not move. His fist stayed closed. The cold against his palm passed beyond pain, into numbness.

That other Dirk, the younger one, Gwen's Dirk. He *had* promised. But so had she, he remembered. Long ago on Avalon. The old esper, a wizened Emereli with a very minor Talent and red-gold hair, had cut two jewels. He had read Dirk t'Larien, had felt all the love Dirk had for his Jenny, and then had put as much of that into the gem as his poor psionic powers allowed him to. Later, he had done the same for Gwen. Then they had traded jewels.

It had been his idea. *It may not always be so,* he had told her, quoting an ancient poem. So they had promised, both of them: Send this memory, and I will come. No matter where I am, or when, or what has passed between us. I will come, and there will be no questions.

But it was a shattered promise. Six months after she had left him, Dirk had sent her the jewel. She had not come. After that, he could never have expected her to invoke *his* promise. Yet now she had.

Did she really expect him to come?

And he knew, with sadness, that the man he had been back then, *that* man would come to her, no matter what, no matter how much he might hate her —or love her. But that fool was long buried. Time and Gwen had killed him.

But he still listened to the jewel and felt his old

feelings and his new weariness. And finally he looked up and thought, Well, perhaps it is not too late after all.

There are many ways to move between the stars, and some of them are faster than light and some are not, and all of them are *slow*. It takes most of a man's lifetime to ship from one end of the manrealm to the other, and the manrealm—the scattered worlds of humanity and the greater emptiness in between—is the very smallest part of the galaxy. But Braque was close to the Veil, and the outworlds beyond, and there was some trade back and forth, so Dirk could find a ship.

It was named the *Shuddering of Forgotten Enemies,* and it went from Braque to Tara and then through the Veil to Wolfheim and then to Kimdiss and finally to Worlorn, and the voyage, even by ftl drive, took more than three months standard. After Worlorn, Dirk knew, the *Shuddering* would move on, to High Kavalaan and ai-Emerel and the Last Stars, before it turned and began to retrace its tedious route.

The spacefield had been built to handle twenty ships a day; now it handled perhaps one a month. The greater part of it was shut, dark, abandoned. The *Shuddering* set down in the middle of a small portion that still functioned, dwarfing a nearby cluster of private ships and a partially dismantled Toberian freighter.

A section of the vast terminal, automated and yet lifeless, was still brightly lit, but Dirk moved through it quickly, out into the night, an empty outworld night that cried for want of stars. They were there, waiting for him, just beyond the main doors, more or less as he had expected. The captain of the *Shuddering* had lasered on ahead as soon as the ship emerged from drive into normal space.

Gwen Delvano had come to meet him, then, as he had asked her to. But she had not come alone. Gwen and the man she had brought with her were talking to each other in low, careful voices when he emerged from the terminal.

Dirk stopped just past the door, smiled as easily as he could manage, and dropped the single light bag he carried. "Hey," he said softly. "I hear there's a Festival going on."

She had turned at the sound of his voice, and now she laughed, a so-well-remembered laugh. "No," she said. "You're about ten years too late."

Dirk scowled and shook his head. "Hell," he said. Then he smiled again, and she came to him, and they embraced. The other man, the stranger, stood and watched without a trace of self-consciousness.

It was a short hug. No sooner had Dirk wrapped his arms about her than Gwen pulled back. After the break they stood very close, and each looked to see what the years had done.

She was older but much the same, and what changes he saw were probably only defects in his memory. Her wide green eyes were not quite as wide or green as he remembered them, and she was a little taller than he recalled and perhaps a bit heavier. But she was close enough; she smiled the same way, and her hair was the same, fine and dark, falling past her shoulders in a shimmering stream blacker than an outworld night. She wore a white turtleneck pullover and belted pants of sturdy chameleon cloth, faded to night-black now, and a thick headband, as she had liked to dress on Avalon. Now she wore a bracelet too, and that was new. Or perhaps the proper word was armlet. It was a massive thing, cool silver set with jade, that covered half her left forearm. The sleeve of her pullover was rolled back to display it.

"You're thinner, Dirk," she said.

He shrugged and thrust his hands into his jacket pockets. "Yes," he said. In truth, he was almost gaunt, though still a little round-shouldered from slouching too much. The years had aged him in other ways as well; now his hair had more gray than brown, when once it had been the other way around, and he wore it nearly as long as Gwen, though his was a mass of curls and tangles.

"A long time," Gwen said.

"Seven years, standard," he replied nodding. "I didn't think that . . ."

The other man, the waiting stranger, coughed then, as if to remind them that they were not alone. Dirk glanced up, and Gwen turned. The man came forward and bowed politely. Short and chubby and very blond—his hair looked almost white—he wore a brightly colored silkeen suit, all green and yellow, and a tiny black knit cap that stayed in place despite his bow.

"Arkin Ruark," he said to Dirk.

"Dirk t'Larien."

"Arkin is working with me on the project," Gwen said.

"Project?"

She blinked. "Don't you even know why I'm here?"

He didn't. The whisperjewel had been sent from Worlorn, so he had known not much else than where to find her. "You're an ecologist," he said. "On Avalon . . ."

"Yes. At the Institute. A long time ago. I finished there, got my credentials, and I've been on High Kavalaan since. Until I was sent here."

"Gwen is with the Ironjade Gathering," Ruark said. He had a small, tight smile on his face. "Me, I'm representing Impril City Academy. Kimdiss. You know?"

Dirk nodded. Ruark was a Kimdissi then, an outworlder, from one of their universities.

"Impril and Ironjade, well, after the same thing, you know? Research on ecological interaction on Worlorn. Never really done properly during the Festival, the outworlds not being so strong on ecology, none of them. A science ai-forgotten, as the Emereli say. But that's the project. Gwen and I knew each other from before, so we thought, well, here for the same reason, so it is good sense to work together and learn what we can learn."

"I suppose," Dirk said. He was not really overly interested in the project just then. He wanted to talk to Gwen. He looked at her. "You'll have to tell me all about it later. When we talk. I imagine you want to talk."

She gave him an odd look. "Yes, of course. We do have a lot to talk about."

He picked up his bag. "Where to?" he asked. "I could probably do with a bath and some food."

Gwen exchanged glances with Ruark. "Arkin and I were just talking about that. He can put you up. We're in the same building. Only a few floors apart."

Ruark nodded. "Gladly, gladly. Pleasure in doing for friends, and both of us are friend to Gwen, are we not?"

"Uh," said Dirk. "I thought, somehow, that I would stay with you, Gwen."

She could not look at him for a time. She looked at Ruark, at the ground, at the black night sky, before her eyes finally found his. "Perhaps," she said, not smiling now, her voice careful. "But not right now. I don't think it would be best, not immediately. But we'll go home, of course. We have a car."

"This way," Ruark put in, before Dirk could frame his words. Something was very strange. He had played through the reunion scene a hundred times on board the *Shuddering* during the months of his voyage, and sometimes he had imagined it tender and loving, and sometimes it had been an angry confrontation, and often it had been tearful—but it had never been quite like this, awkward and at odd angles, with a stranger present throughout it all. He began to wonder exactly who Arkin Ruark was, and whether his relationship with Gwen was quite what they said it was. But then, they had hardly said anything. Without knowing what to say or to think, he shrugged and followed as they led him to their aircar.

The walk was quite short. The car, when they

reached it, took Dirk aback. He had seen a lot of different types of aircars in his travels, but none quite like this one; huge and steel-gray, with curved and muscled triangular wings, it looked almost alive, like a great aerial manta ray fashioned in metal. A small cockpit with four seats was set between the wings, and beneath the wingtips he glimpsed ominous rods.

He looked at Gwen and pointed. "Are those lasers?"

She nodded, smiling just a little.

"What the hell are you flying?" Dirk asked. "It looks like a war machine. Are we going to be assaulted by Hrangans? I haven't seen anything like that since we toured the Institute museums back on Avalon."

Gwen laughed, took his bag from him, and tossed it into the back seat. "Get in," she told him. "It is a perfectly fine aircar of High Kavalaan manufacture. They've only recently started turning out their own. It's supposed to look like an animal, the black banshee. A flying predator, also the brother-beast of the Iron-jade Gathering. Very big in their folklore, sort of a totem."

She climbed in, behind the stick, and Ruark followed a bit awkwardly, vaulting over the armored wing into the back. Dirk did not move. "But it has *lasers!*" he insisted.

Gwen sighed. "They're not charged, and never have been. Every car built on High Kavalaan has weapons of some sort. The culture demands it. And I don't mean just Ironjade's. Redsteel, Braith, and the Shanagate Holding are all the same."

Dirk walked around the car and climbed in next to Gwen, but his face was blank. "What?"

"Those are the four Kavalar holdfast-coalitions," she explained. "Think of them as small nations, or big families. They're a little of both."

"But why the lasers?"

"High Kavalaan is a violent planet," Gwen replied.

Ruark gave a snort of laughter. "Ah, Gwen," he said. "That is utter wrong, *utter!*"

"Wrong?" she snapped.

"Very," Ruark said. "Yes, utter, because you are close to truth, half and not everything, worst lie of all."

Dirk turned in his seat to look back at the chubby blond Kimdissi. "What?"

"High Kavalaan *was* a violent planet, truth. But *now,* truth is, the violence is the Kavalars. Hostile folk, each and every among them, xenophobes often, racists. Proud and jealous. With their highwars and their code duello, yes, and *that* is why Kavalar cars have guns. To fight with, in the air! I warn you, t'Larien—"

"Arkin!" Gwen said between her teeth, and Dirk started at the edged malice in her tone. She threw on the gravity grid suddenly, touched the stick, and the aircar wrenched forward and left the ground with a whine of protest, rising rapidly. The port below them was bright with light where the *Shuddering of Forgotten Enemies* stood among the lesser starships, shadowy everywhere else. Around it was darkness to the unseen horizon where black ground blended with blacker sky. Only a thin powder of stars lit the night above. This was the Fringe, with intergalactic space above and the dusky curtain of the Tempter's Veil below, and the world seemed lonelier than Dirk had ever imagined.

Ruark had subsided, muttering, and a heavy silence lay over the car for a long moment.

"Arkin is from Kimdiss," Gwen said finally, and she forced a chuckle. Dirk remembered her too well to be fooled, however; she was not one bit less tense than when she had snapped at Ruark a moment before.

"I don't understand," Dirk said, feeling quite stupid, since everyone seemed to think he should.

"You are no outworlder," Ruark said. "Avalon, Baldur, whatever world, it doesn't matter. Your people inside the Veil don't know Kavalars."

"Or Kimdissi," Gwen said, a little more calmly.

Ruark grunted. "A sarcasm," he told Dirk. "Kimdissi and Kavalars, well, we don't get on, you know?

So Gwen is telling you I'm all prejudiced and not to believe me."

"Yes, Arkin," she said. "Dirk, he doesn't know High Kavalaan, doesn't understand the culture or the people. Like all Kimdissi, he'll tell you only the worst, but everything is more complex than he would credit. So remember that when this glib scoundrel starts working on you. It should be easy. In the old days, you were always telling me that every question has thirty sides."

Dirk laughed. "Fair enough," he said, "and true. Although these last few years I've begun to think that thirty is a bit low. I still don't understand what this is all about, however. Take the car—does it come with your job? Or do you have to fly something like this just because you work for the Ironjade Gathering?"

"Ah," Ruark said loudly. "You do not work for the Ironjade Gathering, Dirk. No, you are of them, you are not—two choices only. You are not *of* Ironjade, you do not work for Ironjade!"

"Yes," said Gwen, the edge returning to her voice. "And I am *of* Ironjade. I wish you'd remember that, Arkin. Sometimes you begin to annoy me."

"Gwen, Gwen," Ruark said, sounding very flustered. "You are a friend, a soulmate, very. We have tussled great problems, us two. I would never offend, do not mean to. You are *not* a Kavalar though, never. For one, you are too much a woman, a true woman, not merely an *eyn-kethi* nor a *betheyn*."

"No? I'm not? I wear the bond of jade-and-silver, though." She glanced toward Dirk and lowered her voice. "For Jaan," she said. "This is really his car, and that's why I fly it, to answer your original question. For Jaan."

Silence. The wind was the only noise, moving around them as they fell upward into blackness, tossing Gwen's long straight hair and Dirk's tangles. It knifed right through his thin Braqui clothing. He wondered briefly why the aircar had no bubble canopy, only a thin windscreen that was hardly any use at all.

Then he folded his arms tight against his chest, and slid down into the seat. "Jaan?" he asked quietly. A question. The answer would come, he knew, and he dreaded it, just from the way that Gwen had spoken the name, with a sort of strange defiance.

"He doesn't know," Ruark said.

Gwen sighed, and Dirk could see her tense. "I'm sorry, Dirk. I thought you would know. It has been a long time. I thought, well, one of the people we both knew back on Avalon, one of them surely has told you."

"I never see anyone anymore," Dirk said carefully. "That we knew, together. You know. I travel a lot. Braque, Prometheus, Jamison's World." His voice rang hollow and inane in his ears. He paused and swallowed. "Who is Jaan?"

"Jaantony Riv Wolf high-Ironjade Vikary," Ruark said.

"Jaan is my . . ." She hesitated. "It is not easy to explain. I am *betheyn* to Jaan, *cro-betheyn* to his *teyn* Garse." She looked over, a brief glance away from the aircar instruments, then back again. There was no comprehension on Dirk's face.

"Husband," she said then, shrugging. "I'm sorry, Dirk. That's not quite right, but it is the closest I can come in a single word. Jaan is my husband."

Dirk, huddled low in his seat with his arms folded, said nothing. He was cold, and he hurt, and he wondered why he was there. He remembered the whisper-jewel, and he still wondered. She had some reason for sending for him, surely, and in time she would tell him. And really, he could hardly have expected that she would be alone. At the port he had even thought, quite briefly, that perhaps Ruark . . . and that hadn't bothered him.

When he had been silent for too long, Gwen looked over once again. "I'm sorry," she repeated. "Dirk. Really. You should never have come."

And he thought, She's right.

The three of them flew on without speaking. Words had been said, and not the words that Dirk had wanted, but words that had changed nothing. He was here on Worlorn, and Gwen was still beside him, though suddenly a stranger. They were both strangers. He sat slumped in his seat, alone with his thoughts, while a cold wind stroked his face.

On Braque, somehow, he had thought that the whisperjewel meant she was calling him back, that she wanted him again. The only question that concerned him was whether he would *go,* whether he could return to her, whether Dirk t'Larien still could love and be loved. That had not been it at all, he knew now.

Send this memory, and I will come, and there will be no questions. That was the promise, the only promise. Nothing more.

He became angry. Why was she doing this to him? She had held the jewel and felt his feelings. She could have guessed. No need of hers could be worth the price of this remembering.

Then, finally, calm came back to Dirk t'Larien. With his eyes tight shut, he could see the canal on Braque again, and the lone black barge that had seemed so briefly important. And he remembered his resolve, to try again, to be as he *had* been, to come to her and give whatever he could give, whatever she might need—for himself, as well as for her.

He straightened with an effort, unfolded his arms, opened his eyes, and sat up into the biting wind. Then, deliberately, he looked at Gwen and smiled his old shy smile for her. "Ah, Jenny," he said, "I'm sorry too. But it doesn't matter. I didn't know, but that doesn't matter. I'm glad I came, and you should be glad too. Seven years is too long, right?"

She glanced at him, then back at her instruments, and licked her lips nervously. "Yes. Seven years is too long, Dirk."

"Will I meet Jaan?"

She nodded. "And Garse too, his *teyn.*"

Below, somewhere, he heard water, a river lost in the darkness. It was gone quickly; they were moving quite fast. Dirk peered over the side of the aircar, down past the wings into the rushing black, then up. "You need more stars," he said thoughtfully. "I feel as though I'm going blind."

"I know what you mean," Gwen said. She smiled, and quite suddenly Dirk felt better than he had for a long time.

"Remember the sky on Avalon?" he asked.

"Yes. Of course."

"Lots of stars there. It was a beautiful world."

"Worlorn has a beauty too," she said. "How much do you know of it?"

"A little," Dirk replied, still looking at her. "I know about the Festival, and that the planet is a rogue, and not much else. A woman on the ship told me that Tomo and Walberg discovered the place on their jaunt to the end of the galaxy."

"Not quite," said Gwen. "But the story has a certain charm to it. Anyway, everything you'll see is part of the Festival. The whole planet is. All the worlds of the Fringe took part, and the culture of each is reflected here in one of the cities. There are fourteen cities, for the fourteen worlds of the Fringe. In between you've got the spacefield and the Common, which is sort of a park. We're flying over it now. The Common is not very interesting, even by day. They had fairs and games there in the years of the Festival."

"Where is your project?"

"The wilderness," Ruark said. "Beyond the cities, beyond the mountainwall."

Gwen said, "Look."

Dirk looked. At the horizon he could vaguely make out a row of mountains, a jagged black barrier that climbed out of the Common to eclipse the lower stars. A spark of bloody light sat high upon one peak, and it grew as they drew near. Taller and higher it became, though not more brilliant; the color stayed a múrky, threatening red that reminded Dirk somehow of the whisperjewel.

"Home," Gwen announced as the light swelled. "The city Larteyn. *Lar* is Old Kavalar for sky. This is the city of High Kavalaan. Some people call it the Firefort."

He could see why at a glance. Built into the shoulder of the mountain, rock beneath it and rock to its back, the Kavalar city was also a fortress—square and thick, massively walled, with narrow slit windows. Even the towers that rose behind the city walls were heavy and solid. And short; the Mountain loomed above them, its dark stone stained bloody by reflected light. But the lights of the city itself were not reflected; the walls and streets of Larteyn burned with a dull glowering fire of their own.

"Glowstone," Gwen told him in answer to his unvoiced question. "It absorbs light during the day and gives it back at night. On High Kavalaan, it was used mostly for jewelry, but they quarried it by the ton and shipped it off to Worlorn for the Festival."

"Baroque impressive," Ruark said. "Kavalar impressive." Dirk only nodded.

"You should have seen it in the old days," Gwen said. "Larteyn drank from the seven suns by day and lit the range by night. Like a dagger of fire. The stones are fading now—the Wheel grows more distant every hour. In another decade the city will go dark as a burnt-out ember."

"It doesn't look very big," Dirk said. "How many people did it hold?"

"A million, once. You're just seeing the tip of the iceberg. The city is built into the mountain."

"Very Kavalar," Ruark said. "A deep holding, a fastness in stone. But empty now. Twenty people, last count, us including."

The aircar passed over the outer wall, set flush to the cliff on the edge of the wide mountain ledge, to make one long straight drop past rock and glowstone. Below them Dirk saw wide walkways, and rows of slowly stirring pennants, and great carved gargoyles with burning glowstone eyes. The buildings were white stone and ebon wood, and on their flanks the rock fires were reflected in long red streaks, like open wounds on some hulking dark beast. They flew over towers and domes and streets, twisting alleys and wide boulevards, open courtyards and a huge many-tiered outdoor theater.

Empty, all empty. Not a figure moved in the red-drenched ways of Larteyn.

Gwen spiraled down to the roof of a square black tower. As she hovered and slowly faded the gravity grid to bring them in, Dirk noted two other cars in the airlot beneath them: a sleek yellow teardrop and a formidable old military flyer with the look of century-old war surplus. It was olive-green, square and sheathed in armor, with lasercannon on the foward hood and pulse-tubes on the rear.

She put their metal manta down between the two cars, and they vaulted out onto the roof. When they reached the bank of elevators, Gwen turned to face him, her face flushed and strange in the brooding reddish light. "It is late," she said. "We had all better rest."

Dirk did not question the dismissal. "Jaan?" he said.

"You'll meet him tomorrow," she replied. "I need a chance to talk to him first."

"Why?" he asked, but Gwen had already turned and started toward the stairs. Then the tube arrived and Ruark put a hand on his shoulder and pulled him inside.

They rode downward, to sleep and to dreams.

chapter 2

He got very little rest that night. Each time he started off to sleep, his dreams would wake him: fitful visions laced with poison and only half remembered when he woke, as he did, time and time again throughout the night. Finally he gave up. Instead, he began to rummage through his belongings until he found the jewel in its wrappings of silver and velvet, and he sat with it in the darkness and drank from its cold promises.

Hours passed. Then Dirk rose and dressed, slid the jewel into his pocket, and went outside alone to watch the Wheel come up. Ruark was sound asleep, but he had the door coded for Dirk, so there was no problem getting in or out. He took the tubes back up to the roof and waited through the last dregs of night, sitting on the cold metal wing of the gray aircar.

It was a strange dawn, dim and dangerous, and the day it birthed was murky. First only a vague cloudy glow suffused the horizon, a red-black smear that faintly echoed the glowstones of the city. Then the first sun came up: a tiny ball of yellow that Dirk watched with naked eyes. Minutes later, a second appeared, a little larger and brighter, on another part of the horizon. But the two of them, though recognizably more than stars, still cast less light than Braque's fat moon.

A short time later the Hub began to climb above the Common. It was a line of dim red at first, lost in the ordinary light of dawn, but it grew steadily brighter until at last Dirk saw that it was no reflection, but the crown of a vast red sun. The world turned crimson as it rose.

He looked down into the streets below. The stones of Larteyn had all faded now; only where the shadows fell could the glow still be seen, and there only dimly. Gloom had settled over the city like a grayish pall tinged slightly with washed-out red. In the cool weak light the nightflames all had died, and the silent streets echoed death and desolation.

Worlorn's day. Yet it was twilight.

"It was brighter last year," said a voice behind him. "Now each day is darker, cooler. Of the six stars in the Hellcrown, two are hidden now behind Fat Satan, and are of no use at all. The others grow small and distant. Satan himself still looks down on Worlorn, but his light is very red and growing feeble. So Worlorn lives in slow-declining sunset. A few more years and the seven suns will shrink to seven stars, and the ice will come again."

The speaker stood very still as he regarded the dawn, his boots slightly apart and his hands on his hips. He was a tall man, lean and well muscled, barechested even in the chill morning. His red-bronze skin was made even redder by the light of Fat Satan. He had high angular cheekbones, a heavy square jaw, and receding shoulder-length hair as black as Gwen's. And on his forearms—his dark forearms matted with fine black hair—he wore two bracelets, equally massive. Jade and silver on his left arm, black iron and red glowstone on his right.

Dirk did not stir from the wing of the manta. The man looked down at him. "You are Dirk t'Larien, and once you were Gwen's lover."

"And you are Jaan."

"Jaan Vikary, of the Ironjade Gathering," the other said. He stepped forward and raised his hands, palms outward and empty.

Dirk knew the gesture from somewhere. He stood and pressed his own palms against the Kavalar's. As he did, he noticed something else. Jaan wore a belt of black oiled metal, and a laser pistol was at his side.

Vikary caught his look and smiled. "All Kavalars go armed. It is a custom—one we value. I hope you are not as shocked and biased as Gwen's friend, the Kimdissi. If so, that is your failure, not ours. Larteyn is part of High Kavalaan, and you cannot expect our culture to conform to yours."

Dirk sat down again. "No. I should have expected it, perhaps, from what I heard last night. I do find it strange. Is there a war on somewhere?"

Vikary smiled very thinly—an even, deliberate baring of teeth. "There is always a war somewhere, t'Larien. Life itself is a war." He paused. "Your name: t'Larien. Unusual. I have not heard its like before, nor has my *teyn* Garse. Where is your homeworld?"

"Baldur. A long way off, on the other side of Old Earth. But I scarcely remember it. My parents came to Avalon when I was very young."

Vikary nodded. "And you have traveled, Gwen has told me. Which worlds have you seen?"

Dirk shrugged. "Prometheus, Rhiannon. Thisrock, Jamison's World, among others. Avalon, of course. A dozen altogether, mostly places more primitive than Avalon, where my knowledge is in demand. It's usually easy to find work if you've been to the Institute, even if you're not especially skilled or talented. Fine with me. I like traveling."

"Yet you have never been beyond the Tempter's Veil until now. Only in the jambles, and never to the outworlds. You will find things different here, t'Larien."

Dirk frowned. "What was that word you used? Jambles?"

"The jambles," Vikary repeated. "Ah. Wolfman slang. The jambled worlds, the jumbled worlds, what you will. A phrase that I acquired from several Wolfmen who were among my friends during my studies on Avalon. It refers to the star sphere between the outworlds and the first- and second-generation colonies near Old Earth. It was the jambles where the Hrangans saturated the stars and ruled their slaveworlds and fought the Earth Imperials. Most of the planets you named were known then, and they were touched hard by the ancient war and jumbled by the collapse. Avalon itself is a second-generation colony, once a sector capital. That is some distinction, do you think, for a world so very far in these centuries ai-shattered?"

Dirk nodded agreement. "Yes. I know the history, a little. You seem to know a lot of it."

"I am a historian," Vikary said. "Most of my work has been devoted to making history out of the myths of my own world, High Kavalaan. Ironjade sent me to Avalon at great expense to search the data banks of the old computers for just that purpose. Yet I spent two years of study there, had much free time, and developed an interest in the broader history of man."

Dirk said nothing but only looked out again toward the dawn. The red disc of Fat Satan was half risen now, and a third yellow star could be seen. It was slightly to the north of the others, and it was only a star. "The red star is a supergiant," Dirk mused, "but up there it seems only a bit larger than Avalon's sun. It must be pretty far away. It should be colder, the ice should be here now. But it's only chilly."

"That is our doing," Vikary told him with some pride. "Not High Kavalaan, in truth, yet outworld work nonetheless. Tober preserved much of the lost forcefield technology of the Earth Imperials during the collapse, and the Toberians have added to it in the centuries since then. Without their shield no Festival could ever have been held. At perihelion, the heat of the Hellcrown and Fat Satan would have burned off Worlorn's atmosphere and boiled its sea, but the Toberian shield blocked off that fury and we had a long bright summer. Now, in like manner, it helps to hold in the heat. Yet it has its limits, as does everything. The cold will come."

"I did not think we'd meet like this," Dirk said. "Why did you come up here?"

"A chance. Long years ago Gwen told me that you liked to watch the dawn. And other things as well, Dirk t'Larien. I know far more of you than you of me."

Dirk laughed. "Well, that's true. I never knew you existed until last night."

Jaan Vikary's face was hard and serious. "But I do exist. Remember that, and we can be friends. I hoped to find you alone and tell you this before the others woke. This is not Avalon now, t'Larien, and today is not yesterday. It is a dying Festival world, a world without a code, so each of us must cling tightly to whatever codes we bring with us. Do not test mine. Since my years on Avalon, I have tried to think of myself as Jaan Vikary, but I am still a Kavalar. Do not force me to be Jaantony Riv Wolf high-Ironjade Vikary."

Dirk stood up. "I'm not sure what you mean," he said. "But I think I can be cordial enough. I certainly have nothing against you, Jaan."

That seemed to be enough to satisfy Vikary. He nodded slowly, and reached into the pocket of his trousers. "An emblem of my friendship and concern for you," he said. In his hand was a black metal collar pin, a tiny manta. "Will you wear it during your time here?"

Dirk took it from his hand. "If you want me to," he said, smiling at the other's formality. He fixed it to his collar.

"Dawn is gloomy here," Vikary said, "and day is not

much better. Come down to our quarters. I will rouse the others, and we can eat."

The apartment that Gwen shared with the two Kavalars was immense. The high-ceilinged living room was dominated by a fireplace two meters high and twice as long, and above was a slate-gray mantel where glowering gargoyles perched to guard the ashes. Vikary led Dirk past them, over an expanse of deep black carpet, into a dining chamber that was nearly as large. Dirk sat in a high-backed wooden chair, one of twelve along the great table, while his host went to fetch food and company.

He returned shortly, bearing a platter of thinly sliced brown meat and a basket of cold biscuits. He set them in front of Dirk, then turned and left again.

No sooner had he gone than another door opened and Gwen entered, smiling sleepily. She wore an old headband, faded trousers, and a shapeless green top with wide sleeves. He could see the glint of her heavy jade-and-silver bracelet, tight on her left arm. With her, a step behind, came another man, nearly as tall as Vikary but several years younger and much more slender, clad in a short-sleeved jumpsuit of brown-red chameleon cloth. He glanced at Dirk out of intense blue eyes, the bluest eyes that Dirk had ever seen, set in a gaunt hatchet face above a full red beard.

Gwen sat down. The red beard paused in front of Dirk's chair. "I am Garse Ironjade Janacek," he said. He offered his palms. Dirk rose to press them.

Garse Ironjade Janacek, Dirk noted, wore a laser pistol at his waist, slung in a leather holster on a silvery mesh-steel belt. Around his right forearm was a black bracelet, twin to Vikary's—iron and what looked to be glowstone.

"You probably know who I am," Dirk said.

"Indeed," Janacek replied. He had a rather malicious grin. Both of them sat down.

Gwen was already munching on a biscuit. When Dirk resumed his seat, she reached out across the table and fingered the little manta pin on his collar, smiling at some secret amusement. "I see that you and Jaan found each other," she said.

"More or less," Dirk replied, and just then Vikary returned, with his right hand wrapped awkwardly around the handles of four pewter mugs, and his left hand holding a pitcher of dark beer. He deposited it all in the center of the table, then made one last trip to the kitchen for plates and ironware and a glazed jar of sweet yellow paste that he told them to spread on the biscuits.

While he was gone, Janacek pushed the mugs across the table at Gwen. "Pour," he said to her, in a rather peremptory tone, before turning his attention back to Dirk. "I am told you were the first man she knew," he said while Gwen was pouring. "You left her with an imposing number of vile habits," he said, smiling coolly. "I am tempted to take insult and call you out for satisfaction."

Dirk looked baffled.

Gwen had filled three of the four mugs with beer and foam. She set one in front of Vikary's place, the second by Dirk, and took a long draft from the third. Then she wiped her lips with the back of her hand, smiled at Janacek, and handed him the empty mug. "If you're going to threaten poor Dirk because of my habits," she said, "then I suppose I must challenge Jaan for all the years I've had to suffer yours."

Janacek turned the empty beer mug in his hands and scowled. "*Betheyn*-bitch," he said in an easy conversational voice. He poured his own beer.

Vikary was back an instant later. He sat down, took a swipe from his own mug, and they began to eat. Dirk discovered very soon that he liked having beer for breakfast. The biscuits, smeared over with a thick coating of the sweet paste, were also excellent. The meat was rather dry.

Janacek and Vikary questioned him throughout the meal, while Gwen sat back and looked bemused, saying very little. The two Kavalars were a study in contrasts. Jaan Vikary leaned forward as he spoke (he was still bare-chested, and every so often he yawned and scratched himself absently) and maintained a tone of general friendly interest, smiling frequently, seemingly much more at ease than he had been up on the roof. Yet he struck Dirk as somehow deliberate, a tight man who was making a conscious effort to loosen; even his informalities—the smiles, the scratching—seemed studied and formal. Garse Janacek, while he sat more erect than Vikary and never scratched and had all the formal Kavalar mannerisms of speech, nevertheless seemed more genuinely relaxed, like a man who *enjoyed* the restrictions his society had laid on him and would not even think of trying to break free. His speech was animated and abrasive; he tossed off insults like a flywheel tossing sparks, most of them directed at Gwen. She tossed a few back, but feebly; Janacek played the game much better than she did. A lot of it gave the appearance of casual, affectionate give-and-take, but several times Dirk thought he caught a hint of real hostility. Vikary tended to frown at every exchange.

When Dirk happened to mention his year on Prometheus, Janacek quickly seized on it. "Tell me, t'Larien," he said, "do you consider the Altered Men human?"

"Of course," Dirk said. "They are. Settled by the Earth Imperials way back during the war. The modern Prometheans are only the descendants of the old Ecological Warfare Corps."

"In truth," Janacek said, "yet I would disagree with your conclusion. They have manipulated their own genes to such a degree that they have lost the right to call themselves men at all, in my opinion. Dragonfly men, undersea men, men who breathe poison, men who see in the dark like Hruun, men with four arms, hermaphrodites, soldiers without stomachs, breeding sows without sentience—these creatures are not men. Or *not-men,* more precisely."

"No," Dirk said. "I've heard the term *not-man.* It's

common parlance on a lot of worlds, but it means human stock that's been mutated so it can no longer interbreed with the basic. The Prometheans have been careful to avoid that. The leaders—they're fairly normal themselves, you know, only minor alterations for longevity and such—well, the leaders regularly swoop down on Rhiannon and Thisrock, raiding, you know. For ordinary Earth-normal humans—"

"Yet even Earth is less than Earth-normal these past few centuries," Janacek interrupted. Then he shrugged. "I should not break in, should I? Old Earth is too far away, in any event. We only hear century-old rumors. Continue."

"I made my point," Dirk said. "The Altered Men are still human. Even the low castes, the most grotesque, the failed experiments discarded by the surgeons—all of them can interbreed. That's why they sterilize them, they're afraid of offspring."

Janacek took a swallow of beer and regarded him with those intense blue eyes. "They do interbreed, then?" He smiled. "Tell me, t'Larien, during your year on that world did you ever have occasion to test this personally?"

Dirk flushed and found himself glancing toward Gwen, as if it were somehow all her fault. "I haven't been celibate these past seven years, if that's what you mean," he snapped.

Janacek rewarded his answer with a grin, and looked at Gwen. "Interesting," he said to her. "The man spends several years in your bed and then immediately turns to bestiality."

Anger flashed across her face; Dirk still knew her well enough to recognize *that*. Jaan Vikary looked none too pleased either. "Garse," he said warningly.

Janacek deferred to him. "My apologies, Gwen," he said. "No insult was intended. T'Larien no doubt acquired a taste for mermaids and mayfly women quite independently of you."

"Will you be going out into the wild, t'Larien?"

Vikary asked loudly, deliberately wrenching the conversation away from the other Kavalar.

"I don't know," Dirk said, sipping his beer. "Should I?"

"I'd never forgive you if you didn't," Gwen said, smiling.

"Then I'll go. What's so interesting?"

"The ecosystem—it's forming and dying, all at the same time. Ecology was a forgotten science in the Fringe for a long time. Even now the outworlds boast less than a dozen trained eco-engineers between them. When the Festival came, Worlorn was seeded with life forms from fourteen different worlds with almost no thought as to the interaction. Actually *more* than fourteen worlds were involved, if you want to count multiple transplants—animals brought from Earth to Newholme to Avalon to Wolfheim, and thence to Worlorn, that sort of thing.

"What Arkin and I are doing is a study of how things have worked out. We've been at it a couple years already, and there's enough work to keep us busy for a decade more. The results should be of particular interest to farmers on all the outworlds. They'll know which Fringe flora and fauna they can safely introduce to their homeworlds, and under what conditions, and which are poison to an ecosystem."

"The animals from Kimdiss are proving particularly poisonous," Janacek growled. "Much like the manipulators themselves."

Gwen grinned at him. "Garse is annoyed because it looks as though the black banshee is heading toward extinction," she told Dirk. "It's a shame, really. On High Kavalaan itself they've been hunted to the point where the species is clearly endangered, and it had been hoped that the specimens turned loose here twenty years ago would establish themselves and multiply, so they could be recaptured and taken back to High Kavalaan before the cold came. It hasn't worked out that way. The banshee is a fearful predator, but at home it can't compete with man, and on Worlorn it has had its niche appropriated by an infestation of tree-spooks from Kimdiss."

"Most Kavalars think of the banshee only as a plague and a menace," Jaan Vikary explained. "In its natural habitat it is a frequent man-killer, and the hunters of Braith and Redsteel and the Shanagate Holding think of banshee as the ultimate game, with a single exception. Ironjade has always been different. There is an ancient myth, of the time Kay Iron-Smith and his *teyn* Roland Wolf-Jade were fighting alone against an army of demons in the Lameraan Hills. Kay had fallen, and Roland, standing over him, was weakening by the moment, when from over the hills the banshees came, many of them flying together, black and thick enough to block out the sun. They fell hungrily onto the demon army and consumed them, one and all, leaving Kay and Roland alive. Later, when that *teyn*-and-*teyn* found their cave of women and established the first Ironjade holdfast, the banshee became their brother-beast and sigil. No Ironjade has ever killed a banshee, and legend says that whenever a man of Ironjade is in danger of his life, a banshee will appear to guide and protect him."

"A pretty story," Dirk said.

"It is more than a story," Janacek said. "There is a bond between Ironjade and banshee, t'Larien. Perhaps it is psionic, perhaps the things are sentient, perhaps it is all instinct. I do not pretend to know. Yet the bond exists."

"Superstition," Gwen said. "You really must not think too badly of Garse. It's not his fault that he never got much of an education."

Dirk spread paste across a biscuit and looked at Janacek. "Jaan mentioned that he was a historian, and I know what Gwen does," he said. "What about you? What do you do?"

The blue eyes stared coldly. Janacek said nothing.

"I get the impression," Dirk said, continuing, "that you are not an ecologist."

Gwen laughed.

"That impression is uncannily correct, t'Larien," Janacek said.

"What are you doing on Worlorn, then? For that matter"—he shifted his gaze to Jaan Vikary—"what does a historian find to do in a place like this?"

Vikary cradled his beer mug between two large hands and drank from it thoughtfully. "That is simple enough," he said. "I am a highbond Kavalar of the Ironjade Gathering, bonded to Gwen Delvano by jade-and-silver. My *betheyn* was sent to Worlorn by vote of the highbond council, so it is natural that I am here too, and my *teyn*. Do you understand?"

"I suppose. You keep Gwen company, then?"

Janacek appeared very hostile. "We *protect* Gwen," he said icily. "Usually from her own folly. She should not be here at all, yet she is, so we must be here as well. As to your earlier question, t'Larien, I am an Ironjade, *teyn* to Jaantony high-Ironjade. I can *do* anything that my holdfast might require of me: hunt or farm, duel, make highwar against our enemies, make babies in the bellies of our *eyn-kethi*. That is what I do. What I am you already know. I have told you my name."

Vikary glanced at him and bid him silent with a short chopping motion of his right hand. "Think of us as late tourists," he told Dirk. "We study and we wander, we drift through the forests and the dead cities, we amuse ourselves. We would cage banshees so they might be brought back to High Kavalaan, except that we have not been able to find any banshees." He rose, draining his mug as he did so. "The day ages and we sit," he said after he had set it back on the table. "If you would go off to the wild, you should do it soon. It will take time to cross the mountains, even by aircar, and it is not wise to stay out after dark."

"Oh?" Dirk finished his own beer and wiped his mouth with the back of his hand. Napkins did not seem to be part of a Kavalar table setting.

"The banshees were never the only predator on Worlorn," Vikary said. "There are slayers and stalkers from fourteen worlds in the forests, and they are the least of it. The humans are the worst. Worlorn is an easy, empty world today, and its shadows and its barrens are full of strangeness."

"You would do best to go armed," Janacek said. "Or better still, Jaan and I should go with you, for the sake of your safety."

But Vikary shook his head. "No, Garse. They must go alone, and talk. It is better that way, do you understand? It is my wish." Then he picked up an armful of plates and walked toward the kitchen. But near the door he paused and glanced back over his shoulder, and briefly his eyes met Dirk's.

And Dirk remembered his words, out on the rooftop at dawn. *I do exist,* Jaan had said. *Remember that.*

"How long since you rode a sky-scoot?" Gwen asked him a short time later when they met on the roof. She had changed into a one-piece chameleon cloth coverall, a belted garment that covered her from boots to neck in dusky grayish red. The headband that held her black hair in place was the same fabric.

"Not since I was a child," Dirk said. His own clothing was twin to hers; she'd given it to him so they could blend into the forest. "Since Avalon. But I'm willing to try. I used to be pretty good."

"You're on, then," Gwen said. "We won't be able to go very far or very fast, but that shouldn't matter." She opened the storage trunk on the gray manta-shaped aircar and took out two small silvery packages and two pairs of boots.

Dirk sat on the aircar wing again while he changed into the new boots and laced them up. Gwen unfolded the scoots, two small platforms of soft tissue-thin metal barely large enough to stand upon. When she spread them on the ground, Dirk could trace the crosshatched wires of the gravity grids built into their undersides. He stepped on one, positioning his feet carefully, and the metal soles of his boots locked tightly in place as the platform went rigid. Gwen handed him the control device and he strapped it around his wrist so that it flipped out into the palm of his hand.

"Arkin and I use the scoots to get around the forests," Gwen told him while she knelt to lace up her own boots. "An aircar has ten times the speed, of course, but it isn't always easy to find a clearing big enough to land. The scoots are good for close-in detail work, as long as we don't try to carry too much equipment or get in too much of a hurry. Garse says they're toys, but . . ." She stood up, stepped onto her platform, and smiled. "Ready?"

"You bet," Dirk said, and his finger brushed the silver wafer in the palm of his right hand. Just a little too hard. The scoot shot up and out, dragging his feet with it and whipping him upside down when the rest of him lagged behind. He barely missed cracking his head on the roof as he flipped, and ascended into the sky laughing wildly and dangling from underneath his platform.

Gwen came after him, standing on her platform and climbing up the twilight wind with skill born of long practice, like some outworld djinn riding a silver carpet remnant. By the time she reached Dirk, he had played with the controls long enough to right himself, though he was still flailing back and forth in a wild effort to keep his balance. Unlike aircars, sky-scoots had no gyros.

"Wheeee," he shouted as she closed. Laughing, Gwen moved in behind him and slapped him heartily on the back. That was all he needed to flip over again, and he began careening through the sky above Larteyn in a mad cartwheel.

Gwen was behind him, shouting something. Dirk blinked and noticed that he was about to crash into the side of a tall ebony tower. He played with his controls and shot straight up, still fighting to steady himself.

He was high above the city and standing upright when she caught him. "Stay away," he warned with a grin, feeling stupid and clumsy and playful. "Knock me over again and I'll get the flying tank and laser you out of the sky, woman!" He tilted to one side, caught himself, then overcompensated and swung to the other side yelping.

"You're drunk," Gwen shouted at him through the keening wind. "Too much beer for breakfast." She was above him now, arms folded against her chest, watching his struggles with mock disapproval.

"These things seem much more stable when you hang from them upside down," Dirk said. He had finally achieved a semblance of balance, although the way he held his arms out to either side made it clear that he was dubious about maintaining it.

Gwen settled down to his level and moved in beside him, sure-footed and confident, her dark hair streaming behind her like a wild black banner. "How you doing?" she yelled as they flew side by side.

"I think I've got it!" Dirk announced. He was still upright.

"Good. Look down!"

He looked down, past the meager security of the platform under his feet. Larteyn with its dark towers and faded glowstone streets was no longer beneath him. Instead there was a long *long* drop through an empty twilight sky to the Common far below. He glimpsed a river down there, a thread of wandering dark water in the dim-lit greenery. Then his head swam dizzily, his hands tightened, and he flipped over again.

This time Gwen dipped underneath him as he hung upside down. She crossed her arms again and smirked up at him. "You sure are a dumbshit, t'Larien," she told him. "Why don't you fly right side up?"

He growled at her, or tried to growl, but the wind took away his breath and he could only make faces. Then he turned himself over. His legs were getting sore from all of this. "There!" he shouted, and looked down defiantly to prove that the height would not spook him a second time.

Gwen was beside him again. She looked him over and nodded. "You are a disgrace to the children of Avalon, and sky-scooters everywhere," she said. "But you'll probably survive. Now, do you want to see the wild?"

"Lead me, Jenny!"

"Then turn. We're going the wrong way. We have to clear the mountains." She held out her free hand and took his and together they swung around in a wide spiral, up and back, to face Larteyn and the mountain-wall. The city looked gray and washed-out from a distance, its proud glowstones a sun-doused black. The mountains were a looming darkness.

They rode toward them together, gaining altitude steadily until they were far over the Firefort, high enough to clear the peaks. That was about top altitude for the sky-scoots; an aircar, of course, could ascend much higher. But it was high enough for Dirk. The chameleon cloth coveralls they wore had gone all gray and white, and he was thankful for their warmth; the wind was chill and the dubious day of Worlorn not much hotter than its night.

Holding hands and shouting infrequent comments, leaning this way and that into the wind, Gwen and Dirk rode up over one mountain and down its far slope into a shadowed rocky valley, then up and down another and still another, past dagger-sharp outcroppings of green and black rock, past high narrow waterfalls and higher precipices. At one point Gwen challenged him to race, and he shouted his acceptance, and then they streaked forward as fast as the scoots and their skill could take them until finally Gwen took pity on him and came back to take his hand again.

The range dropped off as suddenly to the west as it had risen in the east, throwing up a tall barrier to shield the wild from the light of the still-climbing Wheel. "Down," Gwen said, and he nodded, and they began a slow descent toward the jumbled dark greenery below. By then they had been up for more than an hour; Dirk was half numb from the bite of the Worlorn wind, and most of his body was protesting this mal-treatment.

They landed well inside the forest, beside a lake they had seen as they came down. Gwen swooped down gracefully in a gentle curve that left her standing on a mossy beach beside the water's edge. Dirk, afraid of smashing into the ground and breaking a leg, flicked off his grid a moment too soon and fell the last meter.

Gwen helped him detach his boots from the sky-scoot, and together they brushed damp sand and moss from his clothes and from his hair. Then she sat down beside him and smiled. He smiled back and kissed her.

Or tried to. As he reached and put his arm around her, she pulled away, and he remembered. His hands fell, and the shadows swept across his face. "I'm sorry," he said, mumbling. He looked away from her, toward the lake. The water was an oily green, and islands of violet fungus dotted the still surface. The only motion was the half-seen stirrings of insects skimming the shallows nearby. The forest was even darker than the city, for the mountains still hid most of Fat Satan's disc.

Gwen reached out and touched him on the shoulder. "No," she said softly. "I'm sorry. I forgot too. It was almost like Avalon."

He looked at her and forced a faint smile, feeling lost. "Yes. Almost. I've missed you, Gwen, despite it all. Or should I be saying that?"

"Probably not," she said. Her eyes avoided his again and went wandering from him, out across the lake. The far side was lost in haze. She gazed into the distance for a long time, not moving except once, when she shivered briefly from the cold. Dirk watched her clothing slowly fade to a mottled off-white and green to match the shade of the ground she sat upon.

Finally he reached to touch her, his hand unsure. She shrugged it away. "No," she said.

Dirk sighed and picked up a handful of cool sand, running it through his fingers as he thought. "Gwen." He hesitated. "Jenny, I don't know . . ."

She glanced at him and frowned. "That's not my

name, Dirk. It never was. No one ever called me that except you."

He winced, hurt. "But why—"

"Because it isn't me!"

"No one else," he said. "It just came to me, back on Avalon, and it fit you and I called you that. I thought you liked it."

She shook her head. "Once. You don't understand. You never understand. It came to mean more to me than it did at first, Dirk. More and more and more, and the things that name meant to me were not good things. I tried to tell you, even then. But that was a long time ago. I was younger, a child. I didn't have the words."

"And now?" His voice was edged with overtones of anger. "Do you have the words *now,* Gwen?"

"Yes. For you, Dirk. More words than I can use." She smiled at some secret joke and shook her head so her hair tossed in the wind. "Listen, private names are fine. They can be a special sharing. With Jaan it is like that. The highbonds have long names because they fill many roles. He can be Jaan Vikary to a Wolfman friend on Avalon, and high-Ironjade in the councils of Gathering, and still Riv in worship and Wolf in high-war and yet another name in bed, a private name. And there is a rightness to it, because all those names are him. I recognize that. I like some of him better than other parts, like Jaan more than Wolf or high-Ironjade, but they are all true for him. The Kavalars have a saying, that a man is the sum of all his names. Names are very important on High Kavalaan. Names are very important everywhere, but the Kavalars know that truth better than most. A thing without a name has no substance. If it existed, it would have a name. And, likewise, if you give a thing a name, somewhere, on some level, the thing named will exist, will come to be. That's another Kavalar saying. Do you understand, Dirk?"

"No."

She laughed. "You're as muddled as ever. Listen,

when Jaan came to Avalon he was Jaantony Ironjade Vikary. That was his name, his whole name. The most important part of it was the first two words—Jaantony is his true name, his birth name, and Ironjade is his holdfast and his alliance. Vikary is a made-up name he took at puberty. All of the Kavalars take such names, usually the names of highbonds they admire, or mythic figures, or personal heroes. A lot of Old Earth surnames have survived that way. The thought is that by taking the name of a hero the boy will gain some of the man's qualities. On High Kavalaan it actually seems to work.

"Jaan's chosen name, Vikary, is a bit unusual in several respects. It sounds like an Old Earth hand-me-down, but it isn't. From all accounts Jaan was an odd child—dreamy, very moody, much too introspective. He liked to listen to the *eyn-kethi* sing and tell stories when he was very little, which is bad for a Kavalar boy. The *eyn-kethi* are the breeding women, the perpetual mothers of the holdfast, and a normal child is not supposed to associate with them any more than he has to. When Jaan was older he spent all his time alone, exploring caves and abandoned mines in the mountains. Safely away from his holdfast-brothers. I don't blame him. He was always an object of torment, essentially friendless, until he met Garse. Who is notably younger, but still wound up as Jaan's protector through the later stages of his childhood. Eventually that all changed. When Jaan approached the age when he would be subject to the code duello, he turned his attention to weaponry and mastered it very quickly. He is really a fantastic study; today he is terribly fast and considered deadly, better even than Garse, whose skill is mainly instinctual.

"It wasn't always like that, however. Anyway, when it came time for Jaantony to choose a name, he had two great heroes, but he did not dare name either one to the highbonds. Neither of them were Ironjades, and worse, both were semi-pariahs, villains of Kavalar history, charismatic leaders whose causes had lost and then been subjected to generations of oral abuse. So Jaan sort of shoved their names together and juggled the sounds around until the product looked like an old family name imported from Earth. The highbonds accepted it without a thought. It was only his chosen name, the least important part of his identity. It's the part that comes last, after all."

She frowned. "Which is the point of this whole story. Jaantony Ironjade Vikary came to Avalon, and he was mostly Jaantony Ironjade. Except that Avalon is a surname-conscious world, and there he found that he was mostly Vikary. The Academy registered him under that name, and his instructors called him Vikary, and it was a name he had to live by for two years. Pretty soon he became Jaan Vikary, in addition to being Jaantony Ironjade. I think he rather liked it. He's always tried to stay Jaan Vikary ever since, although it was not easy after we returned to High Kavalaan. To the Kavalars he'll always be Jaantony."

"Where did he get all the other names?" Dirk found himself asking, despite himself. Her story fascinated him and seemed to offer new insights into what Jaan Vikary had said that dawn, up on the roof.

"When we were married, he brought me back to Ironjade with him and became a highbond, automatically a member of the highbond council," she said. "That put a 'high' in his name, and gave him the right to own private property independent of the holdfast, and to make religious sacrifices, and to lead his *kethi*, his holdfast-brothers, in war. So he got a war name, sort of a rank, and a religious name. Once those kinds of names were very important. Not so much anymore, but the customs linger."

"I see," Dirk said, although he didn't, not completely. The Kavalars seemed to set unusually great store on marriage. "What has this got to do with us?"

"A lot," Gwen said, becoming very serious again. "When Jaan reached Avalon and people started calling him Vikary, he changed. He became Vikary, a hybrid of his own iconoclastic idols. That's what names can do, Dirk. And that was our downfall. I loved you, yes. Much. I loved you, and you loved Jenny."

"You were Jenny!"

"Yes, no. Your Jenny, your Guinevere. You said that, over and over again. You called me those names as often as you called me Gwen, but you were right. They were your names. Yes, I liked it. What did I know of names or naming? Jenny is pretty enough, and Guinevere has the glow of legend. What did I know?

"But I learned, even if I never had the words for it. The problem was that you loved Jenny—only Jenny wasn't me. Based on me, perhaps, but mostly she was a phantom, a wish, a dream you'd fashioned all on your own. You fastened her on me and loved us both, and in time I found myself becoming Jenny. Give a thing a name and it will somehow come to be. All truth is in naming, and all lies as well, for nothing distorts like a false name can, a false name that changes the reality as well as the seeming.

"I wanted you to love me, not her. I was Gwen Delvano, and I wanted to be the best Gwen Delvano I could be, but still myself. I fought being Jenny, and you fought to keep her, and never understood. And that was why I left you." She finished in a cool, even voice, her face a mask, and then she looked away from him again.

And he did understand, at last. For seven years he never had, but now, briefly, he grasped it. This then, he thought, was why she sent the whisperjewel. Not to call him back, no, not that. But to tell him, finally, why she had sent him away. And there was a sense to it. His anger had suddenly faded into weary melancholy. Sand ran cold and unheeded through his fingers.

She saw his face, and her voice softened. "I'm sorry, Dirk," she said. "But you called me Jenny again. And I had to tell you the truth. I have never forgotten, and I can't imagine you have, and I've thought of it over the years. It was *so* good, when it was good, I kept thinking. How could it go wrong? It scared me, Dirk.

It really scared me. I thought, If *we* could go wrong, Dirk and I, then nothing is sure, nothing can be counted on. That fear crippled me for two years. But finally, with Jaan, I understood. And now it came out, the answer I found. I'm sorry if it is a painful answer for you. But you had to know."

"I had hoped . . ."

"Don't," she warned. "Don't start it, Dirk. Not again. Don't even try. We're over. Recognize that. We'll kill ourselves if we try."

He sighed, blocked at every turn. Through all the long conversation, he had never even touched her. He felt helpless. "I take it that Jaan doesn't call you Jenny?" he asked finally with a bitter smile.

Gwen laughed. "No. As a Kavalar, I have a secret name, and he calls me that. But I've taken the name, so there's no problem. It is *my* name."

He only shrugged. "You're happy, then?"

Gwen rose and brushed loose sand from her legs. "Jaan and I—well, there is a lot that is hard to explain. You were a friend once, Dirk, and maybe my best friend. But you've been gone a long time. Don't press too hard. Right now I need a friend. I talk to Arkin, and he listens and tries, but he can't help much. He's too involved, too blind about Kavalars and their culture. Jaan and Garse and I have problems, yes, if that's what you're asking. But it's hard to speak of them. Give me time. Wait, if you will, and be my friend again."

The lake was very still in the perpetual red-gray sunset. He watched the water, thick with its spreading scabs of fungus, and he flashed back to the canal on Braque. Then she did need him, he thought. Perhaps it was not as he had hoped, but there was still something he could give her. He clung to that tightly; he wanted to give, he had to give. "Whatever," he said as he rose. "There's a lot I don't understand, Gwen. Too much. I keep thinking that half the conversation of the past day has gone past me, and I don't even know the right questions to ask. But I can try. I owe you, I guess. I owe you for something or other."

"You'll wait?"

"And listen, when the time comes."

"Then I'm glad you've come," she said. "I needed someone, an outsider. You're well timed, Dirk. A luck."

How strange, he thought, to send off for a luck. But he said nothing. "Now what?"

"Now let me show you the forest. That was why we came here, after all."

They picked up their sky-scoots and walked away from the silent lake, toward the thick of the waiting forest. There was no trail to follow, but the underbrush was light and walking easy, with many paths to choose from. Dirk was quiet, studying the woods around him, his shoulders slumped and his hands shoved deep into his pockets. Gwen did all the talking; the little there was. When she spoke, her voice was low and reverent as a child's whisper in a great cathedral. But mostly she just pointed and let him look.

The trees around the lake were all familiar friends that Dirk had seen a thousand times before. For this was the so-called forest of home, the wood that man carried with him from sun to sun and planted on all the worlds he walked. It had its roots on Old Earth, the homeforest, but it was not all of Earth. On each new planet humanity found new favorites, plants and trees that soon were as much a part of the blood as those that came out from Earth in the beginning. And when the starships moved on, seedlings from those worlds went with the twice-uprooted grandchildren of Terra, and so the homeforest grew.

Dirk and Gwen passed through that forest slowly, as others had walked through the same forest on a dozen other worlds. And they knew the trees. Sugar maples there, and fire maples, and mockoak and oak itself, and silverwood and poison pine and asten. The outworlders had brought them here even as their ancestors had brought them to the Fringe, to add a touch of home, wherever home might be.

But here these woods looked different.

It was the light, Dirk realized after a time. The drizzling light that leaked so meager from the sky, the wan red gloom that passed for Worlorn's day. This was a twilight forest. In the slowness of time—in a far-extended autumn—it was dying.

He looked closer then and saw that the sugar maples were all bare, their faded leaves beneath his feet. They would not green again. The oaks were barren too. He paused and pulled a leaf from a fire maple, and saw that the fine red veins had turned to black. And the silverwoods were really dusty gray.

Rot would come next.

To parts of the forest, rot had come already. In one forlorn glen where the humus was thicker and blacker than elsewhere, Dirk noticed a smell. He looked at Gwen, asking. She bent and brought a handful of the black stuff to his nose, and he turned away.

"It was a bed of moss," she told him, sorrowing. "They brought it all the way from Eshellin. A year ago it was all green and scarlet, alive with little flowers. The black spread quickly."

They moved farther into the forest, away from the lake and the mountainwall. The suns were nearly overhead by now, Fat Satan dim and bloated like a blood-drenched moon, unevenly ringed by four small yellow star-suns. Worlorn had receded too far and in the wrong direction; the Wheel effect was lost.

They had been walking for more than an hour when the character of the forest around them began to change. Slowly, subtly, the change seeped in, almost too gradual for Dirk to notice. But Gwen showed him. The familiar blend of homeforest was giving way, yielding to something stranger, something unique, something wilder. Gaunt black trees with gray leaves, high walls of red-tipped briar, drooping weepers of pale phosphorescent blue, great bulbous shapes infested with dark flaking splotches; to each of these

Gwen pointed and gave a name. One type became more and more common: a towering yellowish growth that sprouted tangled branches from all over its waxy trunk, and smaller offshoots from those branches, and still smaller ones from those, until it had built itself into a tight wooden maze. "Chokers," Gwen called them, and Dirk soon saw why. Here in the deep of the wood one of the chokers had grown alongside a regal silverwood, sending out crooked yellow-wax branches to mingle with straight, stately gray ones, burrowing roots under and around those of the other tree, constricting its rival in an ever-tightening vise. And now the silverwood could scarce be seen: a tall dead stick lost in the swelling choker.

"The chokers are native to Tober," Gwen said. "They're taking over the forests here, just as they did there. We could have told them it would happen, but they wouldn't have cared. The forests were all doomed anyway, even before they were planted. Even the chokers will die, though they'll be the last to go."

They walked on, and the chokers grew steadily thicker, until soon they dominated the forest. Here the woods were denser, darker; passage was more difficult. Half-buried roots tripped them underfoot, while tangled branches interlocked above them like the straining arms of giant wrestlers. Where two or three or more chokers grew close together, they seemed to merge into a single twisted knot, and Gwen and Dirk were forced to detour. Other plant life was scarce, except for beds of black and violet mushrooms near the feet of the yellow trees, and ropes of parasitic scumweb.

But there were animals.

Dirk saw them moving through the dark twistings of the chokers and heard their high, chittering call. Finally he saw one. Sitting just above their heads on a swollen yellow branch, looking down on them; fist-sized, dead still, and somehow—transparent. He touched Gwen's shoulder and nodded upward.

But she just smiled for him and laughed lightly.

Then she reached up to where the little creature sat and crumpled it in her hand. When she offered it to Dirk, her palm held only dust and dead tissue.

"There's a nest of tree-spooks around," she explained. "They shed their skins four or five times before maturity and leave the husks as guards to scare away other predators." She pointed. "There's a live one, if you're interested."

Dirk looked and caught a fleeting glimpse of a tiny yellow scampering thing with sharp teeth and enormous brown eyes. "They fly too," Gwen told him. "They've got a membrane that goes from arm to leg and lets them flit between the trees. Predators, you know. They hunt in packs, can bring down creatures a hundred times their size. But generally they won't attack a man unless he blunders into their nest."

The tree-spook was gone now, lost beneath a labyrinth of choker branches, but Dirk thought he saw another, briefly, from the corner of his eye. He studied the woods around him. The transparent skin husks were everywhere, staring fiercely into the twilight from their perches, all small grim ghosts. "These are the things that get Janacek so upset, aren't they?" he asked.

Gwen nodded. "The spooks are a pest on Kimdiss, but here they've really found their element. They blend perfectly with the chokers, and they can move through the tangles faster than anything I've ever seen. We studied them pretty thoroughly. They're cleaning out the forests. In time, they would kill off all the game and starve themselves to death, but they won't have time. The shield will fail before that, and the cold will come." She moved her shoulders in a tiny weary shrug and rested her forearm on a low-drooping limb. Their coveralls had long ago become the same dirty yellow color as the woods around them, but her sleeve slid up and back as she brushed the branch, and Dirk saw the dull sheen of jade-and-silver gleaming against the choker.

"Is there much animal life left?"

"Enough," she said. Pale red light made the silver

strange. "Not as much as there used to be, of course. Most of the wildlife has deserted the homeforest. Those woods are dying, and the animals know it. But the outworld trees are sterner, somehow. Where the forests of the Fringe were planted, you'll find life, still strong, still hanging on. The chokers, the ghost trees, the blue widowers—they'll flourish right until the end. And they'll have their tenants, old and new, until the cold comes."

Gwen moved her arm idly, this way and that, and the armlet winked at him, screamed at him. Bond and reminder and denial, all at once, love sworn in jade-and-silver. And he had only a small whisper-jewel shaped like a tear and full of fading memories.

He looked up, past a wild crisscross of yellow choker branches, to where the Helleye sat in a murky slice of sky, looking more tired than hellish, more sorry than satanic. And he shivered. "Let's go back," he told Gwen. "This place depresses me."

He got no argument. They found a clear spot away from the chokers that pressed around them, a place to spread the silver-metal tissue of their scoots. Then they rose together for the long flight back to Larteyn.

chapter **3**

They raced again above the mountains, and Dirk did better this time, losing by less than he had before, but the improvement did not lighten his mood. For most of the weary trip they flew in silence, apart, Gwen meters ahead of him. Their backs were to the broken, muted Wheel of Fire as they went, and Gwen was a witch figure vague against the sky and always out of reach. The melancholy of Worlorn's dying forests had seeped into his flesh, and he saw Gwen through tainted eyes, a doll figure in a suit as faded as despair, her black hair oily with red light. Thoughts came in a colored chaos as the wind swept past him, and one more often than the others. She was not his Jenny, was not and never had been.

Twice during their flight Dirk saw—or thought he saw—the jade-and-silver flashing, tormenting, as it had tormented him in the wood. He forced his eyes away each time and watched black clouds, long and thin, skitter across the barren, empty sky.

The gray manta aircar and the olive-green war machine were both gone from the rooftop lot when they reached Larteyn. Only Ruark's yellow teardrop was unmoved. They landed nearby—Dirk's landing yet another clumsy stumble, now oddly humorless, only stupid—and left the sky-scoots and flight boots out on the roof where they removed them. Near the tubes they spoke briefly, but Dirk forgot the words even as he said them. Then Gwen left him.

In his rooms at the base of the tower, Arkin Ruark was waiting patiently. Dirk found a recliner amid the pastel walls and sculpture and the potted Kimdissi plants. He reclined, wanting only to rest and not to think, but Ruark was there, chuckling and shaking his head so the white-blond hair danced, thrusting a tall green glass into his hand. Dirk took it and sat up again. The glass was a fine thin crystal, plain and unadorned except for a fast-melting coat of frost. He drank, and the wine was very green and cold, incense and cinnamon down his throat.

"Utter tired you look, Dirk," the Kimdissi said after he had found a drink of his own and seated himself with a plop in a slung-web chair beneath the shadow of a drooping black plant. The spear-shaped leaves cast striped darkness on his plump, smiling face. He sipped, sucking the drink noisily, and very briefly Dirk despised him.

"A long day," he said noncommittally.

"Truth," Ruark agreed. "A day of Kavalars, heh, always long. Sweet Gwen and Jaantony and last Garsey, enough to make any day last forever. What do you say?"

Dirk said nothing.

"But now," Ruark said, smiling, "you have seen. Me, I wanted that, for you to see. Before I told you. But I was sworn to tell you, yes, a swearing to myself. Gwen, she has told me. We talk, you know, as friends, and I have known her and Jaan too since Avalon. But here we've grown closer. She cannot talk of it easily, ever, but she talks to me, or has, and I can tell you. Not violating trust. You are the one to know, I think."

The drink sent icy fingers down into his chest, and Dirk felt his weariness lifting. It seemed as if he had been half asleep, as if Ruark had been talking for a long time and he had missed it all. "What are you talking about?" he said. "What should I know?"

"Why Gwen needs you," Ruark said. "Why she sent . . . the thing. The red tear. You know. I know. She has told me."

Suddenly Dirk was quite alert, interested and puzzled. "She told you," he began, then stopped. Gwen had asked him to wait, and long ago the promise he had made—but it fit. Perhaps he should listen, perhaps it was simply hard for her to tell him. Ruark would know. Her friend, she had said in the forests, the only one she could talk to. "What?"

"You must help her, Dirk t'Larien, somehow. I don't know."

"Help her how?"

"To be free. To escape."

Dirk set his drink down and scratched his head. "From who?"

"Them. The Kavalars."

He frowned. "Jaan, you mean? I met him this morning, him and Janacek. She loves Jaan. I don't understand."

Ruark laughed, sucked from his drink, laughed again. He was dressed in a three-piece suit of alternating brown and green squares, like motley, and as he sat spouting nonsense Dirk wondered if the short ecologist was indeed a fool.

"Loves him, yes, she said that?" Ruark said. "You are sure of it, are you? Well?"

Dirk hesitated, trying to remember her words when they had talked by the still, green lake. "I'm not sure," he said. "But something to that effect. She is— What was it?"

"*Betheyn?*" Ruark suggested.

Dirk nodded. "Yes, *betheyn,* wife."

Ruark chuckled. "No, utter wrong. In the car I listened. Gwen said it wrong. Well, not really, but you took the wrong impression. *Betheyn* is not wife. Part truth the biggest lie of all, remember? What do you think *teyn* is?"

The word stopped him. *Teyn.* He had heard the word a hundred times on Worlorn. "Friend?" he guessed, not knowing what it meant.

"*Betheyn* is more of wife than *teyn* is friend," Ruark said. "Learn the outworlds better, Dirk. No. *Betheyn* is woman-to-man word in Old Kavalar, for a heldwife bound by jade-and-silver. Now, there can be much affection in jade-and-silver, much love, yes. Though, you know, the word used for that, the standard Terran word, there is no like word in Old Kavalar. Interesting, eh? Can they love without a word for it, t'Larien friend?"

Dirk did not reply. Ruark shrugged and drank and continued. "Well, no matter, but think of it. I spoke of jade-and-silver and yes, often the Kavalars have love in that bond, love from *betheyn*-to-highbond, from highbond-to-*betheyn* sometimes. Or liking, if not love. But not always, and not necessarily! You see?"

Dirk shook his head.

"Kavalar bonds are custom and obligation," Ruark said, leaning forward very intently, "with love late-coming accident. Violent folk, I told you. Read history, read legends. Gwen met Jaan on Avalon, you know, and she did not read. Not enough. He was Jaan Vikary of High Kavalaan, and what was that, some planet? She never knew. Truth. So their liking grew—call it love, perhaps—and sex happens and he offers her jade-and-silver wrought in his pattern, and suddenly she is *betheyn* to him, still not quite knowing. Trapped."

"Trapped? How trapped?"

"Read history! The violence of High Kavalaan is

long past, the culture is unchanged. Gwen is *betheyn* to Jaan Vikary, *betheyn* heldwife, his wife, yes, his lover, and more. Property and slave, she is that too, and gift. She is his gift to Ironjade Gathering, with her he bought his highnames, yes. She must have children if he orders, whether she wishes or no. She must take Garse as lover also, whether she wishes or no. If Jaan dies in duel with a man of a holdfast other than Ironjade, a Braith or a Redsteel, Gwen passes to that man like baggage, property—to become his *betheyn,* or a mere *eyn-kethi* if the victor already wears jade-and-silver. If Jaan dies of natural causes, or in duel with another Ironjade, Gwen goes to Garse. Her will in the matter is no concern. Who cares that she hates him? Not the Kavalars. And when Garsey dies, eh? Well, when that time comes, she is an *eyn-kethi,* holdfast breeder, degraded forever, free to use for any of the *kethi. Kethi* meaning holdfast-brothers, more or less, the men of the family. Ironjade Gathering is all huge family, thousands and thousands of family, and any can have her. What did she call Jaan, husband? No. Jailer. That is what he is, he and Garse, loving jailers maybe if you think that such can love truly as you or I would. Jaantony honors our Gwen, and should, for he is high-Ironjade now, she is his *betheyn*-gift, and if she dies or leaves him, he is fre-Ironjade, an old man, mocked, empty-armed, without voice in council. But he slaves her, does not love her, and she is years after Avalon now, older and wiser, and now she knows." Ruark had delivered the last in a breathless fury, his lips drawn tight.

Dirk hesitated. "He doesn't love her, then?"

"As you love your property, so a highbond and his *betheyn*. It is a tight bond, jade-and-silver, never to be broken, but it is a bond of obligation and possession. No love. That is elsewhere, if the Kavalars have it at all, to be found in chosen-brother, the shield and soulmate and lover and warrior twin, the ever-loyal bringer-of-pleasure and taker-of-blows and lifter-of-pain, the lifetime strongbond."

"Teyn," Dirk said, a little numbly, his mind racing ahead.

"Teyn!" Ruark nodded. "The Kavalars, all violent as they are, have great poetry. Much celebrates the *teyn,* the bond of iron-and-glowstone, none the jade-and-silver."

Things fell smoothly into place. "You are saying," Dirk began, "that she and Jaan don't love each other, that Gwen is all but a slave. Yet she doesn't leave?"

Ruark's chubby face was flushed. *"Leave?* Utter nonsense! They would only force her back. A highbond must keep and protect his *betheyn.* And kill the one who tries to steal her."

"And she sent the jewel to me . . ."

"Gwen talks to me, I know. What other hope has she? The Kavalars? Jaantony has twice killed in duels. No Kavalar would touch her, and what good if they did? Me? Am I a hope?" His soft hands swept down his body, and he dismissed himself in contempt. "You, t'Larien, you are Gwen's hope. You who owe her. You who loved her once."

Dirk heard his own voice, as if from far away. "I still love her," he said.

"Good. I think, you know, that Gwen . . . though she would never say it, yet I think . . . she too still feels. As she did. As she never has for Jaantony Riv Wolf high-Ironjade Vikary."

The drink, the odd green wine, had touched him more than he would have imagined. Only one glass, a single tall glass, and strange the room ran around him, and Dirk t'Larien held himself upright with an effort and heard impossible things and began to wonder. Ruark made no sense, he thought, but then he made too much sense. He explained everything, really, and it was all so shining clear, and clear too what Dirk must do. Or was it? The room wavered, grew dark and then light again, dark and then light, and Dirk was one second very sure and the next not sure at all. What must he do? Something, something for

Gwen. He must find out the truth of things, and then ...

He raised a hand to his forehead. Beneath the dangling locks of gray-brown hair his brow was beaded with sweat. Ruark stood suddenly, alarm across his face. "Oh," the Kimdissi said, "the wine has made you sick! Utter fool I am! My fault. Outworld wine and Avalon stomach, yes. Food will help, you know. Food." He scurried off, brushing the potted plant as he went so the black spears bobbed and danced behind him.

Dirk sat very still. Far off in the distance he heard a clatter of plates and pots but paid it no mind. Still sweating, his forehead was furrowed in thought, thought that was strangely difficult. Logic seemed to elude him, and the clearest things faded even as he grabbed hold of them. He trembled while dead dreams woke to new life, while the choker-woods withered in his mind and the Wheel burned hot and fiery above the new-flowering noonday woods of Worlorn. He could make it happen, force it, wake it, put an end to the long sunset, and have Jenny, his Guinevere, forever by his side. Yes. *Yes!*

When Ruark came back with forks and bowls of soft cheese and red tubers and hot meat, Dirk was calmer, cool again. He took the bowls and ate in half a trance while his host prattled on. Tomorrow, he promised himself. He would see them at breakfast, talk to them, learn what truth he could. Then he could act. Tomorrow.

". . . no insult is intended," Vikary was saying. "You are not a fool, Lorimaar, but in this I think you act foolishly."

Dirk froze in the doorway, the heavy wooden door that he had opened without thinking swinging away before him. All of them turned to regard him, four pairs of eyes, Vikary's last and not until he had finished what he was saying. Gwen had told him to come up to breakfast when they had parted the night be-

fore (him only, since Ruark and the Kavalars preferred
to avoid each other whenever possible), and this was
the correct time, just shortly after dawn. But the scene
was not one he had expected to enter.

There were four of them in the cavernous living
room. Gwen, hair unbrushed and eyes full of sleep,
was seated on the edge of the low wood-and-leather
couch that stretched in front of the fireplace and its
gargoyle guards. Garse Janacek stood just behind her
with his arms crossed and a frown on his face, while
Vikary and a stranger confronted each other by the
mantel. All three of the men were dressed formally,
and armed. Janacek wore leggings and shirt of soft
charcoal-gray, with a high collar and a double row of
black iron buttons down his chest. The right sleeve of
his shirt had been cut away to display the heavy
bracelet of iron and dimly blazing glowstones. Vikary
was also all in gray, but without the row of buttons;
the front of his shirt was a V that swooped almost to
his belt, and against the dark chest hair a jade me-
dallion hung on an iron chain.

The newcomer, the stranger, was the first to address Dirk. His back was to the door, but he turned
when the others looked up, and he frowned. Taller by
a head than either Vikary or Janacek, he towered over
Dirk, even at a distance of several meters. His skin
was a hard brown, very dark against the milk-white
suit he wore beneath the pleated folds of a violet
half-cape. Gray hair, shot through with white, fell to
his broad shoulders, and his eyes—flints of obsidian
set in a brown face with a hundred lines and wrinkles
—were not friendly. Neither was his voice. He looked
Dirk over quickly, then said, very simply, "Get out."

"What?" No reply could be as stupid as his was,
Dirk thought even as he said it, but nothing else came
to mind.

"I said get out," the giant in white repeated. Like
Vikary, both of his forearms were bare to display the
bracelets, the almost-twins of jade-and-silver on his left
arm and iron-and-fire on his right. But the patterns

and settings of the stranger's armlets were very different. The only thing that was the same, exactly, was the gun on his hip.

Vikary folded his arms, just as Janacek had already folded his. "This is my place, Lorimaar high-Braith. You have no right to be rude to those who come at my invitation."

"An invitation you yourself lack, Braith," Janacek added with a tiny venomous smile.

Vikary looked over at his *teyn,* shook his head sharply and vigorously. *No.* But to what? Dirk wondered.

"I come to you in high grievance, Jaantony high-Ironjade, with serious talking to do," the white-suited Kavalar rumbled. "Must we treat before an off-worlder?" He glanced at Dirk again, still frowning. "A mockman, for all I know."

Vikary's voice was quiet but stern when he replied. "We are done dealing, friend. I've told you my answer. My *betheyn* has my protection, and the Kimdissi, and this man too"—he indicated Dirk with a wave of his hand, then folded his arms again—"and if you take any among these, then prepare to take me."

Janacek smiled. "He is no mockman either," the gaunt red-bearded Kavalar said. "This is Dirk t'Larien, *koruriel of Ironjade,* whether you like it or no." Janacek turned very slightly in Dirk's direction and indicated the stranger in white. "T'Larien, this is Lorimaar Reln Winterfox high-Braith Arkellor."

"A neighbor of ours," Gwen said from the couch, speaking for the first time. "He lives in Larteyn too."

"Far from you, Ironjades," the other Kavalar said. He was not happy. The frown was deep-graven in his face, and his black eyes moved from one of them to the next, full of cold anger, before coming to rest on Vikary. "You are younger than me, Jaantony high-Ironjade, and your *teyn* younger still, and I would not willingly go to face you and yours in duel. Yet code has its demands, as you know and I, and neither of us should venture too far. You young highbonds oft press that line closely, I feel, and the highbonds of Ironjade most of all, and—"

"And I most of all the highbonds of Ironjade," Vikary said, finishing for the other.

Arkellor shook his head. "Once, when I was but an unweaned child in the holdfasts of Braith, it was duel to so much as interrupt another, as you have done now to me. Truly, the old ways have gone. The men of High Kavalaan turn soft before my eyes."

"You think me soft?" Vikary asked quietly.

"Yes and no, high-Ironjade. You are a strange one. You have a hardness none can deny, and that is good, but Avalon has put the stench of the mockman on you, touched you with the weak and foolish. I do not like your *betheyn*-bitch, and I do not like your 'friends.' Would that I were younger. I would come at you in fury and teach you again the old wisdoms of the holdfast, the things that you forget so easy."

"Do you call us to duel?" Janacek asked. "You speak strongly."

Vikary unfolded his arms and waved casually with his hand. "No, Garse. Lorimaar high-Braith does not call us to duel. Do you, friend, highbond?"

Arkellor waited several heartbeats too long before his answer came. "No," he said. "No, Jaantony high-Ironjade, no insult is intended."

"And none is taken," Vikary said, smiling.

The Braith highbond did not smile. "Good fortunes," he said begrudgingly. He went to the door in long strides, pausing only long enough to let Dirk step hurriedly aside, then proceeded out and up the roof stairs. The door closed behind him.

Dirk started toward the others, but the scene was quickly breaking up. Janacek, with a frown and a shake of his head, turned and left quickly for another room. Gwen rose, pale and shaken, and Vikary took a step toward Dirk.

"That was not a good thing for you to witness," the Kavalar said. "But perhaps it will be enlightening to you. Still, I regret your presence. I would not have you think of High Kavalaan as the Kimdissi do."

"I didn't understand," Dirk said. Vikary put an arm around his shoulder and drew him off toward the dining room, Gwen just behind them. "What was he talking about?"

"Ah, much. I will explain. But I must tell you a second regret also, that your promised breakfast is not set and ready for you." He smiled.

"I can wait." They went into the dining room and sat, Gwen still silent and troubled. "What did Garse call me?" Dirk asked. "*Kora*-something, what does that mean?"

Vikary appeared hesitant. "The word is *korariel*. It is an Old Kavalar word. Its meanings have changed over the centuries. Today, here in this place, when used by Garse or myself, it means protected. Protected by us, protected of Ironjade."

"That is what you would like it to mean, Jaan," Gwen said, her voice barbed and angry. "Tell him the real meaning!"

Dirk waited. Vikary crossed his arms and his eyes went from one of them to the other. "Very well, Gwen, if you wish it." He turned to Dirk. "The full, older meaning is protected property. I can only hope you do not take insult at this. None is intended. *Korariel* is a word for people not part of a holdfast, yet still guarded and valued."

Dirk remembered the things Ruark had told him the night before, the words dimly perceived through a haze of green wine. He felt anger creeping like a red tide up his neck, and fought to hold it down. "I am not accustomed to being property," he said bitingly, "no matter how highly valued. And who are you supposed to be protecting me against?"

"Lorimaar and his *teyn* Saanel," Vikary said. He leaned forward across the table and took Dirk's arm in a powerful grip. "Garse used the word perhaps too hastily, t'Larien, yet to him it no doubt seemed right at that moment, an old word for an old concept.

Wrong—yes, I can recognize the wrongness—wrong in that you are a human, a person, no one's property. Yet it was an apt word to use to one like Lorimaar high-Braith, who understands such things and little else. If it disturbs you so greatly, as I know the concept disturbs Gwen, then I am grievously sorry my *teyn* used it."

"Well," Dirk said, trying to be reasonable, "I thank you for the apology, but that's not good enough. I still don't know what's going on. Who was Lorimaar? What did he want? And why do I have to be protected against him?"

Vikary sighed and released Dirk's arm. "It will not be a simple matter to answer your questions. I must tell you of the history of my people, a little that I know and much that I have guessed." He turned to Gwen. "We can eat while we talk, if no one objects. Will you bring food?"

She nodded and left, returning several minutes later carrying a large tray piled high with black bread and three kinds of cheese and hard-cooked eggs in bright blue shells. And beer, of course. Vikary leaned forward so that his elbows rested on the tabletop. He talked while the others ate.

"High Kavalaan has been a violent world," he said. "It is the oldest outworld except for the Forgotten Colony, and all its long histories are histories of struggle. Sadly, those histories are also largely fabrication and legend, full of ethnocentric lies. Yet these tales were believed right up until the time that the starships came again, following the interregnum.

"In the holdfasts of the Ironjade Gathering, for example, boys were taught that the universe has only thirty stars, and High Kavalaan is its center. Mankind originated there, when Kay Iron-Smith and his *teyn* Roland Wolf-Jade were born of a mating between a volcano and a thunderstorm. They walked steaming from the lips of the volcano into a world full of demons and monsters, and for many years they wandered far and near, having various adventures. At last they

came across a deep cave beneath a mountain, and inside they found a dozen women, the first women in the
world. The women were afraid of the demons and
would not come out. So Kay and Roland stayed, sciz-
ing the women roughly and making them *eyn-kethi.*
The cave became their holdfast, the women birthed
them many sons, and thus began Kavalar civilization.

"The path upward was no easy one, the stories say.
The boys born of the *eyn-kethi* were all the seed of
Kay and Roland, hot-tempered and dangerous and
strong-willed. There were many quarrels. One son, the
wily and evil John Coal-Black, habitually killed his
kethi, his holdfast-brothers, in fits of envy because he
could not hunt as well as they. Then, hoping to gain
some of their skill and strength, he fell to eating their
bodies. Roland found him engaged in such a feast one
day, and chased the child across the hills, beating him
with a great flail. Afterwards John did not return to
Ironjade, but started his own holdfast in a coal mine
and took to *teyn* a demon. That was the origin of the
cannibal highbonds of the Deep Coal Dwellings.

"Other holdfasts were founded in like manner, although the Ironjade histories give the other rebels a
good deal more credit than Black John. Roland and
Kay were stern masters, not easy to live with. Shan the
Swordsman, for example, was a good strong boy who
left with his *teyn* and *betheyn* after a violent fight with
Kay, who would not respect his jade-and-silver. Shan
was the founder of the Shanagate Holding. Ironjade
recognizes his line as fully human, and always did. So
it was with most of the great holdfasts. Those that died
out, like the Deep Coal Dwellings, fared less well in
the legends.

"Those legends are quite extensive, and many are
enlightening. There is the tale of the disobedient *kethi,*
as an instance. The first Ironjade knew that the only fit
home for a man was deep under rock, a fastness in
stone, a cave or a mine. Yet those who came later did
not believe; the plains looked open and inviting to their
naive eyes. So they went out, with *eyn-kethi* and chil-

dren, and erected tall cities. That was their folly. Fires fell from the sky to destroy them, melting and twisting the towers they had thrown up, burning the city men, sending the survivors fleeing underground in terror to where the flames could not reach. And when their *eyn-kethi* gave them births, the children were demons, not men at all. Sometimes they ate their way free of the womb."

Vikary paused and took a drink from his mug. Dirk, almost finished with his breakfast, pushed a few crumbs of cheese aimlessly across his plate and frowned. "This is all fascinating," he said, "but I don't see the relevance, I'm afraid."

Vikary drank again and took a quick bite of cheese. "Be patient," he said.

"Dirk," Gwen said dryly, "the histories of the four surviving holdfast-coalitions differ in many respects, but there are two great events on which they agree. Those are the milestones of Kavalar myth. All of them have a version of that last story—the burning of the cities. It is called the Time of Fire and Demons. A later story, the Sorrowing Plague, is also repeated virtually word for word in every holdfast."

"Truth," Vikary said. "These stories—these were the only accounts of ancient days that I was given to work with. By the time of my birth, no sane Kavalar believed any of this."

Gwen coughed politely.

Vikary glanced at her and smiled. "Yes, Gwen corrects me," he said. *"Few* sane Kavalars believed any of this." He went on. "Yet the doubters had nothing else to believe, no alternate truth to adhere to. Most of them did not particularly care. When star travel resumed, and the Wolfmen and Toberians and later the Kimdissi came to High Kavalaan, they found us eager to learn the lost arts of technology, and that is what they taught us in return for our gems and heavy metals. Soon we had starships, but still no history." He smiled. *"I* found what truth we now have during my studies on Avalon. It was little enough, and yet sufficient. Hidden in the great data banks of the Academy I found records of the original colonization of High Kavalaan.

"It was fairly late in the Double War. A group of settlers left from Tara for a world beyond the Tempter's Veil, where they hoped to find safety from the Hrangans and the Hrangan slaveraces. The computers indicate that for a time they did. They discovered a planet harsh and strange, yet rich. Quickly they built a high-level colony, based on mining operations. There are records of trade between Tara and the colony for about twenty years, then the planet beyond the Veil abruptly vanished from human history. Tara hardly noticed. Those were the cruelest years of the war."

"And you think the planet was High Kavalaan?" Dirk asked.

"It is known for a fact," Vikary replied. "The coordinates match, and other fascinating pieces of data as well. The colony was named Cavanaugh, for example. Perhaps even more intriguing, the leader of the first expedition was a starship captain named Kay Smith. A woman."

Gwen smiled at that.

"There was something else I discovered as well," Vikary continued, "quite by chance. You must remember that most of the outworlds were never involved in the Double War. The Fringe civilizations are children of the collapse, or even post-collapse. No Kavalar had ever seen a Hrangan, much less any of the various slaveraces. I had not, until I went to Avalon and grew interested in the broader aspects of human history. Then, in one account of the conflict in the jambles, I lucked upon illustrations of the various semi-sentient slaves the Hrangans used as shock troops on worlds they did not deem worthy of their own immediate attention. Undoubtedly, being a man of the jambles, you know these alien races, Dirk. The nocturnal Hruun, heavy-gravity warriors of immense strength and savagery, who see well into the infrared. Winged dactyloids, who got their name from some chance resemblance to a beast of human prehistory. Worst of all, the *githyanki,* the soulsucks, with their terrible psionic powers."

Dirk was nodding. "I've seen a Hruun or two during my travels. The other races are pretty much extinct, aren't they?"

"Perhaps," Vikary said. "I looked at the illustrations I had found for a long time, and returned to them again and again. There was a quality about them that disturbed me. Finally, I puzzled out the truth. The Hruun, the dactyloids, the *githyanki*—each bore a vague semblance to the gargoyles that sit at the door of every Kavalar holdfast. They were the demons of our myth cycles, Dirk!"

Vikary stood up and began to pace slowly up and down the length of the room, still talking, his voice even and controlled, his excitement showing only in the act of pacing. "When Gwen and I returned to Ironjade I put forward my theory, based on the old legends, the *Demonsong* cycle of the great poet-adventurer Jamis-Lion Taal, and on the Academy data banks. Consider its truth: The colony Cavanaugh stands, with its cities on the plains and its far-flung mining operations. The Hrangans level the cities with a nuclear bombardment. Survivors live only in the deep shelters and out in the wild, in the mines. To make the planet their own, the Hrangans also land contingents of their slaveraces. Then they depart, not to return for a century. The mines become the first holdfasts, others are built later, carved deep into stone. Their cities gone, the miners revert to a more primitive level of technology, and soon establish a rigid survival-oriented culture. For endless generations they war against the slaveraces and against each other. At the same time, beneath the radioactive ruins of the cities, human mutations begin to arise . . ."

Now Dirk stood up. "Jaan," he said.

Vikary stopped his pacing, turned, frowned.

"I have been very damn patient," Dirk said. "I understand that all this is of great concern to you. It's your work. But I want some answers and I want them now." He raised his hand and ticked off the questions on his fingers. "Who is Lorimaar? What did he want? And why do I have to be protected against him?"

Gwen rose too. "Dirk," she said, "Jaan is only giving you the background you need to understand. Don't be so—'

"No!" Vikary quieted her with a wave of his hand. "No, t'Larien is correct, I grow too enthusiastic whenever I speak of these matters." To Dirk he said, "I will answer you directly, then. Lorimaar is a very traditional Kavalar, so traditional that he is out of place even on High Kavalaan itself. He is a creature of another age. Do you recall yesterday morning, when I gave you my pin to wear, and Garse and I both expressed concern about your safety after dark?"

Dirk nodded. His hand went up and touched the small pin, snugly fastened to his collar. "Yes."

"Lorimaar high-Braith and others like him were the cause of our concern, t'Larien. The reasons are not easy to tell."

"Let me," Gwen said. "Dirk, listen. The highbond Kavalars, the holdfast folk, always respected each other throughout the centuries— Oh, they fought and warred, so much that some twenty-odd holdfasts and coalitions were destroyed utterly, leaving only the four great surviving holdfasts of modern times. Still, they recognized each other as human, subject to the rules of highwar and the Kavalar code duello. But there were others, you see—solitary people in the mountains, people who dwelled under the ruined cities, farmers. Those are just guesses—mine and Jaan's— but the point is such people *did* exist, survivors outside the mining camps that became the holdfasts—those survivors the highbonds would not recognize as men and women. Jaan left something out of all that history, you see— Oh, don't fidget so. I know it was a long story, but it was important. You remember all that about the Hrangan slaveraces corresponding to the three demons of Kavalar myth? Well, the only problem with that is there are three slaveraces, but *four* kinds of demons. The worst and most evil demons of all were the mockmen."

Dirk frowned. "Mockmen. Lorimaar called me a mockman. I thought it was something like not-man, more or less."

"No," Gwen said. "Not-man is a common term, mockman is unique to High Kavalaan. Shape-changers, the legends say, weres and liars. They can wear any form, but most often that of men, and they want to infiltrate the holdfasts. Inside, disguised as humans, they can secretly strike and kill.

"Those other survivors—the farmers and the mountain families and the mutants and the unlucky, the other humans on Cavanaugh—those were the mockmen, the werefolk. They were not allowed to surrender, the rules of highwar did not apply. The Kavalars exterminated them, never trusting any to be human. They were alien animals. After centuries, those that remained were hunted for sport. The holdfast men always hunted in pairs, *teyn*-and-*teyn,* so each could swear to the humanity of the other when they returned."

Dirk looked aghast. "Does this still go on?"

Gwen shrugged. "Seldom. Modern Kavalars admit the sins of their history. Even before the starships came, the Ironjade Gathering and Redsteel, the most progressive coalitions, had banned the taking of mockmen. The hunters had a custom. When they did not wish to kill a mockman immediately, for whatever reason, but wanted him as their personal prey later, they would brand him *korariel,* and no one else would touch him under penalty of duel. The Ironjade and Redsteel *kethi* went out and ran down all the mockmen they could, set them up in villages, and tried to bring them back to civilization from the savagery they had fallen into. All they caught they named *korariel.* There was a brief highwar over it, Ironjade against Shanagate. Ironjade won, and *korariel* took on a new meaning, protected property."

"And Lorimaar?" Dirk demanded. "How does he fit in?"

She smiled wickedly, for a second reminding him of Janacek. "In any culture, a few diehards remain, true believers and fundamentalists. Braith is the most conservative coalition, and about a tenth of them— Jaan's estimate—still believe in mockmen. Mostly hunters, who *want* to believe, and nearly all of them from Braith. Lorimaar and his *teyn* and a handful of his *kethi* are here to hunt. The game is more varied than on High Kavalaan, and no one enforces any game laws. In fact, there are no laws. The Festival pacts ended long ago. Lorimaar can kill anything he wants to."

"Including humans," Dirk said.

"If they can find them," she said. "Larteyn has twenty citizens, I believe—twenty-one with you. Us, and a poet named Kirak Redsteel Cavis who lives in an old watchtower, and a pair of legitimate hunters from Shanagate. The rest are Braiths. Hunting mockmen, and other game when they can't find mockmen. A generation older than Jaan, chiefly, and quite bloodthirsty. Except for stories they heard in their holdfasts, and maybe a few illicit man-kills in the Lameraan Hills, they know nothing of the old hunts except the legends. All of them are bursting with tradition and frustration." She smiled.

"And this goes on? No one does anything?"

Jaan Vikary crossed his arms. "I have a confession to make, t'Larien," he said gravely. "We lied to you yesterday, Garse and I, when you asked us why we are here. In truth, I was the one who lied. Garse told at least the partial truth—we must protect Gwen. She is an offworlder, no Kavalar, and the Braiths would gladly kill her for a mockman without the shield of Ironjade. The same is truth for Arkin Ruark, who knows nothing of this, not even that he has our protection. Yet he does. He too is *korariel* of Ironjade.

"Our reasons for being here go beyond that, however. It was vital that I leave High Kavalaan at the time I did. When I took on my highnames and published my theories, I became at once very powerful and celebrated in highbond council, and very hated. Many religious men took personal insult from my contention that Kay Iron-Smith was a woman. I was challenged six times on that account alone. In the last duel, Garse killed a man, while I wounded his *teyn* so badly that he will never walk again. I was not willing to let this go on. Worlorn was empty of enemies, it seemed. At my urging, the Ironjade council dispatched Gwen on her ecological project.

"Yet, at the same time, I became aware of Lorimaar's activity here. He had already taken his first trophy, and word had come back to Braith and spread to us. Garse and I discussed the matter and determined to stop it. The situation is explosive in the extreme. If the Kimdissi should learn that the Kavalars are hunting mockmen again, they would gladly spread the news to all the outworlds. There is little love lost between Kimdiss and High Kavalaan, as you may know. We do not fear the Kimdissi themselves, who espouse a religion and a philosophy as nonviolent as the Emereli. Other Fringe worlds are more dangerous. The Wolfmen are always volatile and erratic; the Toberians might end their trade agreements if they learn that Kavalars are hunting their laggardly tourists. Perhaps even Avalon would turn against us, should the news go beyond the Veil, and we would be barred from the Academy. These risks cannot be taken. Lorimaar and his fellows do not care, and the holdfast councils can do nothing. They have no authority here, and only the Ironjades have even the slightest concern about events light-years away, on a dying world. Thus Garse and I act against the Braith hunters alone.

"Up to now, it has not come to open conflict. We travel as widely as we can, visiting each of the cities, searching for those who remain on Worlorn. Any we find we make *korariel*. We have found only a few— a wild child lost during the Festival, a few lingering Wolfmen in Haapala's City, an ironhorn hunter from Tara. To each I give a token of my esteem"—he smiled—"a little black iron pin shaped like a banshee. It is a proximity beacon, to warn a hunter who gets too close. Should they touch any wearing such a pin, any of my *korariel,* it would be a dueling offense. Lorimaar may rant and rage, but he will not duel us. It would be his death."

"I see," said Dirk. He reached up to his collar, unfastened the little iron pin, and tossed it on the table amid the remains of their breafast. "Well, that's lovely, but you can have your little pin. I am nobody's property. I've been taking care of myself for a long time, and I can keep on taking care of myself."

Vikary frowned. "Gwen," he said, "can you not convince him that it would be safer if—"

"No," she said sharply. "I appreciate what you are trying to do, Jaan, you know that. But I understand Dirk's feelings. I don't like being protected either, and I refuse to be property." Her voice was curt, decisive.

Vikary regarded them helplessly. "Very well," he said. He picked up Dirk's discarded pin. "I should tell you something, t'Larien. We have had better luck in finding people than the Braiths simply because we search the cities while they hunt the forests, hopeless slaves to old habits. They seldom find anyone in the wild. Up to now they have had no inkling as to what Garse and I were doing. But this morning Lorimaar high-Braith came to me in grievance because the previous day he had come across likely game while hunting with his *teyn,* and had been prevented from taking that game.

"The prey he sought was a man on a sky-scoot, flying alone above the mountains." He held up the banshee-shaped pin. "Without this," he said, "he would have forced you down or lasered you from the sky, run you through the wilderness, and finally killed you." He put the pin into his pocket, stared at Dirk meaningfully for a minute, and left them.

chapter 4

"It's unfortunate that you had to stumble into Lorimaar this morning," Gwen said after Jaan had gone. "There was no reason for you to get involved, and I had hoped to spare you all the grisly details. I hope you will keep this confidential after you leave Worlorn. Let Jaan and Garse take care of the Braiths. No one else will do anything anyway, except talk about it and slander innocent people on High Kavalaan. Above all, don't tell Arkin! He despises Kavalars, and he'd be off to Kimdiss in a shot." She stood up. "For the present, I'd suggest we talk of more pleasant things. We have a short time together; I can only be your tour guide so long before I have to return to my work. There is no reason to let those Braith butchers spoil the few days we have."

"Whatever you say," Dirk answered, anxious to please but still shaken by the whole business with Lorimaar and his mockmen. "You have something planned?"

"I could take you back to the forests," Gwen told him. "They go on and on forever, and there are hundreds of fascinating things to see in the wild: lakes full of fish larger than either of us, insect mounds bigger than this building erected by insects smaller than your fingernail, an incredible cave system that Jaan discovered beyond the mountainwall— He's a born caver, Jaan. Still, today I think we should play it safe. We don't want to pour too much salt into Lorimaar's wound, or he and his fat *teyn* might hunt us both and Jaan be damned. Today I'll show you the cities. They have a fascination too, and a kind of macabre beauty. As Jaan said, Lorimaar has not yet thought to hunt there."

"All right," Dirk said, with little enthusiasm.

Gwen dressed quickly and took him up to the roof. The sky-scoots still lay where they had discarded them a day earlier. Dirk bent to retrieve them, but Gwen took the silver-metal tissues from his hands and tossed them into the back of the gray manta aircar. Then she got the flight boots and controls and chucked them in afterwards. "No scoots today," she said. "We'll be covering too much ground."

Dirk nodded, and both of them vaulted over the car's wings into the front seat. Worlorn's sky made him feel as if he should be coming in from an expedition instead of just setting out on one.

The wind shrieked around the aircar wildly, and Dirk briefly took the stick so Gwen could tie back her long black hair. His own gray-brown mop whipped around in mad convulsions as they raced across the sky, but thought had him too abstracted to notice, much less be annoyed.

Gwen kept them high over the mountainwall and bore south. The placid Common with its gentle grassy hills and meandering rivers stretched far away to their right, until the sky came down to meet it. On the distant left, when the mountains dropped off, they could glimpse the edge of the wilderness. The choker-infested areas were obvious even from this altitude

—yellow cancers spreading through the darker green.

For nearly an hour they rode in silence, Dirk lost in his thoughts, trying to put one thing together with the next and failing. Until finally Gwen looked at him with a smile. "I like flying an aircar," she said. "Even this one. It makes me feel free and clean, cut off from all the problems down there. You know what I mean?"

Dirk nodded. "Yes. You're not the first one to say that. Lots of people feel that way. Myself included."

"Yes," she said. "I used to take you flying, remember? On Avalon? I'd fly for hours and hours, from dawn until dark that one time, and you'd just sit with an arm out the window, staring far and away with that dreamy look on your face." She smiled again.

He did remember. Those trips had been very special. They never spoke much, just looked at each other from time to time, and whenever their eyes met they'd grin. It was inevitable; no matter how hard he fought it, that grin had always come. But now it all seemed terribly far off, and lost.

"What made you think of that?" he asked her.

"You," she said, and gestured. "Sitting there, slouched, with one hand hanging over the side. Ah, Dirk. You cheat, you know. I think you did it deliberately, to make me think of Avalon, and smile, and want to hug you again. Bah."

And they laughed together.

And Dirk, almost unthinking, slid over in his seat and put his arm around her. She looked briefly into his face, then gave a small shrug, and her frown melted into a sigh of resignation and finally a reluctant smile. And she did not pull away.

They went to see the cities.

The city of the morning was a soft pastel vision set in a wide green valley. Gwen put the aircar down in the center of one of its terraced squares, and they strolled the broad boulevards for an hour. It was a gracious city, carved from delicately veined pink marble and pale stone. The streets were wide and sinuously curved, the buildings low and seemingly fragile structures of polished wood and stained glass. Everywhere they found small parks and wide malls, and everywhere art: statues, paintings, murals on sidewalks and along the sides of buildings, rock gardens, and living tree-sculptures.

But now the parks were desolate and overgrown, the blue-green grass gone wild. Black creepers snaked across the sidewalks, the parkside plinths were empty more often than not, and the sturdier tree-sculptures had grown into grotesque shapes that their shapers never dreamed of.

A slow-moving blue river divided and subdivided the city, wandering this way and that in a course as meandering and tortuous as the streets along its bank. Gwen and Dirk sat near the water for a while, beneath the shadow of an ornate wooden footbridge, and watched the reflection of Fat Satan float red and sluggish on the water. And while they sat, she told him of how the city once had been, in the days of the Festival, before either of them had come to Worlorn. The people of Kimdiss had built it, she said, and they called it the Twelfth Dream.

Perhaps the city was dreaming now. If so, its sleep was the final one. Its vaulted halls all echoed empty, its gardens were grim jungles, soon to be graveyards. Where laughter had once filled the streets, now the only sound was the rustling whisper of dead leaves blown by the wind. If Larteyn was a dying city, Dirk reflected while he sat beneath the bridge, then Twelfth Dream was a dead one.

"This is where Arkin wanted to set up our base of operations," Gwen said. "We vetoed him, though. If he and I were going to work together, it was clearly best that we live in the same city, and Arkin wanted it to be Twelfth Dream. I wouldn't go along, and I don't know if he's ever forgiven me. If the Kavalars built Larteyn as a fortress, the Kimdissi crafted this city as a work of art. It was even more beautiful in the old days, I understand. They dismantled the best buildings and took the finest sculpture from the squares when the Festival ended."

"You voted for Larteyn?" Dirk said. "To live in?"

She shook her head. Her hair, unbound now, tossed gently, and touched Dirk with a smile. "No," she said. "Jaan wanted that, and Garse. Me—well, I didn't vote for Twelfth Dream either, I'm afraid. I could never have lived here. The scent of decay is too strong. I agree with Keats, you know. Nothing is quite so melancholy as the death of beauty. There was more beauty here than ever in Larteyn, though Jaan would growl to hear me say it. So this is the sadder place. Besides, in Larteyn there is *some* company, at least, if only Lorimaar and his sort. Here there's no one left but ghosts."

Dirk looked out over the water, where the great red sun, drained and captured, bobbed eerily up and down in the slow roll of the waves. And he could almost see the ghosts she spoke of then, phantoms who pressed the riverbank on both sides and sang laments for things long lost. And another too, a ghost uniquely his: a Braque bargeman, advancing down the river, pushing a long black pole. He was coming for Dirk, that bargeman, coming on and on. And the black boat that he rode was low in the water, very full of emptiness.

So he stood up and pulled Gwen up with him, saying nothing except he wanted to move on. And they ran from the ghosts, back to the terrace where the gray aircar waited.

Then it took them up again, for a second interlude of wind and sky and silent thought. Gwen flew them farther south and then east, and Dirk watched and brooded and was quiet, and at intervals she would look over at him and, never meaning to, she would smile.

They came at last to the sea.

The city of the afternoon was built along the shore of a jagged bay where dark green waves crested to break against rotting wharfs. Once it was called Musquel-by-the-Sea, Gwen said as they circled above it in low, looping spirals. Though it had risen with the other cities of Worlorn, there was an air of the ancient about it. The streets of Musquel were broken-backed snakes, twisting cobbled alleys between leaning towers of multicolored bricks. It was a brick city. Blue bricks, red bricks, yellow, green, orange, bricks painted and striped and speckled, bricks slammed together with mortar as black as obsidian or as red as Satan above, slammed together in crazy clashing patterns. Even more gaudy were the painted canvas awnings of the merchant stalls that still lined the rambling streets and sat deserted on the abandoned wooden piers.

They landed on a pier that looked stronger than most, listened to the breakers for a time, and then strolled into the city. All empty—all dust. The streets were windswept and vacant, the domes and onion towers deserted, and the fat red sun above washed out all the once-gay colors. The bricks crumbled as well; dust was everywhere, multicolored and choking. Musquel was not a well-built city, and now it was as dead as Twelfth Dream.

"It's primitive," Dirk said, amid the remains. They stood at the juncture of two alleys where a deep well had been sunk and ringed with stone. Black water splashed below. "The whole feel is pre-space, and the signs say the same thing about the culture. Braque is like this, but not to this degree. They have a little of the old technology, bits and pieces where they aren't forbidden by religion. Musquel looks as if it had nothing."

She nodded, running her hand lightly along the top of the well, sending a stream of dust and pebbles to tumble into darkness. The jade-and-silver shone dull red on her left arm, catching Dirk's eye and making him wince and wonder once again. What was it? A slave's mark, or a token of love, what? But he pushed the thought aside, reluctant to consider it.

"The people who built Musquel had very little,"

she was saying. "They came from the Forgotten Colony, which is sometimes called Letheland by the other outworlders, and is always called Earth by its own people. On High Kavalaan the people themselves are called the Lostfolk. Who they are, how they got to their world, where they came from . . ." She smiled and shrugged. "No one knows. They were here before the Kavalars, though, and possibly before the *Mao Tsetung,* which history records as the first human starship to breach the Tempter's Veil. The traditional Kavalars are certain all the Lostfolk are mockmen and Hrangan demons, but they have proved that they can interbreed with other human stocks from better-known worlds. But mostly the Forgotten Colony is a solitary globe, with not much interest in the rest of space. They have a Bronze Age culture, fisherfolk mostly, and they keep to themselves."

"I'm surprised they even came here at all then," Dirk said, "or bothered to build a city."

"Ah," she said, smiling and brushing loose more crumbling stone to fall into the well with tiny splashes. "But everyone had to build a city, all fourteen outworld cultures. That was the idea. Wolfheim had found the Forgotten Colony a few centuries ago, and so Wolfheim and Tober between them dragged the Lostfolk here. They had no starships of their own. Fisherfolk back on their homeworld so were they made fisherfolk here. Again it was Wolfheim, with the World of the Blackwine Ocean, who stocked the seas for them. They fished with woven nets from little boats, small black men and women bare to the waist, and they fried the catch in open pits for the visitors. They had bards and street singers to bring their alleys joy. Everyone stopped at Musquel during the Festival to listen to their odd myths and eat the fried fish and rent boats. But I don't think the Lostfolk loved the city much. Within a month of the Festival's end, every one of them was gone. They didn't even take down their awnings, and you can still find fish knives and clothing and a bone or two if you prowl through the buildings."

"Have you?"

"No. But I hear stories. Kirak Redsteel Cavis, the poet who lives in Larteyn, stayed here once and wandered and wrote some songs."

Dirk looked around, but there was nothing to see. Fading bricks and empty streets, unglassed windows like the sockets of a thousand blind eyes, painted awnings flapping loudly in the wind. Nothing. "Another city of ghosts," he commented.

"No," Gwen said. "No, I don't think so. The Lostfolk never gave their souls to Musquel, or to Worlorn. Their ghosts all went home with them."

Dirk shivered, and the city felt suddenly even emptier than it had a moment before. Emptier than empty. It was a strange idea. "Is Larteyn the only city that has any life at all?" he asked.

"No," she said, turning from the wall. They walked down the alley together, back in the direction of the waterfront. "No, I'll show you life now, if you'd like. Come on."

Airborne again, they were on another ride through the gathering gloom. They had consumed most of the afternoon reaching Musquel and wandering through it; Fat Satan was low on the western horizon, and one of the four yellow attendants had already sunk out of sight. It was twilight again, in fact as well as in appearance.

Very restless, Dirk took the controls this time, while Gwen sat at his side with her arm resting very lightly on his, giving curt directions. Most of the day was gone already, and he had so much to say, so much to ask, so many things to decide. Yet he had done none of it. Soon, though, he promised himself as he flew. Soon.

The aircar purred very softly, almost inaudibly, beneath his gentle touch. The ground grew dark below, and the kilometers raced by. Life, Gwen told him, would be found ahead, west, due west, toward the sunset.

The city of the evening was a single silver building with its feet in the rolling hills far beneath them and its head in the clouds two kilometers up. It was a city of light, its flanks metallic and windowless and shimmering with white-hot brilliance. Coruscating, flashing, the light climbed the vaulting shaft in waves, beginning at the far bottom where the city was anchored deep into the primal rock, then climbing and climbing and growing steadily brighter as the city rose and narrowed like the vast needle it was. Faster and higher the wave of light would ascend, up all that incredible climb, until it reached that cloud-crusted silver spire in a burst of blinding glory. And by then, three later waves had already begun to follow it up.

"Challenge," Gwen named the city as they approached. Its name and its intent. It was built by the urbanites of ai-Emerel, whose home cities are black steel towers set amid rolling plains. Each Emereli city was a nation-state, all in a single tower, and most Emereli never left the building they were born in (although those that did, Gwen said, often became the greatest wanderers in all of space). Challenge was all those Emereli towers in one, silver-white instead of black, twice as haughty and three times as tall—ai-Emerel's arcological philosophy embodied in metal and plastic—fusion-powered, automatic, computerized, and self-repairing. The Emereli boasted that it was immortal, a final proof that the glories of Fringe technology (or Emereli technology, at any rate) gleamed no less bright than that of Newholme or Avalon or even Old Earth itself.

There were dark horizontal slashes in the body of the city—airlot landing decks, each ten levels from the last. Dirk homed in on one, and when he reached it the black slit blazed into light for his approach. The opening was easily ten meters high; he had no trouble setting them down in the vast airlot on the hundredth level.

As they climbed out, a deep bass voice spoke to them from nowhere. "Welcome," it said. "I am the Voice of Challenge. May I entertain you?"

Dirk glanced back over his shoulder, and Gwen laughed at him. "The city brain," she explained. "A supercomputer. I told you this city still lived."

"May I entertain you?" the Voice repeated. It came from the walls.

"Maybe," Dirk said tentatively. "I think we're probably hungry. Can you feed us?"

The Voice did not answer, but a wall panel rolled back several meters away and a silent cushioned vehicle moved out and stopped before them. They got in and the vehicle moved off through another obliging wall.

They rolled on soft balloon tires through a succession of spotless white corridors, past countless rows of numbered doors, while music played soothingly around them. Dirk remarked briefly that the white lights were a harsh contrast to the dim evening sky of Worlorn, and instantly the corridors became a soft, muted blue.

The fat-tired car let them off at a restaurant, and a robowaiter who sounded much like the Voice offered them menus and wine lists. Both selections were extensive, not limited to cuisine from ai-Emerel or even to the outworlds, but including famous dishes and vintage wines from all the scattered worlds of the manrealm, including a few that Dirk had never heard of. Each dish had its world of origin printed in small type beneath it on the menu. They mulled the selection for a long time. Finally Dirk chose sand dragon broiled in butter, from Jamison's World, and Gwen ordered bluespawn-in-cheese, from Old Poseidon.

The wine they picked was clear and white. The robot brought it frozen in a cube of ice and cracked it free, and somehow it was still liquid and quite cold.

That, the Voice insisted, was the way it should be served. Dinner came on warm plates of silver and bone. Dirk pulled a clawed leg from his entree, peeled back the shell, and tasted the white, buttery meat.

"This is incredible," he said, nodding down at his plate. "I lived on Jamison's World for a while, and those Jamies do love their fresh-broiled sand dragon, and this is as good as any I had. Frozen? Frozen and shipped here? Hell, the Emereli must have needed a fleet to move all the food they'd need for this place."

"Not frozen," came the reply. It wasn't Gwen, though she stared at him with a bemused grin. The Voice answered him. "Before the Festival, the trading ship *Blue Plate Special* from ai-Emerel visited as many worlds as it could reach, collecting and preserving samples of their finest foodstuffs. The voyage, long planned, took some forty-three standard years, under four captains and as many crews. Finally the ship came to Worlorn, and in the kitchens and bio-tanks of Challenge the collected samples were cloned and recloned to feed the multitudes. Thus were the fishes and loaves multiplied by no false prophet but by the scientists of ai-Emerel."

"It sounds very smug," Gwen said with a giggle.

"It sounds like a set speech," Dirk said. Then he shrugged and went back to his dinner, as did Gwen. The two of them ate alone, except for their robowaiter and the Voice, in the center of the restaurant built to hold hundreds. All around them, empty but immaculate, other tables sat waiting with dark-red tablecloths and bright silver dinnerware. The customers were gone a decade ago; but the Voice and the city had infinite patience.

Afterwards, over coffee (black and thick with cream and spices, a blend from Avalon of fond memory), Dirk felt mellow and relaxed, perhaps more at ease than he had been since coming to Worlorn. Jaan Vikary and the jade-and-silver—it gleamed dark and beautiful in the dim lights of the restaurant, exquisitely wrought yet oddly drained of menace and meaning—

had shrunk somehow in importance now that he was back with Gwen. Across from him, sipping from a white china mug and smiling her dreamy faraway smile, she looked very approachable, very like the Jenny that he had known and loved once, the lady of the whisperjewel.

"Nice," he said, nodding, meaning everything around them.

And Gwen nodded back at him. "Nice," she agreed, smiling, and Dirk ached for her, Guinevere of the wide green eyes and the endless black hair, she who had cared, his lost soulmate.

He leaned forward and stared down into his cup. There were no omens in the coffee. He had to talk to her. "It's all been nice tonight," he said. "Like Avalon."

When she murmured, agreeing yet again, he continued. "Is there anything left, Gwen?"

She regarded him levelly and sipped at her coffee. "Not a fair question, Dirk, you know that. There is always something left. If what you had was real to begin with. If not, well, then it doesn't matter. But if it was real, then something, a chunk of love, a cup of hate, despair, resentment, lust. Whatever. But something."

"I don't know," Dirk t'Larien said, sighing. His eyes looked down and inward. "Maybe you're the only reality I've had, then."

"Sad," she said.

"Yes," he said. "I guess." His eyes came up. "I've got a lot left, Gwen. Love, hate, resentment, all of that. Like you said. Lust." He laughed.

She only smiled. "Sad," she said again.

He was not willing to let it go. "And you? Something, Gwen?"

"Yes. Can't deny it. Something. And it's been growing, off and on."

"Love?"

"You're pressing," she said gently, setting down her

cup. The robowaiter at her elbow filled it again, already creamed and spiced. "I asked you not to."

"I have to," he said. "Hard enough to be so close to you, and talk about Worlorn or Kavalar customs or even hunters. That's not what I want to talk about!"

"I know. Two old lovers standing together talking. That's a common situation and a common strain. Both of them afraid, not knowing whether to try to open old gates again, not knowing if the other one wants them to reawaken those sleeping thoughts or let them go. Every time I think a thought of Avalon and almost say it, I wonder, Does he want me to talk about it or is he praying that I won't?"

"I suppose that depends on what you were going to say. Once I tried to start it all again. Remember? Just afterwards. I sent you my whisperjewel. You never answered, never came." His voice was even, with a faint tinge of reproach and regret, but no anger. Somehow he had lost his anger, just for now.

"Did you ever think why?" Gwen said. "I got the jewel and cried. I was still alone then, hadn't met Jaan yet, and I wanted someone so badly. I would have gone back to you if you'd called me."

"I did call you. You didn't come."

A grim smile. "Ah, Dirk. The whisperjewel came in a small box, and taped to it was a note. 'Please,' the note said, 'come back to me now. I need you, Jenny.' That was what it said. I cried and cried. If you'd only written 'Gwen,' if you'd only loved *Gwen,* me. But no, it was always Jenny, even afterwards, even then."

Dirk remembered, and winced. "Yes," he admitted after a short silence. "I guess I did write that. I'm sorry. I never understood. But I do now. Is it too late?"

"I said so. In the woods. Too late, Dirk, it's all dead. You'll hurt us if you press."

"*All* dead? You said something was left, and growing. Just now you said it. Make up your mind, Gwen. I don't want to hurt you, or me. But I want—"

"I know what you want. It can't be. It's gone."

"Why?" he asked. He pointed across the table at her bracelet. "Because of that? Jade-and-silver forever and ever, is that it?"

"Maybe," she said. Her voice faltered, uncertain. "I don't know. We . . . that is, I . . ."

Dirk remembered all the things that Ruark had told him. "I know it's not easy to talk about," he said carefully, gently. "And I promised to wait. But some things can't wait. You said Jaan is your husband, right? What is Garse? What does *betheyn* mean?"

"Heldwife," she said. "But you don't understand. Jaan is different than other Kavalars, stronger and wiser and more decent. He is changing things, he alone. The old ties, of *betheyn* to highbond, our ties are not like that. Jaan doesn't believe that, no more than he believes in hunting mockmen."

"He believes in High Kavalaan," Dirk said, "and in code duello. Maybe he's atypical, but he's still a Kavalar."

It was the wrong thing to say. Gwen only grinned at him and rallied. "Pfui," she said. "Now you sound like Arkin."

"Do I? Maybe Arkin is right, though. One other thing. You say Jaan doesn't believe in many of the old ways, right?"

Gwen nodded.

"Fine. What about Garse, then? I haven't had as much a chance to talk to him. Garse is equally enlightened, no doubt?"

That stopped her. "Garse . . ." she began. She stopped and shook her head dubiously. "Well, Garse is more conservative."

"Yes," said Dirk. Suddenly he seemed to have it all. "Yes, I think he is, and that's a big part of your problem, isn't it? On High Kavalaan it's not man and woman. No, it's man and man and maybe woman, but even then she's not so terribly important. You may love Jaan, but you don't care for Garse Janacek all that damn much, do you?"

"I feel a lot of affection for—"

"Do you?"

Gwen's face went hard. "Stop it," she said.

Her voice frightened him. He drew back, suddenly and sickeningly aware of the way he had been leaning across the table, pressing, pushing, jabbing, attacking, and taunting her, he who had come to care and to help. "I'm sorry," he blurted.

Silence. She was staring at him, her lower lip trembling, while she drew herself together and gathered strength. "You're right," she finally said. "Partly, anyway. I'm not . . . well . . . not entirely happy with my lot." She gave a forced ironic chuckle. "I guess I fool myself a lot. A bad idea, fooling yourself. Everyone does it, though, everyone. I wear the jade-and-silver and tell myself I'm more than a heldwife, more than other Kavalar women. Why? Just because Jaan says so? Jaan Vikary is a good man, Dirk, really he is, in many ways the best man I have ever known. I did love him, maybe I still do. I don't know. I'm very confused right now. But whether I love him or not, I owe him. Debt and obligation, those are the Kavalar bonds. Love is only something Jaan picked up on Avalon, and I'm not quite sure he's mastered it yet, either. I would have been his *teyn,* if I could. But he already had a *teyn.* Besides, not even Jaan would go that far against the customs of his world. You heard what he said about the duels—and all because he searched some old computer banks and found out one of their Kavalar folk heroes had tits." She smiled grimly. "Imagine what would happen if he took me to *teyn!* He would lose everything, just everything. Ironjade is relatively tolerant, yes, but it will be centuries before any holdfast is ready for that. No woman has ever worn the iron-and-glowstone."

"Why?" Dirk said. "I don't understand. All of you keep making these comments—about breeding women and heldwives and women hiding in caves afraid to come out, all that stuff. And I keep not quite believing it. How did High Kavalaan get so twisted up anyway? What do they have against women? Why is it so critical that the founder of Ironjade was female? Lots of people are, you know."

Gwen gave him a wan smile and rubbed her temples gently with her fingertips, as if she had a headache she was hoping to massage away. "You should have let Jaan finish," she said. "Then you'd know as much as we do. He was only warming up. He hadn't even gotten to the Sorrowing Plague." She sighed. "It is all a very long story, Dirk, and right now I don't have the goddamn energy. Wait till we get back to Larteyn. I'll hunt up a copy of Jaan's thesis and you can read it all for yourself."

"All right," Dirk said. "But there are a few things I'm not going to be able to read in any thesis. A few minutes ago you said you weren't sure if you loved Jaan anymore. You certainly don't love High Kavalaan. I think you hate Garse. So why are you doing all this to yourself?"

"You have a way of asking nasty questions," she said sourly. "But before I answer, let me correct you on a few points. I may hate Garse, as you say. Sometimes I'm quite sure that I hate Garse, though it would kill Jaan to hear me say that. At other times, however— I wasn't lying before when I told you that I feel considerable affection for him. When I first arrived on High Kavalaan, I was as dewy-eyed and innocent and vulnerable as I could be. Jaan had explained everything to me beforehand, of course, very patiently, very thoroughly, and I had accepted it. I was from Avalon, after all, and you can't get more sophisticated than Avalon, can you? Not unless you're an Earther. I'd studied all the weird cultures humanity has spread among the stars, and I knew that anyone who steps into a starship has got to be prepared to adapt to widely different social systems and moralities. I knew that sexual-familial customs vary and that Avalon was not necessarily wiser than High Kavalaan in that area. I was very wise, I thought.

"But I wasn't ready for the Kavalars, oh no. As long as I live I will never forget a second of the fear and the trauma of my first day and night in the hold-fasts of Ironjade, as Jaan Vikary's *betheyn*. Especially the first night." She laughed. "Jaan had warned me, of course, and— Hell, I just wasn't ready to be *shared*. What can I say? It was bad, but I lived. Garse helped. He was honestly concerned for me, and very much for Jaan. You might even say he was tender. I confided in him; he listened and cared. And the next morning the verbal abuse started. I was frightened and hurt; Jaan was baffled and gloriously angry. He threw Garse halfway across the room the first time he called me *betheyn*-bitch. Garse was quiet for a little while after that. He rests fairly often, but he never stops. He is truly remarkable, in a way. He would challenge and kill any Kavalar who insulted me half so badly as he does. He knows that his jokes enrage Jaan and provoke terrible quarrels—or at least they did. By now Jaan has become dulled to it all. Yet he persists. Maybe he can't help himself, or maybe he honestly loathes me, or maybe he just enjoys inflicting pain. If so, I haven't given him much joy these past few years. One of the first things I decided was that I wasn't going to let him make me cry anymore. I haven't. Even when he comes out and says something that makes me want to split his head with an axe, I just smile and grit my teeth and try to think of something unpleasant to say back to him. Once or twice I've managed to throw him off his stride. Usually he leaves me feeling like a crushed bug.

"Yet, in spite of everything, there are *other* moments as well. Truces, little ceasefires in our never-ending war, times of surprising warmth and compassion. Many of them at night. They always shock me when they come. They're too intense. Once, believe it or not, I told Garse I loved him. He laughed at me. He did not love me, he said loudly, rather I was *cro-betheyn* to him and he treated me as he was obliged to treat me by the bond that existed between us. That was the last time I even came close to crying. I fought and I fought, and I won. I did not cry. I just shouted something at him and rushed out into the corridor. We lived underground, you know. Everyone lives underground on High Kavalaan. I wasn't wearing much except my bracelet, and I ran around crazy, and finally this man tried to stop me—a drunk, an idiot, a blind man who could not see the jade-and-silver, I don't know. I was so furious I pulled his sidearm out of its holster and smashed him across the face with it, the first time I'd ever hit another human being in anger, and just then Jaan and Garse arrived. Jaan seemed calm, but he was very upset. Garse was almost happy, and spoiling for a fight. As if the man I'd overpowered hadn't been insulted enough, Garse had to tell me that I should pick up all the teeth I'd knocked out and hand them back, that I had quite enough already. They were lucky to avoid a duel over that comment."

"How the hell did you ever get involved in a situation like this, Gwen?" Dirk demanded. He was struggling to keep his voice from breaking. He was angry with her, hurt for her, and yet oddly—or perhaps not so oddly—elated. It was all true, everything Ruark had told him. The Kimdissi was her good friend and her confidant; no wonder she had sent for him. Her life was a misery, she was a slave, and he could set it right, *him*. "You must have had some idea what it would be like."

She shrugged. "I lied to myself," she said, "and I let Jaan lie to me, although I think he honestly believes all the lovely falsehoods he tells me. If I had it to do over— But I don't. I was ready for him, Dirk, and I needed him, and I loved him. And he had no iron-and-fire to give me. That he had given already, so he gave me jade-and-silver, and I took it just to be near him, with only the vaguest knowledge of what it meant. I'd lost you not long before. I didn't want Jaan to go as well. So I put on the pretty little bracelet and said very loudly, 'I am more than *betheyn*,' as if that made a difference. Give a thing a name and it will somehow come to be. To Garse, I am Jaan's *betheyn* and his *cro-betheyn,* and that is all. The names define the bonds and duties. What more could there possibly be? To every other Kavalar it is the same. When I try to grow, to step beyond the name, Garse is there, angry, shouting *betheyn!* at me. Jaan is different, only Jaan, and sometimes I can't help myself and I begin to wonder how *he* really feels."

Her hands came up on the tablecloth and became two small fists, side by side. "The same damn thing, Dirk. You wanted to make me into Jenny, and I saved myself by rejecting the name. But like a fool I took the jade-and-silver, and now I am heldwife and all the denials I can utter won't change that. *The same damn thing!*" Her voice was shrill, her fists clutched so tightly the knuckles were turning white.

"We can change it," Dirk said quickly. "Come back to me." He sounded inane, hopeful, despairing, triumphant, concerned; his tone was everything at once.

At first Gwen did not answer. Finger by finger, very slowly, she unclenched her fists and stared at her hands solemnly, breathing deeply, turning her hands over and over again as if they were some strange artifacts that had been set before her for inspection. Then she put them flat on the table and pushed, rising to her feet. "Why?" she said, and the calm control had come back to her voice. "Why, Dirk? So you can make me Jenny again? Is that why? Because I loved you once, because something may be left?"

"Yes! No, I mean. You confuse me." He rose too.

She smiled. "Ah, but I loved Jaan once also, more recently than you. And with him now there are other ties, all the obligations of jade-and-silver. With you, well, only memories, Dirk." When he did not reply—he stood and waited—Gwen started toward the door. He followed her.

The robowaiter intercepted them and blocked the way, its face a featureless metal ovoid. "The charge," it said. "I require the number of your Festival accounts."

Gwen frowned. "Larteyn billing, Ironjade 797-742-

677," she snapped. "Register both meals to that number."

"Registered," the robot said as it moved out of their way. Behind them the restaurant went dark.

The Voice had their car waiting for them. Gwen told it to take them back to the airlot, and it set off through corridors that suddenly swam with cheerful colors and happy music. "The damn computer registered tension in our voices," she said, a little angrily. "Now it's trying to cheer us up."

"It's not doing a very good job," Dirk said, but he smiled as he said it. Then, "Thank you for the meal. I converted my standards to Festival scrip before I arrived, but it didn't come to much, I'm afraid."

"Ironjade is not poor," Gwen said. "And there isn't much to pay for on Worlorn, in any case."

"Hmm. Yes. I never thought there would be, until now."

"Festival programming," Gwen said. "This is the only city that still runs that way. The others are all shut down. Once a year ai-Emerel sends a man to clear all charges from the banks. Although soon it will reach the point where the trip will cost more than he picks up."

"I'm surprised that it doesn't already."

"Voice!" she said. "How many people live in Challenge today?"

The walls answered. "Presently I have three hundred and nine legal residents and forty-two guests, including yourselves. You may, if you wish, become residents. The charge is quite reasonable."

"Three hundred nine?" Dirk said. "Where?"

"Challenge was built to hold twenty million," Gwen said. "You can hardly expect to run into them, but they're here. In the other cities as well, though not as many as in Challenge. The living is easiest here. The dying will be easy too, if the highbonds of Braith ever think to begin hunting the cities instead of the wild. That has always been Jaan's great fear."

"Who are they?" Dirk demanded, curious. "How do

they live? I don't understand at all. Doesn't Challenge lose a fortune every day?"

"Yes. A fortune in energy, wasted, squandered. But that was the point of Challenge and Larteyn and the whole Festival. Waste, defiant waste, to prove that the Fringe was rich and strong, waste on a grand scale such as the manrealm had never before known, a whole planet shaped and then abandoned. You see? As for Challenge, well, if truth be known, its life is all empty motion now. It powers itself from fusion reactors and throws off the energy in fireworks no one sees. It harvests tons of food every day with its huge farming mechs, but no one eats except the handful— hermits, religious cultists, lost children turned savage, whatever dregs remain from the Festival. It still sends a boat to Musquel every day to pick up fish. There are never any fish, of course."

"The Voice doesn't rewrite the program?"

"Ah, the crux of the matter! The Voice is an idiot. It can't really think, can't program itself. Oh, yes, the Emereli wanted to impress people, and the Voice is big, to be sure. But really it's very primitive compared to the Academy computers on Avalon or the Artificial Intelligences of Old Earth. It can't think, or change very well. It does what it was told, and the Emereli told it to go on, to withstand the cold as long as it could. It will."

She looked at Dirk. "Like you," she said, "it keeps on long after its persistence has lost point and meaning, it keeps on pushing—for nothing—after everything is dead."

"Oh?" said Dirk. "But, *until* everything is dead, you have to push. That's the point, Gwen. There is no other way, is there? I rather admire the city, even if it is an overgrown idiot like you say."

She shook her head. "You would."

"There's more," he said. "You bury everything too soon, Gwen. Worlorn may be dying, but it isn't dead yet. And us, well, we don't have to be dead either. What you said back at the restaurant, about Jaan and me, I think you should think about it. Decide what's left, for me, for him. How heavy that bracelet weighs on your arm"—he pointed—"'and what name you like best, or rather who is more likely to give you your *own* name. You see? Then tell me what's dead and what's alive!"

He felt very satisfied with the little speech. Surely, he thought, she could see that he could give up Jenny and let her be Gwen far more easily than Jaantony Vikary could make her a female *teyn* instead of a mere *betheyn*. It seemed very clear. But she only looked at him, saying nothing, until they reached the airlot.

Then she got out of the vehicle. "When the four of us chose where we would live on Worlorn, Garse and Jaan voted for Larteyn and Arkin for Twelfth Dream," she said. "I voted for neither. Nor for Challenge, for all its life. I don't like living in a warren. You want to know what's dead and what's alive? Come, then, I'll show you *my* city."

Then they were outside once more, Gwen tight-lipped and silent behind the controls, the sudden cold of the night air all around them, Challenge's shining shaft vanishing behind. Now it was deep darkness again, as it had been on the night when the *Shuddering of Forgotten Enemies* had brought Dirk t'Larien to Worlorn. Only a dozen lonely stars swung through the sky, and half of those were hidden by the churning clouds. The suns had all set.

The city of the night was vast and intricate, with only a few scattered lights to pierce the darkness it was set in, as a pale jewel is set on soft black felt. Alone among the cities it stood in the wild beyond the mountainwall, and it belonged there, in the forests of chokers and ghost trees and blue widowers. From the dark of the wood, its slim white towers rose wraithlike toward the stars, linked by graceful spun bridges that glittered like frozen spiderwebs. Low domes stood lonely vigils amid a network of canals whose waters caught the tower lights and the twinkle of infrequent far-off stars, and ringing the city were a number of strange buildings that looked like thin-fleshed angular hands clutching up at the sky. The trees, such as there were, were outworld trees; there was no grass, only thick carpets of dimly glowing phosphorescent moss.

And the city had a song.

It was like no music Dirk had ever heard. It was eerie and wild and almost inhuman, and it rose and fell and shifted constantly. It was a dark symphony of the void, of starless nights and troubled dreams. It was made of moans and whispers and howls, and a strange low note that could only be the sound of sadness. For all of this, it *was* music.

Dirk looked at Gwen, wonder in his eyes. "How?"

She was listening as she flew, but his question tore her loose from the drifting strains, and she smiled faintly. "Darkdawn built this city, and the Darklings are a strange people. There is a gap in the mountains. Their weather wardens made the winds blow through it. Then they built the spires, and in the crest of each there is an aperture. The wind plays the city like an instrument. The same song, over and over. The weather control devices shift the winds, and with each shift, some towers sound their notes while others fall silent.

"The music—the symphony was written on Dark-dawn, centuries ago, by a composer named Lamiya-Bailis. A computer plays it, they say, by running the wind machines. The odd thing about it is that the Darklings never used computers much and have very little of the technology. Another story was popular during the days of the Festival. A legend, say. It claimed that Darkdawn was a world always perilously close to the edge of sanity, and that the music of Lamiya-Bailis, the greatest of the Darkling dreamers, pushed the whole culture over into madness and despair. In punishment, they say, her brain was kept alive, and can now be found deep under the mountains of Worlorn, hooked up to the wind machines and playing her own masterpiece over and over, forever." She shivered. "Or at least until the atmosphere freezes. Even the weather wardens of Darkdawn can't stop that."

"It's . . ." Dirk, lost in the song, could find no words. "It fits, somehow," he finally said. "A song for Worlorn."

"It fits now," Gwen said. "It's a song of twilight and the coming of night, with no dawn again, ever. A song of endings. In the high day of the Festival the song was out of place. Kryne Lamiya—that was this city's name, Kryne Lamiya, although it was often called the Siren City, in much the same way that Larteyn was called the Firefort—well, it was never a popular place. It looks big, but it isn't really. It was built to house only a hundred thousand, and it was never more than a quarter full. Like Darkdawn itself, I suppose. How many travelers ever go to Darkdawn, right on the edge of the Great Black Sea? And how many go in winter, when the Darkdawn sky is almost totally empty, with nothing to see by but the light of a few far galaxies? Not many. It takes a peculiar sort of person for that. Here too, to love Kryne Lamiya. People said the song disturbed them. And it never stopped. The Darklings didn't even soundproof the sleeping rooms."

Dirk said nothing. He was looking at the fairy spires and listening to them sing.

"Do you want to land?" Gwen asked.

He nodded, and she spiraled down. They found an open landing slit in the side of one of the towers. Unlike the airlots in Challenge and Twelfth Dream, this one was not completely empty. Two other aircars rested there, a stub-winged red sportster and a tiny black-and-silver teardrop, both of them long abandoned. The windblown dust was thick on their hoods and canopies, and the cushions inside the sportster had gone to rot. Out of curiosity, Dirk tried them both. The sportster was dead, burned-out, its power vanished years ago. But the little teardrop still warmed under his touch, and the control panel lit up and flickered, showing that a small reserve of power was left. The huge gray manta from High Kavalaan was bigger and heavier than the two derelicts combined.

From the airlot they went out into a long gallery where gray-and-white light-murals swirled and spun in dim patterns that matched the echoing music. Then they climbed to a balcony they had spied when coming in.

Outside, the music was all around them, calling to them with unearthly voices, touching them and playing with their hair, booming and beckoning like passion-thunder. Dirk took Gwen's hand in his own and listened as he stared blindly out across the towers and domes and canals toward the forests and the mountains beyond. The music-wind seemed to pull at him as he stood there. It spoke to him softly, urging him to jump, it seemed—to end it all, all the silly and undignified and ultimately meaningless futility that he called his life.

Gwen saw it in his eyes. She squeezed his hand, and when he looked at her she said, "During the Festival, more than two hundred people committed suicide in Kryne Lamiya. Ten times the number of any other city. Despite the fact that this city had the smallest population of all."

Dirk nodded. "Yes. I can feel it. The music."

"A celebration of death," Gwen said. "Yet, you know, the Siren City itself is *not* dead, not like Musquel or Twelfth Dream at all. It still lives, stubbornly, if only to exalt despair and glorify the emptiness of the very life it clings to. Strange, eh?"

"Why would they build such a place? It's beautiful, but—"

"I have a theory," Gwen said. "The Darklings are black-humored nihilists, chiefly, and I think that Kryne Lamiya is their bitter joke on High Kavalaan and Wolfheim and Tober and the other worlds that pushed so hard for the Festival of the Fringe. The Darklings came, all right, and they built a city that said it was all worthless. *All* worthless—the Festival, human civilization, life itself. Think of it! What a trap for a smug tourist to walk into!" She threw back her head and began to laugh wildly, and Dirk briefly felt a sudden irrational fear, as if his Gwen had gone mad.

"And you wanted to live here?" he said.

Her laughter faded as abruptly as it had begun; the wind snatched it from her. Away on their right, a needle-tower sounded a brief piercing note that wavered like the wail of an animal in pain. Their own tower answered with the low mournful moan of a foghorn, lingering, lingering. The music swirled around them. Far off, Dirk thought he could hear the pounding of a single drum, short dull booms, evenly spaced.

"Yes," Gwen said. "I wanted to live here." The foghorn faded; four reedy spires across the canal, tied together by drooping bridges, began to ululate wildly, each note higher than the one preceding, until they finally climbed up into the inaudible. The drum persisted, unchanging: boom, boom, boom.

Dirk sighed. "I understand," he said, in a voice very tired. "I would live here too, I suppose, though I wonder how long I'd live if I did. Braque was a little like this, the faintest echo, mostly at night. Maybe that was why I lived *there*. I had gotten very weary, Gwen. Very. I guess I'd given up. In the old days, you know, I was always searching—for love, for fairy gold, for the secrets of the universe, whatever. But after you left me . . . I don't know, everything went wrong, turned sour in my mouth. And when something *did* go right, I'd find it didn't matter, didn't make any difference. It was all empty. I tried and tried, but all I got was tired and apathetic and cynical. Maybe that was why I came here. You . . . well, I was better then, when I was with you. I hadn't given up on quite so many things. I thought that maybe, if I found you again, maybe I could find *me* again as well. It hasn't worked quite that way. I don't know that it's working at all."

"Listen to Lamiya-Bailis," Gwen said, "and her music will tell you that *nothing* works, that nothing means anything. I did want to live here, you know. I voted

. . . well, I didn't plan to vote this way, but we were talking it over when we first landed, and it just came out. It scared me. Maybe you and I are still a lot alike, Dirk. I've gotten tired too. Mostly it doesn't show. I have my work to keep me busy, and Arkin is my friend, and Jaan loves me. But then I come here . . . or sometimes I just slow down and think a bit too long, and then I wonder. It's not enough, the things I have. Not what I wanted."

She turned toward him and took his hand in both of hers. "Yes, I've thought of you. I've thought that things were better when you and I were together back on Avalon, and I've thought that maybe it was still *you* I loved and not Jaan, and I've thought that you and I could bring the magic back, make it all make sense again. But don't you see? It isn't *so,* Dirk, and all your pushing won't make it so. Listen to the city, listen to Kryne Lamiya. There's your truth. You think about me, and I sometimes about you, only because it's dead between us. That's the only reason it seems better. Happiness yesterday and happiness tomorrow, but never today, Dirk. It can't be, because it's only an illusion after all, and illusions only look real from a distance. We're over, my dreamy lost love, *over,* and that's the best thing of all, because it's the only thing that makes it good."

She was weeping; slow tears moved trembling down her cheeks. Kryne Lamiya wept with her, the towers crying their lament. But it mocked her too, as if to say, Yes, I see your grief, but grief has no more meaning than anything else, pain is as empty as pleasure. The spires wailed, thin gratings laughed insanely, and the low far-off drum went: boom, boom, boom.

Again, more strongly this time, Dirk wanted to jump —off the balcony toward the pale stone and dark canals below. A dizzy fall, and then rest at last. But the city sang him for a fool: *Rest?* it sang, there is no rest in death. Only nothing. Nothing. Nothing. The drum, the winds, the wailings. He trembled, still holding

Gwen's hands. He looked down toward the ground below.

Something was moving down the canal. Bobbing and floating, drifting easily, coming toward him. A black barge, with a solitary pole-man. "No," he said.

Gwen blinked. "No?" she repeated.

And suddenly the words came, the words that the *other* Dirk t'Larien would have said to his Jenny, and the words were in *his* mouth, and though he was no longer quite sure that he could believe them, he found himself saying them all the same. *"No!"* he said, all but shouting it at the city, throwing a sudden rage back at the mocking music of Kryne Lamiya. "Damn it, Gwen, all of us have something of this city in us, yes. The test is how we meet it. All this is frightening"—he let loose of her hands and gestured out at the darkness, the sweep of his hand taking in everything—"what it *says* is frightening, and worse is the fear you get when part of you agrees, when you feel that it's all true, that you belong here. But what do you do about it? If you're weak, you ignore it. Pretend it doesn't exist, you know, and maybe it'll go away. Busy yourself in the daylight with trivial tasks, and never think about the darkness outside. That's the way you let it win, Gwen. In the end it swallows you and all your trivia, and you and the other fools lie to each other blithely and welcome it. You can't be like that, Gwen, you *can't* be. You have to try. You're an ecologist, right? What's ecology all about? Life! You have to be on the side of life, everything you *are* says so. This city, this damn bone-white city with its death hymn, denies everything you believe in, everything you are. If you're strong, you'll face it and fight it and call it by name. Defy it."

Gwen had stopped weeping. "It is no use," she said, shaking her head.

"You're wrong," he answered. "About this city, and about us. It's all tied up, you see? You say you want to live here? Fine! *Live* here! To live in this city would be a victory all in itself, a philosophical victory. But live here because you know that life itself refutes

Lamiya-Bailis, live here and laugh at this absurd music of hers, *don't* live here and agree with this damn wailing lie." He took her hand again.

"I don't know," she said.

"I do," he said, lying.

"Do you *really* think that . . . that we could make it work again? Better than before?"

"You won't be Jenny," he promised. "Never again."

"I don't know," she repeated in a low whisper.

He took her face in both hands and raised it so her eyes looked at his. He kissed her, very lightly, the barest driest touching of their lips. Kryne Lamiya moaned. The foghorn sounded deep and sorrowing around them, the distant towers screamed and keened, and the solitary drum kept up its dull, meaningless booming.

After the kiss they stood amid the music and stared at each other. "Gwen," he finally said, in a voice not one half as strong and sure as it had been just a moment before. "I don't know either, I guess. But maybe it would be worth it just to try . . ."

"Maybe," she said, and her wide green eyes looked away and down again. "It would be hard, Dirk. And there's Jaan to think of, and Garse, so many problems. And we don't even know if it would be worth it. We don't know if it will make the slightest bit of difference."

"No, we don't," he said. "Lots of times in these last few years I've decided that it doesn't matter, that it's not worth trying. I don't feel good then, just tired, endlessly tired. Gwen, if we don't try, we'll never know."

She nodded. "Maybe," she said, and nothing more. The wind blew cold and strong; the music of the Darkling madness rose and fell. They went inside, then down the stairs from the balcony, past the fading, flickering walls of gray-white light, to where the solid sanity of their aircar rested, waiting to carry them back to Larteyn.

chapter 5

They flew from the white towers of Kryne
Lamiya to the fading fires of Larteyn in a lonely silence, not touching, both thinking their own thoughts.
Gwen left the aircar in its usual place on the roof, and
Dirk followed her downstairs to her door. "Wait," she
said in a quick whisper, when he had expected her to
say good night. She vanished inside; he waited, puzzled. There were noises from the other side of the door
—voices—then abruptly Gwen was back, pressing a
thick manuscript into his hand, an impressively heavy
mass of paper hand-bound in black leather. Jaan's thesis. He had almost forgotten. "Read it," she whispered,
leaning out the door. "Come up tomorrow morning,
and we'll talk some more." She kissed him lightly on
the cheek and closed the heavy door with a small click.
Dirk stood for a moment turning the bound manuscript
over in his hands, then turned toward the tubes.

He was only a few steps down the hall when he
heard the first shout. Then, somehow, he could not

continue; the sounds drew him back, and he stood listening at Gwen's door.

The walls were thick, and very little of what was said came through. The words and the meanings he lost entirely, but the voices themselves carried, and the tones. Gwen's voice dominated: loud, sharp-edged—at times she was shouting—close to the edge of hysteria. In his mind Dirk could see her pacing the living room before the gargoyles, the way she always paced when she was angry. Both of the Kavalars would be present, berating her—Dirk was sure he heard two other voices—one quiet and sure, without anger, questioning relentlessly. That had to be Jaan Vikary. His cadence gave him away, the rhythms of his speech distinctive even through the wall. The third voice, Garse Janacek, spoke infrequently at first, then more and more, with increasing volume and anger. After a time the quiet male voice was virtually silent, while Gwen and Garse screamed at one another. Then it said something, a sharp command. And Dirk heard a noise, a fleshy thud. A blow. Someone hitting someone, it could be nothing else.

Finally Vikary giving orders, followed by silence. The light went off inside the room.

Dirk stood quietly, holding Vikary's manuscript and wondering what to do. There did not seem to be anything he *could* do, except talk to Gwen the next morning and find out who had hit her, and why. It had to be Janacek, he thought.

Ignoring the tubes, he decided to walk downstairs to Ruark's rooms.

Once in bed, Dirk found he was immensely tired and badly shaken by the events of the day. So much all at once, he could hardly cope with it. The Kavalar hunters and their mockmen, the strange bitter life Gwen lived with Vikary and Janacek, the sudden dizzy possibility of her return. Unable to sleep, he thought about it all for a long time. Ruark was already asleep; there was no one to talk to. Finally Dirk picked up the thick manuscript Gwen had given him and began to leaf through the first few pages. There was nothing like a good chunk of scholarly writing to put a man to sleep, he reflected.

Four hours and a half-dozen cups of coffee later, he put down the manuscript, yawned, and rubbed his eyes. Then he shut off the light and stared at the darkness.

Jaan Vikary's thesis—*Myth and History: Origins of Holdfast Society As Based on an Interpretation of the* Demonsong *Cycle of Jamis-Lion Taal*—was a worse indictment of his people than anything that Arkin Ruark could possibly say, Dirk thought. He had laid it all out, with sources and documentation from the computer banks on Avalon, with lengthy quotations from the poetry of Jamis-Lion Taal and even lengthier dissertations on what Jamis Taal had meant. All of the things that he and Gwen had told Dirk that morning were there, in detail. Vikary supplied theories on theories, attempted to explain everything. He even explained the mockmen, more or less. He argued that during the Time of Fire and Demons some survivors from the cities had reached the mining camps and sought shelter. Once taken in, however, they proved dangerous. Some were victims of radiation sickness; they died slowly and horribly, and possibly passed the poison on to those who nursed them. Others, seemingly healthy, lived and became part of the proto-holdfast, until they married and produced children. Then the taint of radiation showed up. It was all conjecture on Vikary's part, with not even a line or two from Jamis-Lion to support it, yet it seemed a glib and plausible rationalization of the mockman myth.

Vikary also wrote at length of the event the Kavalars called the Sorrowing Plague—and what he carefully called "the shift to contemporary Kavalar sexual-familial patterns."

According to his hypothesis, the Hrangans had returned to High Kavalaan approximately a century after their first raid. The cities they had bombed were still slag; there was no sign of new building on the part of the humans. Yet the three slaveraces they had dropped to seed the planet were nowhere in evidence: decimated, extinct. Undoubtedly the Hrangan Mind commanding concluded that some of the humans still lived. To effect a final wiping up, the Hrangans dropped plague bombs. That was Vikary's theory.

Jamis-Lion's poems had no mention of Hrangans, but many mentions of sickness. All the surviving Kavalar accounts agreed on that. There was a Sorrowing Plague, a long period when one horrible epidemic after another swept through the holdfasts. Each turn of the season brought a new and more dreadful disease—the ultimate demon-enemy, one the Kavalars could not fight or kill.

Ninety men died out of every hundred. Ninety men, and ninety-nine women.

One of the many plagues, it seemed, was female-selective. The medical specialists Vikary had consulted on Avalon had told him that, based on the meager evidence he gave them—a few ancient poems and songs—it seemed likely that the female sex hormones acted as a catalyst for the disease. Jamis-Lion Taal had written that young maids were spared the bloody wasting because of their innocence, while the rutting *eyn-kethi* were struck down horribly and died in shuddering convulsions. Vikary interpreted this to mean that prepubescent girls were left untouched, while sexually mature women were devastated. An entire generation was wiped out. Worse, the disease lingered; no sooner did girl children reach puberty than the plague struck. Jamis-Lion made this a truth of vast religious significance.

Some women escaped—the naturally immune. Very few at first. More later; because they lived, producing sons and daughters, many of whom were also immune, while those who did not share the resistance died at puberty. Eventually all Kavalars were immune, with rare exceptions. The Sorrowing Plague ended.

But the damage had been done. Entire holdfasts had been wiped out; those that clung to life had seen their populations decline far below the numbers necessary to maintain a viable society. And the social structure and sexual roles had been warped irrevocably away from the monogamous egalitarianism of the early Taran colonists. Generations had grown to maturity in which men outnumbered women ten to one; little girls lived all through childhood with the knowledge that puberty might mean death. It was a grim time. On that both Jaan Vikary and Jamis-Lion Taal spoke with one voice.

Jamis-Lion wrote that sin had finally passed from High Kavalaan when the *eyn-kethi* were safely locked away from the daylight, back in the caves from which they had issued, where their shame could not be seen. Vikary wrote that the Kavalar survivors had fought back as best they could. They no longer had the technological skills to construct airtight sterilized chambers; but no doubt rumors of such places had drifted down the years to them, and they still hoped that such places could be proof against disease. So the surviving women were secured in prisonlike hospitals deep under the ground, in the safest part of the holdfast, the farthest from the contaminated wind and rain and water. Men who had once roamed and hunted and warred with their wives by their sides now teamed with other men, both grieving for lost partners. To relieve the sexual tensions—and maintain the gene pool as best they could, if they even understood such things—the men who lived through the Sorrowing Plague made their women sexual property of all. To insure as many children as possible, they made them perpetual breeders who lived their lives safe from danger and in constant pregnancy. The holdfasts that did not adopt such measues failed to survive; those that did passed on a cultural heritage.

Other changes took root as well. Tara had been a religious world, home of the Irish-Roman Reformed Catholic Church, and the urge to monogamy died hard. The patterns appeared in two mutated forms; the strong emotional attachments that grew up between male hunting partners became the basis for the intense total relationship of *teyn*-and-*teyn,* while those men who desired a semi-exclusive bond with a woman created *betheyns* by capturing females from other holdfasts. The leaders encouraged such raidings, Jaan Vikary said; new women meant new blood, more children, a larger population, and thus a better chance of survival. It was unthinkable that any man take exclusive possession of one of the *eyn-kethi;* but a man who could bring a woman in from outside was rewarded with honors and a seat in the councils of leadership and, perhaps most importantly, the woman herself.

These were the likely events, Vikary argued, self-evident truths that produced modern Kavalar society. Jamis-Lion Taal, wandering the face of the world many generations later, had been so much a child of his culture that he was unable to conceive of a world in which women held any status other than what he saw; and when he was forced to think otherwise by the folklore he collected, he thought the idea intolerably wicked. Thus he rewrote all the oral literature as he cast his *Demonsong* cycle. He transformed Kay Iron-Smith into a thundering giant of a man, made the Sorrowing Plague a ballad of *eyn-kethi* wickedness, and generally created the impression that the world had always been the way he found it. Later poets built on the foundations he had laid.

The forces that had produced the holdfast society of High Kavalaan had long ago vanished. Today, women and men numbered roughly the same, the epidemics were only grisly fables, most of the dangers of the planet's surface had been conquered. Nonetheless the holdfast-coalitions continued. The men fought duels and studied the new technology and worked on the farms and in the factories and sailed the Kavalar starships, while the *eyn-kethi* lived in vast subterranean barracks as sexual partners for all the men of the holdfast, laboring at whatever tasks the high-bond councils deemed safe and suitable, and having babies, though fewer now. Kavalar population was strictly controlled. Other women lived slightly freer lives under the protection of jade-and-silver, but not many. A *betheyn* had to come from outside the holdfast, which in practice meant that an ambitious youngster had to challenge and kill a highbond of another coalition, or lay claim to one of the *eyn-kethi* in an enemy holdfast and face a defender chosen in council. The second route was rarely successful; highbond councils invariably chose the holdfast's most accomplished duelist to champion the *eyn-kethi*. In fact, the designation was a singular honor. A man who did succeed in winning a *betheyn* immediately took his highnames and his place among the rulers. It was said that he had given his *kethi* the gift of the two bloods—the blood of death, a slain enemy, and the blood of life, a new woman. The woman enjoyed the status of jade-and-silver until such time as her highbond was killed. If he was slain by one of his own holdfast, she became an *eyn-kethi;* if the killer was an outsider, she passed to him.

Such was the status that Gwen Delvano had taken when she clasped Jaan's bracelet around her wrist.

Dirk lay awake for a long time, thinking of everything he had read and staring up at the ceiling, growing more and more angry the more he thought. By the time the first dawn light began to filter slowly through the window above his head, he had decided. In a sense it no longer mattered if Gwen returned to him or not, so long as she left Vikary and Janacek and the whole sick society of High Kavalaan. But alone she could not make the break, much as she might wish to. Very well then, Arkin Ruark was right; he would help her. He would help her to be free. And afterwards there would be time to consider their own relationship.

Finally, his resolve fixed firmly in his mind, Dirk slept.

It was midday when he awoke, suddenly, with a snap of guilt. He sat up and blinked and remembered he had promised Gwen that he would come up that morning, and here the morning was gone and he had overslept. Hurriedly he rose and dressed, looked around briefly for Ruark—the Kimdissi was gone, no clue as to where or for how long—and then went up to Gwen's apartment, Vikary's thesis tucked firmly under his arm.

Garse Janacek answered his knock.

"Yes?" the red-bearded Kavalar said, frowning. He was bare to the waist, dressed only in snug-fitting black trousers and the eternal bracelet of iron-and-glowstone on his right arm. Dirk saw at a glance why Janacek did not wear the sort of V-necked shirts that Vikary seemed to favor; the left side of his chest, from his armpit to his breast, bore a long crooked scar, slick and hard.

Janacek saw his stare. "A duel that went wrong," he snapped. "I was too young. It will not happen again. Now, what do you require?"

Dirk flushed. "I want to see Gwen," he said.

"She is not here," Janacek said, his ice eyes hard and unfriendly. He started to shut the door.

"Wait." Dirk stopped the door with his hand.

"More? What is it?"

"Gwen. I was supposed to see her. Where is she?"

"In the wilderness, t'Larien. I would be pleased if you would remember that she is an ecologist, sent here by the highbonds of Ironjade to do important work. She has neglected that work for two full days to guide you hither and yon. Now, as is proper, she has returned to it. She and Arkin Ruark took their instruments and went off into the forests."

"She didn't say anything last night," Dirk insisted.

"She is not required to inform you of her plans," Janacek said. "Nor must she secure your permission for anything. There is no bond between you."

Remembering the argument he had overheard the night before, Dirk was suddenly suspicious. "Can I come in?" he said. "I want to give this back to Jaan, talk to him about it," he added, showing Garse the leather-bound thesis. Actually he hoped to look for Gwen, to find out if she was being kept from him. But it would hardly have been polite to say this; Janecek was dripping hostility, and an attempt to push past him would be very unwise.

"Jaan is not presently at home. No one is here but me. I am about to leave." He reached out and snatched the thesis from Dirk's hands. "I will take this, however. Gwen should never have given it to you."

"Hey!" Dirk said. He had an impulse. "The history was very interesting," he said suddenly. "Can I come in and talk to you about it? A second or two—I won't keep you."

Abruptly Janacek seemed to change. He smiled and gave way, beckoning Dirk into the apartment.

Dirk looked around quickly. The living room was deserted, the fireplace cold; nothing seemed amiss or out of place. The dining room, visible through an open archway, was also empty. The whole apartment was very quiet. No sign of Gwen or Jaan. From what he could see, it appeared Janacek had been telling the truth.

Uncertain, Dirk wandered across the room, pausing before the mantel and its gargoyles. Janacek watched him wordlessly, then turned and left, returning shortly. He had strapped on his mesh-steel belt with its heavy holster and was buttoning up the front of a faded black shirt when he re-entered.

"Where are you going?" Dirk asked.

"Out," Janacek replied with a brief grin. He undid the latch flap of his holster and drew out the laser pistol within, checked the power reading on the side of its butt, then reholstered and drew again—a smooth flowing motion with his right hand—and sighted down on Dirk. "Do I alarm you?" he asked.

"Yes," Dirk said. He moved away from the mantel.

Janacek's grin came back again. He slid the laser into its holster. "I am quite good with a dueling laser," he said, "though in truth my *teyn* is better.

Of course, I must use only my right arm. The left still pains me. The scar tissue pulls, so the chest muscles on that side cannot move so far or so easily as those on my right. Yet it matters little. I am chiefly right-handed. The right arm is always more than the left, you know." His right hand rested on the laser pistol as he spoke, and the glowstones in their black iron setting shone like dim red eyes along his forearm.

"Too bad about your injury."

"I made a mistake, t'Larien. I was too young, perhaps, but my mistake was none the less serious for my age. Such mistakes can be very grave matters, and in some ways I escaped easily." He was staring very fixedly at Dirk. "One should be careful that one does not make mistakes."

"Oh?" Dirk affected an innocent smile.

For a time Janacek did not reply. Then, finally, he said, "I think you know what I am speaking about."

"Do I?"

"Yes. You are not an unintelligent man, t'Larien. Nor am I. Your childish ruses do not amuse me. You have nothing to discuss with me, for example. You simply wanted to gain admittance to this chamber for some reasons of your own."

Dirk's smile vanished. He nodded. "All right. A lousy trick, clearly, since you saw right through it. I wanted to look for Gwen."

"I told you that she was out in the wild, at work."

"I don't believe you," Dirk said. "She would have said something to me yesterday. You're keeping me from her. Why? What's going on?"

"Nothing that need concern you," said Janacek. "Understand me, t'Larien, if you will. Perhaps to you, as to Arkin Ruark, I seem an evil man. You may think that of me. I care very little. I am not an evil man. That is why I warn you against mistakes. That is why I admitted you, though I know full well that you have nothing to say to me. For *I* have things to say to you."

Dirk leaned against the back of the couch and nodded. "All right, Janacek. Go ahead."

Janacek frowned. "Your problem, t'Larien, is that you know little and understand less of Jaan and myself and our world."

"I know more than you think."

"Do you? You have read Jaan's writings on the *Demonsong,* and no doubt people have told you things. Yet what is that? You are no Kavalar. You do not understand Kavalars, I would guess, yet you stand here and I see judgment in your eyes. By what right? Who are you to judge us? You scarcely know us. I will give you an instance. Just a second ago you called me Janacek."

"That's your name, isn't it?"

"That is part of my name, the last part, the least and smallest part of who I am. It is my chosen-name, the name of an ancient hero of the Ironjade Gathering who lived a long and fruitful life, many times honorably defending his holdfast and his *kethi* in highwar. I know why you use it, of course. On your world and in your naming system it is customary to address those toward whom you feel distance or hostility by the final component of their names—an intimate you would call by his first name, would you not?"

Dirk nodded. "More or less. It's not quite that simple, but you're close enough."

Janacek smiled thinly; the blue eyes seemed to sparkle. "You see, I *do* understand your people, only too well. I give you the benefit of your own ways—I call you t'Larien because I am hostile to you, and that is correct. You do not reciprocate, however. You address me as Janacek, without an instant of thought or concern, quite deliberately imposing your own naming system on me."

"What should I call you then? Garse?"

Janacek made a sharp, impatient gesture. "Garse is my true name, but it is not proper from you. In Kavalar custom, use of that name alone would indicate a relationship that does not in fact exist between us.

Garse is a name for my *teyn* and my *cro-betheyn* and my *kethi,* not for an offworlder. Properly you should call me Garse Ironjade, and my *teyn* Jaantony high-Ironjade. Those are traditional and correct from an equal, a Kavalar of another house with whom I am on speaking terms. I give you the benefit of many doubts." He smiled. "Now understand, t'Larien, that I tell you this as illustration only. I care precious little whether you call me Garse or Garse Ironjade or Mister Janacek. Call me whatever makes your heart happiest, and I will take no insult. The Kimdissi Arkin Ruark has even been known to call me *Garsey,* yet I have resisted the urge to prick him and see if he pops.

"These matters of courtesy and address— I do not need Jaan to tell me that they are old things, legacies of days both more elaborate and more primitive, dying in this modern time. Today Kavalars sail ships from star to star, talk and trade with creatures we would once have exterminated as demons, even shape planets as we have shaped Worlorn. Old Kavalar, the language of the holdfasts for thousands of your standard years, is scarcely spoken anymore, though a few terms linger on and will continue to linger, since they name realities that can be named only clumsily or not at all in the tongues of the star travelers—realities that would soon vanish if we gave up their names, the Old Kavalar terms. Everything has changed, even we of High Kavalaan, and Jaan says that we must change still more if we are to fulfill our destiny in the histories of man. Thus the old rules of names and namebonds break down, and even highbonds grow lax in their speech, and Jaantony high-Ironjade goes about calling himself Jaan Vikary."

"If it doesn't matter," Dirk said, "then what's your point?"

"The point was illustration, t'Larien, a simple and elegant illustration of how much of your own culture you wrongly presume to be part of ours, of how you press your judgments and your values on us with every word and action. That was the point. There are more important matters in question, but the pattern is the same; you make the same mistake, a mistake you ought not make. The price might be greater than you can afford. Do you think I do not know what you are trying to do?"

"*What* am I trying to do?"

Janacek smiled again, his eyes small and hard, tiny wrinkles creasing the skin at their corners. "You try to take Gwen Delvano away from my *teyn*. Truth?"

Dirk said nothing.

"It is truth," Janacek said. "And it is wrong. Understand that it will never be permitted. *I* will not permit it. I am bonded by iron-and-fire to Jaantony high-Ironjade, and I do not forget that. We are *teyn*-and-*teyn,* we two. No bond that you have ever known is as strong."

Dirk found himself thinking of Gwen and of a deep red teardrop full of memories and promises. He thought it a pity that he could not give the whisper-jewel to Janacek to hold for a moment, so the arrogant Kavalar could taste just how strong a bond Dirk had had with his Jenny. But such a gesture would be useless. Janacek's mind would have no resonances with the patterns esper-etched in the stone; it would be only a gem to him. "I loved Gwen," he said sharply. "I doubt that any bond of yours is more than that."

"Do you? Well, you are no Kavalar, no more than Gwen is, you do not understand the iron-and-fire. I first encountered Jaantony when each of us was quite young. I was even younger than he, in truth. He was fond of play with children younger than himself rather than his agemates, and he came frequently to our creche. I held him in great esteem from the first, as only a boy can, because he was older than me and thus closer to being a highbond, and because he led me on adventures into strange corridors and caves, and because he told fascinating stories. When I was older, I learned why he came among the younger children so often, and I was shocked and shamed. He was afraid of those as old as he, because they taunted him and often beat him. Yet by the time I learned that, a bond existed between us. You might call it friendship, but you would be wrong to do so; you would be imposing your own concepts on our lives once more. It was more than your offworlder friendship, there was iron between us already, although we were not yet *teyn*-and-*teyn*.

"The next time that Jaan and I went exploring together—we were far beyond our holdfast, in a cavern he knew well—I surprised him and beat him until every part of his flesh was bruised and swollen. He did not visit my age-barracks for the entire winter, yet at last he returned. We had no bitterness between us. We began to roam and hunt together once more, and he told me more stories, tales of myth and history. For my part, I would assault him randomly, always catching him unready and overwhelming him. In time he began to fight back, and well. In time it became impossible for me to surprise him with my fists. One day I smuggled a knife out from Ironjade beneath my shirt, and bared it on Jaan and cut him. Then we both began to carry knives. When he reached his adolescence, the age where he would pick his chosen-names and become subject to the code duello, Jaantony was no longer a subject of easy taunt.

"He was always unpopular. You must understand that he was ever a questioning sort, given to uncomfortable inquiries and unorthodox opinions, a lover of history but openly contemptuous of religion, with much too much unhealthy interest in the offworlders who moved among us. As such, he was challenged again and again that first year he attained dueling age. He always won. When I reached adolescence a few years later, and we became *teyn*-and-*teyn,* I had scarcely anyone to fight. Jaantony had put fear in all of them, so they would not challenge us. I was very disappointed.

"Since that time we have dueled together often. We are bonded for life, and we have been through much, and I do not care to hear you spout comparisons with this meaningless 'love' you offworlders are so enchanted by, this mockman bond that comes and goes with the whim of a moment. Jaantony himself was badly corrupted by the concept during his years on Avalon, and that was in some measure my responsibility because I let him go alone. It was true that on Avalon I would have had no function and no place, yet I should have been there. I failed Jaan in that. I will never fail him again. I am his *teyn* and always his *teyn,* and I will permit no one to kill him or wound him, or twist his mind, or steal his name. These things are my bond and my duty.

"Too often these days Jaan lets his very name be threatened by such as you and Ruark. Jaan is in many ways a perverse and dangerous man, and the quirks of his mind often bring us into peril. Even his heroes— I remembered, one day, some of the stories he had told me in childhood, and was struck by the fact that all of Jaan's favorite heroes were solitary men who suffered ultimate defeat. Aryn high-Glowstone, as an instance, who dominated an entire epoch of history. He ruled by force of personality the most powerful holdfast High Kavalaan ever knew, the Glowstone Mountain; and when his enemies leagued against him in highwar, all hands raised against his, he put swords and shields on the arms of his *eyn-kethi* and took them to battle to swell the size of his army. His foes were broken and humiliated, and so Jaan would tell me the story. Yet later I learned that Aryn high-Glowstone won no victory at all. So many of his holdfast's *eyn-kethi* were slain that day that few remained to birth new warriors. Glowstone Mountain declined steadily in power and in population, and forty years after Aryn's bold stroke the Glowstones fell and highbonds from Taal and Ironjade and Bronzefist took their women and children, leaving the halls abandoned. The truth of Aryn high-Glowstone is that he was a failure and a fool, one of history's pariahs, and such are all Jaan's mad heroes."

"Aryn sounds heroic enough to me," Dirk said

sharply. "On Avalon we'd probably credit him with freeing the slaves, even if he didn't win."

Janacek glowered at him, his eyes like blue sparks set in his narrow skull. He tugged at his red beard in annoyance. "T'Larien, that comment is precisely what I warned you of. *Eyn-kethi* are not slaves, they are *eyn-kethi*. You judge wrongly and your translations are false."

"According to you," Dirk said. "According to Ruark—"

"Ruark." Janacek's tone was contemptuous. "Is the Kimdissi the source of all your information about High Kavalaan? I see that I have wasted time and words on you, t'Larien. You are already poisoned and you have no interest in understanding. You are a tool of the manipulators of Kimdiss. I will lecture you no more."

"Fine," Dirk said. "Just tell me where Gwen is."

"I told you."

"When will she be back, then?"

"Late, and then she will be tired. I am certain that she will not wish to see you."

"You *are* keeping her from me!"

Janacek was silent for a moment. "Yes," he said finally, his mouth grim. "It is the best course, t'Larien, for you as well as her, although I do not expect you to believe that."

"You have no right."

"In your culture. I have every right in mine. You will not be alone with her again."

"Gwen is not part of your damned sick Kavalar culture," Dirk said.

"She was not born into it, yet she took the jade-and-silver, and the name *betheyn*. Now she is Kavalar."

Dirk was trembling, his control gone, "What does she say to that?" he demanded, stepping closer to Janacek. "What did she say last night? Did she threaten to leave?" He jabbed the Kavalar with his finger. "Did she say she was coming with me, was that it? And you hit her and carried her off?"

Janacek frowned and brushed Dirk's hand away

forcefully. "So you spy on us too. You do it poorly, t'Larien, but it is offensive nonetheless. A second mistake. The first was Jaan's, in telling you the things he did, in trusting you and lending you his protection."

"I don't need anyone's protection!"

"So you say. An idiot's misplaced pride. Only those who are strong should reject the protections given the weak; those who are truly weak need them." He turned away. "I will waste no more time with you," he said, walking toward the dining chamber. There was a thin black carrying case lying on the table. Janacek opened it, clicking back both locks simultaneously and flipping up the lid. Inside Dirk saw five rows of the black iron banshee pins on red felt. Janacek held one up. "Are you quite certain that you do not want one of these? *Korariel?*" He grinned.

Dirk crossed his arms and did not dignify the question with an answer.

Janacek waited a moment for a reply. When none came, he slipped the banshee pin back into its place and closed the case. "The jelly children are not so choosy as you are," he said. "Now I must bring these to Jaan. Get out of here."

It was early afternoon. The Hub burned dimly in the center of the sky, with the scattered small lights of the four visible Trojan Suns arrayed unevenly around it. A strong wind was blowing from the east, building into a gale, it seemed. Dust swirled through the gray and scarlet alleys.

Dirk sat on one corner of the roof, his legs hanging out over the street, mulling his possibilities.

He had followed Garse Janacek up to the airlot and had seen him depart, carrying the case of banshees and flying his massive squared-off military relic in its olive-green armor. The other two aircars, the gray manta-wing and the bright yellow teardrop, were gone as well. He was stranded here in Larteyn, with no idea of where Gwen was or what they were doing to her. He wished briefly that Ruark was somewhere around.

He wished he had an aircar of his own. No doubt he could have rented one in Challenge, if he had thought of it, or even at the spacefield the night he had come in. Instead he was alone and helpless; even the sky-scoots were missing. The world was red and gray and pointless. He wondered what to do.

Abruptly it came to him as he sat and thought about aircars. The Festival cities he had seen were all very different, but they had one thing in common: none of them had nearly enough landing space to accommodate an aircar population equal to their human population. Which meant the cities had to be linked by some other kind of transportation network. Which meant that maybe he had some freedom of action after all.

He got up and went to the tubes and then down to Ruark's quarters in the base of the tower. Between two black-barked ceiling-high plants in earthenware pots, a wallscreen waited, just as he remembered seeing it, dark and unlit, as it had been since Dirk arrived; there were very few people left on Worlorn to call or be called. But no doubt there was an information circuit. He studied the double row of buttons beneath the screen, selected one, and punched. The darkness gave way to a soft blue light, and Dirk breathed a little easier; the communications grid, at least, was still operational.

One of the buttons was marked with a question mark. He tried it and was rewarded. The blue light cleared and suddenly the screen was full of small script, a hundred numbers for a hundred basic services, everything from medical aid and religious information to offplanet news.

He punched the sequence for "visitor transport." Figures flowed across the screen, and one by one Dirk's hopes withered. There were aircar rental facilities at the spacefield and at ten of the fourteen cities. All closed. The functional aircars had left Worlorn with the Festival crowds. Other cities had provided hovercraft and hydrofoil boats. No longer. At

Musquel-by-the-Sea, visitors could sail upcoast and down in a genuine wind-powered ship from the Forgotten Colony. Service terminated. The intercity airbus line was closed down, the nuclear-powered stratoliners of Tober and the helium dirigibles of Eshellin were all grounded and gone. The wallscreen showed him a map of the high-speed subways that had run from beneath the spacefield out to each of the cities, but the map was drawn all in red, and the legend below it explained that red meant "Depowered—No Longer Operational."

There was no transportation left on Worlorn except walking, it seemed. Plus whatever late visitors had brought with them.

Dirk scowled and killed the readout. He was about to turn off the screen when another thought hit him. He punched for "Library" and got a query sign and instructions. Then he coded in "jelly children" and "define." He waited.

It was a short wait and he hardly needed the vast bulk of information the library threw at him, the details of history and geography and philosophy. The critical information he took in quickly, the rest he disregarded. "Jelly children," it seemed, was a popular nickname for the followers of a pseudo-religious drug cult on the World of the Blackwine Ocean. They were so called because they spent years at a time living in the cavernous inner dampness of kilometer-long gelatinous slugs that crept with infinite slowness along the bottom of their seas. The cultists called the creatures Mothers. The Mothers fed their children with sweet hallucinogenic secretions and were believed to be semi-sentient. The belief, Dirk noted, did not stop the jelly children from killing their host when the quality of her dream secretions began to decline, which invariably happened as the slugs aged. Free of one Mother, the jelly children would then seek another.

Quickly Dirk cleared the screen of that data and consulted the library again. The World of the Blackwine Ocean had a city on Worlorn. It lay beneath an artificial lake fifty kilometers around, under the same dark, teeming waters that covered the surface of the Blackwiners' homeworld. It was called the City in the Starless Pool, and the surrounding lake was full of lifeforms brought in for the Festival of the Fringe. Including Mothers, no doubt.

Out of curiosity, Dirk found the city on a map of Worlorn. He had no way of getting there, of course. He killed the wallscreen and walked into the kitchen to mix himself a drink. As he tossed it down—it was a thick off-white milk from some Kimdissi animal, very cold, bitter but refreshing—he drummed his fingers very impatiently on the bar. The restlessness was growing in him, the urge to do something. He felt trapped here, waiting for one of the others to return, not knowing which it would be or what would happen then. It seemed as though he had been moved back and forth at the whim of others ever since he had first come down on the *Shuddering of Forgotten Enemies*. He had not even come of his own volition; Gwen had called him with her whisperjewel, although she had hardly seemed to welcome him when he arrived. That, at least, he had begun to understand. She was trapped in a very complex web, a web that was political and emotional at the same time; and he seemingly had been pulled in with her, to stand helpless while half-understood storms of psychosexual and cultural tension swirled all around them. He was very tired of standing helpless.

Abruptly, he thought of Kryne Lamiya. In a windswept landing deck two aircars sat abandoned. Dirk put his glass down thoughtfully, wiped his lip with the back of his hand, and went back to the wallscreen.

It was a simple matter to find the location of all aircar landing facilities in Larteyn. There were airlots atop all of the larger residential towers, and a big public garage deep within the rock beneath the city. The garage, the city directory informed him, could be reached from any of twelve undertubes spaced evenly through Larteyn; its concealed doors opened in the middle of the plunging cliff that loomed above the Common. If the Kavalars had left any aircars at all in the shell of their city, that was where he would find them.

He took the tubes down to ground level and the street. Fat Satan had climbed past zenith and was sinking toward the horizon. The glowstone streets were faded and black where the red gloom fell, but when Dirk walked through the shadows between the square ebon towers he could still see the cold fires of the city beneath his feet, the soft red glow of the rock, fading yet still persisting. In the open, he himself threw shadows, dim dark wraiths that piled clumsily atop one another—almost but not quite coinciding—and scuttled too swiftly at his heels to wake the sleeping glowstone into life. He saw no one else during his walk, although he wondered uneasily about the Braiths, and once he passed what must have been a dwelling. It was a square building with a domed roof and black iron pillars at its door, and chained to one of those pillars was a hound that stood taller than Dirk, with bright red eyes and a long hairless face that reminded him somehow of a rat's. The creature was worrying a bone, but it stood when he walked past and growled deep in its throat. Whoever lived in that building clearly did not relish the idea of visitors.

The undertubes still functioned. He fell and daylight vanished, and he got out again in the lower passages, where Larteyn had the greatest resemblance to the holdfasts of High Kavalaan itself: echoing stone halls with wrought-iron hangings, metal doors everywhere, chambers within chambers. A fastness in stone, Ruark had said once. A fortress, no part of which could be taken easily. But now abandoned.

The garage was multileveled and dimly lit, with space enough for a thousand aircars on each of its ten levels. Dirk wandered through the dust for a half-hour before he found even one. It was useless to him. Another beast-car, fashioned of blue-black metal in the grotesque likeness of a giant bat, it was more realistic and frightening than Jaan Vikary's rather stylized manta-banshee. But it was also a burned-out hulk. One of the ornamental batwings was twisted and half melted, and of the aircar itself only the body remained. The interior appointments, the power plant, and the weaponry were all gone, and Dirk suspected the gravity grid would be missing as well, though he could not see the underside of the derelict. He walked around it once and passed on.

The second aircar he found was in even worse shape. In fact, it could hardly be called a car at all. Nothing remained but a bare metal frame and four rotting seats squatting in the midst of the tubing—a skeleton gutted of even its skin. Dirk passed by that one too.

The next two wrecks he came to were both intact, but ghosts. He could only guess that their owners had died here on Worlorn, and the aircars had waited in the depths of the city long after they had been forgotten, until all power was gone. He tried both of them, and neither responded to his touch and his tinkerings.

The fifth car—by then a full hour had passed—responded much too quickly.

Thoroughly Kavalar, the car was a stubby two-seater with short triangular wings that looked even more useless than the wings on other aircars of High Kavalaan manufacture. It was all silver and white enamel, and the metal canopy was shaped to resemble a wolf's head. Lasercannon were mounted on both sides of the fuselage. The car was not locked; Dirk pushed up on the canopy, and it swung open easily. He climbed in, snapped it shut, and looked out of the wolf's great eyes with a wry smile on his face. Then he tried the controls. The aircar still had full power.

Frowning, he killed that power again and sat back to think. He had found the transportation he was looking for, if he dared to take it. But he could not fool himself; this car was not a derelict like the others he had discovered. Its condition was too good. No doubt it belonged to one of the other Kavalars still in Larteyn. If colors meant anything—he wasn't sure about that—then it probably belonged to Lorimaar or one of the other Braiths. Taking it was not the safest course he could choose, not by a long margin.

Dirk recognized the danger and considered it. Waiting did not appeal to him, but neither did the prospect of danger. Jaan Vikary or no Jaan Vikary, stealing an aircar might just provoke the Braiths into action.

Reluctantly, he swung back the canopy and climbed out, but no sooner had he emerged than he heard the voices. He eased the aircar canopy down and it closed with a faint but audible click. Dirk crouched and made for the safety of the shadows a few meters beyond the wolf-car.

He could hear the Kavalars talking, and their footsteps noisily echoing, long before he saw them; there were only two, but they sounded like ten. By the time they had moved into the light near the aircar, Dirk was pressed flat against a niche in the garage wall, a small cavity full of hooks where tools had once been hung. He was not quite sure why he was hiding, but he was very glad of it. The things that Gwen and Jaan had told him of the other residents of Larteyn had not reassured him.

"Are you sure of all this, Bretan?" one of them, the taller, was saying as they came into sight. He was not Lorimaar, but the resemblance was striking; this man had the same imposing height, the same tan and wrinkled face. But he ran more to fat than Lorimaar high-Braith, and his hair was pure white where the other's had been mostly gray, and he had a small toothbrush of a mustache. Both he and his companion wore short white jackets over pants and shirt of chameleon cloth that had darkened to near-black in the dimness of the garage. And they both had lasers.

"Roseph would not jape me," the second Kavalar said in a voice that rasped like sandpaper. He was much shorter than the other man, close to Dirk's own height, and younger as well, very lean. His jacket had the sleeves cut off to display powerful brown arms and a thick iron-and-glowstone armlet. As he moved to the aircar, he came full into the light for an instant and seemed to stare at the darkness where Dirk was hidden. He had only half a face; the rest was all twitching scar tissue. His left "eye" moved restlessly as his face turned, and Dirk saw the telltale fire: a glowstone set in an empty socket.

"How do you know this?" the older man said as the two paused briefly by the side of the wolf-car. "Roseph is fond of japes."

"I am not fond of japes," said the other, the one who had been called Bretan. "Roseph might jape you, or Lorimaar, or even Pyr, but he dare not jape me." His voice was horribly unpleasant; there was a grating rawness to it that offended the ear, but with the scars as thick as they were up and down his neck, Dirk found it surprising that the man could talk at all.

The taller Kavalar pushed up against the side of the wolf's head, but the canopy did not lift. "Well, if this is truth, then we must hurry," he said querulously. "The lock, Bretan, the lock!"

One-eyed Bretan made an odd noise partway between a grunt and a growl. He tried the canopy himself. "My *teyn*," he rasped. "I left the head slightly ajar . . . I . . . it only took a moment to come up and find you."

In the shadows Dirk pressed back hard against the wall, and the hooks dug painfully into his back between the shoulder blades. Bretan frowned and knelt, while his older companion stood and looked puzzled.

Then suddenly the Braith was standing again, and his laser pistol was snug in his right hand, trained on Dirk. His glowstone eye smoldered faintly. "Come out and let us discover what you are," he announced. "The trail you left in the dust is very plain to see."

Dirk, silent, raised his hands above his head and emerged.

"A mockman!" the taller Kavalar said. "Down here!"

"No," Dirk said carefully. "Dirk t'Larien."

The tall one ignored him. "This is rare good fortune," he said to his companion with the laser. "Those jelly men of Roseph's would have been poor prey at best. This one looks fit."

His young *teyn* made the odd noise again, and the left side of his face twitched. But his laser hand was quite steady. "No," he told the other Braith. "Sadly, I do not think he is ours to hunt. This can only be the one that Lorimaar spoke of." He slid his laser pistol back into his holster and nodded at Dirk, a very slight and deliberate motion, more a shifting of his shoulders than of his head. "You are grossly careless. The canopy locks automatically when full-closed. It may be opened from the inside, but—"

"I realize that now," Dirk said. He lowered his hands. "I was only looking for an abandoned car. I needed transportation."

"So you sought to steal our aircar."

"No."

"Yes." The Kavalar's voice made every word a painful effort. "You are *korariel* of Ironjade?"

Dirk hesitated, his denial caught in his throat. Either answer seemed likely to get him in trouble.

"You have no answer to that?" said the scarred one.

"Bretan," the other cautioned. "The mockman's words are no matter to us. If Jaantony high-Ironjade names him *korariel,* then such is truth. Such animals have no voice about their status. Whatever he might say cannot lift the name, so the reality is the same regardless. If we slay him, we have stolen Ironjade property and they will surely issue challenge."

"I urge you to consider the possibilities, Chell," Bretan said. "This one, this Dirk t'Larien, he can be man or mockman, *korariel* of Ironjade or not. Truth?"

"Truth. But he is no true man. Listen to me, my

teyn. You are young, but I know of these things from *kethi* long dead."

"Consider nonetheless. If he is mockman and the Ironjades name him *korariel,* then he is *korariel* whether he admits it or no. But if that is truth, Chell, then you and I must go against the Ironjades in duel. He was trying to steal from us, remember. If he is Ironjade property, then that is an Ironjade theft."

The big white-haired man nodded slowly, reluctantly.

"If he is mockman but not *korariel* then we have no problem," Bretan continued, "since then he may be hunted. And what if he is a true man, human as a highbond, and no mockman at all?"

Chell was much slower than his *teyn.* The older Kavalar frowned thoughtfully and said, "Well, he is no female, so he cannot be owned. But if he is human, he must have a man's rights and a man's name."

"Truth," Bretan agreed. "But he cannot be *korariel,* so his crime would be his alone. I would duel *him,* not Jaantony high-Ironjade." The Braith gave his strange grunt-growl again.

Chell was nodding, and Dirk was almost numb. The younger of the two hunters seemed to have worked things out with a nasty precision. Dirk had told both Vikary and Janacek in no uncertain terms that he rejected the tainted shield of their protection. At the time, it had been an easy enough thing to do. On sane worlds like Avalon it would unquestionably have been the right thing as well. On Worlorn, things were not quite so clear.

"Where shall we take him?" Chell said. The two Braiths spoke as if Dirk had no more volition than their aircar.

"We must take him to Jaantony high-Ironjade and his *teyn,*" Bretan said in his sandpaper growl. "I know their tower by sight."

Briefly Dirk considered running. It did not seem feasible. There were two of them, with sidearms and even an aircar. He would not get far. "I'll come," he said when they started toward him. "I can show you the way." It seemed that he would be given some time to think, in any event; the Braiths did not seem to know that Vikary and Janacek were already out at the City of the Starless Pool, no doubt trying to protect the hapless jelly children from the other hunters.

"Show us, then," Chell said. And Dirk, not knowing what else to do, led them toward the undertubes. On the way up he reflected bitterly that all this had come about because he was tired of waiting. And now, it seemed, he would wait after all.

chapter **6**

At first, the waiting was sheer hell.

They took him to the airlot on top of the empty tower after they discovered that the Ironjades were not to be found, and they forced him to sit in a corner of the windswept roof. The panic was rising in him by then, and his stomach was a painful knot. "Bretan," he began, in a voice laced by hysteria, but the Kavalar only turned on him and delivered a stinging open-handed blow across the mouth.

"I am not 'Bretan' to you," he said. "Call me Bretan Braith if you must address me, mockman."

After that, Dirk was silent. The broken Wheel of Fire limped oh-so-slowly across the sky of Worlorn, and as he watched it crawl, it seemed to Dirk that he was very close to a breaking point. Everything that had happened to him seemed unreal, and the Braiths and the events of the afternoon were the least real of all, and he wondered what would happen if he were to suddenly leap to his feet and vault over the edge of the roof into the street. He would fall and fall, he thought, as one does in a dream, but when he smashed on the dark glowstone blocks below there would be no pain, only the shock of a sudden awakening. And he would find himself in his bed on Braque, drenched with sweat and laughing at the absurdities of his nightmare.

He played with that thought and others like it for a time that seemed like hours, but when he looked up at last, Fat Satan had hardly sunk at all. He began to tremble then; the cold, he told himself, the cold Worlorn wind, but he knew that it was not the cold, and the more he fought to control it the more he shook, until the Kavalars looked at him strangely. And still the waiting went on.

And finally the shakes ran their course, as had the thoughts of suicide and the panic before them, and an odd sort of calm swept over him. He found himself thinking again, but thinking of nonsensical things: speculating idly—as if he were soon going to place a wager—on whether the gray manta or the military flyer would return first, on how Jaan or Garse would fare in a duel with one-eyed Bretan, on what had happened to the jelly children in the distant Black-winer city. Such matters seemed terribly important, though Dirk didn't know why.

Then he began to watch his captors. That was the most interesting game of all, and it served to pass the time as well as any other. As he watched, he noticed things.

The two Kavalars had hardly spoken since they escorted him up to the rooftop. Chell, the tall one, sat on the low wall that surrounded the airlot only a meter away from Dirk, and when Dirk began to study him, he saw that he was quite an old man indeed. The resemblance to Lorimaar high-Braith was very deceptive. Although Chell walked and dressed like a younger man, he was at least twenty years senior to Lorimaar, Dirk guessed. Seated, his years weighed on him heavily. A distinct paunch bulged over the soft-shining metal of his mesh-steel belt, and his wrinkles were carved very deep into his worn brown face, and Dirk saw blue veins and splotches of grayish-pink skin on the back of Chell's hands as they rested on his knees. The long useless wait for the Ironjades' return had touched him too, and it was more than boredom. His cheeks seemed to sag, and his wide shoulders had unconsciously fallen into a tired slouch.

He moved once, sighing, and his hands came off his knees and twined together, and he stretched. That was when Dirk saw his armlets. The right arm was iron-and-glowstone, twin to the one displayed so proudly by one-eyed Bretan, and the left was silver. But the jade was missing. It had been there once, but the stones had been torn from their settings, and now the silver bracelet was riddled by holes.

While weary old Chell—it seemed suddenly hard for Dirk to see him as the menacing martial figure he had been just a short time ago—sat and waited for something to happen, Bretan (or Bretan Braith, as he demanded he be called) paced the hours away. He was all restless energy, worse than anyone that Dirk had ever known, even Jenny, who had been quite a pacer in her time. He kept his hands deep in the slit pockets of his short white jacket and walked back and forth across the rooftop, back and forth, back and forth. Every third trip or so he would glance up impatiently, as if he were reproaching the twilight sky because it had not yet yielded up Jaan Vikary to him.

They were a strange pair, Dirk decided as he watched them. Bretan Braith was as young as Chell was old—surely no older than Garse Janacek and probably younger than Gwen and Jaan or himself. How had he come to be *teyn* to a Kavalar so many years his senior? He was no high, either, he had given no *betheyn* to Braith; his left arm, covered by fine reddish hairs that glinted now and then when he walked very close and let them catch the sunlight, had no bracelet of jade-and-silver.

His face, his strange half-face, was ugly beyond anything that Dirk had ever seen, but as the day waned and false dusk became real, he found himself getting used to it. When Bretan Braith paced in one direction, he looked utterly normal: a whip-lean youth, full of nervous energy held tightly in check, so tightly that Bretan almost seemed to crackle. His face on that side was unlined and serene; short black curls pressed tightly around his ear and a few ringlets dropped to his shoulder, but he had no hint of a beard. Even his eyebrow was only a faint line above a wide green eye. He appeared almost innocent.

Then, pacing, he would reach the edge of the roof and turn back the way he had come, and everything would be changed. The left side of his face was inhuman, a landscape of twisted plains and angles that no face ought to have. The flesh was seamed in a half-dozen places, and elsewhere it was shiny-slick as enamel. On this side, Bretan had no hair whatsoever, and no ear—only a hole—and the left half of his nose was a small piece of flesh-colored plastic. His mouth was a lipless slash, and worst of all, it moved. He had a twitch, a grotesque tic, and it touched the left corner of his mouth at intervals and rippled up his bare scalp over the hills of scar tissue.

In the daylight the Braith's glowstone eye was as dark as a piece of obsidian. But slowly night was coming, the Helleye sank, and the fires were stirring in his socket. At full darkness, Bretan would be the Helleye, not Worlorn's tired supergiant of a sun; the glowstone would burn a steady, unwinking red, and the half-face around it would become a black travesty of a skull, a fit home for an eye such as that.

It all seemed very terrifying until you remembered —as Dirk remembered—that it was all quite deliberate. Bretan Braith had not been forced to have a glowstone for an eye; he had chosen it, for his own reasons, and those reasons were not hard to comprehend.

Dirk's mind raced back to the earlier part of the afternoon and the conversation by the wolf's-head air-car. Bretan was quick and shrewd, no doubt about that, but Chell might easily be in the early years of senility. He had been painfully slow to grasp anything, and his young *teyn* had led him by the hand at every point, Dirk recalled. Suddenly the two Braiths seemed much less fearful, and Dirk could only wonder why he had ever been so terrified of them. They were almost amusing. Whatever Jaan Vikary might say when he returned from the City in the Starless Pool, surely nothing could happen; there was no real danger from such as these.

As if to underline the point, Chell began to mumble, talking to himself without realizing it, and Dirk glanced over and tried to hear. The old man jiggled a little as he spoke, his eyes vacantly staring. His words made no sense at all. It took Dirk several minutes to think things through, but he did, and it finally dawned on him that Chell was speaking in Old Kavalar. A tongue that evolved on High Kavalaan during the long centuries of interregnum, when the surviving Kavalars had no contact with other human worlds, it was a language that was quickly melting back into standard Terran, though enriching the mother language with words that had no equivalents. Hardly anyone spoke Old Kavalar anymore, Garse Janacek had told him, and yet here was Chell, an elderly man from the most traditional of the holdfast-coalitions, mumbling things he had no doubt heard in his youth.

And so too Bretan, who slapped Dirk soundly because he used the wrong form of address, a form permitted only to *kethi*. Another dying custom, Garse had said; even the highbonds were growing lax. But not Bretan Braith, young and not high at all, who clung to traditions that men generations older than himself had already discarded as dysfunctional.

Dirk almost felt sorry for them. They were misfits, he decided, more outcast and more alone than Dirk himself, worldless in a sense, because High Kavalaan had moved beyond them and could be *their* world no longer. No wonder they came to Worlorn; they belonged here. They and all their ways were dying.

Bretan in particular was a figure of pity, Bretan who tried so hard to be a figure of fear. He was young, perhaps the last true believer, and he might live to see a time when no one felt as he did. Was that why he was *teyn* to Chell? Because his peers rejected him and his old man's values? Probably, Dirk decided, and that was grim and sad.

One yellow sun still glinted in the west. The Hub was a vague red memory on the horizon, and Dirk was thoughtful and in control, beyond all fear, when they heard the aircars approach.

Bretan Braith froze and looked up, and his hands came out of his pockets. One of them came to rest, almost automatically, on the holster of his laser pistol. Chell, blinking, got slowly to his feet and suddenly seemed to shed a decade. Dirk rose as well.

The cars came in. Two of them together, the gray car and the olive-green one, flying with an almost military precision side by side.

"Come here," Bretan rasped, and Dirk walked over to him, and Chell joined them so that the three were standing together, with Dirk in the center like a prisoner. The wind bit at him. All around, the glowstones of the city Larteyn were radiant and bloody, and Bretan's eye—so close—shone savagely in its scarred nesting place. The twitching had stopped, for some reason; his face was very still.

Jaan Vikary hovered the gray manta and let it float gently down, then vaulted over the side and came to them with quick strides. The square and ugly military machine, roofed over and armored so the pilot was not visible, landed almost simultaneously. A thick metal door swung open in its side, and Garse Janacek emerged, ducking his head a trifle and looking around to see what was the problem. He saw, straightened, and slammed the door with a resounding *clang,* then came over to stand at Vikary's right arm.

Vikary greeted Dirk first, with a curt nod and a vague smile. Then he looked at Chell. "Chell Nim Coldwind fre-Braith Daveson," he said formally. "Honor to your holdfast, honor to your *teyn.*"

"And to yours," the old Braith said. "My new *teyn* guards my side, and you know him not." He indicated Bretan.

Jaan turned, weighed the scarred youth quickly with his eyes. "I am Jaan Vikary," he said, "of the Ironjade Gathering."

Bretan made his noise, his peculiar noise. There was an awkward silence.

"More properly," Janacek said, "my *teyn* is Jaantony Riv Wolf high-Ironjade Vikary. And I am Garse Ironjade Janacek."

Now Bretan responded. "Honor to your holdfast, honor to your *teyn.* I am Bretan Braith Lantry."

"I would never have known," Janacek said with the barest trace of a smile. "We have heard of you."

Jaan Vikary threw him a warning glance. There seemed to be something wrong with Jaan's face. At first Dirk thought it was a trick of the light—darkness was coming fast now—but then he saw that Vikary's jaw was slightly swollen on one side, giving his profile a puffed look.

"We come to you in high grievance," said Bretan Braith Lantry.

Vikary looked at Chell. "This is so?"

"It is so, Jaantony high-Ironjade."

"I am sorry we must quarrel," Vikary replied. "What is the problem?"

"We must question you," Bretan said. He put his hand on Dirk's shoulder. "This one, Jaantony high-Ironjade. Tell us, is he *korariel* of Ironjade, or no?"

Now Garse Janacek grinned openly and his hard blue eyes met Dirk's, laughing just a little in their icy depths, as if to say, Well, well, what have you done now?

Jaan Vikary only frowned. "Why?"

"Does your truth depend on our reasons, high-bond?" Bretan asked harshly. His scarred cheek twitched violently.

Vikary looked at Dirk. Clearly he was not pleased.

"You have no cause to delay or deny us your answer, Jaantony high-Ironjade," Chell Daveson said. "The truth is yes or the truth is no; there cannot be more to it than that." The old man's voice was quite even; he at least had no nervousness to conceal, and his code dictated each word that he would say.

"Once you were correct, Chell fre-Braith," Vikary began. "In the old days of the holdfasts, truth was a simple matter, but these are new times and full of new things. We are a people of many worlds now, not simply of one, and so our truths are more complex."

"No," said Chell. "This mockman is *korariel* or this mockman is not *korariel*. That is not complex."

"My *teyn* Chell speaks the truth," Bretan added. "The question I have put to you is quite simple, high-bond. I demand your answer."

Vikary would not be pushed. "Dirk t'Larien is a man from the distant world of Avalon, far within the Tempter's Veil, a human world where I once studied. I did name him *korariel,* to give him my protection and the protection of Ironjade against those who would do him harm. But I protect him as a friend, as I would protect a brother in Ironjade, as a *teyn* protects a *teyn*. He is not my property. I make no claim to own him. Do you understand?"

Chell did not. The old man pressed his lips together beneath his little stiff mustache and mumbled something in Old Kavalar. Then he spoke aloud. Too loud, in fact, almost shouting. "What is this nonsense? Your *teyn* is Garse Ironjade, not this strange one. How can you shield him as a *teyn?* Is he of Ironjade? He is not even armed! Is he a man at all? Why, if he is, he cannot be *korariel;* and if he is not and he is *korariel,* then you must own him. I do not hear any sense in your mockman words."

"I am sorry of that, Chell fre-Braith," Vikary

said, "but it is your ears that fail, and not my words. I try to do you honor, but you do not make it easy."

"You jape me!" Chell said, accusingly.

"No."

"You do!"

Bretan Braith spoke then, and his voice had none of Chell's anger, but it was very hard. "Dirk t'Larien, as he calls himself and you call him, has done us wrong. This is the heart of the matter, Jaantony high-Ironjade. He has laid hands upon the property of Braith without any word of Braith permission. Now, who pays for this? If he is a mockman and *korariel* to you, then here and now I issue challenge. Ironjade has done wrong to Braith. If he is not *korariel,* then, well . . ." He stopped.

"I see," Jaan Vikary said. "Dirk?"

"For one thing, all I did was sit in the damned aircar for a second," Dirk said uneasily. "I was looking for a derelict, an abandoned car still in working order. Gwen and I found one like that in Kryne Lamiya, and I thought maybe I could find another."

Vikary shrugged and looked at the two Braiths. "It seems that small wrong has been done, if any. Nothing was taken."

"Our car was *touched!*" old Chell bellowed. "By him, by a mockman; he had no right! Small wrong, you call this? He might have flown it off. Would you have me close my eyes like a mockman and be thankful he did so little?" He turned to Bretan, his *teyn.* "The Ironjades jape us, insult us," he said. "Perhaps they are not true men, but mockmen themselves. They are full of mockman words."

Garse Janacek responded immediately. "I am *teyn* to Jaantony Riv Wolf high-Ironjade, and I vouch for him. He is no mockman." The words came quickly, a rote formula.

From the way that Janacek then looked toward Vikary, it seemed clear to Dirk that he expected his *teyn* to repeat the same words. Instead Jaan shook his head and said, "Ah, Chell. There are no mockmen."

He sounded immensely tired, and there was a slump to his broad shoulders.

The tall, elderly Braith looked as though Jaan had struck him. Again he muttered low hoarse words in Old Kavalar.

"This cannot go on," Bretan Braith said. "We get nowhere. Did you name this man *korariel,* Jaantony high-Ironjade?"

"I did."

"I rejected the name," Dirk said quietly. He felt compelled to, and the time seemed right. Bretan half turned and glared at him, and the Braith's green eye seemed to have as much fire in it as its glowstone counterpart.

"He rejected only the suggestion of property," Vikary said very quickly. "My friend asserted his humanity, but he still wears the shield of my protection."

Garse Janacek grinned and shook his head. "No, Jaan. You were not home this morning. T'Larien wants none of our protection, either. He said so."

Vikary looked at him, furious. "Garse! This is no time for jokes."

"I do not joke," said Janacek.

"It's true," Dirk admitted. "I said I could take care of myself."

"Dirk, you do not know what you are saying!" Vikary said.

"For a change, I think I do."

Bretan Braith Lantry made his noise, quite loudly and suddenly, while Dirk and the two Ironjades argued and his *teyn* Chell stood stiff with fury. "Silence," the sandpaper voice demanded, and it got it. "This is of no consequence. Things are the same. You say he is human, Ironjade. If so, he cannot be *korariel* and you cannot protect him. If he wants it or no, you cannot protect him. My *kethi* will see that you do not." He spun on his heel to face Dirk full front. "I challenge you, Dirk t'Larien."

Everyone was quiet. Larteyn smoldered all around,

and the wind was very cold. "I meant no insult," Dirk said, remembering words that the Ironjades had used at other times. "Am I allowed to apologize, or what?" He offered his palms to Bretan Braith, up and open and empty.

The scarred face twitched. "Insult was taken."

"You must duel him," Janacek said.

Dirk's palms sank slowly. At his side they became fists. He said nothing.

Jaan Vikary was staring at the ground mournfully, but Janacek was still animated. "Dirk t'Larien knows nothing of the dueling customs," he told the two Braiths. "Such customs do not prevail on Avalon. Will you allow me to instruct him?"

Bretan Braith nodded, the same curiously awkward motion of head and shoulders that Dirk had noticed that afternoon in the garage. Chell did not even seem to hear; the old Braith was still facing Vikary, mumbling and glaring.

"There are four choices to make, t'Larien," Janacek said to Dirk. "As challenged, you make the first. I urge you to make the choice of weapons, and to choose blades."

"Blades," Dirk said softly.

"I make the choice of mode," Bretan rasped, "and I choose the death-square."

Janacek nodded. "You have the third choice also, t'Larien. Since you have no *teyn,* the choice of numbers is dictated. It must be singles. You may say that, or you may choose the place."

"Old Earth?" Dirk said hopefully.

Janacek grinned. "No. This world only, I fear. Other choices are not legal."

Dirk shrugged. "Here, then."

"I make the choice of numbers," Bretan said. It was fully dark now, with only the thin scattering of outworld stars to light the black sky above. The Braith's eye flamed, and strange reflected light glistened wetly on his scars. "I choose singles, as it must be."

"It is set then," Janacek said. "You two must agree on an arbiter, and then . . ."

Jaan Vikary looked up. His features were dim and shadowy, with only the pale light of the glowstones to shine on them, but his swollen jaw cast an odd silhouette. "Chell," he said very quietly, in a deliberate and even tone.

"Yes," the old Braith replied.

"You are a fool to believe in mockmen," Vikary told him. "All of you who believe such are fools."

Dirk was still facing Bretan Braith when Vikary spoke. The scarred face twitched once, twice, a third time.

Chell sounded as if he were in a trance. "Insult is taken, Jaantony high-Ironjade, false Kavalar, mockman. I issue challenge."

Bretan whirled and tried to shout. His voice was not capable of it, and he sputtered and choked instead. "You . . . duel breaker! Ironjade . . . I . . ."

"It is within the code," Vikary replied halfheartedly. "Though perhaps, if Bretan Braith could overlook the small trespass of an ignorant offworlder, then I might find it in myself to beg forgiveness from Chell fre-Braith."

"No," Janacek said darkly. "Begging has no honor."

"No," Bretan echoed. His face *was* a skull now. His jewel-eye gleamed and his cheek was twisted in fury. "I have bent as far as I may bend for you, false Kavalar. I will not make jape of all the wisdom of my holdfast. My *teyn* was more right than I. In truth, I was bitter wrong to even try to avoid duel with you, liar. Mockman. There was great shame in it. But now I will be clean. We will kill you, Chell and I. We will kill all three of you."

"Perhaps that is truth," Vikary said. "It will soon be done, and then we will see.'

"And your *betheyn*-bitch too," Bretan said. He could not shout; his voice broke when he tried. So he spoke as low as ever, and the rawness caught in his throat, and he could not be held. "When we have done with you, we will wake our hounds and hunt her and her fat Kimdissi through the forests they know so well."

Jaan Vikary ignored him. "I am challenged," he said to Chell fre-Braith. "The first of the four choices is mine. I make the choice of numbers. We will fight *teyn*ed."

"I make the choice of weapons," Chell replied. "I choose sidearms."

"I make the choice of mode," said Vikary. "I choose the death-square."

"Last the choice of place," Chell said. "Here, then."

"The arbiter will chalk only one square," Janacek said. Of the five men on the roof, only he was still smiling. "We need an arbiter still. The same for both duels?"

"One man will do," Chell said. "I suggest Lorimaar high-Braith."

"No," said Janacek. "He came to us in high grievance only yesterday. Kirak Redsteel Cavis."

"No," Bretan said. "He writes fair poetry, but I have no other use for Kirak Redsteel."

"There are two of the Shanagate Holding," Janacek said. "I am not certain of their names."

"We would prefer a Braith," Bretan said, twitching. "A Braith will rule well, uphold all the honor of the code."

Janacek glanced at Vikary; Vikary shrugged. "Agreed," Janacek said, facing Bretan once more. "A Braith, then. Pyr Braith Oryan."

"Not Pyr Braith," Bretan said.

"You are not easy to please," Janacek said dryly. "He is one of your *kethi*."

"I have had frictions with Pyr Braith," Bretan said.

"A highbond would make a better choice," old Chell said. "A man of stature and wisdom. Roseph Lant Banshee high-Braith Kelcek."

Janacek shrugged. "Agreed."

"I will ask him," said Chell. The others nodded.

"Tomorrow, then," said Janacek.

"All is done," Chell said.

And while Dirk stood and watched, feeling lost and out of place, the four Kavalars took their farewell. And strangely, before parting, each of them kissed his two enemies lightly on the lips.

And Bretan Braith Lantry, scarred and one-eyed, his lip half gone—Bretan Braith Lantry kissed Dirk.

When the Braiths had gone, the others went downstairs. Vikary opened the door to his apartment and turned on the lights. Then, in methodical silence, he began to build a fire in the great hearth beneath the mantel, taking logs of twisted black wood from a concealed storage cabinet in a nearby wall. Dirk sat on one end of the couch frowning. Garse Janacek sat on the other end with a vague smile on his face, his fingers tugging absently at the orange-red hairs of his beard. No one spoke.

The fire woke to blazing life, orange and blue-tipped tongues of flame licking around the logs, and Dirk felt the sudden heat on his face and hands. A scent like cinnamon filled the room. Vikary stood up and left.

He came back with three glasses, brandy snifters as black as obsidian. A bottle was under his arm. He handed one glass to Dirk and one to Garse, put the third down on a nearby table, and yanked the cork with his teeth. The wine within was a deep red in color, very pungent. Vikary poured all three glasses very full, and Dirk passed his under his nose. The vapors burned, but he found them oddly pleasant.

"Now," Vikary said, before any of them had tasted the wine. He had set down the bottle and lifted his own glass. "Now I am going to ask something very difficult of both of you. I am going to ask each of you to go beyond his own little culture for a time, and be something he has not been before, something strange to him. Garse, I ask you—for the good of each of us—to be friend to Dirk t'Larien. There is no word for it in Old Kavalar, I know. There is no need of such on High Kavalaan, where a man has his holdfast and his *kethi* and most of all his *teyn*. But we are all on Worlorn, and tomorrow we duel. Perhaps we do not duel all together, yet we have common enemies. So I ask you, as my *teyn,* to take the name and namebonds of friend with t'Larien."

"You ask a good deal of me," Janacek replied, holding his wine in front of his face and watching the flames dance in the black glass. "T'Larien has spied upon us, has attempted to steal my *cro-betheyn* and your name, and now has involved us in his quarrel with Bretan Braith. I am tempted to issue challenge against him myself for all he has done. And you, my *teyn,* you ask me to take the bond of friend instead."

"I do," Vikary said.

Janacek looked at Dirk, then tasted his wine. "You are my *teyn,*" he said. "I yield to your wishes. What obligations must I fulfill in the namebond of friend?"

"Treat a friend as you would a *keth*," Vikary said. He turned slightly to face Dirk. "And you, t'Larien, you have been the cause of very great trouble, but I am not sure how much of it, if any, you must truly bear the weight for. I ask something of you also. To be holdfast-brother, for a time, to Garse Ironjade Janacek."

Dirk never got the chance to respond; Janacek beat him to it. "You cannot do that. Who is he, this t'Larien? How can you think him worthy, bring him into Ironjade? He will be false, Jaan. He will not keep the bonds, will not defend the holdfast, will not return with us to the Gathering. I protest this."

"If he accepts, I think he will keep the bonds for a time," Vikary said.

"For a time? *Kethi* are linked forever!"

"Then this will be a new thing, a new sort of *keth*, a friend for a time."

"It is more than new," said Janacek. "I will not allow it."

"Garse," said Jaan Vikary, "Dirk t'Larien is now your friend. Or have you forgotten so soon? You do wrong to try to block my offer. You break the bonds that you have just taken. You would not act such to a *keth*."

"You would not be inviting a *keth* to be a *keth*," Janacek grumbled. "He would be already, so the whole thing has no sense to it. He is an outbonder. The high-bond council would rebuke you, Jaan. This is wrong, clearly."

"The highbond council is seated on High Kavalaan, and this is Worlorn," Vikary said. "Only you are here to speak for Ironjade. Will you hurt your friend?"

Janacek did not reply.

Vikary turned again to Dirk. "Well, t'Larien?"

"I don't know," Dirk said. "I think I know what it would mean, to be a holdfast-brother, and I suppose that I appreciate the honor, or whatever. But we have a lot of things between us, Jaan."

"You are speaking of Gwen," Vikary said. "She is indeed between us. But Dirk, I am asking you to be a new and special sort of holdfast-brother. Only for so long as you are on Worlorn, and only to Garse, not to myself or any other Ironjade. Do you understand?"

"Yes. That makes it easier." He glanced at Janacek. "Even with Garse, though, I've got problems. He was the one who tried to make property of me, and just now he wasn't exactly trying to get me *out* of that duel."

"I spoke only truth," Janacek said, but Vikary waved him quiet.

"Those things I could forgive, I guess," Dirk said. "But not the business with Gwen."

"That matter will be resolved by myself and you and Gwen Delvano," Vikary said calmly. "Garse has no voice in it, though he may tell you that he has."

"She is my *cro-betheyn*," Garse complained. "I have a right to speak and act. I have an obligation."

"I'm talking about last night," Dirk said. "I was at the door. I heard. Janacek hit her, and since then the two of you have had her locked up away from me."

Vikary smiled. "He hit her?"

Dirk nodded. "I heard it."

"You heard an argument and a blow, of that I have

no doubt," Vikary said. He touched his swollen jaw. "How dŏ you think *this* transpired?"

Dirk stared, and suddenly felt incredibly dense. "I . . . I thought . . . I don't know. The jelly children . . ."

"Garse hit *me,* not Gwen," Vikary said.

"I would do it again," Janacek added in a surly voice.

"But," said Dirk, "but then, what was going on? Last night? This morning?"

Janacek rose and walked to Dirk's end of the couch to loom over him. "Friend Dirk," he said in slightly venomous tones, "this morning I told you the truth. Gwen went out with Arkin Ruark, to work. The Kimdissi had been calling for her all throughout yesterday. He was most frantic. The tale he told to me was that a column of armor-bugs had begun to migrate, undoubtedly in response to the growing cold. This is said to be very rare even on Eshellin. On Worlorn, of course, such an event is unique and cannot be recreated, and Ruark felt that it had to be studied at once. *Now* do you comprehend, my *friend* Dirk t'Larien, *now?*"

"Uh," said Dirk. "She would have said something."

Janacek returned to his seat with his gaunt hatchet face screwed up in a scowl. "My friend calls me a liar," he said.

"Garse speaks the truth," Vikary said. "Gwen said she would leave word for you, a note or a tape. Perhaps in the excitement of her preparation she forgot. Such things happen. She is very involved in her work, Dirk. She is a good ecologist."

Dirk looked at Garse Janacek. "Hold on," he said. "This morning you *said* you were keeping her from me. You admitted it."

Vikary looked puzzled also. "Garse?"

"Truth," Janacek said grudgingly. "He came up and pressed and pressed, forced his way inside with a transparent lie. More, he clearly wanted to believe that Gwen was being held captive by the foul Ironjades. I doubt that he would have believed anything else." He sipped carefully at his wine.

"*That,*" Jaan Vikary said, "was not wise, Garse."

"Untruth given, untruth returned," Janacek said, looking smug.

"You are not being a good friend."

"I will henceforth be better," said Janacek.

"That pleases me," Vikary said. "Now, t'Larien, will you be *keth* to Garse?"

Dirk considered it for a long moment. "I guess," he finally said.

"Drink then," Vikary said. The three men raised their glasses simultaneously—Janacek's was already half drained—and the wine flowed hot and a little bitter over Dirk's tongue. It was not the best wine he had ever tasted. But it was good enough.

Janacek finished his glass and stood. "We must talk of the duels."

"Yes," Vikary said. "This has been a bitter day. Neither of you has been wise."

Janacek leaned up against the mantel below one of the leering gargoyles. "The greatest lack of wisdom was yours, Jaan. Understand me, I have no fear of duel with Bretan Braith and Chell Empty-Arms, but it was not needed. You deliberately provoked it. The Braith had to issue challenge after your words, lest even his own *teyn* spit upon him."

"It did not go as I had hoped," Vikary said. "I thought perhaps Bretan feared us, that he might let pass his duel with t'Larien in order to avoid us. He did not."

"No," said Janacek, "he did not. I could have told you, had you asked. You pushed him too far and came perilously close to duel-breaking."

"It is within the code."

"Perhaps. Yet Bretan was correct; there would have been great shame for him if he had ignored t'Larien's trespass in fear of you."

"No," said Vikary. "That is where you and all our people are wrong. There should be no shame in avoiding a duel. If we are ever to achieve our destiny, we must learn that. Yet, in a sense, you are right—in consideration of who and what he was, he could give no other answer. I misjudged him."

"A serious misjudgment," Janacek said. A grin split his red beard. "It would have been better to let t'Larien duel. I saw to it that they will fight with blades, did I not? The Braith would not have slain him for such a trifling offense. A man like Dirk, ah, there would have been no honor in it. One blow only, I would have said. A cut would do t'Larien good. A lesson for him, a lesson about mistakes. It would add character to his face, a small cut." He looked at Dirk. "Now, of course, Bretan Braith will kill you."

He was still grinning and he made his final comment with casual élan. Dirk tried not to choke on his wine. "What?"

Janacek shrugged. "As first-challenged, you must duel first, so you cannot hope that Jaan and I will slay them before they get to you. Bretan Braith Lantry is as widely known for his skill in duel as he is for his striking good looks. In truth, he is notorious. I suppose he is here hunting mockmen with Chell, but he is not really much a hunter. He is more comfortable in the death-square than in the wild, from all that I have heard of him. Even his own *kethi* find him difficult. In addition to being ugly, he took Chell fre-Braith to *teyn*. Chell was once a highbond of great power and honor. He outlived his *betheyn* and his original *teyn*. Today he is a superstitious dodderer with a small mind and great wealth. The holdfast rumors say the wealth is the reason Bretan Braith wears Chell's iron-and-fire. No one tells this to Bretan openly, of course. He is said to be quite touchy. And now Jaan has made him angry as well, and perhaps he is a bit frightened. He will have no mercy for you. I hope that you can manage to cut him a bit before you die. That would make it easier for us in the duel to follow."

Dirk was remembering the confidence that had filled him up on the roof; he had been quite certain that neither of the Braiths was a real danger. He understood them; he felt sorry for them. Now he began to feel sorry for himself. "Is he right?" he asked Vikary.

"Garse jokes and exaggerates," Vikary said, "yet you are in danger. No doubt Bretan will try to kill you, if you let him. This need not happen. The rules of your mode and weaponry are quite simple. The arbiter will chalk a square upon the street, five meters by five, and you and your enemy will start from opposite corners. At a word from the arbiter, each of you will advance with your sword toward the center. When you meet, you fight. To satisfy the requirements of honor, you must take one blow and deal one. I would advise you to cut at his foot or at his leg, since this will indicate that you have no wish for a true death-duel. Then, after you have taken his first blow—try to deflect it with your sword, if you can—you can walk to the perimeter of the square. Do not run. There is no honor in running, and the arbiter will rule the duel a death-victory for Bretan, and then the Braiths will kill you. You must walk, calmly. At the perimeter line, once beyond it, you are safe."

"To achieve this safety you must *reach* the perimeter line," Janacek said. "Bretan will kill you first."

"If I deal my one blow, and take one, then can I drop my sword and walk away?" Dirk asked.

"In such a case Bretan will kill you with a puzzled look on his face, or what remains of it," said Janacek.

"I would not do that," Vikary cautioned.

"Jaan's suggestions are folly," Janacek said. He walked slowly back to the couch, retrieved his glass, and poured himself more wine. "You should keep your sword and fight him. Consider, the man is blind on one side. Surely he is vulnerable there! And see how awkwardly he nods or turns his head."

Dirk's glass was empty. He held it out and Janacek filled it with wine. "How will *you* duel them?" Dirk asked.

"The rules for our mode and weaponry differ from yours," Vikary said. "The four of us must stand at the four corners of the death-square with dueling lasers or other sidearms. We may not move except to step backwards, outside the square, to safety. And that we may not do until each man within the square had taken one shot. That done, the choice is ours. Those who remain within, if they still stand, may continue to fire. It can be a harmless mode, or a very deadly one, depending on the will of those participating."

"Tomorrow," Janacek promised, "it must be deadly." He drank again.

"I would wish otherwise," Vikary said with a rueful shake of his head, "but I fear you speak the truth. The Braiths are too full of anger for us to fire into the air."

"Indeed," Janacek said with a small smile. "They took the insult too deeply. Chell Empty-Arms, at least, will not forgive."

"Can't you shoot to wound?" Dirk suggested. "Disarm them?" The words came easily, but it was odd to hear himself say it. The situation was so totally outside his experience, and yet he found himself accepting it, becoming strangely comfortable with the two Kavalars and their wine and their quiet talk of death and maiming. Perhaps it meant something, to be one of the *kethi*; perhaps that was why his unease was fading. All Dirk knew was that he felt peaceful, and at home.

Vikary looked troubled. "Wound them? I might wish that too, but it cannot be. The hunters fear us now. They spare *korariel* of Ironjade because of that fear. We save lives. That will not be possible if we are too easy on the Braiths tomorrow. The others might not hold back their hunting if they thought that all they risked was a small wound. No, sadly, I think we must kill Chell and Bretan if we can."

"We can," Janacek said confidently. "And, friend t'Larien, it is not so easy or so wise to wound an enemy in duel as you might think it is. Disarming them, well, you jape us. That is virtually impossible. We fight with dueling lasers, friend, not with war weapons. Such sidearms fire in half-second pulses and require a full fifteen seconds to recycle between firings. You understand? A man who hurries his shot, or makes it needlessly difficult, a man who shoots to disarm—he is soon dead. Even at five meters you can still miss, and your enemy will kill you clean before your laser is ready for a second shot."

"It can't be done?" Dirk said.

"Many people are only wounded in duel," Vikary told him. "Far more than are killed, in truth. Yet in most cases this is not the intended result. Sometimes yes. When a man fires into the air, and his enemy decides to punish him, then horrible scars can be inflicted. But this does not happen often."

"We might wound Chell," Janacek said. "He is old and slow, his sidearm will not rise quickly to his hand. But Bretan Braith is another matter. He is said to have a half-dozen kills already."

"He will be my concern," said Vikary. "See that Chell's laser stays dark, Garse, and that will be enough."

"Perhaps." Janacek looked toward Dirk. "If you could cut Bretan only a little, t'Larien, in the arm or hand or shoulder—give him a single painful gash, slow him a bit. That would make a difference." He grinned.

Despite himself, Dirk found that he was returning the smile. "I can try," he said, "but remember, I know damn little about dueling and less about swords, and my first concern is going to be staying alive."

"Don't fret over the impossible," Janacek said, still grinning. "Just do as great a damage as you can."

The door opened. Dirk turned and looked up, and Janacek fell silent. Gwen Delvano stood framed in the doorway, her face and clothing streaked with dust. She looked uncertainly from one face to the next, then came slowly into the room. A sensor pack was slung over one shoulder. Arkin Ruark followed her in, carrying two heavy cases of instruments under his arms. He was sweaty and panting, dressed in heavy green pants and jacket and hood, and he looked much less foppish than usual.

Gwen lowered the sensor pack to the ground gently,

but her hand kept its hold on the strap. "Damage?" she said. "What was this? Who is going to do damage to who?"

"Gwen," Dirk began.

"No," Janacek interrupted. He stood very stiffly. "The Kimdissi must leave."

Ruark looked around, white-faced and puzzled. He threw back his hood and began to mop his forehead beneath his white-blond hair. "Utter trash, Garsey," he said. "What is this, big Kavalar secret, eh? A war, a hunt, a duel, some violence, yes? I would not pry such things, no, not me. I give you privacy then, yes, yours to keep." He started back toward the door.

"Ruark," Jaan Vikary said. "Wait."

The Kimdissi paused.

Vikary faced his *teyn.* "He must be told. If we fail—"

"We will not fail!"

"If we fail, they have promised to hunt them. Garse, the Kimdissi is too involved. He must be told."

"You know what will happen. On Tober, on Wolfheim, on Eshellin, all throughout the Fringe. He and his kind will spread lies, and all Kavalars will be Braiths. It is the way of the manipulators, the mockmen." Janacek's voice had none of the savage humor with which he had jabbed Dirk; he was cold serious now.

"His life is at stake in this, and Gwen's," Vikary said. "They must be told."

"Everything?"

"The charade is over," Vikary said.

Ruark and Gwen spoke simultaneously.

"Jaan, what—" she started.

"Charade, life, hunting, what is all this? Tell!" Jaan Vikary turned and told him.

chapter 7

"Dirk, Dirk, you cannot be serious. No, I do not believe it. All along I have thought, well, yes, that you were better than them. And you say *this* to me? No, I dream. This is utter folly!" Ruark had recovered somewhat. In his long dressing gown, green silkeen embroidered with owls, he looked more like himself, although he was woefully out of place amid the clutter of the workroom. He sat on a high stool with his back to the dark rectangular screens of the computer console; his slippered feet were crossed at the ankles, and his chubby hands held a tall frosted glass of green Kimdissi wine. The bottle was behind him, sitting next to two empty glasses.

Dirk was on top of a wide plastic worktable, his legs folded under him and his elbow resting on a sensor pack. He had cleared a space for himself by shoving the pack to one side and a stack of slides and papers to the other. The room was in incredible disarray. "I don't see what the folly is," he said stubbornly. Even as he spoke, his eyes were wandering. He had never seen the workroom before. It was about the same size as the living room in the Kavalar compartment, but seemed much smaller. A bank of small computers lined one wall. Across from it was a huge map of Worlorn in a dozen different colors, stuck full of various pins and markers. In between were the three worktables. This was where Gwen and Ruark pieced together the bits of knowledge they hunted down in the wilds of the dying Festival world, but it looked more like a military headquarters to Dirk's eyes.

He still wasn't quite sure why they were there. After Vikary's long explanation and the acrimonious discussion that had followed between Ruark and the two Kavalars, the Kimdissi had stomped down to his own apartment, taking Dirk with him. The time had not seemed right to talk to Gwen. But no sooner had Ruark changed clothes and quieted his nerves with a slug of wine than he insisted that Dirk accompany him back upstairs to the workroom. He brought along three glasses, but Ruark himself was the only one drinking. Dirk still remembered the last time, and he had tomorrow to consider; he had to be sharp. Besides, if Kimdissi wine mixed with its Kavalar counterpart the way the Kimdissi mixed with Kavalars, it would be sheer suicide to drink one after the other.

So Ruark drank alone. "The folly," the Kimdissi said after one sip of the green stuff, "is you dueling like a Kavalar. I say it, I hear myself, I cannot believe it! Jaantony, yes, Garsey by all means, and of course these Braiths. Xenophobe animals, violent folk. But *you,* ah! Dirk, you, a man of Avalon, this is beneath you. Think, I beg you, yes, I beg, for me, for Gwen, for you yourself. How *how* can you be serious? Tell me, I must know. From Avalon! You grew up with the Academy of Human Knowledge, yes, with the Avalon Institute for the Study of Non-Human Intelligence, that too. The world of Tomas Chung, the home base of the Kleronomas Survey, all that history and knowledge all about you, as much as is left anywhere except perhaps Old Earth or Newholme maybe. You are traveled, cultured, you have seen different worlds, many scattered folks. Yes! You know better. You must, no? Yes!"

Dirk frowned. "Arkin, you don't understand. I didn't pick this fight. It's all some sort of mistake. I tried to apologize, but Bretan wouldn't listen. What else am I supposed to do?"

"Do? Why, leave, of course. Take sweet Gwen and leave; get off Worlorn as soon as you can. You owe her, Dirk, you know it, truth. She needs you, yes, no one else can help. How do you help her? By being as bad as Jaan? By killing yourself? Eh? You tell me, Dirk, you tell me."

It was getting all confused again. When he had been drinking with Janacek and Vikary, everything had seemed so very clear, so easy to accept. But now Ruark was saying it was all wrong. "I don't know," Dirk replied. "I mean, I turned down Jaan's protection. So I have to protect myself, don't I? Who else is responsible? I made the choices and all that; the duel is set. I can't very well back out now."

"Of course you can," Ruark said. "Who is to stop you? What law, eh? No law on Worlorn, no, none. Utter truth! Could these beasts hunt us with a law? No, but is no law, so everyone is in trouble, but you don't have to duel unless you want to."

The door clicked open, and Dirk turned in time to see Gwen enter. His eyes narrowed, while Ruark beamed. "Ah, Gwen," the Kimdissi said, "come with me, talk sense into t'Larien. This utter fool intends to duel, truth, like he was Garsey himself."

Gwen came forward and stood between them. She wore pants of chameleon cloth (dark gray now) and a black pullover, with a green scarf knotted in her hair. Her face was freshly scrubbed and serious. "I told them I was coming down to run over some data," she said, the tip of her tongue flicking nervously over her lips. "I don't know what to say. I asked Garse about

Bretan Braith Lantry. Dirk, the chances are very good that he'll kill you out there."

Her words chilled him. Somehow hearing it from Gwen made it different. "I know," he said. "It doesn't change anything, Gwen. I mean, if I wanted to be safe, I could just be *korariel* of Ironjade, right?"

She nodded. "Yes. But you rejected it. Why?"

"What did you say in the forest? And later, again? About names? I didn't want to become anyone's property, Gwen. I am not *korariel*."

He watched her. Very briefly her face darkened, and her eyes flicked down to the jade-and-silver. "I understand," she said in a voice that was almost a whisper.

"*I* do not," Ruark said in a snort. "So be *korariel*. What is it? Some word only! Then you are alive, eh?"

Gwen looked at him, up on his perch on his stool. He looked faintly comic in his long gown, clutching his drink and scowling. "No, Arkin," she said. "That was my mistake. I thought *betheyn* was only a word."

He flushed. "All right, so! So Dirk is no *korariel*, fine, he is no one's property. It does not mean he must duel, no, utter not. The Kavalar honor code is nonsense, great high stupidness in truth. So, you are bound to be stupid, Dirk? To die and be stupid?"

"No," Dirk said. Ruark's words bothered him. He did not believe in the code of High Kavalaan. Why then? He was far from sure. To prove something, he thought, but he did not know what or to whom. "I have to, that's all. It is the right thing to do."

"Words!" Ruark said.

"Dirk, I don't want to see you dead," Gwen said. "Please. Don't put me through that."

The pudgy Kimdissi chuckled. "No, we will talk him out of it, us two, eh?" He sucked at his wine. "Listen to me, Dirk, will you do that much?"

Dirk nodded sullenly.

"Good. First, answer me this, do you believe in code duello? As a social institution? As a moral thing? Tell me, in truth, do you?"

"No," Dirk said. "But I don't think Jaan does either, from some of the comments he's made. Still, he duels when he has to. Anything else would be cowardice."

"No, no one thinks you are a coward, or him even. Jaantony may be Kavalar, with all the bad that is in that, but even I do not say he is coward. But there are different kinds of courage, no? If this tower caught fire, would you risk your life to save Gwen and maybe me? Garse too, perhaps?"

"I'd hope so," Dirk said.

Ruark nodded. "See then, you are courageous man. It is not needed, a suicide, to prove that."

Gwen nodded. "Remember what you said that night in Kryne Lamiya, Dirk, about life and death. You can't go off and kill yourself after that, can you?"

He frowned. "Damn it, this isn't suicide."

Ruark laughed. "No? Same thing, close enough. You think you will outduel him, maybe?"

"Well, no but—"

"If he drops his sword, sweat on his fingers, or such, will you kill him?"

"No," Dirk said. "I—"

"That would be wrong, yes, in truth? Yes! Well, to let him kill you, that is just as wrong. Even to give him the chance. Stupid. You are no Kavalar either, so point me not at Jaantony. Misgivings or no, he is still a killer. You are better, Dirk. And he has an excuse, something he thinks he fights for maybe, to change his people. A big savior complex, Jaan, but we will not mock at him, no. But you, Dirk, you have no reason like that. Do you?"

"I guess not. But damnit, Ruark, he's doing the right thing. You didn't look so good up there when he told you how the Braiths would have hunted you down except for his protection."

"No, and I did not feel so good either, no lie. That changes nothing. So I am *korariel* maybe, so the Braiths are worse than the Ironjades, so Jaan uses violence to stop worse violence, maybe. Is that right? Ah,

I cannot say. Tough moral issue, utter truth! Maybe Jaan's duels serve some purpose, eh, for his people, for us. But *your* duel is utter folly, serves nothing, just gets you dead. And Gwen stays with Jaan and Garse forever, until they lose a duel maybe, and then it is not so pleasant for her."

Ruark paused and finished his wine, then swiveled around on his stool to pour himself another glass. Dirk sat very still, Gwen's eyes on him, her patient stare heavy enough to feel. His head pounded. Ruark was confusing everything, he thought again. He had to do the right thing, but what was it? Suddenly all his insights and his decisions had evaporated on him. The silence lay thick over the workroom.

"I won't run," Dirk said at last. "I won't. But I won't duel, either. I'll go there and tell them my decision, refuse to fight."

The Kimdissi swirled his wine and chuckled. "Well, a certain moral courage is in that. Utter truth. Jesus Christ and Socrates and Erika Stormjones and now Dirk t'Larien, great martyrs of history, yes. Maybe the Redsteel poet will write something on you."

Gwen gave a more serious answer. "These are Braiths, Dirk, Braith highbonds of the old school. On High Kavalaan itself you might never be challenged to duel. The highbond councils recognize that offworlders don't adhere to their code. But this is different. The arbiter will rule you forfeit, and Bretan Braith and his holdfast-brothers will kill you or hunt you down. By refusing to duel, in their eyes, you'll have proven yourself a mockman."

"*I can't run,*" Dirk repeated. His arguments were all gone suddenly; he had nothing left but emotion, a determination to face the dawn and see it through.

"You push away your only sanity, yes, in truth. It is no cowardice, Dirk. The bravest choice of all, think that way, to risk their scorn by flight. Even then, you face peril. Probably they hunt you, Bretan Braith if he lives, the others if not, you know? But you'll live, avoid them maybe, help Gwen."

"I can't," Dirk said. "I promised them, Jaan and Garse."

"Promise? What? That you'd die?"

"No. Yes. I mean, Jaan had me promise to be a brother to Janacek. They wouldn't be in this duel if Vikary hadn't been trying to get me out of trouble."

"After Garse pushed you in," Gwen said bitterly, and Dirk started at the sudden venom in her quiet tones.

"They could die tomorrow too," Dirk said uncertainly. "And I'm responsible for that. Now you say I should desert them."

Gwen stepped very close to him and lifted her hands. Her fingers lightly grazed his cheeks as she brushed gray-brown hair back from his forehead, and the wide green eyes stared into his. Suddenly he remembered other promises: the whisperjewel, the whisperjewel. And times long gone came flashing back, and the world spun, and right and wrong began to melt and run together.

"Dirk, listen to me," Gwen said slowly. "Jaan has been in six duels because of me. Garse, who doesn't even love me, has shared four of those. They've killed for me, for my pride, my honor. I didn't ask it, no more than you asked for their protection. It was *their* conception of my honor, not my own. But still, those duels were for me as much as this one is for you. Despite that, you asked me to leave them, to return to *you*, to love you again."

"Yes," Dirk said. "But— I don't know. I've left a trail of broken promises." His voice was anguished. "Jaan named me *keth*."

Ruark snorted. "If he named you *dinner*, you would jump into the oven, eh?"

Gwen just shook her head sadly. "You feel what? A duty? An obligation?"

"I guess," he said reluctantly.

"Then you've answered yourself, Dirk. You've told me what my answer to *you* must be. If you feel so strongly that you have to fulfill the duties of a short-term *keth,* a bond that doesn't even have any reality on High Kavalaan, how can you ask me to discard the jade-and-silver? *Betheyn* means more than *keth.*"

Her soft hands left his face. She stepped back.

Dirk's hand shot out and caught her by the wrist. The left wrist. His grip closed around cold metal and polished jade. "No," he said.

Gwen said nothing. She waited.

For Dirk, Ruark was forgotten, the workroom had faded to darkness. There was only Gwen, staring at him, eyes green and wide and full of—what? Promises? Threats? Lost dreams? She waited, all silent, and he fumbled over his words, never knowing what he would say next. And the jade-and-silver was cool in his hand, and he was remembering:

Red teardrops full of love, wrapped in silver and velvet, burning fiercely cold.

Jaan's face: high cheekbones, the clean square jaw, the receding black hair, and the easy smile. His voice, quiet as steel, always even: *But I do exist.*

The white ghost towers of Kryne Lamiya, wailing, mocking, singing bright despair while a distant drum sounded its low, meaningless booms. In the middle of it all, defiance, resolution. Briefly he had known what to say.

The face of Garse Janacek: distant (the eyes blue smoke, the head held stiffly, the mouth set), hostile (ice in his sockets, a savage smile at play behind his beard), full of bitter humor (his eyes snapping, his teeth bared in death's own grin).

Bretan Braith Lantry: a tic and a glowstone eye, a figure of fear and pity with a cold and frightening kiss.

Red wine in obsidian goblets, vapors that stung the eye, drinking in a room full of cinnamon and a strange fellowship.

Words. *A new and special kind of holdfast-brother,* Jaan said.

Words. *He will be false,* Garse promised.

Gwen's face, a younger Gwen, slimmer, with eyes somehow wider. Gwen laughing. Gwen crying. Gwen in orgasm. Holding him, her breasts flushed and red, the blush spreading over her body. Gwen whispering to him, *I love you, I love you.* Jenny!

A solitary black shadow, poling a low barge down an endless dark canal.

Remembering.

His hand trembled where it gripped her. "If I do not duel," he said, "you will leave Jaan, then? And come with me?"

Her answering nod was painfully slow. "Yes. I thought of it all day, talked about it with Arkin. We had planned it so he would bring you up here, and I'd tell Jaan and Garse that I had to work."

Dirk unfolded his legs from beneath him, and they tingled to the jabs of a hundred tiny knives as the sleep and the stiffness ran out of them. He stood up, and he was decided. "You were going to do this anyway, then? It's not just because of the duel?"

She shook her head.

"Then I'll go. How soon can we leave Worlorn?"

"Two weeks and three days," Ruark said. "No ship till then."

"We'll have to hide," Gwen said. "All things considered, it's the only safe course. I wasn't sure this afternoon whether I should tell Jaan my decision or simply leave. I thought maybe we would talk, then go up together to face him. But the duel business settles it. You would not be allowed to leave now."

Ruark climbed down off his stool. "Go, then," he said. "I'll stay, keep watch, you can call and I tell you what happens. Safe enough for me, unless Garsey and Jaantony lose their duel. Then I'd come quick, run and join you, eh?"

Dirk took Gwen's hands. "I love you," he said. "Still. I do."

She smiled gravely. "Yes. I'm glad, Dirk. Maybe it will work again. But we have to move fast, lose ourselves thoroughly. From now on, all Kavalars are poison to us."

"All right," he said. "Where?"

"Go down and get your things, you'll need warm clothing. Then meet me up on the roof. We'll take the aircar and decide after we're on our way."

Dirk nodded and kissed her quickly.

They were airborne over the dark rivers and rolling hills of the Common when the first blush of dawn touched the sky, a crimson glow low in the east. Soon the first yellow sun rose, and the darkness below turned to a gray morning mist that was fast dissolving. The manta aircar was open, as ever, and Gwen had pushed its speed to maximum, so the chill wind rushed about loudly, making it impossible to talk. While she flew, Dirk slept by her side, huddled up in a patchwork brown greatcoat that Ruark had given him before they left.

She woke him when the shining spear of Challenge came into sight ahead of them, by pushing gently against his shoulder. He had been sleeping lightly, uneasily. At once he straightened and yawned. "We're there," he said, unnecessarily.

Gwen did not answer. The manta slackened in speed as the Emereli city grew larger and nearer.

Dirk looked off toward the dawn. "Two suns are up," he said, "and look, you can almost see Fat Satan. I guess they know we've gone." He thought of Vikary and Janacek, waiting for him at the death-square chalked on the street, waiting with the Braiths. Bretan would have paced impatiently, no doubt, and then made his odd noise. His eye would be drained and cold in the morning, a dead ember in his scarred face. Maybe he was dead as well by now, or Jaan, or Garse Janacek. Briefly Dirk flushed with shame. He moved closer to Gwen and put an arm around her.

Challenge swelled before them. Gwen took the aircar up in a sharp ascent through a bank of wispy white clouds. The black maw of a landing deck lit at their approach and Dirk saw the numbers as Gwen took them in. The 520th level, an airlot vast and immaculate and deserted.

"Welcome," a familiar tone said as the manta hovered and sank to the floor plates. "I am the Voice of Challenge. May I entertain you?"

Gwen killed the aircar's power and climbed out over the wing. "We want to become temporary residents."

"The charge is quite reasonable," the Voice said.

"Take us to a compartment then."

A wall opened, and another of the balloon-tired cars rolled out to meet them. In everything except color, it was twin to the one that had carried them during their last visit. Gwen got in, and Dirk began to load the vehicle with the luggage from the back seat of the aircar: a sensor pack that Gwen had brought along, three bags jammed with clothing, a package of field supplies for jaunts into the wild. The two sky-scoots, complete with flight boots, were on the bottom of the pile, but Dirk left them in the aircar.

The vehicle set off, and the Voice began to tell them about the various kinds of living quarters that it could provide. Challenge had rooms furnished in a hundred different styles, to make offworlders feel at home, although the flavor of ai-Emerel predominated.

"Something simple and cheap," Dirk told it. "A double bed and cooking facilities and a wet-shower will do."

The Voice deposited them in a small cubicle with pastel blue walls two levels up. It did have a double bed, which filled most of the room, plus a kitchenette built into one wall and a huge color viewscreen that filled three-quarters of another.

"Real Emereli splendor," Gwen said sarcastically when they entered. She set down her sensor pack and clothing, and fell gratefully onto the bed. Dirk stashed the bags he was carrying behind a sliding panel-closet, then sat by Gwen's feet on the edge of the bed and regarded the wallscreen.

"A wide selection of library tapes is available for your viewing pleasure," the Voice said. "I regret to inform you that all regular Festival programming has been terminated."

"Don't you ever go away?" Dirk snapped.

"Basic monitoring functions continue at all times, for your safety and protection; but if you wish, my service function can be temporarily deactivated in your vicinity. Some residents prefer it this way."

"Including me," Dirk said. "Deactivate."

"If you should change your mind or require some service," the Voice said, "simply push the button marked with a star on any nearby wallscreen, and I will again be at your command." Then it fell silent.

Dirk waited briefly. "Voice?" he said. No response. He nodded with satisfaction and went back to his inspection of the screen. Gwen, behind him, was already asleep, her hands cradling her head as she lay curled up on one side.

He wanted to call Ruark desperately, to find out what had happened at the duel, who had lived and who had died. But he did not think it would be safe yet. One of the Kavalars—or more than one—might be keeping Ruark company in either his quarters or the workroom, and a call could give away their location. He would have to wait. Before they had taken off, the Kimdissi had given them the call number of a deserted apartment two floors above his own, and told Dirk to try that number just past dusk. If it was safe, he promised to be there and respond to the buzz. If not, there would be no answer. In any case, Ruark did not know where the two fugitives had gone, so the Kavalars could not possibly force the information out of him.

Dirk was very tired. Despite his nap in the aircar en route, exhaustion weighed heavily on him, tinged with the dark colors of guilt. He had Gwen back at his side again at last, but he felt no exultation. Perhaps that would come later, when his other concerns had faded and they had begun to know each other once more, as they had known each other on Avalon seven long years ago. Yet that might not be until they were safely off Worlorn, away from Jaan Vikary and Garse Janacek and all the other Kavalars, away from the dead cities and the dying forests. They would go back inside the

Tempter's Veil, Dirk thought then as he sat and looked absently at the blank screen, leave the Fringe entirely, go to Tara or Braque or some other sane planet, maybe back to Avalon, maybe farther in than that, to Gulliver or Vagabond or Old Poseidon. There were a hundred worlds he had never seen, a thousand, more—worlds of men and not-men and aliens, all sorts of distant romantic places where no one had ever heard of High Kavalaan or Worlorn. He and Gwen could see those worlds together now.

Too tired to sleep, restless and ill at ease, Dirk began to play with the viewscreen, idly testing its capabilities. He flicked it on and punched the button marked with a query as he had the day before in Ruark's apartment in Larteyn, and the same list of services flashed before him in figures three times the size. He studied them carefully, to learn what he could learn. Perhaps he might pick up some bit of knowledge that could be useful, become aware of something that could help them.

The list included a call number for planetary news. He tapped it out, hoping that the dawn duel in Larteyn would have been noted, maybe as an obituary. But the screen went gray on him, and white letters flashed "Service Terminated" on and off until he wiped them.

Frowning, Dirk tried another sequence, for spaceport information, to check Ruark's data on the ship. This time he had better luck. There were three ships due within the next two standard months. The earliest, as the Kimdissi had said, would come in a little over two weeks from now, a Fringe shuttle named *Teric neDahlir*. What Ruark hadn't mentioned, however, was that the ship was outbound, coming from Kimdiss and headed on toward Eshellin and the World of the Blackwine Ocean and finally ai-Emerel, its point of origin. A week after that a supply ship was due in from High Kavalaan. Then there was nothing until the *Shuddering of Forgotten Enemies* returned, inbound.

There was no question of waiting that long, however; he and Gwen would simply have to catch the *Teric neDahlir* and switch ships on some other world farther out. Getting to the ship was going to be the biggest risk they faced, Dirk had decided. The Kavalars had virtually no chance of finding them here in Challenge, with an entire planet to search, but Jaan Vikary would certainly guess that they intended to go offworld as soon as possible. That meant he could be waiting for them at the spacefield when the time came. Dirk didn't know how they would deal with that. He could only hope they would not have to.

Dirk cleared the screen and tried other numbers, noting which functions had been shut down entirely, which had been stripped to a skeleton status—medical emergency service, for one—and which still operated at Festival levels. Often there was a city-by-city breakdown, which convinced him that they had chosen correctly in coming to Challenge. The Emereli had been determined to prove their tower-city immortal, and they had left nearly everything on in defiance of the cold and the dark and the coming ice. This would be an easy place to live. The other cities were in sorry shape by comparison. Four of the fourteen were entirely dark and depowered, and one of those had suffered so much erosion from wind and weather that it was already crumbling into dusty ruins.

For a time Dirk continued to punch buttons, but finally the game began to wear on him, and he grew bored and restive. Gwen slept on. It was still morning, impossible to call Ruark. He turned off the wallscreen, washed briefly in the waste cubicle, and then went back to the bed, flicking off the light panels. It was some time before he went to sleep. He lay in the warm darkness staring at the ceiling and listening to Gwen's faint breathing, but his mind was far away and troubled.

Soon everything will be good again, he told himself, the way things were on Avalon. Yet he could not believe it. He did not feel like the old Dirk t'Larien, Gwen's Dirk, the one he had promised himself he would become again. He felt, instead, as if nothing had changed; he labored on, as wearily, as hopelessly, as he had on Braque and the other worlds before it. His Jenny was with him again, and he should be full of joy, but he only knew a sick, tired feeling. As if he had failed her once again.

Dirk pushed the thoughts aside and closed his eyes.

When he woke, it was late afternoon. Gwen was already up and about. Dirk showered and dressed in soft faded garments of Avalon synthetic. Then the two of them went out into the corridors to explore the 522nd level of Challenge. They held hands as they walked.

Their compartment was one of thousands in a residential sector of the building. Around it were other compartments, identical to their own except for the numbers on the black doors. The floors and walls and ceilings of the corridors through which they walked were all carpeted in rich cobalt shades, and the lights that hung down at intersections—dim globes, restful, easy on the eyes—matched the hue.

"This is boring," Gwen said after they had walked for a few minutes. "The sameness is too depressing. And I don't see any maps, either. I'm surprised people don't get lost."

"I imagine they could just ask the Voice for directions," Dirk said.

"Yes. I forgot about that." She frowned. "What happened to the Voice? It hasn't had much to say lately."

"I shut it up," Dirk told her. "But it's still watching."

"Can you get it working again?"

He nodded and stopped, then led her toward the nearest of the black doors. The compartment, as he'd expected, was unoccupied, and opened easily at his touch. Inside, the bed, the layout, the viewscreen—everything was the same.

Dirk turned on the viewscreen, pressed the button marked with a star, then turned the set off again.

"Can I help you?" the Voice asked.

Gwen smiled at him; a thin, strained sort of smile it was. She was as tired as he was, it seemed. There were worry lines around the corners of her mouth.

"Yes," she said. "We want something to do. Entertain us. Keep us busy. Show us the city." Dirk thought that she spoke a trifle too quickly, like someone frantic to distract herself and take her mind off an unpleasant subject. He wondered whether it was fear about their safety he was hearing, or possibly concern about Jaan Vikary.

"I understand," the Voice replied. "Let me be your guide, then, to the wonders of Challenge, the glory of ai-Emerel reborn on distant Worlorn." Then it began to direct them, and they walked to the nearest bank of tubes, out of the realm of endless straight cobalt corridors, into regions more colorful and diverting.

They ascended to Olympus, a plush lounge at the very summit of the city, and stood ankle deep in black carpet while they looked out of Challenge's single vast window. A kilometer below them rows of dark clouds scuttled by, racing on a bitter wind they could not feel. The day was dim and gloomy; the Helleye burned and glowered as always, but its yellow companions were hidden by gray haze smeared across the sky. They could see the distant mountains from their tower, and the faint dark green of the Common far beneath them. A robowaiter served them iced drinks.

They walked to the centershaft, a plunging cylinder that cored the tower-city from top to bottom. Standing on the highest balcony, they held hands and looked down together, past other balconies in never-ending rows that dwindled into dim-lit depths. Then they opened the wrought-iron gate and jumped, and hand-in-hand they floated down in the gentle grip of the warm updraft. The centershaft was a recreational facility, maintained at a trace gravity that was hardly great enough to be called a gravity at all—less than .01 percent Emereli normal.

They strolled the outer concourse, a broad slanting corridor that spiraled around and around the rim of the city like the threading on some vast screw, so that an ambitious tourist could walk from the ground level to the top. Restaurants, museums, and shops lined both sides of the concourse; in between were deserted traffic lanes for both the balloon-tired cars and faster vehicles. A dozen slidewalks—six up, six down—formed the median strip of the gently curving boulevard. When their feet grew tired, they climbed onto a belt, then to a faster one, then onto one faster still. As the scenery slid by, the Voice pointed out items of particular interest, none of which were particularly interesting.

They swam nude in the Emereli Ocean, a fresh-water pseudo sea that occupied most of the 231st and 232nd levels. The water was bright green crystal, so clean that they could see algae twisting in sinuous ropes on the bottom two levels below. It sparkled beneath panels of lights that gave the illusion of bright sunshine. Small scavenger fish darted to and fro in the lower reaches of the ocean; on the surface, floating plants bobbed and drifted like giant mushrooms done up in green felt.

They used power-skis to descend the ramp, a plunging, bracing flight over low-friction plastic that took them from the hundredth level all the way down to the first. Dirk fell twice, only to bounce back up again.

They inspected a free-fall gymnasium.

They looked into darkened auditoriums built for thousands, and declined to view the taped holoplays the Voice offered.

They ate, briefly and without relish, at a sidewalk cafe in the middle of a once-busy shopping mall.

They wandered in a jungle of twisted trees and yellow moss where the animal sounds were all on tape and echoed strangely off the walls of the hot, steamy park.

Finally, still restive and worried and only a little distracted by it all, they allowed the Voice to whisk them up to their room. Outside, they had been told, true dusk was settling over Worlorn.

Dirk stood in the narrow space between the bed and the wall as he pressed the buttons in sequence. Gwen sat just behind him.

Ruark was a long time answering, too long. Dirk wondered apprehensively if something terrible had happened. But just as he thought it, the throbbing blue call signal faded out, and the plump face of the Kimdissi ecologist filled the screen. Behind him, in a grayish pall, was the dirt of a deserted apartment.

"Well?" Dirk said. He glanced back at Gwen. She was chewing the edge of her lip, and her right hand was still, resting on the jade-and-silver bracelet that she wore yet on her left forearm.

"Dirk? Gwen? Is this you? I cannot see you, no, my screen is dark." Ruark's pale eyes flicked back and forth restlessly beneath lank strands of paler hair.

"Of course it's us," Dirk snapped. "Who else would call this number?"

"I cannot see you," Ruark repeated.

"Arkin," Gwen said from where she sat on the bed, "if you could see us, then you'd know where we were."

Ruark's head bobbed. He had just the slightest suggestion of a double chin. "Yes, I did not think, you are right. Best that I do not know, yes."

"The duel," Dirk prompted. "This morning. What happened?"

"Is Jaan all right?" Gwen asked.

"No duel," Ruark told them. His eyes still flicked back and forth, searching for something to look at, Dirk supposed. Or perhaps he was nervous that the Kavalars would burst in on him in the vacant apartment. "I went to see, but no duel, utter truth."

Gwen sighed audibly. "Then everyone is all right? Jaan?"

"Jaantony is alive and well, and Garsey, and the Braiths," Ruark said. "No shooting or killing at all, but when Dirk did not come to die on schedule, everyone got crazy, yes."

"Tell me," Dirk said quietly.

"Yes, well, you were the cause of the other duel being postponed."

"Postponed?" said Gwen.

"Postponed," Ruark replied. "They will still fight, same mode and weapons, but not now. Bretan Braith appealed to the arbiter. He said he had a right to face Dirk first, since he might die in the duel with Jaan and Garsey, so his grievance against Dirk would go unsettled. He demanded that the second duel be stayed till Dirk could be found. The arbiter said yes to him. A Braith tool, the arbiter, yes, agreed with everything the animals wanted. Roseph high-Braith, they called him, an utter malevolent little man."

"The Ironjades," Dirk said. "Jaan and Garse. Did they say anything?"

"Jaantony, no. He said nothing at all, no, just kept standing very still in his corner of the death-square. All the rest of them were running around, shouting and yelling and being Kavalar. Nobody else was even *in* the square but Jaan, no, but he kept standing there looking around, like he expected the duel to start any second. Garsey, now, he got very angry. First, when you did not come, he made jokes about you being sick, then he got very cold and silent for a time, quiet as Jaan was, but later he was a little less angry, I think, so he began to argue with Bretan Braith and the arbiter and the other dueler, Chell. All the Braiths were here, to witness perhaps. I did not know we had so much company in Larteyn, no. Well, I did abstractly, yes, but it is different when they come together all in one place. A pair of Shanagates came also, though not the Redsteel poet, so we were short three, you two and him. Otherwise, perhaps it was a city council meeting, everyone dressed up formally." He chuckled.

"Do you know what's going to happen now?" Dirk said.

"Do not worry," Ruark said. "You two will hide and catch the ship, yes. They cannot track you down, a whole planet to hunt! The Braiths, I think, will not even look. Truth, they had you named a mockman.

Bretan Braith demanded it, and his partner spoke about
old traditions, and others of the Braiths too, and the
arbiter said yes, that if you did not come to duel
you are no true man at all. So they will hunt you,
maybe, but not with special purpose, you are now just
another animal to kill, any other will do as well."

"Mockman," Dirk said hollowly. Oddly, he felt as
if he had lost something.

"To Bretan Braith and those, yes. Garse, I think,
will try harder to find you, but he will not hunt you
like an animal. He swore that you would duel, duel
Bretan Braith and then duel him, or maybe him first."

"What about Vikary?" Dirk said.

"I have told you, he said nothing at all, nothing."

Gwen rose from the bed. "You've only been talking
about Dirk," she said to Ruark. "What about me?"

"You?" Ruark's pale eyes blinked. "The Braiths said
you were mockman too, but Garse would not allow it.
He talked very strong of dueling any who touched you.
Roseph high-Braith waffled. He wanted to call you
mockman as well as Dirk, but Garsey was very angry,
and I understand Kavalar duelers can challenge arbiters
who make bad decisions, though they are still bound
to follow the decision, truth. So, sweet Gwen, you are
still *betheyn* and protected, and they will only bring
you back if they catch you. Afterwards, you will be
punished, but it will be a punishment of Ironjade. In
truth, they did not talk of you overmuch, many more
words were spent on Dirk. You are only a woman,
eh?"

Gwen said nothing.

"We'll call you again in a few days," Dirk said.

"Dirk, it must be a picked time, no? I am not always in this dust hole." Ruark gave another little
chuckle at that.

"In three days, then, at dusk again. We've got to
give some thought to how we're going to get to the
ship. I figure that Jaan and Garse will cover the spacefield when the time comes."

Ruark nodded. "I will think on it."

"Can you get us weapons?" Gwen asked suddenly.

"Weapons?" The Kimdissi made a clucking noise. "Truth, Gwen, the Kavalar is seeping into your blood. I am from Kimdiss. What do I know of lasers and such, violent things? I can try, however, for you, for Dirk my friend. We will talk of it when we speak again; now I must go."

His face dissolved, and Dirk blacked out the wall-screen before turning to face Gwen. "You want to fight them? Is that wise?"

"I don't know," she said. She walked to the door slowly, turned, walked back again. And then stopped; the compartment was so small that it was impossible to pace with any real vehemence.

"Voice!" Dirk said as sudden inspiration struck. "Is there a gun shop in Challenge? A place where we can purchase lasers or other weapons?"

"I regret to inform you that the norms of ai-Emerel prohibit the carrying of personal weaponry," the Voice replied.

"Sport weapons?" Dirk suggested. "For hunting and target practice?"

"I regret to inform you that the norms of ai-Emerel prohibit all blood sports and games based on sublimated violence. If you are a member of a culture where such pursuits are esteemed, please be assured that no insult is intended to your homeworld. These forms of recreation are available elsewhere on Worlorn."

"Forget it," Gwen said. "It was a bad idea anyway."

Dirk put his hands on her shoulders. "We won't need weapons in any case," he said with a smile, "though I'll admit that it might make me feel a little better to be carrying one. I doubt that I'd know how to use it if the time came."

"I would," she said. Her eyes—her wide green eyes—had a hardness in them that Dirk had never seen. For a single strange second he was reminded of Garse Janacek and his icy blue disdain.

"How?" he said.

She waved impatiently and shrugged, so that his hands slid off her shoulders. Then she turned away from him. "In the field, Arkin and I use projectile guns. To fire tracer-needles when we're trying to keep track of an animal, study its patterns of migration. Sleep darts too. And there are sensor implants the size of a thumbnail that will tell you everything you might want to know about a life form—how it hunts, what it eats, mating habits, brain patterns during various stages of the life cycle. Enough clues like that, and you can work out a whole ecosystem from the data that different species are reporting back. But you have to plant your spies first, and you do that by immobilizing the subjects with darts. I've fired thousands of them. I'm good. I only wish I'd thought to lug one along."

"It's different," Dirk said. "Using a weapon for something like that, and shooting a man with a laser. I've never done either, but I don't think they would be at all comparable."

Gwen leaned against the door and regarded him sourly from several meters away. "You don't think I could kill a man?"

"No."

She smiled. "Dirk, I'm not the little girl you knew on Avalon. In between then and now I spent several years on High Kavalaan. They were not easy years. I've had other women spit in my face. I've heard Garse Janacek deliver a thousand lectures on the obligations of jade-and-silver. I've been called mockman and *betheyn*-bitch by other Kavalar men so often that sometimes I find myself answering to them." She shook her head. Beneath the broad headband pulled tight across her forehead, her eyes were hard green stone. Jade, Dirk thought inanely, jade as in the armlet she still wore.

"You're angry," he said. "It's easy to get angry. But I've known you, love, and you're essentially a gentle person."

"I was. I try to be. But it's been a long time, Dirk,

a long, long time, and it's been building, and Jaan Vikary has been the only part of it that's been any good at all. I've told Arkin; he knows how I feel, *what* I've felt. There have been times when I've come so close—*so damned close*. With Garse especially, because in a very odd way he *is* part of me, and very much a part of Jaan, and it hurts more when it's someone who you care about, someone you could almost love if it weren't for . . ."

She stopped. Her arms were crossed tightly across her chest and she was frowning, but she stopped. She must have seen the expression on his face, Dirk thought. He wondered what it was.

"Maybe you're right," she said after a little bit, uncrossing her arms. "Maybe I couldn't kill anyone. But, you know, I feel as if I could sometimes. And right now, Dirk, I would very much like to have a gun." She laughed a small unfunny laugh. "On High Kavalaan, of course, I wasn't allowed to go armed. Why does a *betheyn* need a sidearm? Her highbond and his *teyn* protect her. And a woman with a gun might shoot herself. Jaan . . . well, Jaan has fought to change a lot of things. He tries. I'm here, after all. Most women never leave the safe stone of their holdfasts once they take the jade-and-silver. But for all his trying, and I do respect it, Jaan doesn't understand. He's a highbond, after all, and he's fighting other things as well, and for everything I tell him, Garse tells him something else. Sometimes Jaan doesn't even notice. And the small things, like my going armed, he says aren't important. I talked to him about it once, and he pointed out that I objected to the whole practice of going armed, the whole big artifice of code duello, which is true. And yet—Dirk, you know, I did understand what you were saying to Arkin last night, about wanting to face Bretan even if you don't feel yourself bound by his code. I've felt the same way at times."

The room lights flickered briefly, dimming, then flaring back to full intensity. "What?" Dirk said, looking up.

"Residents should not be alarmed," the Voice said in its even bass tones. "A temporary power failure affecting your level has now been rectified."

"Power failure!" A picture flashed through Dirk's mind, a picture of Challenge—sealed, windowless, totally contained Challenge—without power. He did not like the idea. "What's going on?"

"Please do not be alarmed," the Voice repeated, but the overhead lights gave the lie to its words. They went out entirely, and for a brief second Gwen and Dirk stood in frighteningly total darkness.

"I think we had better leave," Gwen said when the lights came back on. She turned and slid open the wall panel and began to remove their bags. Dirk went to help her.

"Please do not panic," the Voice said. "For your own safety, I urge you to remain within your compartment. The situation is under control. Challenge has many built-in safeguards, as well as back-ups for every important system."

They finished packing. Gwen went to the door. "Are you on secondary power now?" she asked.

"Levels one through fifty, 251 through 300, 351 through 451, and 501 through 550 are on secondary power at present," the Voice admitted. "This is no cause for alarm. Robotechs are repairing primary power as quickly as possible, and other standby systems exist in the unlikely event that secondary power should fail."

"I don't understand," Dirk said. "*Why?* What's the cause of the failures?"

"Please do not be alarmed," the Voice said.

"Dirk," Gwen said calmly. "Let's go." She went out, a bag in her right hand and her sensor pack slung over her left shoulder on a strap. Dirk picked up the other two bags and followed her out into the cobalt-blue corridors. They hurried toward the tubes, Gwen two steps ahead, the carpets swallowing the sounds of their footfalls.

"Residents who panic are more likely to harm themselves than those who remain within the safety of their own compartments during the duration of this small inconvenience," the Voice chided them.

"Tell us what's going on and we might reconsider," Dirk said. They did not stop or slow up.

"Emergency regulations are now in effect," the Voice said. "Warders have been dispatched to conduct you back to your own compartment. This is for your own protection. I repeat, warders have been dispatched to conduct you back to your own compartment. The norms of ai-Emerel prohibit . . ." The words abruptly began to slur, and the bass voice rose and squeaked and became a grating whine that clawed briefly at their ears. It ended in a sudden shuddering silence.

The lights went off.

Dirk stopped for an instant, then took two steps forward in the thick darkness and bumped into Gwen. "What?" he said. "Sorry."

"Quiet," Gwen whispered. She began to count off the seconds. At thirteen, the hanging globes at the cross corridors came on again. But the blue radiance was a dim ghost glow, barely enough to see by.

"Come on," Gwen said. She began walking again, more slowly this time, treading carefully in the blue gloom. The tubes were not far ahead.

When the walls spoke to them, the voice was not the Voice.

"This is a large city," it said, "yet it is not large enough to hide you, t'Larien. I am waiting in the lowest of the Emereli cellars, the fifty-second sublevel. The city is mine. Come to me, now, or all power will die around you, and in the darkness my *teyn* and I will come hunting."

Dirk recognized the speaker. He could hardly be mistaken. On Worlorn, or anywhere, it would not be easy to duplicate the twisted, rasping voice of Bretan Braith Lantry.

chapter 8

They stood in the shadowed corridor as if paralyzed. Gwen was a dim blue silhouette, her eyes black pits. Her mouth twitched at the corner, reminding Dirk horribly of Bretan and *his* twitch. "They found us," she said.

"Yes," Dirk said. Both of them were whispering, out of fear that Bretan Braith—like the displaced Voice of Challenge—would hear them if they spoke aloud. Dirk was acutely aware that speakers surrounded him, and cars as well, and maybe eyes—all invisible behind the carpeted walls.

"How?" said Gwen. "They couldn't have. It's impossible."

"They did. It must be possible. But what do we do now? Do I go to them? What's down on the fifty-second sublevel anyway?"

Gwen frowned. "I don't know. Challenge wasn't my city. I know the subsurface levels weren't residential, though."

"Machines," Dirk suggested. "Power. Life support."

"Computers," Gwen added, in a small hollow whisper.

Dirk set down the bags he was carrying. It seemed silly to cling tightly to clothing and possessions at this point. "They killed the Voice," he said.

"Maybe. If it can be killed. I thought it was a whole network of computers, scattered throughout the tower. I don't know. Maybe it was only one large installation."

"In any case they got the central brain, the nerve center, whatever. No more friendly advice from the walls. And Bretan can probably see us right now."

"No," Gwen said.

"Why not? The Voice could."

"Yes, maybe, though I don't think the Voice's sensing devices had to include visual sensors, by any means. I mean, it didn't need them. It had other senses, things humans don't have. That's not the point. The Voice was a supercomputer, built to handle billions of bits of information simultaneously. Bretan can't do that. No human can. Besides, the inputs weren't intended to make sense to him, or to you or to me. Only to the Voice. Even if Bretan is standing where he has access to all of the data the Voice was getting, it will mostly be meaningless gibberish to him, or it will flood by so fast as to be useless. Maybe a trained cyberneticist could make something out of it, though I doubt it. Not Bretan, though. Not unless he knows some secret we don't."

"He knew how to find us," Dirk said. "And he knew where the brain of Challenge was, and how to short-circuit it."

"I don't know how he found us," Gwen replied, "but it was no great trick to get to the Voice. The lowest sublevel, Dirk! It was just a guess on his part, it had to be. Kavalars build their holdfasts deep into stone, and the lowest level is always the safest, the most secure. That's where they quarter the women, and other holdfast treasures."

Dirk was thoughtful. "Wait a minute. He *can't* know

exactly where we are. Otherwise, why try to get us down to the basement, why threaten to hunt us?"

Gwen nodded.

"If he's in a computer center, though," Dirk continued, "we have to be careful. He might be able to find us."

"Some of the computers must still be functioning," Gwen said, glancing toward the dim blue globe a few meters away. "The city is still alive, more or less."

"Can he ask the Voice where we are? If he brings it back?"

"Maybe, but would it tell him? I don't think so. We're legal residents, unarmed, he's a dangerous intruder violating all the norms of ai-Emerel."

"He? You mean they. Chell is with him. Maybe others as well."

"A party of intruders, then."

"But there can't be more than—what? Twenty? Less? How could they take over a city this size?"

"Ai-Emerel is a world singularly without violence, Dirk. And this is a Festival world. I doubt that Challenge had many defenses. The warders . . ."

Dirk looked around suddenly. "Yes, warders. The Voice mentioned them. It was sending one for us." He almost expected to see something large and menacing wheel into sight from a cross corridor, as if on cue. But there was nothing. Shadows and cobalt globes and blue silence.

"We can't just stand here," Gwen said. She had stopped whispering. So had he. Both of them realized that if Bretan Braith and his fellows could hear every word they spoke, then they could surely be located in a dozen other ways as well. If so, their case was hopeless. Whispering was a wasted gesture. "The aircar is only two levels away," she said.

"The Braiths might be two levels away too," Dirk replied. "Even if they're not, we have to avoid the aircar. They have to know we've got one, and they'll be expecting us to run for it. Maybe that was why Bretan made his little speech, to flush us out into the air, where we'd be easy prey. His holdfast-brothers are probably out there waiting to laser us down." He paused, thoughtful. "But we can't just stay here, either."

"Not around our own compartment," she said. "The Voice knew where we were, and Bretan Braith might be able to find out. But we have to stay in the city; you're right about that."

"We hide, then," Dirk said. "Where?"

Gwen shrugged. "Here, there, and everywhere. It's a big city, as Bretan Braith said."

Gwen quickly knelt and went through her bag, discarding all the cumbersome clothing but retaining her field supplies and sensor pack. Dirk put on the heavy greatcoat that Ruark had given him and abandoned everything else. They walked toward the outer concourse; Gwen was anxious to get as far from their compartment as possible, and neither of them was willing to risk using the tubes.

The lights above the wide concourse boulevard still burned bright and white, and the slidewalks were humming evenly; the corkscrew road seemed to have an independent power supply. "Up or down?" Dirk asked.

Gwen did not seem to hear; she was listening to something else. "Quiet," she said. Her mouth twitched.

Above the steady hum of the slidewalks then Dirk heard the *other* noise, faint but unmistakable.

A howl.

It came from the corridor behind them, Dirk was positive of that. It came like a chill breath from out of the warm blue stillness, and it seemed to hang in the air far longer than it should have. Dim, distant shouts followed close on its heels.

There was a short silence. Gwen and Dirk looked at each other and stood very still, listening. The howl came again, louder, more distinct, echoing a bit this time. It was a furious shriek of a howl, long and high pitched.

"Braith hounds," Gwen said, in a voice that was much steadier than it had any right to be.

Dirk remembered the beast he had encountered when he walked through the streets of Larteyn—the horse-sized dog that had snarled at his approach, the creature with the hairless rat's face and the small red eyes. He looked down the corridor behind them with apprehension, but nothing moved in the cobalt shadows.

The sounds were growing louder, closer.

"Down," Gwen said. "And quickly."

Dirk needed no persuasion. They hurried to the median strip of the concourse, across the width of the silent boulevard, and got onto the first and slowest of the descending slidewalks. Then they began to move in, hopping from belt to belt until they were riding the swiftest of the descenders. Gwen unslung her field supplies and opened the packet, rummaging through the contents while Dirk stood above her, one hand resting on her shoulder, and watched the level numbers slide by, black sentinels mounted above the dusk-dark maws that led off into the interior corridors of Challenge. The numbers flashed past at regular intervals, growing steadily smaller.

They had just passed into the 490s when Gwen stood, holding a palm-sized rod of blue-black metal in her right hand. "Take off your clothes," she said.

"What?"

"Take off your clothes," she repeated. When Dirk only looked at her, she shook her head impatiently and tapped his chest with the point of the rod. "Null-scent," she told him. "Arkin and I use it in the wild. Spray ourselves before going out. It will kill the body scent for about four hours, and hopefully throw the hounds off the trail."

Dirk nodded and began to strip. When he was naked, Gwen made him stand with his legs far apart and his arms raised over his head. She touched one end of the metal rod, and from the other a fine gray mist issued, its soft touch tingling his bare skin. He felt cold and foolish and very vulnerable as she treated him, back and front, head to toe. Then she knelt and sprayed his clothing as well, inside and out, everything except the heavy greatcoat that Arkin had given him, which she carefully set to one side. When she was finished, Dirk dressed again—his clothes were dry and dusty with the ashen powder—while Gwen stripped in turn, and let him spray her.

"What about the coat?" he said while she got back into her clothes. She had treated everything: the sensor pack, the field supplies, her jade-and-silver armlet—everything except Arkin's patched brown greatcoat. Dirk nudged it with the toe of his boot.

Gwen picked it up and tossed it over the guardrail, onto the swiftly moving belt of an ascending slidewalk. They watched as it receded from them, out of sight. "You don't need it," Gwen said when the coat was gone. "Maybe it will lead the pack in the wrong direction. They're certain to have followed us as far as the concourse."

Dirk looked dubious. "Maybe," he said, with a glance at the inner wall. Level 472 came and went. "I think we should get off," he said suddenly. "Get away from the concourse."

Gwen looked at him, questioning.

"You said it yourself," he said. "Whoever is behind us will get at least as far as the concourse. If they've already started down, my coat won't fool them much. They'll see it sailing past, and laugh."

She smiled. "Conceded. But it was worth a try."

"So assume they're coming down after us . . ."

"We'll have built a good lead by this point," she interrupted. "They'll never get a pack of hounds onto a slidewalk, which means they'll be on foot."

"So? The concourse still isn't safe, Gwen. Look, that can't be Bretan up there, he's down in the sublevels. It probably isn't Chell either, is it?"

"No. A Kavalar hunts with his *teyn*. They do not split."

"I figured as much. So we've got one pair playing games with the power way below us, another pair at our backs. How many others are after us? Can you answer that?"

"No."

"I'd guess a few, at least; and even if it isn't so, we'd be better off to assume the worst and work from there. If there are other Braiths loose in the city, and if they're in contact with the hunters behind us, the ones above us will tell the others to close off the concourse."

Her eyes narrowed. "Maybe not. Hunting parties seldom work together. Each pair want the kill for themselves. *Damn,* but I wish I had a weapon!"

Dirk ignored her final comment. "We shouldn't take any chances," he said. Even as he said it, the bright lights above them began to flicker, fading down abruptly into a dim lingering grayness, and simultaneously the slidewalk beneath them jerked and began to slow. Gwen stumbled. Dirk caught her and held her in his arms. The slowest belt stopped first, then the one next to it, and finally the descender they were riding.

Gwen shivered and looked up at him, and Dirk hugged her more tightly, drawing desperately needed reassurance from the warmth and closeness of her body.

Below them——Dirk swore that the sound came from *below* them, from the direction the slidewalk had been taking them—a shrill scream rang briefly, and not so very far away.

Gwen pulled loose of him. They did not speak. They moved from belt to belt, across the shadowed, empty traffic lanes, toward the passage that led away from the dangerous concourse and into the corridors again. He glanced up at the numbers as they passed from gray dimness into blue: level 468. When the carpets swallowed their footsteps once again, they began to run, moving quickly down the first long corridor, then turning again and yet again, sometimes right and sometimes left, choosing at random the directions they took. They ran until both of them were short of breath, and then they paused and sank into the carpets beneath the light of a dusky bluish globe.

"What was it?" he said at last, when his breath returned to him.

Gwen was still heaving and panting with the effort of their run. They had come a long way. She fought to catch her breath. Silent tears left wet trails down her face in the blue light. "What do you *think* it was?" she said at last, with an edge in her voice. "That was a mockman, screaming."

Dirk opened his mouth and tasted salt. He touched the wetness on his own cheeks then, and wondered how long he had been crying. "More Braiths, then," he said.

"Below us," she said. "And they've found a victim. Damn, damn, *damn!* We led them here, we're to blame. How could we have been so stupid? Jaan was always afraid they would start to hunt the cities."

"They started yesterday," Dirk said, "with the Blackwiner jelly children. It was only a matter of time until they came here. Don't get all . . ."

She turned her face up to his, her features tight with anger, her cheeks streaked by tears. "What?" she spat. "You don't think we're responsible? Who else, then? Bretan Braith followed *you,* Dirk. Why did we come here? We could have gone to Twelfth Dream, to Musquel, to Esvoch. Empty cities. No one would have gotten hurt. Now the Emereli will be— How many residents did the Voice say were left?"

"I don't remember. Four hundred, I think. Something like that." He tried to put his arm around her and pull her to him, but she shrugged it off and glared at him.

"It's our fault," she said. "We have to do something."

"All we can do is try to stay alive," he told her. "They're after us too, remember? We can't worry about the others."

Gwen was staring at him, her face hard with—

what?—perhaps contempt, Dirk thought. The look startled him.

"I don't believe what you're saying," she said. "Can't you think of anyone besides yourself? Damn it, Dirk, we've got the null-scent going for us, if nothing else. The Emereli, they've got nothing at all. No weapons, no protection. They're mockmen, game, that's all. *We've got to do something!*"

"What? Commit suicide? Is that what? You didn't want me to go against Bretan this morning, in the duel, but now you—"

"Yes! Now we have to. You wouldn't have talked this way back on Avalon," she said, her voice rising until it was almost a shout. "You were different then. *Jaan* wouldn't . . ."

She stopped, suddenly aware of her words, and looked away from him. Then she began to sob. Dirk sat very still.

"So that's it," he said after a time. His voice was quiet. "Jaan wouldn't think of himself, right? Jaan would play the hero."

Gwen looked at him again. "He would, you know."

He nodded. "He would. Maybe I would have, once. Maybe you're right. Maybe I've changed. I don't know anything anymore." He felt sick and weary and defeated then, and very shamed. His thoughts went back and forth and round and round. They were both right, he kept thinking. They *had* brought the Braiths down on Challenge, on hundreds of innocent victims. The guilt was theirs; Gwen was right. And yet, *he* was right, too, they could do nothing now, nothing. If that was selfish, it was no less true.

Gwen was crying openly. He reached for her once more, and this time she let him hold her and try to comfort her with his hands. But all the while, as he stroked her long black hair and fought to hold back his own tears, he knew that it was no good, that it changed nothing. The Braiths were hunting, killing—and he could not stop them. He could hardly save himself. He was not the old Dirk after all, the Dirk of Avalon, no. And the woman in his arms was not Jenny. Both of them were only prey.

Then suddenly it came to him. "Yes," he said loudly.

Gwen looked at him, and Dirk got unsteadily to his feet, pulling her up after him.

"Dirk?" she said.

"We can do something," he said, and he led her to the door of the nearest compartment. It opened easily. Dirk went to the viewscreen by the bed. The room lights were all out; the only illumination was the long rectangle of faded blue that fell from the open doorway. Gwen stood in the frame, uncertain, a bleak dark silhouette.

Dirk turned on the screen, hoping (he could do nothing else), and it lit under his hands, and he breathed easier. He turned to Gwen.

"What are you going to do?" she asked him.

"Tell me your home call number," he said.

She understood. Slowly she nodded, and she told him the numbers, and he punched them out, one by one, and waited. The throbbing call signal brightened the room. When it dissolved, the patterns of light reshaped themselves into the strong-jawed features of Jaan Vikary.

No one spoke. Gwen came forward to stand behind Dirk, one hand up on his shoulder. Vikary looked at them in silence, and Dirk was afraid for a long moment that he would blank the screen and leave them to their fate.

He did not. He said to Dirk, "You were a holdfast-brother. I trusted you." Then his eyes shifted to Gwen. "And you I loved."

"Jaan," she said, quick and soft, in a voice so much a whisper that Dirk doubted that Vikary could hear. Then she broke and turned and walked swiftly from the room.

Still Vikary did not close out the connection. "You are in Challenge, I see. Why have you called, t'Larien? You know what we must do, my *teyn* and I?"

"I know," Dirk said. "I risk it. I had to tell you. The

Braiths have followed us. Somehow, I don't know how, we never thought we would be traced. But they are here. Bretan Braith Lantry has knocked out the city computer, and seems to control much of the remaining power. The others—they have hunting packs here. They are in the corridors."

"I understand," Vikary said. Emotion—unreadable, strange—flickered across his face. "The residents?"

Dirk nodded. "Will you come?"

Vikary smiled very faintly, and there was no joy in it. "You ask my help, Dirk t'Larien?" He shook his head. "No, I should not jape, it is not you who asks, not for yourself. I understand that. For the others, the Emereli, yes, Garse and I will come. We will bring our beacons, and those such as we find before the hunters we shall make *korariel* of Ironjade. Yet it will take time, too long perhaps. Many will die. Yesterday, at the City in the Starless Pool, a creature called a Mother died a sudden death. The jelly children— Do you know of the Blackwiner jelly children, t'Larien?"

"Yes. I know enough."

"They burst forth from their Mother to find another, and discovered none. During the decades they have lived inside their vast host, others of their world had caught the creature and brought it to Worlorn from the World of the Blackwine Ocean, and lastly abandoned it. There is scant love lost between the jelly children and other Blackwiners not of the cult. So they stumbled forth, a hundred of them or more, overrunning their city, filling it with a sudden life, knowing nothing of where they were or why. Most were old, quite old. In panic, they began to wake their dead city, so Roseph high-Braith found them. I did what I could do, protected some. The Braiths found many others, because it took time. It will be the same in Challenge. Those that take to the corridors and run, those will be hunted down and slain, long before my *teyn* and I can help. Do you understand?"

Dirk nodded.

"It is not enough to call me," Vikary said. "You must act yourself. Bretan Braith Lantry wants you badly, you and no other. He may even allow you to duel. The others want only to hunt you, as a mockman, but even they value you high above any other prey. Come into the open, t'Larien, and they will come after you. For the Emereli hiding around you, the time will be important."

"I see," Dirk said. "You want Gwen and me . . ."

Vikary flinched visibly. "No, not Gwen."

"Me, then. You want me to draw attention to myself? Without a weapon?"

"You have a weapon," Vikary said. "You stole it yourself, giving insult to Ironjade. Whether you choose to use it or not is a decision that only you can make. I will not trust you to make the correct choice. I trusted you once. I simply tell you. One other thing, t'Larien. Whatever you do, or do not do, it changes nothing between you and me. This call changes nothing. You know what we must do."

"You said that," Dirk replied.

"I say it a second time. I want you to remember." Vikary frowned. "And now I will go. It is a long flight to Challenge, a long cold flight."

The screen went dark before Dirk could frame an answer.

Gwen was waiting just outside the door, leaning up against the carpeted wall, her face in her hands. She straightened when Dirk came out. "Are they coming?" she asked.

"Yes."

"I'm sorry I . . . left. I couldn't face him."

"It doesn't matter."

"It *does*."

"No," he said sharply. His stomach ached. He kept imagining far-off screams. "It doesn't. You made it clear before—how you feel."

"Did I?" She laughed. "If you know how I feel, you know more than me, Dirk."

"Gwen, I don't— No, listen, it doesn't matter.

You were right. We have to . . . Jaan said we have a weapon."

She frowned. "He did? Does he think I took my dart gun? Or what?"

"No, I don't think so. He only said that we have a weapon, that we stole it ourselves and insulted Iron-jade."

She closed her eyes. "What?" she said. "Of course." Her eyes opened again. "The aircar. It's armed with lasercannon. That has to be what he meant. They aren't charged. I don't even think they're connected. That was the aircar I used most of the time, and Garse . . ."

"I understand. But you think the lasers can be fixed? Made to work?"

"Maybe. I don't know. But what else could Jaan have meant?"

"The Braiths may have found the car, of course," Dirk said. His voice was cool and even. "We'll have to take that chance. Hiding—we can't hide, they'll find us. Bretan may be on his way right now, if my transmission to Larteyn registered anywhere down below. No, we double back to the aircar. They won't expect that, if they know we were headed down along the concourse."

"The aircar is fifty-two levels above us," Gwen pointed out. "How do we get to it? If Bretan has as much control over the power as we think he does, he has surely killed the tubes. He stopped the slidewalks."

"He knew we were using the slidewalks," Dirk said. "Or at least that we were on the concourse. The ones tracking us told him. They *are* in contact, Gwen. The Braiths. They have to be, the belts stopped too conveniently. But that makes it easy."

"Easy? What?"

"For us to draw attention to ourselves," he said. "For us to get them after us, to save the goddamned Emereli. That's what Jaan wants us to do. Isn't that what you want us to do?" His voice was sharp.

Gwen paled slightly. "Well," she said. "Yes."

"Then you win. We're going to do it."

She looked thoughtful. "The tubes, then? If they are still working?"

"We couldn't trust the tubes," Dirk said. "Even if they were working. Bretan might stop them while we were inside one."

"I don't know of any stairs," she said. "And we'd never find them without the Voice even if they do exist. We could walk up the concourse, but . . ."

"We know of at least two Braith hunting parties roaming the concourse. There are probably more. No."

"What then?"

"What's left?" He frowned. "The centershaft."

Dirk leaned forward across the wrought-iron railing, looked up and then down, and grew dizzy. The centershaft seemed to go on forever in both directions. It was only two kilometers from top to bottom, he knew, but everything about it gave the feeling of all but infinite distance. The rising currents of warm air that gave buoyancy to the feather-light floaters also filled the echoing shaft with a gray-white mist, and the balconies that lined the circumference—level on level on level —were all identical, giving the illusion of unending repetition.

Gwen had taken something from her sensor pack, a palm-sized silvery metallic instrument. She stood next to Dirk by the railing and tossed it lightly out into the shaft. Both of them watched it travel, spinning over and over, winking at them with reflected light. It sailed halfway across the diameter of the great cylinder before it began to fall—slowly, gently, half supported by the rising air, a mote of metal dust dancing in the artificial sunlight. They watched it for a eon before it vanished in the gray gulf below them. "Well," Gwen said after it was lost to sight, "the gravity grid is still on."

"Yes. Bretan doesn't know the city. Not well enough." Dirk glanced up again. "I guess we should get started. Who goes first?"

"After you," she said.

Dirk opened the balcony gate and retreated to the wall. He brushed a tangle of hair out of his eyes impatiently, shrugged, and ran forward, kicking as hard as he could when his boot touched the edge.

The leap took him out and up and *up*. For one wild moment it was like falling, and Dirk's stomach wrenched, but then he looked and saw and felt, and it was not like falling at all, it was flying, soaring. He laughed aloud, suddenly giddy, and he brought his arms in front of him and swept them back in powerful strokes, swimming higher and faster. The rows of empty balconies went by: one level, two, five. Sooner or later he would begin to drop, a slow curving descent into gray-shrouded distance, but he would scarcely have time to fall far. The other side of the centershaft was only thirty meters off, an easy jump against the paperclip chains of the shaft's trace gravity.

Finally the curving wall grew near, and he bounced off one black iron railing, spinning out and tumbling upward absurdly before he reached and caught a post of the balcony just above the one he'd hit. It was easy to pull himself in. He'd come clear across the centershaft, and eleven levels up. Smiling and strangely elated, he sat and gathered strength for a second leap while he watched Gwen come after him. She flew like some graceful impossible bird, her black hair shimmering behind her as she soared. She also outjumped him by two levels.

By the time he reached the 520th level, Dirk was bruised in a half-dozen places where he'd banged up against the iron railings, but he felt almost good. At the end of his sixth dizzy leap across the plunging shaft he was half reluctant to pull himself onto the target balcony and return to normal gravity. But he did. Gwen was already there waiting for him, her sensor pack and field supplies strapped to her back between the shoulder blades. She gave him a hand and helped pull him over the railing.

They went out into the broad corridor that circled the centershaft, into the now-familiar blue shadows.

Globes shone dimly at junctions on either side of them, where long straight passages led away from the city's core like spokes on some great wheel. At random they chose one and began to walk swiftly toward the perimeter. It was a longer walk than Dirk would have thought possible, past numerous other intersections (he lost count at forty) each like the others, past black doors that differed only in their numbering. Neither he nor Gwen spoke. The good feeling that he had touched briefly, the joy of wingless flight, dropped from him as suddenly as it had come while he walked through the murky dimness. In its place, a faint tinge of fear. His ears conjured up phantoms to worry him, far-off howlings and the soft footfalls of pursuers; his eyes made the more distant light globes into something strange and terrible, and found shapes in the cobalt corners where only darkness lay. But they encountered nothing, no one; it was only his mind playing tricks on him.

Yet the Braiths had been here. Close to the perimeter of Challenge, where the cross corridor met the outer concourse, they found one of the balloon-tired vehicles that the Voice used to carry guests back and forth. It was empty and overturned, lying half on the blue carpet and half on the clean cold plastic that floored the concourse proper. When they reached it, they stopped, and Gwen's eyes met Dirk's in wordless comment. The balloon-tired cars, he recalled shortly, had no controls for their passengers; the Voice drove them directly. And here one lay, on its side, without power or motion. He noticed something else as well. Near one rear wheel the blue carpet was damp and smelly.

"Come," Gwen whispered, and they started out across the silent concourse, hoping that the Braiths who had been here were gone out of earshot. The airlot and their car were very close now; it would be cruel irony if they did not reach them. But it seemed to Dirk that their steps echoed horribly loud on the uncarpeted surface of the boulevard; surely the whole building could hear them, even Bretan Braith in the deep cellars kilometers below. When they reached the pedestrian walkway that bridged the median strip of unmoving slidewalks, the two of them began to run. He was not sure who started, Gwen or himself. One instant they were walking side by side, trying to move as quickly as possible with as little noise as they could; then suddenly they were running.

Beyond the concourse—uncarpeted corridor, two turns, a wide door that seemed reluctant to open. Finally Dirk smashed his bruised shoulder against it, and he and it both groaned in protest, but the door gave way, and they stood again on the airlot of Challenge's 520th level.

The night was cold and dark. They could hear Worlorn's eternal wind whining against the Emereli tower, and a single bright star burned in the long low rectangle that framed the outworld sky. Inside, the airlot itself was just as black.

No lights went on when they entered.

But the aircar was still there, hunched in the darkness like a living thing, like the banshee it was intended to resemble, and no Braiths stood guarding it.

They went to it. Gwen took off her sensor pack and field supplies and put them in the back seat, where the sky-scoots still lay. Dirk stood and watched her, shivering as he did so; Ruark's greatcoat was gone, and the air was frigid tonight.

Gwen touched a control on the instrument panel, and a dark crack opened in the center of the manta's hood. Metal panels swung back and up, and the guts of the Kavalar machine were before them. She came around front and turned on a light built into the underside of one of the hood panels. The other panel, Dirk saw, was lined with metal tools in clips.

Gwen stood in a small pool of yellow light studying the intricate machinery. Dirk went to her side.

Finally she shook her head. "No," she said in a tired voice. "It won't work."

"We can draw power from the gravity grid," Dirk suggested. "You have the tools." He pointed.

"I don't know enough," she said. "A little, yes. I hoped I'd be able to figure . . . you know. I can't. It's more than just a matter of power. The wing lasers aren't even connected. They might as well be ornaments for all the good they're going to do us." She looked at Dirk. "I don't suppose you . . . ?"

"No," he said.

She nodded. "We have no weapon, then."

Dirk stood and glanced out past the manta, toward Worlorn's empty sky. "We could fly out of here."

Gwen reached out and caught the hood panels, one in each hand, and brought them down and together again, and once more the dark banshee was whole and fierce. Her voice was toneless. "No. Remember what you said. The Braiths will be outside. Their cars will be armed. We wouldn't have a chance. No." She walked around Dirk and got into the aircar.

After a time he followed her. He sat twisted about in his seat, so that he faced the lonely star in the cold night sky. He was conscious of being very tired, and he knew it was more than physical. Since coming to Challenge, his emotions had washed over him like waves over a beach, one after another, but suddenly it seemed as though the ocean had gone. There were no waves left at all.

"I suppose you were right before, in the corridor," he said in a thoughtful, introspective voice. He was not looking at Gwen.

"Right?" she said.

"About being selfish. About . . . you know . . . about not being a white knight."

"A white knight?"

"Like Jaan. I was never a white knight, maybe, but back on Avalon I liked to think I was. I believed in things. Now I can hardly even remember what they were. Except for you, Jenny. You I remembered. That was why . . . well, you understand. The last seven years, I've done things, nothing terrible, you know, but still things that I might not have done on Avalon. Cynical things, selfish things. But until now I'd never gotten anyone killed."

"Don't flog yourself, Dirk," she said. Her voice was weary too. "It's not attractive."

"I want to do something," Dirk said. "I have to. I can't just . . . you know. You were right."

"We *can't* do anything, except run and die, and that won't help at all. We have no weapon."

Dirk laughed bitterly. "So we wait for Jaan and Garse to come and save us, and then . . . Our reunion was terribly short-lived, wasn't it?"

She leaned forward without answering, and cradled her head against her forearm on the top on the instrument panel. Dirk glanced at her and then looked outward again. He was still cold in his thin clothing, but somehow it did not seem important.

They sat quietly in the manta.

Until finally Dirk turned and put a hand on Gwen's shoulder. "The weapon," he said in a strangely animated voice. "Jaan said we had a weapon."

"The lasers on the aircar," Gwen said. "But—"

"No," Dirk said, suddenly grinning. "No, no, *no!*"

"What else could he have meant?"

In answer Dirk reached out and turned on the aircar's lifters, and the gray metal banshee stirred to life and rose slightly from the floor plates. "The car," he said. "The car itself."

"The Braiths outside have cars," she said. "*Armed* cars."

"Yes," Dirk said. "But Jaan and I weren't talking about the Braiths outside. We were talking about the hunting parties *inside,* the ones roaming around through the concourse killing people!"

Understanding burst across her face like sunlight. She grinned. "Yes," she said savagely, and she reached out to her instruments and the manta growled and from somewhere under its hood bright columns of white light fanned out to chase the darkness before them.

While she hovered a half-meter from the floor, Dirk

vaulted out over the wings, went to the battered door and used his equally battered shoulder to knock loose a second panel, wide enough to give the aircar exit. Then Gwen moved the manta to him and he climbed in again.

A short time later, they were in the concourse, floating above the boulevard, close to where the overturned balloon-tired car lay. The bright beams of the head-lamps swung over the stilled slidewalks and the long-deserted shops to point straight ahead, down the path that would lead around and around and around the tall tower of Challenge until it reached the ground at last.

"You realize," Gwen said before they started, "that we're in the *up* lane. Descending traffic is supposed to stay on the other side of the median." She pointed.

"This is prohibited, no doubt, by the norms of ai-Emerel." Dirk smiled. "But I don't think the Voice will mind."

Gwen gave him a faint smile back, touched her instruments, and the manta beneath them leaped forward with a rush and gathered speed. Then for a long time they made their own wind as they swept through the gray gloom, faster and faster, Gwen pale and tight-lipped at the controls, Dirk beside her idly watching the level numbers as corridor after corridor flicked by.

They heard the Braiths a long time before they saw them—the howling again, the wild baying shrieks unlike any canine that Dirk had ever heard before, made even wilder by the echoes that raced up and down the concourse in their wake. When he first heard the pack, Dirk reached out and snapped off the aircar's lights.

Gwen looked at him, questioning.

"We don't make much noise," he said. "They'll never hear us over the howls and their own shouts. But they might see the light coming up behind them. Right?"

"Right," she said. Nothing more. She was intent on the aircar. Dirk watched her in the pale gray light that remained to them. Her eyes were jade again, hard and polished, as angry as Garse Janacek's could sometimes be. She had her gun at last, and the Kavalar hunters were somewhere ahead.

Close to level 497 they passed an area littered with scraps of torn cloth that fluttered and stirred in the wash of their descent. One piece, bigger than the others, scarcely moved from where it lay in the middle of the boulevard. The remains of a brown patchwork greatcoat, ripped to shreds.

Ahead, the howling came stronger and louder.

A smile passed briefly across Gwen's lips. Dirk saw it, and wondered, and remembered his gentle Jenny of Avalon.

Then they saw the figures, small black shapes on the shadowed concourse, shapes that swelled rapidly into men and dogs as the manta swept forward toward them. Five of the great hounds were loping down the boulevard freely, close on the heels of a sixth, larger than any of them, that strained at the ends of two heavy black chains. Two men were on the far ends of the chains, stumbling behind the pack as the massive leader pulled them along.

They grew. How *fast* they grew!

The hounds heard the aircar coming first. The leader fought to turn, and one of the chains whipped loose from the hands of a hunter. Three of the free-roaming pack hounds spun, snarling, and a fourth began bounding back up the concourse toward the fast-descending car. The men briefly seemed confused. One was tangled in the chain he was holding when the lead dog reversed directions. The other, empty-handed, began to reach for something at his hip.

Gwen turned on the lights. In the semi-darkness, the manta's eyes were blinding.

The aircar ripped into them.

Impressions rolled over Dirk one after another. A lingering howl turned abruptly into a squeal of pain; impact made the manta shudder. Savage red eyes gleaming horridly close, a rat's face and yellow teeth wet with slaver, then impact again, another shudder, a snap. More impacts, sickening fleshy sounds, one, two, three. A scream, a very human scream, then there was a man outlined in the wash of the headlamps. It took them an hour to reach him, it seemed. He was a large square man, no one that Dirk knew, dressed in thick pants and jacket of chameleon cloth that seemed to change color as they neared. His hands were up in front of his eyes, one clutching a useless dueling laser, and Dirk could see the sheen of metal peeking from beneath the man's sleeve. White hair fell to his shoulders.

Then, suddenly, after an eternity of frozen motion, he was gone. The manta shuddered once again. Dirk shook with it.

Ahead was gray emptiness, the long curving boulevard.

Behind—Dirk turned to look—a hound was chasing after them, dragging two chains noisily as it ran. But it dwindled smaller and smaller as he watched. Dark shapes littered the cold plastic street. No sooner had he started to count them than they were gone. A pulse of light flamed briefly overhead, coming nowhere near them.

Shortly he and Gwen were alone again, and there was no sound except the rushing whisper of their descent. Her face was very still. Her hands were steady. His were not. "I think we killed him," he said.

"Yes," she replied. "We did. Some of the hounds as well." She was quiet for a while. Then she said, "His name, as I recall, was Teraan Braith something."

Both of them were quiet. Gwen turned off the headlamps once more.

"What are you doing?" Dirk said.

"There are more ahead of us," she said. "Remember the scream we heard."

"Yes." He thought for a time. "Can the car take any more collisions?"

She smiled faintly. "Ah," she said. "The Kavalar code duello has several aerial modes. Aircars are often chosen as weapons. They are strongly built. This car is constructed to withstand laser fires as long as possible. The armor— Need I go on?"

"No." He paused. "Gwen."

"Yes?"

"Don't kill any more of them."

She glanced at him. "They're hunting the Emereli," she said, "and whoever else is unlucky enough to be left inside of Challenge. They would gladly hunt us."

"Still," he said. "We can draw them off, win some time for the others. Jaan will get here soon. No one need be killed."

She sighed and her hands moved and she slowed the aircar. "Dirk," she started to say. Then she saw something and brought them to a near halt, so they hovered and slid forward slowly. "Here," she said, "look." She pointed.

The light was so dim, it was hard to make things out clearly, until they came closer, and then—a carcass of some sort, or what remained of one. In the center of the concourse, still and bloody. Chunks of meat scattered around it. Dried dark blood on the plastic.

"That has got to be the victim we heard earlier," Gwen explained in conversational tones. "Mockman hunters don't eat their kill, you know. In one breath, they say the creatures aren't human, only some sort of semi-sentient animals, and they believe it too. Yet the stench of cannibalism is too strong, even for them, so they don't dare. Even in the oldest days, on High Kavalaan during the dark centuries, the holdfast hunters never ate the flesh of the mockmen they ran down. They would leave that, for the gods, for the carrion moths, for the sand beetles. After they had given their hounds a taste, of course, as a reward. The hunters do take trophies, however. The head. You see the torso there? Show me the head."

Dirk felt sick.

"The skin too," Gwen continued. "They carry flaying knives. Or they did. Remember, mockman hunting has been banned on High Kavalaan for generations.

Even the highbond council of Braith has ruled against it. Such kills as the remaining hunters made were surreptitious. They have to hide their trophies, except maybe from each other. Here, though, well, let me just say that Jaan expects the Braiths to remain on Worlorn for as long as they can. He has told me there is talk of renouncing Braith, of bringing their *betheyns* from the homeworld's holdfasts, and forming a new coalition here, a gathering that will bring back all the old ways, all the dead and dying ugliness. For a time, a year or two or ten, as long as the Toberian stratoshield can gather in the warmth. Lorimaar high-Larteyn, and the like, with no one to restrain them."

"It would be insane!"

"Perhaps. That won't stop them. If Jaantony and Garse were to leave tomorrow, it would be done. The presence of Ironjade deters them. They fear that if they and the other Braith traditionalists moved here in force, then the progressive faction of Ironjade would also send men in force. There would be nothing to hunt then, and they and their children would face a short, hard life on a dying world, without even the pleasures they covet, the joys of high hunt. No." She shrugged. "But there are trophy rooms in Larteyn even now. Lorimaar alone boasts five heads, and it is said he has two jackets of 'mockman' skin. He doesn't wear them. Jaan would kill him."

She threw the aircar forward again, and once more they began to build up speed. "Now," she said, "do you still want me to swerve aside the next time some of them come up? Now that you know what they are?"

He did not answer.

A very short time later the noises began once more below them, the drawn-out howls and the shouts, echoing down the otherwise empty concourse. They passed another overturned vehicle, its fat soft tires deflated and torn, and Gwen had to turn to pass around it. A little later there was a dead hulk of black metal blocking their descent, a massive robot with four tensed arms frozen in grotesque postures above its head. The upper part of its torso was a dark cylinder studded with glass eyes; the lower part was a base the size of an aircar, on treads. "A warder," Gwen said as they went by the quiet mechanical corpse, and Dirk saw that the hands had been sheared off each of its arms in turn, and that the body was riddled with fused laser holes.

"Was it fighting them?" he asked.

"Probably," she answered. "Which means that the Voice is still alive, still controls some functions. Maybe that's why we haven't heard anything further from Bretan Braith. It could be that they're having trouble down there. The Voice would naturally mass its warders to protect the city's life functions." She shrugged. "But it doesn't matter. The Emereli don't hold with violence. The warders are instruments of restraint. They fire sleep-darts, and I think they can emit tear gas from those grills in their base. The Braiths will win. Always."

Behind them the robot was already gone, and the concourse was empty once more. The noises ahead grew very loud.

This time Dirk said nothing when Gwen bore down upon them and turned on her lights, and the screams and the impacts piled one upon the other. She got both of the Braith hunters, although afterwards she said she was not so sure the second one was dead. He'd been hit a glancing blow that spun him to one side, into one of his own hounds.

And Dirk could find no voice at all, because as the man went stumbling and spinning off their right wing he lost his grip on the thing he had been carrying, and it flew through the air and smashed against the window of a shop, leaving a bloody path on the glass when it slid down to the floor. He had been holding it, Dirk noted, by the hair.

The corkscrew road went around and around the tower that was Challenge, sinking slowly and steadily. It took more time than Dirk could have imagined to sink from level 388—where they surprised the second party of Braiths—to level one. A long flight in gray silence.

They encountered no one else, neither Kavalar nor Emereli.

On level 120 a solitary warder blocked their way, turning all its dim eyes on them and commanding them to halt in the voice—still even and cordial—of the Voice of Challenge. But Gwen did not slow, and when she neared, the warder rolled off out of her way, firing no darts and emitting no gas. Its echoing commands chased them down the concourse.

On level fifty-seven the dim lights above them flickered and went out, and for an instant they flew in total darkness. Then Gwen turned on the headlamps and slackened her speed just a bit. Neither of them spoke, but Dirk thought of Bretan Braith and wondered briefly whether the lights had failed or had been turned off. The latter, he guessed; a survivor above had finally called his holdfast-brothers below.

On level one the concourse ended in a great mall and traffic circle. They could see very little of it; only where the beams of the headlamps touched did shapes leap startlingly out of the ocean of pitch that surrounded them. The center of the mall seemed to be a tree of sorts. Dirk caught glimpses of a massive gnarled trunk, a virtual wall of wood, and they could hear leaves rustling above them. The road curved around the great tree and met itself. Gwen followed it, all around the wide circle.

On the far side of the tree a wide gateway stood open to the night and Dirk felt the touch of wind on his face and realized why the leaves had been rustling. As they swept past the gateway, staying on the circle, he looked out. Beyond the gate a white ribbon of road led away from Challenge.

And an aircar was moving low over the road, quickly, toward the city. Toward them. Dirk glimpsed it only for an instant. It was dark—but everything was dark in the meager outworld starlight—and metallic, some misshapen Kavalar beast he could not even begin to identify.

It was not the Ironjades, of that he was sure.

chapter **9**

"We have succeeded," Gwen said dryly after they had moved beyond the gate. "They're after us."

"They saw us?"

"They had to. Our light, as we went past the open gateway. They couldn't miss that."

Thick darkness rushed by them on either side, and the leaves still rustled above their heads. "We run?" Dirk said.

"Their car will have working lasers, and ours doesn't. The outer concourse is the only road open to us. The Braith aircar will chase us up, and somewhere above us the hunters will be waiting. We only killed two, maybe three. There will be more. We're trapped."

Dirk was thoughtful. "We can loop around the circle again, go out the gate after they've entered."

"Yes, that's an obvious try. Too obvious, though. There will be another aircar outside waiting for us, I'd guess. I have a better idea." As she spoke, she slowed the manta and brought it to a halt. Immediately before them the road forked, amid the bright wash of the headlamps. To the left the traffic circle curved back on itself; to the right was the outer concourse, beginning its two-kilometer ascent.

Gwen turned off the lights and darkness engulfed them. When Dirk started to speak, she quieted him with a sharp "Sssh!"

The world was very black. He had gone blind. Gwen, the aircar, Challenge—everything had vanished. He heard leaves brushing against each other, and he thought he heard the other aircar, the Braiths, coming down on them, but that had to be his mind, for surely he would first have seen their lights.

There was a gentle rocking motion, as if he were sitting in a small boat. Something hard touched his arm, and Dirk started, and then other somethings scraped against his face.

Leaves.

They were rising, right up into the low-hanging dense foliage of the great spreading Emereli tree.

A branch, pushed down and then released, whipped him painfully across the cheek, drawing blood. Leaves pressed all around him. Finally there was a soft thud as the wings of the manta came hard against the bulk of a massive limb. They could rise no more. They hovered, blind, enveloped by darkness and unseen foliage.

A very short time later a blur of light flashed by beneath them, curving off to the right, up the concourse. No sooner was it gone than another came into sight—from the *left*—turned sharply up the fork, and followed the first. Dirk was very grateful that Gwen had ignored his suggestion.

They hovered amid the leaves for an endless time, but no other cars appeared. Finally Gwen lowered them back to the road. "That won't lose them permanently," she said. "When their trap closes and we're not in it, they'll begin to wonder."

Dirk was dabbing at the wetness on his cheek with his shirttail. When his fingers finally told him that the thin trickle of blood had dried, he turned in the direction of Gwen's voice. He was still blind. "So they'll hunt for us," he said. "That's good. While they're being bothered by trying to figure out where we went, they won't be killing any Emereli. And Jaan and Garse should get here soon. Now is the time for us to hide, I think."

"Hide or run," came Gwen's answer from the darkness. She still had not touched the aircar lights.

"I have an idea," Dirk said. He touched his cheek again. Then, satisfied, he began to tuck away his shirttails. "When you were swinging around the circle I noticed something. A ramp, with a sign. Just saw it briefly in the headlamps, but it reminded me. Worlorn has a subway network, right? Intercity?"

"True," Gwen said. "It's dismantled, though."

"Is it? I know the trains don't run, but what about the tunnels? Did they fill them in?"

"I don't know. I hardly think so." Suddenly the aircar's headlamps woke again, and Dirk blinked at the sudden light. "Show me this sign," Gwen said, and once more they began the wide circuit around the central tree.

It was a subway entrance, as Dirk had guessed. A shallow ramp led down into darkness. Gwen stopped their forward motion and left them hovering a few meters away while she played the headlamps over the sign. "It will mean abandoning the aircar," she said at last. "Our only weapon."

"Yes," Dirk said. The entrance was much too narrow for the gray metal manta to pass; clearly the subway builders had not counted on anyone wanting to fly through their tunnels. "But that might be best. We can't leave Challenge, and inside the city the car limits our mobility pretty severely. Right?" When Gwen did not answer immediately, he rubbed his head wearily. "It sounds right to me, but maybe I'm not thinking so clearly. I'm tired and I'd probably be scared if I stopped to think about this. I've got bruises and cuts and I want to get some sleep."

"Well," Gwen said, "the subway might be worth a chance then. We can put a few kilometers between us and Challenge, and sleep. I don't think the Braiths will think to hunt for us there, down in the tunnels."

"It's decided, then," Dirk said.

They went about it very methodically. Gwen set the aircar down next to the subterranean ramp and got the sensor pack and the field supplies out of the back seat. They took the sky-scoots as well, changing into the flight boots and discarding their own footwear. And among the tools mounted on the underside of the banshee's hood was a small hand torch, a metal-and-plastic rod as long as a man's forearm that gave off a pale white light.

When they were ready to depart, Gwen treated them both with null-scent again, then had Dirk wait by the subway entrance while she flew the aircar halfway around the great circle and left it standing in the center of the roadway near one of the largest first-level corridors. Let the Braiths think they had gone off into the interior labyrinths of Challenge; they'd have a fine long hunt ahead of them.

Dirk waited in darkness while Gwen walked the long walk back around the tree, lighting her path with the hand torch. Then, together, they went down the ramp to the abandoned subway terminal. The descent was longer than Dirk had expected. They went at least two levels below the surface, he guessed, walking quietly while their light reflected off featureless walls of pastel blue. He thought of Bretan Braith, some fifty levels below even them, and hoped briefly and insanely that the tunnels would still be powered, being (after all) something outside of the Emereli tower-city and thus beyond Bretan's reach.

But of course the subway system had been de-powered long before Bretan and the other Braiths had even come to Worlorn; below they found nothing but a vast echoing platform and massive stone wormholes rushing away to infinity. Infinity seemed very close at hand in the dark. The terminal was still, and its stillness seemed steeped in death, much more so than the quiet corridors of Challenge. It was like walking through a tomb. There was dust everywhere. The Voice had permitted no dust in Challenge, Dirk realized, but the subways were not of Challenge, not the work of ai-Emerel at all. As they walked, their footsteps sounded horribly loud.

Gwen studied a systems map very carefully before they set off into the tunnels. "There are two lines down here," she said, whispering for some reason. "One line connects all the Festival cities in a great circuit. Trains, it appears, used to run along it in both directions. The other line is a shuttle service connecting Challenge with the spaceport. Each city had its own spaceport shuttle. So which way should we go?"

Dirk was exhausted and irritable. "I don't care," he said. "What difference does it make? We can't very well walk to the next city anyway. Even with the skyscoots, the distances are too much."

Gwen nodded thoughtfully, still looking at the map. "Two hundred thirty kilometers to Esvoch in one direction, three hundred eighty to Kryne Lamiya if we go the other way. More than that to the spaceport. I guess you're right." She shrugged and turned and picked a direction at random. "That way," she said.

They wanted speed and distance. Sitting on the edge of the platform above the track, they locked their boots into the tissue-metal platforms of their skyscoots, then set off slowly in the direction Gwen had indicated. She went first, staying a bare quarter-meter off the ground and trailing her left hand along the tunnel wall lightly. Her right held the hand torch. Dirk stayed behind her, flying a little higher so that he could see over her shoulder. The tunnel they had chosen was a great gentle curve, veering away ever so slightly to their left. There was nothing to see, nothing to remark on. At times Dirk lost the sensation of motion entirely, so even and uneventful was their flight.

Then it seemed to him that he and Gwen were floating in some timeless limbo, while the walls crawled steadily past.

But at last, when they had come a good three kilometers from Challenge, they dropped to the bottom of the tunnel and stopped. By then neither of them had anything to say. Gwen leaned the hand torch up against a rough-hewn stone wall while they sat in the dirt and removed their boots. Wordless, she unslung her field supplies and used the packet as a pillow. No sooner did her head touch it than she was asleep, gone from him.

And apart from him too.

His own weariness did not lift, but Dirk found it difficult to sleep. Instead he sat by the edge of the small circle of pale light—Gwen had left the hand torch on—and watched her, watched her breathe, watched the shadows play along her cheeks and in her hair when she moved restlessly in sleep. He grew aware then of how very far she lay from him, and he remembered that they had not touched or talked all the way from Challenge. He did not think about it; his mind was too fogged by fear and fatigue for thought. But he felt it, like a weight upon his chest, and the dark pressed very heavy on him in the long dusty hollow beneath the world.

Finally he shut off the torch and all sight of his Jenny, and tried to sleep himself. It came in time. But nightmares came with it. He dreamed he was with Gwen, kissing her, holding her closely. But when his lips met hers, it was not Gwen at all; it was Bretan Braith he was kissing, Bretan whose lips were dry and hard, whose glowstone eye flamed frighteningly close in the blackness.

And after that he was running again, running down some endless tunnel, running to nowhere. But at his back he could hear the rush of water, and when he looked over his shoulder he thought he could glimpse a solitary bargeman poling an empty barge. The bargeman was floating down an oily black stream, and Dirk was running over dry stone, but somehow in the dream that seemed not to matter. He ran and he ran, but always the barge loomed closer, and finally he could see that the bargeman had no face, no face at all.

There was a quiet after that, and for the rest of the long night Dirk did not dream.

A light was shining where no light ought to be.

It reached him even through his closed eyelids and his slumber: a wavering yellow radiance, close at hand and then receding a bit. Dirk was aware of it only dimly when it first intruded on his hard-earned sleep. He mumbled and rolled away from it. Voices muttered nearby, and someone laughed a small sharp laugh. Dirk ignored it.

Then they kicked him, quite hard, across the face.

His head snapped sideways and the chains of sleep dissolved in a blur of pain. Lost and hurt, not knowing where he was, he struggled to sit up. His temple throbbed. Everything was too bright. He threw an arm across his eyes to block out the light and shield himself from further kicks. There was another laugh.

Slowly the world took form.

They were Braiths, of course.

One of them, a gangling bony man with a frizz of black hair, stood on the far side of the tunnel holding Gwen with one hand and a laser pistol with the other. Another laser, a rifle, was slung across his shoulders on a strap. Gwen's hands had been bound behind her back, and she stood silently with her eyes downcast.

The Braith who was standing over Dirk had not drawn a laser, but in his left hand was a high-powered hand torch that filled the subway with yellow light. The glare of the torch made it difficult for Dirk to make out his features, but he was Kavalar-tall and quite heavy, and seemed to be bald as an egg.

"At last we have won your attention," said the man with the light. The other one laughed, the same laugh Dirk had heard earlier.

With difficulty, Dirk rose to his feet and took a step backwards, away from the Kavalars. He leaned up against the tunnel wall and tried to steady himself, but his skull screamed at him and the scene swam. The bright hot hand torch was an ache eating into his eyes.

"You have injured the game, Pyr," the Braith with the laser commented from the other side of the tunnel.

"Not overly, I would hope," said the heavy man.

"Are you going to kill me?" Dirk asked. The words came with remarkable ease, considering what they were. He was finally beginning to recover from the kick.

Gwen raised her eyes when he spoke. "Eventually they'll kill you," she said in a hopeless voice. "It won't be an easy end. I'm sorry, Dirk."

"Silence, *betheyn*-bitch," said the heavy man, the one called Pyr. Dirk was vaguely conscious of having heard the name before. The man glanced at her casually as he spoke, then looked back toward Dirk.

"What does she mean?" Dirk said nervously. He was pressing himself hard against the stone and trying to tense his muscles inconspicuously. Pyr stood less than a meter away. The Braith seemed cocky and off-guard, but Dirk wondered how true an impression that might be. The man was holding the torch aloft in his left hand, but his right held something else—a baton about a meter long, of some dark wood, with a round hardwood knob at one end and a short blade at the other. He held it lightly between his fingers, his hand around the center shaft, tapping it rhythmically against his leg.

"You have led us a spirited chase, mockman," Pyr said. "I do not say this lightly, or in jape. Few are my equals in the old high hunt. None are my superior. Even Lorimaar high-Braith Arkellor has only half my trophy count. So when I tell you that this hunt has been extraordinary, you know I say truth. I am elated that it is not over."

"What?" Dirk said. "Not over?" The man was so close—he wondered if he could get Pyr between himself and the other man, the one with the laser, and maybe wrest the bladed baton away from him. Perhaps he could even get Pyr's holstered sidearm.

"There is no sport in taking a sleeping mockman, nor is there honor. You will run again, Dirk t'Larien."

"He'll make you his personal *korariel*," Gwen said angrily, looking at the two Braiths with calculated defiance. "No one will be able to hunt you except him and his *teyn*."

Pyr turned toward her again. "I said silence!"

She laughed at him. "Knowing Pyr," she continued, "the hunt will be pure tradition. You'll be cut loose in the forests, probably naked. These two will put away their lasers and aircars and come after you on foot, with knives and throwing-swords and hounds. After they deliver me to my masters, of course."

Pyr was frowning. The other Braith raised his pistol and used it to give Gwen a sharp crack across the mouth.

Dirk tensed, hesitated an instant too long, and jumped.

Even a meter was too far; Pyr was smiling as his head turned again. The baton came up with frightening speed, and the knob caught Dirk square in the gut. He staggered and doubled up and somehow tried to keep going. Pyr stepped daintily backwards and brought his stick around hard, into Dirk's groin. The world vanished in a red haze.

He was vaguely conscious of Pyr standing over him once more after he had collapsed. Then the Braith struck him a third time, an almost casual blow to the side of his head, and then there was nothing.

He hurt. That was the first thing he knew. That was all he knew. He hurt. His head spun and throbbed and shuddered in a strange sort of rhythm; his stomach ached as well, and below that he felt numb. Pain and dizziness were the boundaries of Dirk's world. For the longest time, that was everything.

Gradually, though, a blurred sort of awareness returned to him. He began to notice things. The pain first—it came and went in waves. Up and down it went, up and down. He was going up and down too, he finally realized, jouncing and bouncing. He was lying on something. Being dragged or carried. He moved his hands, or tried to. It was hard. The pain seemed to wipe away all normal sensation. His mouth was full of blood. His ears were ringing, buzzing, burning.

He was being carried, yes. There were voices; he could hear voices, talking and buzzing. The words would not come clear. Ahead, somewhere, a light danced and wavered; everything else was a gray mist.

Little by little the buzzing dwindled. Finally the words began to come.

". . . not be happy," said a voice he did not know. He did not think he knew it, anyway. It was hard to tell. Everything was so terribly distant, and he was bouncing, and the pain came and went, came and went, came and went.

"Yes," said another voice, heavy, clipped, sure.

More buzzing—several voices at once. Dirk understood nothing.

Then one man silenced the others. "Enough," he said. This voice was more removed even than the first two; it came from somewhere ahead, from the wavering light. Pyr? Pyr. "I have no fear of Bretan Braith Lantry, Roseph. You forget who I am. I had taken three heads in the wilds when Bretan Braith was still sucking women's teats. The mockman is mine by all the old rights."

"Truth," the first unknown voice replied. "If you had taken him in the tunnels, none would deny your right. Yet you did not."

"I wish a pure hunt, of the oldest kind."

Someone said something in Old Kavalar. There was a laugh.

"Many the time we hunted together in our youth, Pyr," the strange voice said. "Had you only felt differently about women, we might well have become *teyn*-and-*teyn*, we two. I would not speak you wrong. Bretan Braith Lantry wants this man badly."

"He is no man, he is mockman. You ruled him so yourself, Roseph. The wants of Bretan Braith are nothing to me."

"I did rule him mockman, and so he is. To you and me, he is only one such, one among many. We have the jelly children to hunt, the Emereli, and others. You do not need him, Pyr. Bretan Braith feels differently. He came to the death-square and was made a fool when the man he challenged was no man at all."

"That is truth, but it is not the whole of it. T'Larien is a special sort of prey. Two of our *kethi* are dead at his hands, and Koraat lies dying with a broken spine. No mockman has ever run that way before. I will take him, as is my right. I found him, I alone."

"Yes," said the second new voice, the heavy, clipped one. "That is truth enough, Pyr. How did you discover him?"

Pyr was glad enough of a chance to boast. "I was not misled by the aircar, as you were, and you, and even Lorimaar. He had been too clever, this mockman, and the *betheyn*-bitch who ran at his side. They would not let the car sit like a pointer to the place they had gone. When you had all taken your hounds and fanned out down the corridor, my *teyn* and I began to search the mall by torchlight, looking for a trail. I knew the hounds would be useless. No need for them. I am a better tracker than any hound or hound master. I have tracked mockmen over the bare stone of the Lameraan Hills, through the blasted dead cities, even into the abandoned holdfasts of Taal and Bronzefist and the Glowstone Mountain. These two were pitifully easy. We checked each corridor for a distance of several meters, then moved on to check the next. We found the trail. Scuffmarks on the floor outside a subway ramp, then veritable road signs in the dust. The track vanished when they began to use their flying toys, of course, but by then we had only two possible directions to consider. I feared they might try to fly all the way to Esvoch or Kryne Lamiya, but such was not the truth. It took us most of the day and long walking, yet we caught them."

Dirk was almost alert by then, though his body was still wrapped in a gauze of pain and he doubted that it would respond very efficiently if he tried to move. He could see quite clearly. Pyr Braith was walking in front with the hand torch, talking to a smaller man in white and purple, who must be Roseph, the arbiter of the duels that never were. Between them was Gwen, walking under her own power, her hands still bound. She was silent. Dirk wondered if they had gagged her, but it was impossible to tell, since he could only see her back.

He was lying in a litter of sorts, bouncing with every step. Another Braith in white and purple was holding the front end, his big-knuckled fists wrapped around the wooden poles. The bony laughter, Pyr's *teyn,* was probably behind him, then, at the other end of the litter. They were still in the tunnel, walking; the subway appeared to go on forever, and Dirk had no inkling of how long he had been out. Quite a while, he guessed; there had been no Roseph and no litter when he had tried to tackle Pyr, he was certain of that. His captors had probably waited in the tunnel after calling their holdfast-brothers for help.

No one appeared to have noticed that Dirk had opened his eyes. Or perhaps they had noticed and they simply didn't care. He was in no condition to do anything except maybe scream for help.

Pyr and Roseph continued to talk, with the two others interjecting comments from time to time. Dirk tried to listen, but the pain made it hard to concentrate, and what they were saying was of very little value to Gwen and himself. Chiefly Roseph seemed to be warning Pyr that Bretan Braith would be very upset if Pyr killed Dirk, since Bretan Braith wanted to kill Dirk himself. Pyr didn't care; from his comments, it seemed clear that he had little respect for Bretan, who was two generations younger than the rest of them and therefore suspect. At no time in the conversation did any of the hunters mention the Ironjades, which led Dirk to conclude that either Jaan and Garse had not yet reached Challenge or these four were not yet aware of it.

After a while he stopped straining to understand and let himself slide back into a semi-sleep. The voices became a blur again and went on a long time. Finally, though, they stopped. One end of the litter dropped roughly, and he was jarred back to attention. Strong hands supported him beneath his arms and lifted.

They had reached the terminal beneath Challenge, and Pyr's *teyn* was lifting him to the platform. He did not even try to help. He went limp as he could and let them move him like a piece of dead meat.

Then he was in the litter again and they were carrying him up the ramp into the city proper. They had not handled him gently at the platform; his head was swimming once again. Pastel blue walls went by, and he was reminded of their descent down the ramp last night. For some reason, hiding in the subway had seemed like a terribly good idea at the time.

The walls vanished, and they were in Challenge once again. He saw the great Emereli tree, this time in all of its massive grandeur. It was a gnarled giant, blue and black, its limbs hanging low over the visible curve of the traffic circle while its topmost branches brushed against the shadowed ceiling. Day had come, Dirk realized. The gateway remained open, and through its arch he could see Fat Satan and a single yellow star hanging on the horizon. He was much too lost and weary to know whether they were rising or setting.

Two hulking Kavalar aircars sat on the road near the subway ramp. Pyr halted nearby, and Dirk was lowered to the floor. He struggled to sit up, to no avail. His limbs thrashed weakly and the pain came back, until he surrendered and lay back again.

"Summon the others," Pyr said. "These matters should be settled here and now, so my *korariel* can be made ready for the hunt." He stood over Dirk as he spoke. All of them were clustered around the litter, even Gwen. But she alone looked down, and her eyes caught his. She was gagged. And tired. And hopeless.

It took well over an hour for the other Braiths to assemble; for Dirk an hour of fading light and gathering strength. It *was* sunset, he soon realized; beyond the gateway, Fat Satan sank slowly out of sight. The darkness swelled around them, growing thicker and denser until finally the Kavalars were forced to turn on the headlamps of their aircars. By then Dirk's dizziness had all but passed. Pyr, noticing, had his hands bound behind his back and forced him to sit up against the side of one of the cars. They placed Gwen beside him, but did not remove her gag.

Though Dirk was not gagged, he did not try to speak. He sat with the cold metal to his back and his wrists chafing within their bonds, and he waited and watched and listened. From time to time he would glance toward Gwen, but she sat slumped with her head downcast and did not return his gaze.

Singly and in pairs they came. The *kethi* of Braith. The hunters of Worlorn. From the shadows and dark places they came. Like pale ghosts. A noise and a vague shape at first, before they walked into the small circle of light and turned to men again. Even then they were more and less than human.

The first to come led four tall rat-faced hounds, and Dirk recognized him from the wild gray plunge down the outer concourse. The man chained his hounds to the bumper of Roseph's aircar, gave curt greetings to Pyr and Roseph and their *teyns,* then sat cross-legged on the floor a few meters from the prisoners. He did not speak, not once. His eyes fixed on Gwen and never left her, and he did not move at all. Nearby, Dirk could hear his hounds growling in the shadows, their iron chains twisting and rattling.

Then the others came. Lorimaar high-Braith Arkellor, a brown giant in a pitch-black suit of chameleon cloth fastened with buttons of pale bone, arrived in a massive domed aircar of deep red. Within, Dirk could hear the sounds of a pack of Braith hounds. With Lorimaar was another man, a square fat man twice as heavy as Pyr, his bulk hard and solid as brick, his face pale and porcine. After them, alone and on foot, came a frail-looking oldster, bald and wrinkled and nearly toothless, with one hand of flesh and bone and one three-pronged claw of dark metal. The old man had a child's head slung from his belt; it was still bleeding, and one leg of his white trousers bore the long brown stain of its dripping.

Finally Chell arrived, as tall as Lorimaar, white-haired and mustachioed and very weary, leading a single huge Braith hound. Within the pool of light he stopped and blinked.

"Where is your *teyn?*" Pyr demanded.

"Here." A rasp from the darkness. A few meters away a single glowstone shone dimly. Bretan Braith Lantry came forward and stood next to Chell. His face twitched.

"All have gathered," Roseph high-Braith said to Pyr.

"No," someone objected. "There is Koraat."

The silent hunter spoke up from the floor. "He is no more. He begged ending. I granted it. In truth, he was badly broken. He was the second *keth* I have watched die today. The first was my *teyn,* Teraan Braith Nalarys." As he spoke, his eyes never left Gwen. He finished with a long breathless sentence in Old Kavalar.

"Three of us are gone," the old man said.

"We shall have a silence for them," Pyr said. He was still holding his baton, with its hardwood knob and its short blade, and he tapped it restlessly against his leg as he spoke, just as he had done in the tunnels.

Through her gag, Gwen tried to scream. Pyr's *teyn,* the gangling Kavalar with the wild black hair, came over and stood above her menacingly.

But Dirk, ungagged, had gotten the idea. "I'm not going to keep silence," he shouted. Or tried to. His voice was not quite up to shouting. "They were killers, all of them. Deserved to die."

All of the Braiths were looking at him.

"Gag him and stop his screaming," Pyr said. His *teyn* moved quickly to comply. When it was done, Pyr spoke again. "You shall have time enough to scream, Dirk t'Larien, when you run naked through the forests and you hear my hounds baying behind you."

Bretan's head and shoulders turned awkwardly. Light glistened on his scar tissue. "No," he said. "First claim is mine."

Pyr faced him. "I tracked the mockman. I took him."

Bretan twitched. Chell, still holding the great hound by a chain wrapped about one heavy hand, laid his other hand on Bretan's shoulder.

"This is no matter to me," another voice said. The Braith who sat on the floor. Staring. Unmoving. "What of the bitch?"

The others shifted their attention uneasily. "She can not be at issue, Myrik," said Lorimaar high-Braith. "She is of Ironjade."

The man's lips drew back sharply; for an instant his placid face was wildly distorted, a beast's face, a rictus of emotion. Then it passed. His features settled into pale stillness again, everything held in check. "'I will kill this woman," he said. "Teraan was my *teyn*. She has set his ghost adrift upon a soulless world."

"Her?" Lorimaar's voice was incredulous. "Is this truth?"

"I saw," replied the man on the floor, the one called Myrik. "I fired after her when she rode us down and left Teraan dying. This is truth, Lorimaar high-Braith."

Dirk tried to rise to his feet, but the gangling Kavalar pushed him down again, hard, and slammed his head back against the metal flank of the aircar to underline the point.

The frail oldster spoke then—the clawed ancient who carried the child's head. "Take her then as your personal prey," he said, his voice as thin and sharp as the blade of the flaying knife that hung at his belt. "The wisdom of the holdfasts is old and certain, my brothers. She is no true woman now, if she ever was, neither heldwife or *eyn-keth*. Who is there to vouch for her? She has left her highbond's protection to run with a mockman! If she was flesh of man's flesh once, it is so no longer. You know the ways of the mockmen, the liars, the weres, the great deceivers. Alone with her in the dark, this mockman Dirk would surely have slain her and set in her place a demon like himself, fashioned in her image."

Chell nodded agreement and said something grave in Old Kavalar. The other Braiths looked less certain. Lorimaar traded scowls with his *teyn,* the square fat man. Bretan's hideous face was noncommittal, half a mask of scar tissue, half blank innocence. Pyr frowned and continued to tap restlessly with his baton.

It was Roseph who replied. "I ruled Gwen Delvano human when I was arbiter at the square of death," he said carefully.

"This is truth," Pyr said.

"Perhaps she was human then," the old man said. "Yet she has tasted blood and slept with a mockman, and who will call her human now?"

The hounds began to howl.

The four that Myrik had chained to the aircar started the cacophony, and it was taken up by the pack locked inside Lorimaar's domed vehicle. Chell's massive canine snarled and pulled at his chain, until the elderly Braith jerked back angrily; then the creature sat and joined the howling.

Most of the hunters glanced toward the silent darkness beyond their little circle (Myrik, frozen-faced and immobile, was the notable exception—his eyes never left Gwen Delvano), and more than one touched his sidearm.

On the edge of the circle, beyond the aircars and their pool of light, the two Ironjades stood side by side in shadow.

Dirk's pain—his head was pounding—abruptly

seemed of no consequence. His body trembled and shook. He looked at Gwen; she was looking up, at *them*. At Jaan especially.

He walked into the light then, and Dirk saw that he was staring at Gwen almost as fixedly as the man called Myrik. He seemed to move very slowly, like a figure in some dusty dream, a man asleep. Garse Janacek was alive and liquid at his side.

Vikary was dressed in a mottled suit of chameleon cloth, all shades of black and blacker when he entered the circle of his enemies. By the time the hounds had quieted, he was wearing dusty gray. The sleeves of his shirt ended just above the elbow; iron-and-glowstone embraced his right forearm, jade-and-silver his left. For an endless instant he loomed very large. Chell and Lorimaar both stood a head taller, but somehow, briefly, Vikary seemed to dominate. He flowed past them, a striding ghost—how unreal he was even there—who walked through the Braiths as if he could not see them, and stopped near Gwen and Dirk.

But it was all illusion. The noise subsided, the Braiths began to speak, and Jaan Vikary was just a man again, larger than many but smaller than some.

"You trespass, Ironjades," Lorimaar said in a hard angry tone. "You were not called to this place. You have no right to be here."

"Mockmen," spat Chell "Faloo Kavalais."

Bretan Braith Lantry made his singular noise.

"Your *betheyn* I grant to you, Jaantony high-Ironjade," Pyr said firmly, but his baton moved in nervous haste. "Discipline her as you will, as you must. The mockman is mine to hunt."

Garse Janacek had stopped a few meters away. His eyes moved from one speaker to another, and twice he seemed about to reply. But Jaan Vikary ignored all of them. "Remove the bindings from their mouths," he said, gesturing toward the prisoners.

Pyr's long-limbed *teyn* stood over Dirk and Gwen, facing the Ironjade highbond. He hesitated a long moment, then bent and undid the gags.

"Thanks," Dirk said.

Gwen shook her head to throw loose hair out of her eyes and climbed unsteadily to her feet, her arms still bound behind her back. "Jaan," she said in an uncertain voice. "You heard?"

"I heard," Vikary said. Then, to the Braiths, "Cut loose her arms."

"You presume, Ironjade," Lorimaar said.

Pyr, however, seemed curious. He leaned on his baton. "Cut loose her arms," he said.

His *teyn* pulled Gwen around roughly and used his knife to free her.

"Show me your arms," Vikary said to Gwen.

She hesitated, then brought her hands out from behind her back and extended them, palms down. On her left arm the jade-and-silver shone. She had not removed it.

Dirk watched, bound and helpless, feeling chill. She had not removed it.

Vikary looked down on Myrik, who still sat with his legs crossed and his small eyes set on Gwen. "Rise to your feet."

The man rose and turned to face the Ironjade, taking his gaze from Gwen for the first time since he had arrived. Vikary started to speak.

"No," Gwen said.

She had been rubbing her wrists. Now she stopped and laid her right hand on her bracelet. Her voice was steady. "Don't you understand, Jaan? No. If you challenge him, if you kill him, then I will take it off. I *will*."

For the first time, emotion washed over Jaan's face, and the name of it was anguish. "You are my *betheyn*," he said. "If I do not . . . Gwen . . ."

"No," she said.

One of the Braiths laughed. At the sound, Garse Janacek grimaced, and Dirk saw a savage spasm come and go on the face of the man called Myrik.

If Gwen noticed, she paid no mind. She faced Myrik. "I killed your *teyn*," she said. "Me. Not Jaan.

Not poor Dirk. I killed him, and I admit it. He was hunting us, as you were. And killing the Emereli as well."

Myrik said nothing. Everyone was still.

"If you must duel, then, if you really want me dead, duel *me!*" Gwen continued. "I did it. Fight me if your revenge is so important."

Pyr laughed loudly. An instant later his *teyn* joined him, and Roseph as well, then several of the others —the fat man, Roseph's blocky stern-faced companion, the clawed ancient. All of them were laughing.

Myrik's face went blood-dark, then white, then dark again. *"Betheyn*-bitch," he said. The shuddering rictus passed across his face once more, and this time everyone saw. "You jape me. A duel is . . . my *teyn* . . . and you a woman!"

He ended with a scream that startled the men and set the hounds again to howling. Then he shattered.

His hands rose over his head and clenched and unclenched, and he struck her across the face as she shied away from his fury, and suddenly he was on her. His fingers wrapped around her throat and he dove forward and she went over backwards, and then they were rolling over and over on the floor until they came up hard against the side of an aircar. Myrik came out firmly on top, with Gwen pinned beneath him and his hands digging deep into the flesh of her neck. She hit him then, hard across the jaw, but in his rage he scarcely seemed to feel it. He began to slam her head against the aircar, again and again and again, screaming all the while in Old Kavalar.

Dirk struggled to his feet only to stand uselessly with his hands bound. Garse took two quick steps forward, and Jaan Vikary was finally moving. But it was Bretan Braith Lantry who reached them first and dragged Myrik off her with an arm around his neck. Myrik flailed wildly, until Lorimaar joined Bretan and between them they held the man still.

Gwen lay inert, her head up against the plate-metal door where Myrik had slammed it. Vikary knelt at her side, on one knee, and tried to put an arm around her shoulders. The back of her head left a smear of blood on the side of the aircar.

Janacek knelt too, quickly, and felt her pulse. Satisfied, he rose again and turned back to face the Braiths, his mouth tight with anger. "She wore jade-and-silver, Myrik," he said. "You are a dead man. I issue challenge."

Myrik had stopped screaming, though he was panting. One of the hounds howled and fell silent.

"Does she live?" Bretan asked in his sandpaper voice.

Jaan Vikary looked up at him out of a face as strange and strained as Myrik's had been just a short time before. "She lives."

"Good fortune," said Janacek, "but no thanks to you, Myrik, nor will it make a difference. Make your choices!"

"Let me loose!" Dirk said. No one moved. *"Let me loose!"* he shouted.

Someone sliced apart his bonds.

He went to Gwen, kneeling beside Vikary. Briefly their eyes met. Dirk examined the back of her head, where the dark hair was already beginning to crust with clotted blood. "A concussion at least," he said. "Maybe a fractured skull, maybe worse. I don't know. Are there medical facilities?" He looked at each of them. *"Are* there?"

Bretan answered. "None functional in Challenge, t'Larien. The Voice fought me. The city would not respond. I had to kill it."

Dirk grimaced. "She shouldn't be moved, then. Maybe it's only a concussion. I think she's supposed to rest."

Incredibly, Jaan Vikary left her in Dirk's arms and stood up. He gestured to Lorimaar and Bretan, who held Myrik prisoned between them. "Release him."

"Release. . . ?" Janacek threw Vikary a puzzled glance.

"Jaan," Dirk said, "never mind about him. Gwen—"

"Get her inside an aircar," Vikary said.

"I don't think we should move—"

"It is not safe here, t'Larien. Get her inside an aircar."

Janacek was frowning. "My *teyn?*"

Vikary faced the Braiths again. "I told you to release that man." He paused. "That mockman, as you would call him. He has earned the name."

"What do you intend, high-Ironjade?" Lorimaar said sternly.

Dirk lifted Gwen and laid her gently in the back of the closest of the aircars. She was quite limp, but her breathing was still regular. Then he slid into the driver's seat and waited, massaging his wrists to restore circulation.

Everyone seemed to have forgotten him. Lorimaar high-Braith was still talking. "We recognize your right to face Myrik, but it must be singled, as Teraan Braith Nalarys lies dead. Since your own *teyn* challenged first . . ."

Jaan Vikary had his laser pistol in his hand. "Release him and stand away."

Lorimaar, startled, let go of Myrik's arm and stepped swiftly to the side. Bretan hesitated. "High-Ironjade," he rasped, "for your honor and his, for your holdfast and your *teyn,* set down your weapon."

Vikary aimed at the half-faced youth. Bretan twitched, then released Myrik and fell back with a grotesque shrug.

"What is happening?" the one-handed oldster was demanding in a shrill voice. "What is he doing?" Everyone ignored him.

"Jaan," Garse Janacek said in a horrified tone. "This has disarrayed your thoughts. Lower your gun, my *teyn.* I have challenged. I will kill him for you." He laid his hand on Jaan's arm.

And Jaan Vikary wrenched free and pointed his weapon at Garse. "No. Stand back. You will not interfere, not now. This is for her."

Janacek's face darkened; he had no grins now,

none of his savage wit. His right hand balled into a first, and he slowly raised it straight up in front of his face. Iron-and-glowstone stood shining in the space between the two Ironjades. "Our bond," said Janacek. "Think, my *teyn*. My honor, and yours, and that of our holdfast." His voice was grave.

"What of *her* honor?" Vikary said. Gesturing impatiently with his laser, he forced Janacek away from him and turned again on Myrik.

Alone and confused, Myrik seemed not to know what was expected of him. His rage had deserted him, though he was still breathing hard. A trail of spittle, tinged pink by blood, ran from one corner of his mouth. He wiped it off with the back of his hand and looked uncertainly toward Garse Janacek. "The first of the four choices," he began in a dazed voice. "I make the choice of mode."

"No," said Vikary. "You make no choices. Face *me*, mockman."

Myrik looked from Vikary to Janacek and back again. "The choice of mode," he repeated numbly.

"No," Vikary said again. "You gave Gwen Delvano no choices, she who would have faced you fair, in duel."

Myrik's face twisted into a look of honest bafflement. "She? In duel? I . . . she was a woman, a mockman." He nodded, as if he had settled everything. "She was a *woman*, Ironjade. Have you gone mad? She japed me. A woman does not duel."

"And you do not duel, Myrik. Do you understand? Do you? *You*"—he fired, and a half-second pulse of light took Myrik low, between his legs, so the man screamed—

"do"—and he fired again, and burned Myrik in the neck just beneath his chin, and then waited as the man fell and his laser recycled—

"not"—he continued, fifteen seconds later, and with the word a spurt of light that burned the writhing figure across the chest, and then Vikary was stepping backwards, toward the aircar—

"duel!" he finished, half in and half out of the car, and with the word came a flick of his wrist and a fourth burst of light, and Lorimaar high-Braith Arkellor was falling, his weapon half drawn.

Then the door slammed, and Dirk threw on the the gravity grid, and they jerked forward and up and out, and were halfway to the exit arch when the laser fire began to hiss and burn against their armor.

chapter 10

It was full night above the Common. The air was black crystal, clear and cold. The winds were bad. Dirk was grateful for the heavily armored Braith aircar, with its warm cabin, fully enclosed.

He kept them about a hundred meters above the plains and the gentle hills, and pushed the car as fast as he was able. Once, before Challenge had vanished behind them, Dirk looked back to see if there were any signs of pursuit. He saw none, but the Emereli city caught and held his eye. A tall black spear, soon to be lost against the blacker sky, it reminded him somehow of the great tree that had been caught in a forest fire, its branches and its leaves all gone, nothing left but a charred and soot-dark stick to echo its former glory. He remembered Challenge as Gwen had first shown it to him, when he had asked to see a city with life: bright against the evening, impossibly tall and shining silver, crowned by its ascending bursts of light. A dead husk now, and dead too the dreams of its builders. The hunters of Braith killed more than men and animals.

"They will be after us soon enough, t'Larien," Jaan Vikary said. "You need not search for them."

Dirk turned his attention back to his instruments. "Where are we going? We can't just fly blind above the Common all night, heading for nowhere in particular. Larteyn?"

"We dare not go to Larteyn now," Vikary replied. He had holstered his laser, but his face was as grim as it had been in Challenge when he burned down Myrik. "Are you so much the fool that you do not realize what I did? I broke the code, t'Larien. I am an outbonder now, a criminal, a duel-breaker. They will come after me and kill me as easily as they would a mockman." He knotted his hands together thoughtfully beneath his chin. "Our best hope . . . I do not know. Perhaps we have no hope."

"Speak for yourself. I have quite a bit more hope right now than I did a minute ago, back *there!*"

Vikary looked at him and smiled despite himself. "In truth. Though that is a most selfish viewpoint. It was not for you that I did what I did."

"For Gwen?"

Vikary nodded. "He— He did not even do her the honor of refusing. As if she were an animal. And yet . . . yet by the code, he was correct. The code I have lived by. I could have killed him for it. Garse intended to, as you witnessed. He was angry, because Myrik had . . . had damaged his property, had darkened his honor. He would have avenged the slight, had I let him." He sighed. "Do you understand why I could not, t'Larien? Do you? I have lived on Avalon, and I have loved Gwen Delvano. She lay there, alive only by a quirk of fortune. Myrik Braith would not have cared had she died, nor would the others. Yet Garse would have granted the man who did this thing a clean and decent dying, would have given him the kiss of shared honor before taking his small life. I . . . I care for Garse. Yet I could not let it be, t'Larien, not when Gwen lay so . . . so still, and disregarded. I could not let it be."

Vikary fell silent, brooding. Outside, in the moment of quiet, Dirk could hear the high keening of Worlorn's wind.

"Jaan," Dirk said after a while, "we still need to decide where we're going. We've got to get Gwen to shelter. Some place we can make her comfortable, where she won't be bothered. Maybe get a doctor to look at her."

"I know of no doctors on Worlorn," Vikary said. "Still, we must bring Gwen to a city." He considered the question. "Esvoch is closest, but the city is a ruin. Kryne Lamiya is then our best choice, I think, since it lies second nearest to Challenge. Turn south."

Dirk swung the aircar about in a wide arc, sliding upward and heading for the distant line of the mountainwall. He vaguely remembered the course Gwen had flown from the shining tower of ai-Emerel to the Darkdawn wilderness city and its bleak music.

As they flew on toward the mountains, Vikary fell to brooding again, staring out blind into the blackness of Worlorn's night. Dirk, who had more than a hint of what the Kavalar was suffering, did not attempt to break his melancholy but withdrew into his own sphere of thought and silence. He felt very weak; the ache in his head had returned to pound at him, and he was suddenly conscious of a parched rawness in his mouth and throat. He tried to recall when last he had taken food or water, and failed; somehow, he had lost all track of time.

The great coal peaks of Worlorn loomed up near at hand, and Dirk took the Braith aircar higher, to fly over them, and still neither he nor Jaan Vikary said a word. It was not until the mountains were behind them and the wilderness below that the Kavalar spoke again, and then it was only to give Dirk terse directions on the proper course to fly. Afterwards he lapsed back into silence, and it was in silence that they flew the lonely kilometers to their destination.

This time Dirk knew what to expect, and he listened. The music of Lamiya-Bailis came to his ears, a faint wailing on the wind, long before the city itself rose up out of the forests to engulf them. Outside their armored haven was nothing but the void: the tangled forests of the night below them, the thin-starred and empty sky above. Yet the notes of dark despair came talking, tinkling, and they touched him where he sat.

Vikary heard the music too. He glanced at Dirk. "This is a fitting city for us now, t'Larien."

"No," Dirk said, too loudly, not wanting to believe it.

"For me, then. All my effort has gone to ashes. The folk I thought to save are saved no longer. The Braiths can hunt them at will now, *korariel* of Ironjade or no. I cannot stop them. Garse may, perhaps, but what can one man do alone? He may not even try. It was my obsession, never his. Garse is lost too. He will go back to High Kavalaan alone, I think, and descend alone to the holdfasts of Ironjade, and the highbond council will take away my names. And he must find a knife and cut the glowstones from their settings, and wear empty iron about his arm. His *teyn* is dead."

"On High Kavalaan, perhaps," Dirk said. "But you lived on Avalon too, remember?"

"Yes," said Vikary. "Sadly. Sadly."

The music swelled and boomed around them, and the Siren City itself took shape below: the outer ring of towers like fleshless hands in frozen agony, the pale bridges spanning dark canals, the swards of dimly shining moss, the whistling spires stabbing up into the wind. A white city, a dead city, a forest of sharpened bones.

Dirk circled until he found the same building that Gwen had taken them to and came in for a landing. In the airlot the two derelict cars were still resting undisturbed, deep in dust. They seemed to Dirk like fragments of some other long-forgotten dream. Once, for some reason, they had seemed important; but he and Gwen and the world had all been different then, and now it was difficult to recall what possible relevance these metallic ghosts had had.

"You have been here before," Vikary said, and Dirk looked at him and nodded. "Lead, then," the Kavalar ordered.

"I don't . . ."

But Vikary was already up. He had taken Gwen gently from where she lay and lifted her in his arms, and he stood waiting. "Lead," he said again.

So Dirk led him away from the airlot, into the halls where the gray-white murals danced to the Darkdawn symphony, and they tried door after door until they found one room still furnished. It was a suite, actually, of four connecting rooms, all barren and high-ceilinged and far from clean. The beds—two of the rooms were bedrooms—were circular holes sunk deep into the floor; the mattresses were covered with a seamless oily leather that gave off a faintly unpleasant odor, like sour milk. But they were beds, soft enough and a place to rest, and Vikary arranged Gwen's limp form carefully. When she was resting easily—she looked almost serene—Jaan left Dirk sitting by her side, his legs folded under him on the floor, and went out to search the aircar they had stolen. He returned shortly with a covering for Gwen and a canteen.

"Drink only a swallow," he said, giving the water to Dirk.

Dirk took the cloth-covered metal, twisted off the top, and took a single short pull before handing it back. The liquid was lukewarm and vaguely bitter, but it felt very good trickling down his dry throat.

Vikary wet a strip of gray cloth and began to clean the dry blood from the back of Gwen's head. He dabbed gently at the brownish crust, wetting his rag again and yet again, working until her fine black hair was clean again and lay in a lustrous fan on the mattress, gleaming in the fitful light of the murals. When he was finished, he bandaged her and looked at Dirk. "I will watch," he said. "Go to the other room and sleep."

"We should talk," Dirk said, hesitant.

"Later, then. Not now. Go and sleep."

Dirk could hardly argue; his body was weary, and his own head was still throbbing. He went to the other room and fell gracelessly onto the sour-smelling mattress.

But, despite his pains, sleep did not come easily. Perhaps it was his headache; perhaps it was the uneasy motion of the light that ran within the walls, which haunted him even through closed eyelids. Chiefly, though, it was the music. Which did not leave him, and seemed to echo louder when he closed his eyes, as if that act had trapped it within his skull: thin pipings and wails and whistles, and *still*—forever—the booming of a solitary drum.

Fever dreams stalked that endless night—visions intense and surreal and hot with anxiety. Three times Dirk was shaken from his uneasy sleep, to sit up—trembling, his flesh clammy—and face the song of Lamiya-Bailis once again, never quite remembering what had stirred him. Once on waking he thought he heard voices in the next room. Another time he was quite certain that he saw Jaan Vikary sitting up against a far wall watching him. Neither of them spoke, and it took Dirk almost an hour to fall back into sleep. Only to waken yet again, to an empty echoing room and moving lights. He wondered briefly if they had left him here alone to live or die; the more he thought on it, the more the fear grew, and the worse his trembling became. But somehow he was unable to rise, to walk to the adjoining bedroom and see for himself. Instead he closed his eyes and tried to force all memory away.

And then it was dawn. Fat Satan was halfway up the sky, and feverish light as red and cold as Dirk's nightmares was flooding through a tall stained-glass window (predominantly clear in its center, but bordered all around with an intricate pattern of somber red-brown and smoky gray) to fall across his face. He rolled away from it and struggled to sit up, and Jaan Vikary appeared, offering the canteen.

Dirk took several long swallows, almost choking on the cold water and letting some of it splash over his dry, chapped lips and trickle down his chin. The canteen had been full when Jaan handed it to him; he gave it back half empty. "You found water," he said.

Vikary sealed up the canteen again and nodded. "The pumping stations have been closed for years, so there is no fresh water in the towers of Kryne Lamiya. Yet the canals still run. I went down last night while you and Gwen were sleeping."

Dirk rose to his feet unsteadily, and Vikary lent a hand to help him out of the sunken bed. "Is Gwen. . . ?"

"She regained consciousness early in the night, t'Larien. We spoke together, and I told her what I had done. I think she will recover soon enough."

"Can I talk to her?"

"She is resting now, sleeping normally. Later I am sure she will want to speak to you, but at the moment I do not think you should wake her. She tried to sit up last night and grew very unsteady and finally nauseous."

Dirk nodded. "I see. What about you? Get any sleep?" As he spoke, he looked around their quarters. The Darkdawn music had shrunken somehow. It still sounded, still wailed and moaned and permeated the very air of Kryne Lamiya; but to his ears it seemed fainter and more distant, so perhaps he was finally getting used to it, learning to tune it out of his conscious hearing. The light-murals, like the glowstones of Larteyn, had faded and died at the touch of normal sunlight; the walls were gray and empty. What furnishings there were—a few uncomfortable-looking chairs —flowed from the walls and floor: twisting extrusions that matched the color and tone of the chamber so well that they were almost invisible.

"I have slept enough," Vikary was saying. "That is

not important. I have been considering our position."
He gestured. "Come."

They walked through another chamber, an empty dining room, and out onto one of the many balconies that overlooked the Darkdawn city. By day, Kryne Lamiya was different, less despairing; even Worlorn's wan sunlight was enough to put a sparkle on the swift-flowing waters of the canals, and in the daylong twilight the pale towers were less sepulchral.

Dirk was weak and very hungry, but his headache had gone and the brisk wind felt good against his face. He brushed his hair—knotted and hopelessly filthy—back from his eyes and waited for Jaan to begin.

"I watched from here during the night," Vikary said, with his elbows on the cold railing and his eyes searching the horizon. "They are searching for us, t'Larien. Twice I glimpsed aircars above the city. The first time it was only a light, high in the distance, so perhaps I was wrong. Yet the second could be no mistake. The wolf-head car of Chell's flying near to ground level over the canals, with a searchlight of some sort attached. It passed quite close. There was a hound also. I heard it howling, all wild at the Darkling music."

"They didn't find us," Dirk said.

"In truth," Vikary replied. "I think we are safe enough here, for a while. Unless— I am not sure how they found you in Challenge, and that gives me a fear. If they track us to Kryne Lamiya and comb the city with Braith hounds, our danger will be severe. We have no null-scent now." He looked at Dirk. "How *did* they know where you had fled? Do you have any ideas?"

"No," said Dirk. "No one knew. Certainly no one followed. Maybe they just guessed. It was the most logical choice, after all. Living was more comfortable in Challenge than in any of the other cities. Easier. You know."

"Yes, I know. I do not accept your theory, however. Remember, t'Larien, Garse and I considered this problem too, when you left us shamed and deserted at the death-square. Challenge was the most *obvious* choice, and therefore the least logical, we felt. It seemed more likely that you would go to Musquel and live off what fish you could take, or that Gwen would forage for you both in the wilds she knew so well. Garse even suggested that you might simply have hidden the aircar and remained in some other section of Larteyn itself, so you could laugh at us while we searched the planet for you."

Dirk fidgeted. "Yes. Well, I suppose our choice was stupid."

"No, t'Larien, I did not say that. The only stupid choice, I think, would have been to flee to the City in the Starless Pool, where the Braiths were known to be thick. Challenge was a subtle choice, whether you intended it to be that or not. It seemed such a *wrong* choice that it was actually a right one. Do you understand? I cannot see how the Braiths discovered you by any process of deduction."

"Maybe," Dirk said. He thought a bit. "I remember the first we knew of it was when Bretan spoke to us. He— Well, he wasn't testing a theory, either. He *knew* we were there, somewhere."

"Yet you have no idea how?"

"No. No idea."

"We shall have to live with the fear that they can find us here, then. Otherwise, unless the Braiths can repeat their miracle, we are secure.

"Understand, though, that our position is not without difficulties. We have shelter and unlimited water, but no food to speak of. Our ultimate exit—we must go to the spaceport and leave Worlorn as soon as possible, I have concluded—our ultimate exit is going to be very difficult. The Braiths will anticipate us. We have my laser pistol, and two hunting lasers that I found in the aircar. Plus the vehicle itself, armed and well armored, probably belonging to Roseph high-Braith Kelcek—"

"One of the derelicts in the airlot is still marginally functional," Dirk interjected.

"Then we have two aircars, should we need them," Vikary said. "Against us, at least eight of the Braith hunters still live, and probably nine. I am not sure how seriously I wounded Lorimaar Arkellor. It is possible that I killed him, though I am inclined to doubt it. The Braiths can probably put eight aircars in the sky at once, if they choose to, although it is more traditional to fly together, *teyn*-and-*teyn*. Every car will be armored. They have supplies, power, food. They outnumber us. Possibly, since I am an outbond duel-breaker, they will prevail upon Kirak Redsteel Cavis and the two hunters from the Shanagate Holding to join them in running me down. Finally, there is Garse Janacek."

"Garse?"

"I hope—I pray—that he will cut the glowstones from his arm and return to High Kavalaan. He will be shamed, alone, wearing dead iron. No easy fate, t'Larien. I have disgraced him, and Ironjade. I am sorry for his pain, yet this is how I hope it will be. For there is another possibility, you see."

"Another. . . ?"

"He may hunt for us. He cannot leave Worlorn until a ship comes. That will be some time. I do not know what he will do."

"Surely he won't join the Braiths. They're his enemies, and you are his *teyn,* and Gwen his *cro-betheyn.* He might want to kill me, I don't doubt it, but—"

"Garse is more a Kavalar than me, t'Larien. He always has been. And now more than ever, since I am no Kavalar at all after the thing I have done. The old customs require a man's *teyn,* no less than any other, to bring death to a duel-breaker. It is a custom that only the very strong can follow. The bond of iron-and-fire is too close for most, so they are left alone to mourn. Yet Garse Janacek is a very strong man, stronger than myself in so many ways. I do not know. I do not know."

"And if he does come after us?"

Vikary spoke calmly. "I will not raise a weapon

against Garse. He is my *teyn,* whether I am his or no, and I have hurt him badly enough already, failed him, shamed him. He has worn a painful scar through most of his adult life because of me. Once, when we were both younger, an older man took offense at one of his jokes and issued challenge. The mode was single-shot and we fought *teyn*ed, and in my less-than-infinite wisdom I convinced Garse that our honor would be served if we fired into the air. We did, to our regret. The others decided to teach Garse a lesson about humor. To my shame, I was left untouched while he was disfigured for my folly.

"Yet he never reproached me. The first time I was with him after the duel, when he was still recovering from his wounds, he said to me, 'You were right, Jaantony, they *did* aim for empty air. A pity that they missed.'" Vikary laughed, but Dirk looked at him and saw that his eyes were full of tears, his mouth set grimly. He did not cry, though; as if by some immense effort of will, he kept the tears from falling.

Abruptly Jaan turned and walked back inside, leaving Dirk alone on the balcony with the wind and the white twilight city and the music of Lamiya-Bailis. Off in the far distance the straining white hands rose, holding back the encroaching wilderness. Dirk studied them, thoughtful, reflecting on Vikary's words.

Minutes later the Kavalar returned, dry-eyed and blank-faced. "I am sorry," he began.

"No need to—"

"We must get to the crux, t'Larien. Whether Garse hunts us or not, we face formidable odds. We have weapons, should we have to fight, but no one to use them. Gwen is a good marksman, and fearless enough, but she is injured and unsteady. And you— can I trust you? I put it to you bluntly. I trusted you once, and you betrayed me."

"How can I answer that question?" Dirk said. "You don't have to believe any promise I give you. But the Braiths want to kill me too, remember? And Gwen as well. Or do you think I'd betray her as easily as I . . ." He stopped in horror of his own words.

". . . as easily as you did me," Vikary finished for him with a hard smile. "You are blunt enough. No, t'Larien, I do *not* think you would betray Gwen. Yet I did not think you would desert us either when we had named you *keth* and you had taken the name. We would not have dueled except for you."

Dirk nodded. "I know that. Maybe I made a mistake. I don't know. I would have died, though, if I'd kept faith with you."

"Died a *keth* of Ironjade, with honor."

Dirk smiled. "Gwen appealed to me more than death. That much I expect you to understand."

"I do. She is still between us, ultimately. Face that, and know it for a truth. Sooner or later she will choose."

"She did choose, Jaan, when she left with me. You should face *that*." Dirk said it quickly, stubbornly; he wondered how much he believed it.

"She did not remove the jade-and-silver," Vikary answered. He gestured impatiently. "This is no matter. I *will* trust you, for now."

"Good. What do you want me to do?"

"Someone must fly to Larteyn."

Dirk frowned. "Why are you always trying to talk me into suicide, Jaan?"

"I did not say that you must make the flight, t'Larien," Vikary said. "I will do that myself. It will be dangerous, yes, but it must be done."

"Why?"

"The Kimdissi."

"Ruark?" Dirk had almost forgotten about his erstwhile host and co-conspirator.

Vikary nodded. "He has been a friend to Gwen since our days on Avalon. Though he has never liked me, nor I him, I cannot abandon him entirely. The Braiths . . ."

"I understand. But how will you get to him?"

"Should I reach Larteyn safely, I can summon him

by viewscreen. That is my hope, at least." He gave a vaguely fatalistic shrug.

"And me?"

"Remain here with Gwen. Nurse her, guard her. I will leave you one of Roseph's laser rifles. If she recovers sufficiently, let Gwen use it. She is probably more skillful than you. Agreed?"

"Agreed. It doesn't sound very difficult."

"No," said Vikary. "I expect that you will remain safely hidden, that I will return with the Kimdissi and find you as I leave you. Should it become necessary for you to flee, you will have this other aircar close at hand. There is a cave nearby that Gwen knows of. She can show you the way. Go to that cave if you must leave Kryne Lamiya."

"What if you *don't* come back? That *is* a possibility, you know."

"In that case you will be on your own again, as you were when you first fled Larteyn. You had plans then. Follow them, if you can." He smiled a humorless smile. "I expect to return, however. Remember that, t'Larien. Remember that."

There was an undertone of edged iron in Vikary's voice, an echo that called back another conversation in the same chill wind. With startling clarity, Jaan's old words came back to Dirk: *But I do exist. Remember that . . . This is not Avalon now, t'Larien, and today is not yesterday. It is a dying Festival world, a world without a code, so each of us must cling tightly to whatever codes we bring with us.* But Jaan Vikary, Dirk thought wildly, had brought two codes with him when he came to Worlorn.

While Dirk himself had brought none at all, had brought nothing but his love of Gwen Delvano.

Gwen was still sleeping when the two men went from the balcony. Leaving her undisturbed, they walked together to the airlot. Vikary had unpacked the Braith aircar thoroughly. Roseph and his *teyn* had obviously been planning for a short hunting sojourn in the wild when everything had broken loose. Dirk thought it unfortunate that they had not intended a longer trip.

As it was, Vikary had found only four hard protein bars in the way of food, plus the two hunting lasers and some clothing that had been slung over the seats. Dirk ate one of the bars immediately—he was famished—and slid the other three into the pocket of the heavy jacket he chose. It hung slightly loose on him, but the fit wasn't too bad; Roseph's *teyn* had approximated Dirk in size. And it was *warm*—thick leather, dyed a deep purple, with a collar, cuffs, and lining of soiled white fur. Both sleeves of the jacket were painted in intricate swirling patterns; the right was red and black, the left silver and green. A smaller matching jacket was also found (Roseph's, no doubt), and Dirk appropriated that one for Gwen.

Vikary took out the two laser rifles, long tubes of jet-black plastic with snarling wolves embossed upon the stocks in white. The first he strapped around his own shoulders; the second he gave to Dirk, along with curt instructions on its operation. The weapon was very light and slightly oily to the touch. Dirk held it awkwardly in one hand.

The farewells were brief and overly formal. Then Vikary sealed himself into the big Braith aircar, lifted it from the floor, and shot forward into empty air. Dust rose in great clouds at his departure, and Dirk retreated from the backwash choking, with one hand over his mouth and the other on the rifle.

When he returned to the suite, Gwen was just stirring. "Jaan?" she said, raising her head from the leather mattress to see who had just entered. She groaned and lay back again quickly and began to massage her temples with both hands. "My head," she said in a whimpering whisper.

Dirk stood the laser up against the wall just inside the door and sat by the side of the sunken bed. "Jaan just left," he said. "He's flying back to Larteyn to get Ruark."

Gwen's only reply was another groan.

"Can I get you anything?" Dirk asked. "Water? Food? We've got a couple of these." He took the protein bars out of the pocket of his jacket and handed them down for her inspection.

Gwen gave them a brief glance and grimaced in disgust. "No," she said. "Get them away. I'm not that hungry."

"You should eat something."

"Did," she said. "Last night. Jaan crushed up a couple of those bars in water, made a sort of paste." She lowered her hands from her temples and turned on her side to face him. "I didn't keep it down very well," she said. "I don't feel so good."

"I gathered that," Dirk said. "You can't expect to feel well after what happened. You've probably got a concussion, and you're lucky you're not dead."

"Jaan told me," she said, a little sharply. "About afterwards, too—what he did to Myrik." She frowned. "I thought I hit him pretty good when we fell. You saw, didn't you? It felt like I broke his jaw, either that or my fingers. But he didn't even notice."

"No," said Dirk.

"Tell me about—you know, about afterwards. Jaan just sort of sketched it out. I want to know." Her voice was weary and full of pain, but not to be denied.

So Dirk told her.

"He pointed his gun at Garse?" she said at one point. Dirk nodded, and she subsided again.

When he had finished, Gwen was very silent. Her eyes closed briefly, opened again, then closed and did not reopen. She lay quietly on her side, curled up into a sort of fetal ball, her hands clenched into small fists beneath her chin. Watching her, Dirk felt his eyes drawn to her left forearm, to the cold reminder of the jade-and-silver she still wore.

"Gwen," he said, softly. Her eyes opened again—for a very short time—and she shook her head violently, a silent shouted *no!* "Hey," he said, but by then her lids were shut tight once more, and she was lost within herself, and Dirk was alone with her jewelry and his fears.

The room was soaked in sunlight, or what passed for sunlight here on Worlorn; the sunset tones of high noon were slanting through the window, and dust motes drifted lazily through the broad beam. The light fell so that only one side of the mattress was illuminated; Gwen lay half in and half out of shadow.

Dirk—he did not speak again to Gwen, or look at her—found himself watching the patterns the light made on the floor.

In the center of the chamber everything was warm and red, and it was here the dust danced, drifting in from the darkness and turning briefly crimson, briefly golden, throwing tiny shadows, until it drifted out of the light again and was gone. He raised his hand, held it out for—minutes? hours?—for a time. It grew warm and warmer; dust swirled around it; shadows fell away like water when he twitched and turned his fingers; the sun was friendly and familiar. But suddenly he became aware that the movements of his hand, like the endless whirling of dust, had no purpose, no pattern, and no meaning. It was the music that told him so; the music of Lamiya-Bailis.

He pulled his hand in and frowned.

Around the great center of light and life was a thin twisting border where the sun shone through the window's rim of black and blood stained glass. Or fought through. It was only a small border, but it sealed the land of the stirring dust on every side.

Beyond it were the black corners, the sections of the room that the Hub and the Trojan Suns never reached, where fat demons and the shapes of Dirk's fears hunched obscurely, forever safe from scrutiny.

Smiling and rubbing his chin—stubble covered his cheeks and jaw, and he was starting to itch—Dirk studied those corners and let the Darkdawn music back into his soul. How he had ever tuned it out he was not sure, but now it was back and all around him.

The tower they were in—their home—sounded its long low note. Years away, or centuries, a chorus answered in ringing widows' wails. He heard shuddering throbs, and the screams of abandoned babies, and the slippery sliding sound of knives slicing warm flesh. And the drum. How could the wind beat a drum? he thought. He didn't know. Perhaps it was something else. But it sounded like a drum. So terribly far off, though, and so *alone*.

So horribly endlessly alone.

The mists and the shadows gathered in the farthest, dimmest corner of their room, and then began to clear. Dirk saw a table and a low chair, growing from the walls and floor like strange plastic vegetables. He wondered briefly what he was seeing them by; the sun had moved a little, and only a thin beam of light was trickling through the window now, and finally that snapped off too, and the world was gray.

When the world was gray, he noted, the dust did not dance. No. Not at all. He felt the air to be sure; there was no dust, no warmth, no sunlight. He nodded sagely. It seemed that he had discovered some great truth.

Dim lights were stirring in the walls, ghosts waking for another night. Phantoms and husks of old dreams. All of them were gray and white; color was only for the living, and had no place here.

The ghosts began to move. They were locked into the walls, each of them; from time to time, Dirk thought he could see one stop its furious dancing and beat helplessly and hopelessly against the glass walls that kept it from the room. Wraith hands pounding, pounding, yet the room shook not at all. Stillness was a part of these things; the phantoms were just that, all insubstantial, and pound though they might, finally they must return to dancing.

The dance—the dance macabre—shapeless shadows— Oh, but it was beautiful! Moving, dipping, writhing. Walls of gray flame. So much better than the dust motes, *these* dancers; they had a pattern, and their music was the song of the Siren City.

Desolation. Emptiness. Decay. A single drum, beaten slow. Alone. Alone. Alone. Nothing has meaning.

"Dirk!"

It was Gwen's voice. He shook his head, looked away from the walls, down to where she lay in darkness. It was night. Night. Somehow the day had gone.

Gwen—she had not been sleeping—was looking up at him. "I'm sorry," she said. She was telling him something. But he knew it already, knew it from her silence, knew it from— From the drum perhaps. From Kryne Lamiya.

He smiled. "You never forgot, did you? It wasn't a question of forgetting. There was a reason why you never removed the . . ." He pointed.

"Yes," she said. She sat up in the bed, the coverlet falling down around her waist. Jaan had unsealed the front of her suit, so it hung on her loosely, and the soft curves of her breasts were visible. In the flickering light the flesh was pale and gray. Dirk felt no stirrings. Her hand went to the jade-and-silver. She touched it, stroked it, sighed. "I never thought— I don't know— I said what I had to say, Dirk. Bretan Braith would have killed you."

"Maybe that would have been better," he answered. Not bitterly, but in a bemused, faintly distracted sort of way. "So you never meant to leave him?"

"I don't know. How do I know what I meant? I was going to try, Dirk, really I was. I never really believed, though. I told you that. I was honest. This isn't Avalon, and we've changed. I'm not your Jenny. I never was, and now less than ever."

"Yes," he said, nodding. "I remember you driving. The way you gripped the stick. Your face. Your eyes. You have jade eyes, Gwen. Jade eyes and a silver smile. You frighten me." He glanced away from her, back to the walls. Light-murals moved in chaotic patterns, along with the thin wild music. Somehow the ghosts had gone away. He had only taken his eyes from them for an instant, yet all of them had melted and left. Like his old dreams, he thought.

"Jade eyes?" Gwen was saying.

"Like Garse."

"Garse has blue eyes," she said.

"Still. Like Garse."

She chuckled, and groaned. "It hurts when I laugh," she said. "But it's funny. Me' like Garse. No wonder Jaan——"

"You'll go back to him?"

"Maybe. I'm not sure. It would be very hard to leave him now. Do you understand? He's finally chosen. When he pointed his laser at Garse. After that, after he turned against *teyn* and holdfast and world, I can't just—— You know. But I won't go back to being a *betheyn* to him, not ever. It will have to be more than jade-and-silver."

Dirk felt empty. He shrugged. "And me?"

"You know it wasn't working. Surely. You had to feel it. You never stopped calling me Jenny."

He smiled. "I didn't? Maybe not. Maybe not."

"Never," she said. She rubbed her head. "I'm feeling a little better now," she said. "You still have those protein bars?"

Dirk took one from his pocket and flipped it at her. She snatched it from the air with her left hand, smiled at him, unwrapped it, and began to eat.

He stood up abruptly, jamming his hands deep into his jacket pockets, and walked to the high window. The tops of the bone-white towers still wore a faint, waning reddish tinge—perhaps the Helleye and its attendants were not entirely gone from the western sky. But below, in the streets, the Darkdawn city drank of night. The canals were black ribbons, and the landscape dripped with the dim purple radiance of phosphorescent moss. Through that lambent gloom Dirk glimpsed his solitary bargeman, as he had glimpsed him once before upon those same dark waters. He was leaning on his pole, as ever, letting the current take him, coming on and on, easily, inexorably. Dirk smiled. "Welcome," he muttered, "welcome."

"Dirk?" Gwen had finished eating. She was fastening her jumpsuit tight again, framed in the murky light. Behind her the walls were alive with gray-white dancers. Dirk heard drums, and whispers, and promises. And he knew the last were lies.

"One question, Gwen," he said heavily.

She stared at him.

"Why did you call me back?" he said. "Why? If you thought we were so dead, you and me, why couldn't you leave me alone?"

Her face was pale and blank. "Call you back?"

"You know," he said. "The whisperjewel."

"Yes," she said uncertainly. "It's back in Larteyn."

"Of course it is," he said. "In my luggage. You sent it to me."

"No," she said. "No."

"You met me!"

"You lasered us from your ship. I never— Believe me, that was the first I knew that you were coming. I didn't know what to think of it. I thought you'd get around to telling me, though, so I never pressed."

Dirk said something, but the tower moaned its low note and took his words away from him. He shook his head. "You didn't call me?"

"No."

"But I got the whisperjewel. On Braque. The same one, esper-etched. You can't fake that." He remembered something else. "And Arkin *said*—"

"Yes," she said. She bit her lip. "I don't understand. He must have sent it. But he was my friend. I had to have someone to talk to. I don't understand." She whimpered.

"Your head?" Dirk asked quickly.

"No," she said. "No."

He watched her face. "Arkin sent it?"

"Yes. He was the only one. It had to be. We met on Avalon, right after you and I . . . you know. Arkin helped me. It was a bad time. He was there when you sent your jewel to Jenny. I was crying and all. I told him about it, and we talked. Even later, after I met Jaan, Arkin and I stayed close. He was like a brother!"

"A brother," Dirk repeated. "Why would—"

"I don't *know!*"

Dirk was thoughtful. "When you met me at the spaceport, Arkin was with you. Did you ask him to come along? I was counting on you being alone, I remember."

"It was his idea," she said. "Well, I told him I was nervous. About seeing you again. He . . . he offered to come along and lend me moral support. And he said he wanted to meet you too. You know. After all I had told him on Avalon."

"And the day you and he took off into the wild— you know, when I got into trouble with Garse and then Bretan—what went on?"

"Arkin said . . . an armor-bug migration. It wasn't actually, but we had to check. We rushed away."

"Why didn't you tell me where you were going? I thought that Jaan and Garse had beaten you up, that they were keeping you away from me. The night before, you'd said—"

"I know, but Arkin said he'd tell you."

"And he convinced me to run away," Dirk said. "And you, I suppose he told you that to convince me you should . . ."

She nodded.

He turned toward the window. The last light was gone from the tower tops. Above, a handful of stars sparkled. Dirk counted them. Twelve. An even dozen. He wondered if some of them were really galaxies, away across the Great Black Sea. "Gwen," he said, "Jaan left this morning. From here to Larteyn and back, by aircar—how long should that take?"

When she did not answer, he turned to look at her again.

The walls were full of phantoms, and Gwen trembled in their light.

"He should be back by now, shouldn't he?"

She nodded and lay back again on the pale mattress.

The Siren City sang its lullaby, its hymn to final sleep.

chapter 11

Dirk walked across the room.

The laser rifle was leaning up against the wall. He lifted it, felt once again the vaguely oily texture of the slick black plastic. His thumb brushed over the wolf's head. He raised the weapon to his shoulder, sighted, fired.

The wand of light hung for at least a full second in the air. He moved the rifle slightly, and the pencil beam moved with it. When it faded, and the after-image left his retinas, he saw that he had burned an uneven hole in the window. The wind was whistling through it loudly, making an odd dissonance with the music of Lamiya-Bailis.

Gwen climbed unsteadily out of her bed. "What? Dirk?"

He shrugged at her and lowered the rifle.

"What?" she repeated. "What are you doing?"

"I wanted to make sure I knew how it worked," he explained. "I'm . . . I'm going."

She frowned. "Wait," she said. "I'll find my boots."

He shook his head.

"You too?" Her face was hard, ugly. "I don't need to be protected, damn it."

"It's not like that," he said.

"If this is some idiot move to make yourself a hero in my eyes, it isn't going to work," she said, putting her hands on her hips.

He smiled. "What this is, Gwen, is some idiot move to make myself a hero in *my* eyes. Your eyes . . . your eyes aren't important anymore."

"Why, then?"

He hefted the rifle uncertainly. "I don't know," he admitted. "Maybe because I like Jaan, and owe him. Because I want to make it up to him for running out after he'd trusted me and named me *keth*."

"Dirk," she began.

He waved her quiet. "I know . . . but that isn't all. Maybe I just want to get Ruark. Maybe it's because Kryne Lamiya had more suicides than any other Festival city, and I'm one of them. You can pick your own motive, Gwen. All of the above." A faint smile brushed across his face. "Maybe it's because there are only twelve stars, you know? So it doesn't make any difference, does it?"

"What good can you possibly do?"

"Who knows? And why does it matter? Do you care, Gwen? Do you *really?*" He shook his head, and the motion sent his hair tumbling over his forehead once again, so once more he had to stop and brush it back. "I don't *care* if you care," he said forcefully. "You said, or implied, that I was being selfish back in Challenge. Well, maybe I was. And maybe I am now. I'll tell you something, though. Whatever I'm going to do, I'm not asking to look at your arms first, Gwen. Know what I mean?"

It was a fine exit line, but halfway out the door he softened, hesitated, turned back. "Stay here, Gwen," he told her. "Just stay. You're still hurt. If you have to run, Jaan said something about a cave. You know anything about a cave?" She nodded. "Well, go there if you have to. Otherwise stay here." He waved a clumsy farewell at her with the rifle, then spun and walked away too quickly.

Down in the airlot the walls were just walls—no ghosts, no murals, no lights. Dirk stumbled over the aircar he wanted in the dark, then waited while his eyes adjusted. His derelict was no product of High Kavalaan; it was a cramped two-seater, a black and silver teardrop of plastic and lightweight metal. No armor at all, of course, and the only weapon it carried was the laser rifle he laid across his lap.

It was only a little less dead than the rest of Worlorn, but that little was enough. When he tapped into the power, the car woke, and the instruments lit the cabin with their pale radiance. He ate a protein bar quickly and studied the readings. The energy supply was low, too low, but it would have to do. He would not use the headlamps; he could fly by the scant starlight. And the heater was likewise to be dispensed with, as long as he had his leather jacket to keep him from the chill.

Dirk slammed down the door, sealing himself in, and flicked on the gravity grid. The aircar lifted, rocking a bit unsteadily, but it lifted. He gripped the stick and threw it forward, and then he was outside and airborne.

He had one brief flash of terror. If the grid had been feeble enough, he knew, there would be no flight at all, just a rolling rumble to the moss-choked ground below. The aircar throbbed and dipped alarmingly once clear of the lot, but only for an instant; then the grid caught hold and they rode up on the singing winds, and the only thing left tumbling was his stomach.

Dirk climbed steadily, trying to push the small car as high as it would go. The mountainwall was ahead, and he had to clear it. Besides, he was not anxious to encounter other nocturnal flyers. High up, with his lights doused, he could see any other aircars that passed below him, but the chances were good that he would escape their notice.

He did not look back at Kryne Lamiya, but he felt the city behind him, driving him onward, washing away his fears. Fear was so foolish; nothing mattered, death least of all. Even when the Siren City and its white and gray lights were gone, the music lingered, steadily fading and growing weaker, but always with him, always potent. One note, a thin wavering whistle, outlasted the rest. Some thirty kilometers from the city he was still hearing it, mixed with the deeper whistle of the wind. Finally he realized that the noise was coming from his own lips.

He stopped whistling and tried to concentrate on flying.

When he had been airborne for almost an hour, the mountainwall bulked up before him, or rather beneath him, for he was quite high by that time, and he felt closer to the stars and the pinpoint galaxies above than to the forests far below. The wind had grown shrill and furious as it forced its way through hairline cracks in the door seam, but Dirk was ignoring the sound.

Where the mountains met the wilderness, he saw a light.

He banked the aircar, circled, and began to descend. No lights should shine this side of the mountains, he knew; whatever it was, it should be investigated.

He spiraled down until he was directly above the light, then stilled all forward motion of the aircar, hung hovering for a short moment, and faded his gravity grid. With infinite slowness, he settled, rocking back and forth slightly in the wind, falling quietly.

There were several lights beneath him. The main source of illumination was a fire. He could tell that now; he could see it shifting and flickering as the winds fanned the flames this way and that. But there were other, smaller lights as well—steady and artificial, a circle of them off in the blackness not terribly distant from the fire. Perhaps a kilometer, he estimated, perhaps less.

The temperature in the small cabin began to rise, and Dirk felt sweat on his skin, soaking his clothing beneath the heavy jacket. Smoke assaulted him as well; clouds of it, black and sooty, rose from the fire and obscured his view. Frowning, he moved the aircar until he was no longer directly above the blaze, and continued to descend.

The flames rose up to greet him, long orange tongues, very bright against the plumes of smoke. He saw sparks as well, or embers, or something of that sort; they issued from the fire in hot bright showers, shooting off into the night and then vanishing. Drifting lower, he was treated to yet another display, a furious crackling of blue-white flame that came with a sharp scent of ozone and then was gone again.

Dirk stopped the aircar dead when the fire was still decently below him. There were other people about—the circle of steady artificial lights—and he did not care to be seen. His black and silver aircar, motionless against the black sky, would not be easy to spot, but it would be a different story if he let himself be outlined by the flames. Although he had an unobstructed view from where he hovered, he still could not make out what was burning; the center of the fire was a shapeless darkness from which the sparks issued periodically. Around it he could see the dense tangle of chokers, their waxy limbs shining bright yellow in the reflected glare. Several had fallen into the heart of the conflagration and were contributing most of the black smoke as they shriveled and turned to ash. But the rest, the twisting fence that surrounded the black burning thing, refused to go up. Instead of spreading, the fire was visibly dying out.

Dirk waited and watched it die. He was already fairly certain that he was looking at a fallen aircar; the sparks and ozone smell told him that much. He wanted to know *which* aircar.

After the flames had dwindled and the sparks had

ceased to storm, but before the fire had guttered out entirely and turned to greasy smoke, Dirk saw a shape. Briefly; a wing, vaguely batlike, twisted at a grotesque angle and poking toward the sky, a sheet of fire flaring behind it. That was enough; this was not any aircar he knew, though it was clearly of Kavalar manufacture.

A dark ghost above the forest, he flitted away from the dying fire, toward the ring of man-made illumination. This time he maintained a greater distance. He did not need to go closer. The lights were quite bright, and the scene was etched in fine detail.

He saw a wide clearing, ringed by electric torches, on the edge of some broad body of still water. Three aircars were down there, and he knew all three; the same trio had been down beneath the Emereli tree within Challenge when Myrik Braith had assaulted Gwen. One of them, the great-domed car with dark red armor, belonged to Lorimaar high-Braith. The other two were smaller, almost identical, except they were identical no longer, since one of them was visibly damaged, even seen from this distance. It was lying awkwardly, half submerged in the water, and part of it was misshapen and *glowing*. Its armored door gaped open.

Stick figures moved about the wreck. Dirk would hardly have seen them at all except for their motion, so well did they blend with the background. Nearby, someone was leading Braith hounds from a gate in the flank of Lorimaar's aircar.

Frowning, Dirk touched his grid control and took his own car straight up, until the men and aircars were lost to sight and nothing remained below but a point of light in the forest. Two points, in truth, but the fire was a faint orange ember now, visibly fading.

Safe in the black womb of sky, he paused to think.

The damaged aircar had been Roseph's, the same car they had stolen in Challenge, the car Jaan Vikary had flown to Larteyn that morning. He was sure of that. The Braiths had found him, clearly, and pursued him to the forest, lasered him down. But it seemed unlikely that he was dead; otherwise why the Braith hounds? Lorimaar wasn't just taking his pack for a walk. It was more than likely that Jaan had survived to flee into the forest, and that the Braiths were going to hunt him down.

Dirk considered briefly trying to effect a rescue, but the prospects seemed dim. He had no idea how to find Jaan in the night-shrouded outworld wild. The Braiths were better equipped for that than he was.

He resumed his course toward the mountainwall, and Larteyn beyond. In the forest, armed and alone as he was, he could do Jaan Vikary no particular good. In the Kavalar Firefort, however, he could at the very least settle Ironjade's score with Arkin Ruark.

The mountains slid beneath him, and Dirk relaxed once more, though one hand fell to rest on the laser rifle that still lay across his lap.

The flight took just under an hour; then Larteyn, red and smoldering, shouldered up out of the mountains. It looked very dead, very empty, but Dirk knew that for a lie. He kept low and wasted no time, shooting straight across the low square rooftops and the glowstone plazas to the building that he had once shared with Gwen Delvano, the two Ironjades, and the Kimdissi liar.

Only one other aircar waited on the windswept roof —the armor-clad military relic. Of Ruark's small yellow flyer there was no sign, and the gray manta was missing as well. Dirk briefly wondered what had happened to it, abandoned back in Challenge, then shoved the thought aside as he descended for a landing.

He kept the laser firmly in his grip as he climbed out. The world was still and crimson. He walked swiftly to the tubes, and rode down to Ruark's quarters.

They were empty.

He searched them quite thoroughly, turning things

this way and that, not caring what he disturbed, what he destroyed. All of the Kimdissi's belongings were still in place, but Ruark was not there, nor was there any sign of where he had gone.

Dirk's own possessions remained as well, the few things he had left behind when he and Gwen had run, nothing but a small pile of light clothing he had brought from Braque. Useless here in the chill of Worlorn. He set down the laser, knelt, and began to rummage through the pockets of the soiled pants. It was not until he found it—jammed away, still in its wrappings of silver and velvet—that he really knew what he was looking for, and why he had come back to Larteyn.

In Ruark's bedroom he found a small cache of personal jewelry in a lockbox: rings, pendants, intricate bracelets and crowns, earrings of semi-precious stones. He pawed through the box until he found a thin fine chain with a silver-wire owl frozen in amber and suspended on a clip. It looked about the right size, that clip. Dirk tore away the amber and the owl and replaced them with the whisperjewel.

Then he unsealed his jacket and his heavy shirt and hung the chain around his neck, so the cold red teardrop was next to his bare skin, whispering its whispers, promising its lies. The small stab of ice was painful against his chest, but that was all right; it was Jenny. Very shortly he grew used to it, and it passed. Salt tears rolled down his cheeks. He did not notice. He went upstairs.

The workroom that Ruark had shared with Gwen was as cluttered as Dirk remembered it, but the Kimdissi was not there. Nor was he to be found in the deserted apartment above that where Dirk had called Ruark from Challenge. There was only one more place to search.

Quickly he climbed to the top of the tower. The door was open. He hesitated, and then entered, holding his laser at the ready.

The great living room was chaos and destruction.

The viewscreen had been smashed or had exploded; glass shards were everywhere. The walls were scarred by laser fire. The couch had been overturned and ripped in a dozen places, stuffing pulled out in great handfuls and scattered. Some of it had been thrown into the fireplace, where it contributed to the sodden, smoky mess that choked the hearth. One of the gargoyles, headless and upside down, leaned up against the base of the mantel. Its head, glowstone eyes and all, had been thrown into the sodden ashes of the fire. The air stank of wine and vomit.

Garse Janacek was sleeping on the floor, shirtless, his red beard stained even redder by dribbled wine, his mouth hanging open. He smelled like the room. He was snoring loudly and his laser pistol was still clutched in one hand. Dirk saw his shirt balled up and lying in a pool of vomit that Janacek had tried to mop at halfheartedly.

He walked around carefully and took the laser out of Janacek's limp fingers. Vikary's *teyn* was not quite the iron Kavalar that Jaan imagined him.

Janacek's right arm was still bound by iron-and-glowstones. A few of the red-black jewels had been forced from their settings; the empty holes looked obscene. But most of the bracelet was intact, except where it was marred by long scratches. Janacek's forearm, above the bracelet, was also scarred. The scratches were deep, and often continuous with those scored in the black iron. Arm and armlet both were caked by dried blood.

Near to Janacek's boot Dirk saw the long blood-stained knife. He could imagine the rest. Drunk, no doubt, his left hand made awkward by his old wound, trying to pry the glowstones free, losing patience and stabbing wildly, dropping the blade in his pain and his rage.

Stepping backward lightly, detouring around Janacek's damp shirt, Dirk paused in the door frame, leveled his rifle, and shouted. *"Garse!"*

Janacek did not stir. Dirk repeated his shout. This

time the volume of snoring declined appreciably. Encouraged, Dirk stooped and picked up the nearest object at hand—a glowstone—and lofted it through the air at the Kavalar. It hit Janacek on the cheek.

He sat up slowly, blinking. He saw Dirk and scowled at him.

"Get up," Dirk said. He waved his laser.

Janacek rose shakily to his feet, looked around for his own weapon.

"You won't find it," Dirk told him. "I've got it here."

Janacek's eyes were blurred and weary, but he had slept off most of his drunkenness. "Why are you here, t'Larien?" he said slowly, in a voice tinged more by exhaustion than by wine. "Have you come to mock me?"

Dirk shook his head. "No. I'm sorry for you."

Janacek glared. "Sorry for *me?*"

"You don't think you deserve pity? Look around you!"

"Careful," Janacek told him. "Jape me too much, t'Larien, and I will discover if you have steel enough to fire that laser you hold so awkwardly."

"Don't, Garse," Dirk said. "Please. I need your help."

Janacek laughed, throwing back his head and roaring.

When he had stopped, Dirk told him everything that had happened since Vikary killed Myrik Braith in Challenge. Janacek stood very stiffly as he listened, his arms crossed tightly across his bare, scarred chest. He laughed one more time—when Dirk told him his conclusions about Ruark. "The manipulators of Kimdiss," Janacek muttered. Dirk let him mutter, then finished his story.

"So?" Janacek demanded when he had concluded. "Why do you think any of this is any matter to me?"

"I guess I didn't think you'd let the Braiths hunt Jaan down like an animal," Dirk said.

"He has made himself an animal."

"By Braith lights, I suppose," Dirk replied. "Are you a Braith?"

"I am a Kavalar."

"Are all Kavalars the same now?" He gestured toward the stone head of the gargoyle sitting in the fireplace. "I see you take trophies now, just like Lorimaar."

Janacek said nothing. His eyes were very hard.

"Maybe I was wrong," Dirk said. "But when I came in here and saw all this, it made me think. It made me think that maybe you did have some human feeling for the man who used to be your *teyn*. It reminded me that once you told me that you and Jaan had a bond stronger than any I had ever known. I guess that was a lie, though."

"It was truth. Jaan Vikary broke that bond."

"Gwen broke all the bonds between *us* years ago," Dirk said. "But I came when she needed me. Oh, it turned out that she didn't really need me, and I came for a lot of selfish reasons. But I came. You can't rob me of that, Garse. I kept my promise." He paused. "And I would not let anyone hunt *her,* if I could stop them. It appears that we were bonded by something a lot stronger than your Kavalar iron-and-fire."

"Say what you want, t'Larien. Your words change nothing. The idea of you keeping promises is ludicrous. What of your promises to Jaan and myself?"

"I betrayed them," Dirk said quickly. "I know that. So you and I are even, Garse."

"I have betrayed no one."

"You are abandoning those who stood closest to you. Gwen, who was your *cro-betheyn,* who slept with you and loved you and hated you all at once. And Jaan. Your precious *teyn.*"

"I have never betrayed them," Janacek said hotly. "Gwen betrayed both myself and the jade-and-silver she wore from the day she joined us. Jaan deserted all that was decent in the way he slew Myrik. He ignored me, ignored the duties of iron-and-fire. I owe neither of them."

"You don't, do you?" Beneath his shirt Dirk could feel the whisperjewel hard against his skin, flooding him with words and memories, with a sense of the man he had once been. He was very angry. "And that says it all, right? You don't owe them, so who cares? All your damn Kavalar bonds are, after all, are debt and obligation. Traditions, old holdfast wisdom, like the code duello and mockman hunting. Don't think about them, just follow them. Ruark was right about one thing—there is no love in any of you, except maybe Jaan, and I'm not so sure about him. What the hell was he going to do if Gwen *hadn't* been wearing his bracelet?"

"The same thing!"

"Really? And what about you? Would you have challenged Myrik just because he hurt Gwen? Or was it because he damaged your jade-and-silver?" Dirk snorted. "Maybe Jaan would have done the same thing, but not you, Janacek. You're as Kavalar as Lorimaar himself, as stiff as Chell or Bretan. Jaan wanted to make his folk better, but I guess you were only along for a ride and didn't believe any of it for a minute." He yanked Janacek's laser out of his belt and flung it across the room with his free hand. "Here," he shouted, lowering his rifle. "Go hunt a mockman!"

Janacek, startled, snapped the weapon out of the air almost by reflex. He stood holding it clumsily and frowned. "I could kill you now, t'Larien," he said.

"Do that or do nothing," Dirk said. "It's all the same. If you had ever *really* loved Jaan—"

"I do not *love* Jaan," Janacek snapped, his face flushed. "He is my *teyn!*"

Dirk let the Kavalar's words hang in the air for a long minute. He scratched his chin thoughtfully. "Is?" he said. "You mean Jaan *was* your *teyn,* don't you?"

Janacek's flush faded as suddenly as it had come. Beneath his beard one corner of his mouth twitched in a manner that reminded Dirk of Bretan. His eyes shifted, almost furtively, half ashamed, to the heavy iron bracelet that still hung about his bloodied forearm.

"You never did get all the glowstones out, did you?" Dirk said gently.

"No," Janacek said. His voice was oddly soft. "No, I did not. It means little, of course. The physical iron is nothing when the other iron is gone."

"But it's not gone, Garse," Dirk said. "Jaan spoke of you when we were together in Kryne Lamiya. I know. Maybe he feels himself iron-bound to Gwen too, and maybe that is wrong. Don't ask me. All I know is that for Jaan the other iron is still there. He wore his iron-and-fire bracelet in Kryne Lamiya. He'll be wearing it when the Braith hounds tear him down, I imagine."

Janacek shook his head. "T'Larien," he said, "your mother comes from Kimdiss, I would vow. Yet I cannot resist you. You manipulate too well." He grinned; it was the old grin, the one he had flashed that morning when he aimed his laser at Dirk and asked if it alarmed him. "Jaan Vikary *is* my *teyn,*" he said. "What do you want me to do?"

Janacek's conversion, however reluctant, was thorough enough. The Kavalar took charge almost immediately. Dirk thought they should leave at once and discuss their plans en route, but Janacek insisted that they take time to shower and dress. "If Jaan is still alive, he will be safe enough until dawn. The hounds have poor night sight, and the Braiths will not be eager to go blundering into a dark choker-wood. No, t'Larien, they will camp and wait. A man alone and on foot cannot get far. So we have time enough to meet them like Ironjades."

By the time they were ready to depart, Janacek had removed almost every trace of his drunken rage. He was slim and immaculate in a suit of fur-lined chameleon cloth, his beard cleaned and trimmed, his dark red hair combed carefully back from his eyes. Only his right arm—scrubbed and carefully bandaged, but still conspicuous—gave evidence against him. But the scratches did not seem to have impaired him much; he looked graceful and fluid as he charged and checked his laser and slid it into his belt. In addition to the pistol, Janacek was also carrying a long double-bladed knife and a rifle like Dirk's. He grinned gleefully as he took it up.

Dirk had washed and shaved while waiting, and had also taken the opportunity to eat his first full meal in days. He was feeling almost energetic when they set off for the roof.

The interior of Janacek's huge square aircar was every bit as cramped as that of the tiny derelict Dirk had flown from Kryne Lamiya, although Janacek's machine did have four small seats instead of only two. "The armor," Garse said when Dirk remarked on the limited interior space. He strapped Dirk into a rigid uncomfortable seat with a tight battle harness, did likewise for himself, and took them swiftly aloft.

The cabin was dimly lit and completely enclosed, with gauges and instruments everywhere, even above the doors. No windows; a panel of eight small viewscreens gave the pilot eight different exterior views. The decor was unpainted, unornamented duralloy.

"This vehicle is older than both of us," Janacek said as he took them up. He seemed eager enough to talk, and friendly in his abrasive sort of way. "And it has seen more worlds than even you. Its history is fascinating. This particular model dates to some four hundred standard years ago. It was built by the Wisdoms of Dam Tullian, well within the Tempter's Veil, and used in their wars against Erikan and Rogue's Hope. After a century or so it was disabled and abandoned. The Erikaners salvaged it during a peace and sold it to the Steel Angels on Bastion. They used it in a number of campaigns, until it was finally captured from them by Prometheans. A Kimdissi trader picked it up on Prometheus and sold it to me, and I adapted it to the code duello. No one has challenged me to aerial combat since. Watch." His hand reached out and depressed a glowing button, and suddenly there was a surge of acceleration that pressed Dirk back against his seat. "Auxiliary pulse-tubes for emergency speed," Janacek said with a grin. "We will be there in less than half the time it took you, t'Larien."

"Good," Dirk said. Something was nagging at him. "Did you say you got it from a Kimdissi trader?"

"That is truth," Janacek said. "The peaceful Kimdissi are great arms traders. I have scant regard for the manipulators, as you know, but I am not above taking advantage of a bargain when one is offered."

"Arkin made a great show of being nonviolent," Dirk said. "I suppose that was all another sham."

"No," Janacek said. He glanced at Dirk and smiled. "Startled, t'Larien? The truth is perhaps more bizarre. We do not call the Kimdissi manipulators without reason. You studied history on Avalon, I assume?"

"Some," Dirk said. "Old Earth history, the Federal Empire, the Double War, the expansion."

"Yet no outworld history." Janacek clucked. "It is expected. So many worlds and cultures in the manrealm, so many histories. Even the names are too much to learn. Listen, and I will enlighten you. When you landed on Worlorn, did you notice the circle of flags?"

Dirk looked at him blankly. "No."

"Perhaps they are no longer in place. Once, though, during the Festival itself, the plaza outside the spacefield flew fourteen flags. It was an absurd Toberian conceit, yet it came to pass, in a fashion, though the planetary flags in ten of the fourteen cases represented nothing. Worlds like Eshellin and the Forgotten Colony did not even know what a flag *was,* while at the other extreme the Emereli had a different banner for each of their hundred urban towers. The Darklings laughed at us all and flew a cloth of solid black." He seemed very amused at that. "As for High Kavalaan, we had no flag for all our world. We found one, though. It was taken from history. A rectangle divided into four quadrants of different colors: a green banshee on a field of black for Ironjade,

Shanagate's silver hunting bat on yellow, crossed swords against crimson for Redsteel, and for Braith a white wolf on purple. It was the old standard of the Highbond League.

"The League was created about the time that the starships first returned to High Kavalaan. There was a man, a great leader, named Vikor high-Redsteel Corben. He dominated Redsteel's highbond council for a generation, and when the offworlders came he was convinced that all Kavalars must band together to share knowledge and wealth equally. Thus he formed the Highbond League, whose flag I have described to you. The union was sadly short-lived. Kimdissi traders, fearful of the power of a unified High Kavalaan, contracted to provide modern armaments exclusively to the Braiths. The Braith highbonds had joined the League only from fear; in truth, they wished to shun the stars, which they avowed were all full of mockmen. Yet they did not shrink from taking mockman lasers.

"So we had the last highwar. Ironjade and Redsteel and Shanagate together subjugated Braith, despite the Kimdissi arms, but Vikor high-Redsteel himself was killed, and the cost in lives was hideous. The Highbond League outlasted its founder by only a handful of years. Braith, badly beaten, fastened on the belief that it had been tricked and used by Kimdissi mockmen, and thus cleaved to the old traditions even more firmly than before. To blood the peace and make it lasting, the League—now dominated by highbonds from Shanagate—seized all the Kimdissi traders on High Kavalaan and a ship of Toberians as well, declared all of them to be war criminals—a term the offworlders taught us, by the way—and set them free on the plains to be hunted as mockmen. Banshees killed many of them, others starved, but the hunters took the most and carried the heads home for trophies. It is said that the Braith highbonds took special joy in flaying the men who had armed and advised them.

"We are not proud of that hunt overmuch today, yet we can understand it. The war had been longer and bloodier than any in our history since the Time of Fire and Demons. It was a time of great griefs and towering hatreds, and it destroyed the Highbond League. The Ironjade Gathering withdrew rather than condone the hunting, declaring that the Kimdissi were human. Redsteel soon followed. The mockmen killers were all Braiths and Shanagates, and the Shanagate Holding was thenceforth leagued only to itself. Vikor's banner was soon abandoned and forgotten, until the Festival caused us to remember it." Janacek paused and glanced toward Dirk. "Can you see the truth now, t'Larien?"

"I can see why Kavalars and Kimdissi don't like each other much." Dirk admitted.

Janacek laughed. "It goes beyond our own history," he said. "Kimdiss has fought no wars, but the world has bloody hands. When Tober-in-the-Veil attacked Wolfheim, the manipulators supplied both sides. When civil war flared on ai-Emerel between the urbanites whose universe is a single building and the disaffected star-seekers who urged a broader horizon, Kimdiss was deeply involved, giving the urbanites the means to win conclusively." He grinned. "In truth, t'Larien, there are even tales of Kimdissi plots *within* the Tempter's Veil. It is said it was Kimdissi agents who set the Steel Angels and the Altered Men of Prometheus against each other, who deposed the Fourth Cuchulainn of Tara because he refused to trade with them, who interfered on Braque to keep technology stillborn beneath the weight of the Braqui priests. Do you know the ancient religion of Kimdiss?"

"No."

"You would approve," Janacek said. "It is a peaceful and civilized creed, exceedingly complex. You can use it to justify anything except personal violence. Yet their great prophet, the Son of the Dreamer—accepted as a myth-figure, but they continue to revere him—he said once, 'Remember, your enemy has an enemy.' Indeed he does. That is the heart of Kimdissi wisdom."

Dirk shifted uneasily in his seat. "And you're saying that Ruark—"

"I am saying nothing," Janacek interrupted. "Draw your own conclusions. You need not accept mine. I told all of this to Gwen Delvano once, because she stood *cro-betheyn* to me and I had a concern. She was vastly amused. The history meant nothing, she told me. Arkin Ruark was only himself, not some archetype of outworld history. So she informed me. He was also her friend, I was told, and this bond, this *friendship"* —his voice was acid as he said the word—"somehow transcended the fact that he was a liar and a Kimdissi. Gwen told me to look to my own history. If Arkin Ruark was a manipulator by mere fact of birth on Kimdiss, then I was a taker of mockman heads by simple virtue of being Kavalar."

Dirk considered that. "She was right, you know," he said quietly.

"Oh? Was she?"

"Her argument was right," Dirk said. "It seems as though she was wrong in her assessment of Ruark, but in general—"

"In general it is better to distrust all Kimdissi," Janacek said firmly. "You have been deceived and used, t'Larien, yet you do not learn. You are very like Gwen. Enough of this."

He tapped one of the viewscreens with a knuckle. "We have the mountains close at hand. It will not be long now."

Dirk had been gripping his laser rifle very tightly. He wiped his sweating palms on his trousers. "You have a plan?"

"Yes," said Janacek, grinning. And at that he leaned across the space between them and smoothly snatched the laser from off Dirk's lap. "A very simple plan, in truth," he continued, setting the weapon down carefully out of reach. "I will hand you over to Lorimaar."

chapter 12

Dirk was not startled. Beneath his clothing the whisperjewel was still cold against his skin, reminding him of past promises and past betrayals. He had almost ceased to care. He folded his arms and waited.

Janacek looked disappointed. "You do not seem concerned," he said.

"It doesn't matter, Garse," Dirk answered. "When I left Kryne Lamiya, I expected to die." He sighed. "How is all this going to do Jaan any good?"

Janacek did not answer at once; his blue eyes appraised Dirk carefully. "You are changing, t'Larien," he said at last, the smile gone from his face. "Do you truly care more about Jaan Vikary's fate than about your own?"

"How would I know?" Dirk said. "Get on with your plan!"

Janacek frowned. "I considered a landing in the Braith camp and a direct confrontation. I rejected the idea. My death wish has not waxed so greatly as yours. While I might call one or several of the hunters to duel, it would be too obviously in aid of a criminal outbonder. They would never face me. My own status is tenuous at the moment; because of my words and actions in Challenge, the Braiths still think me human, although in disgrace. Should I openly seek to help Jaan, however, I would taint myself in their eyes. The courtesies of code would no longer rule. I too would become a criminal, a probable mockman.

"A second alternative was to attack them suddenly, without warning, and kill as many as we could. I am not yet so depraved as to consider that idea. Even Jaan's deed against Myrik would be clean compared to such a crime.

"It would be best, of course, if we could fly in and locate Jaan and get him away, safely and secretly. Yet I see little chance of this. The Braiths have hounds. We have none. They are experienced hunters and trackers, particularly Pyr Braith Oryan and Lorimaar high-Braith himself. I am less skilled, and you are useless. The chances are excellent that they would find Jaan before we did."

"Yes," said Dirk. "So?"

"I am being a false Kavalar in aiding Jaan at all," Janacek said in a faintly troubled voice. "Thus I will be just a bit more false. In that lies our best chance. We will fly in openly, and I will hand you over, as I have said. That act should gain at least a grudging trust from them. Then I will join the hunt, and do all that I can short of murder. Perhaps I can provoke a quarrel and call some of them to duel in a manner that will not make it seem as though I am protecting Jaan Vikary."

"You could lose," Dirk pointed out.

Janacek nodded. "Truth enough. I could lose. Yet I do not think so. In singled duel, only Bretan Braith Lantry is a really dangerous antagonist, and he and his *teyn* are not among the hunters, if the aircars you saw are all. Lorimaar has his skills, but Jaan wounded him in Challenge. Pyr is fast and talented with his little stick, but not with a blade or a sidearm. The others are old men and weaklings. I would not lose."

"And if you can't trick them into dueling?"

"Then I can be near when they run down Jaan."

"And then?"

"I do not know. They will not take him, though. I promise you that, t'Larien. They will not take him."

"And meanwhile, what about me?"

Janacek looked over once again, and once more the blue eyes regarded him thoughtfully. "You will be in great danger," the Kavalar said, "but I do not think they will kill you immediately, and certainly not as I will hand you to them, bound and helpless. They will wish to hunt you. Pyr will probably claim you. I hope that they will cut you free and strip you and set you to running in the forest. If some of them elect to hunt you, less will be hunting Jaan. There is another possibility as well. In Challenge, Pyr and Bretan were near to quarreling over you. Should Bretan ever join the hunters, it is likely they would resume their conflict. We can only benefit by that."

Dirk smiled. "Your enemy has an enemy," he said sardonically.

Janacek grimaced. "I am no Arkin Ruark," he said. "I will help you if I can. Before we enter the Braith camp, we will drop—dark and secret, if we can—to this downed aircar you saw, this dead fire. We will leave your laser in the wreck. Then, after they have cut you free and sent you naked into the forest, you can make for the weapon, and hopefully surprise those who come after you." He shrugged. "Your life may depend on how fast and straight you can run, and how accurately you can fire your rifle."

"And whether I can kill," Dirk added.

"And whether you can kill," Janacek acknowledged. "I can give you no better chances, t'Larien."

"I accept the ones you offer," Dirk said. Then they flew in silence for a long time. But when the black knives of the mountainwall had finally fallen behind them, and Janacek had doused all the aircar's lights and begun his slow, careful descent, Dirk turned to speak to him once more. "What would you have done," he asked, "if I had refused to play along with your deceit?"

Garse Janacek swiveled in his seat and laid his right hand on Dirk's arm. The untouched glowstones burned very faintly in the iron of his bracelet. "The bond of fire-and-iron is stronger than any bond you know," the Kavalar said in a grave voice, "and far stronger than any bonds of fleeting gratitude. Had you refused me, t'Larien, I would have cut your tongue from your mouth so you could not tell the Braiths of my plans, and I would have proceeded. Willing or unwilling, you would have played your role. Understand, t'Larien, I do not hate you, though you have earned my hate several times over. At times I have even found myself liking you, as much as an Ironjade may like an outbonder. I would not have hurt you out of malice. Yet I would have hurt you. For I have considered carefully, and my plan is Jaan Vikary's best hope."

As he spoke, not the faintest trace of a smile could be seen on Janacek's face. For once he was not joking.

Dirk did not have long to reflect on Janacek's words. They dropped down through the night like some impossibly light boulder and flitted wraithlike above the tops of the chokers. The wreck still smoldered a dim orange (the light seeping from the core of a blackened, fallen tree), and a haze of smoke obscured its contours. Janacek hovered over the crash, opened one of the great armored doors, and tossed the laser rifle to the forest floor a few meters below. At Dirk's insistence, he also threw out the Braith jacket Dirk had been wearing, whose fur and heavy leather would be a godsend to a man running naked through the forest.

Afterwards they soared straight up again, high into the sky, and Garse bound Dirk hand and foot, the thin cords tight and painful, threatening to cut off circulation, and so very authentic. Then, after flicking on his headlamps and running lights, Janacek took them swooping toward the circle of lights.

The hounds were staked out and sleeping by the water's edge, but they woke when the strange aircar descended, and Janacek landed in the midst of their wild howling. Only one of the Braiths was about, the skin-and-bones hunter whose unkempt black hair stood out as stiffly as if it had been fried to a charcoal crisp. Pyr's *teyn,* Dirk knew, though he did not know his name. The man was sitting by a low campfire near the Braith hounds, a laser rifle by his side, when they first saw him, but he scrambled to his feet swiftly enough as they came down.

Janacek unsealed the massive door again, swinging it up and open and letting the cold night flow into the warmth of the cabin. He pulled Dirk to his feet and shoved him roughly outside, forcing him to kneel in the cool sand.

"Ironjade," the man on guard said harshly. By then his *kethi* had started to gather, pulling themselves from their sleeping bags and piling out of the aircars.

"I have a gift for you," Janacek said, his hands on his hips. "An offering from Ironjade to Braith."

The hunters were six in number, Dirk saw as he looked up from where he knelt; all of them had been in Challenge. Bald, bulky Pyr had been sleeping outside near his *teyn;* he was the first one on hand. Soon afterwards Roseph high-Braith and his quiet muscular companion joined them. They too had been asleep on the ground near their aircar. Lastly Lorimaar high-Braith Arkellor, the left side of his chest wrapped in dark bandages, came slowly from the domed red aircar, leaning on the arm of the fat man who had been with him before. All six of them appeared as they had slept—fully dressed, and armed.

"The gift," Pyr said, "is appreciated, Ironjade." He wore a sidearm on a black metallic belt, but his baton was missing, and he looked almost incomplete without it.

"Your presence is *not* appreciated," Lorimaar said,

as he struggled to join the circle. He was leaning much of his weight on his *teyn,* so that he seemed hunched and broken, no longer quite the giant he had been. And Dirk, looking at him, thought he could see new creases in the dark, deeply lined skin—fresh-carved runnels of pain.

"It is obvious now that the duels for which I was named arbiter will never come to pass," Roseph said evenly, with none of the heavy hostility that thickened Lorimaar's voice, "so I have no particular authority, and I cannot pretend to speak for High Kavalaan, or Braith. Yet I am certain that I speak for all of us. We will not tolerate your interference, Ironjade. Blood-gift or no."

"Truth," Lorimaar said.

"I do not seek to interfere," Janacek told them. "I seek to join you."

"We hunt your *teyn,*" Pyr's companion said.

"He knows that," Pyr snapped.

"I have no *teyn,*" Janacek said. "An animal roams the forest, wearing my iron-and-fire. I would help you kill it, and reclaim the thing that is mine." He sounded very hard, very convincing.

One of the hounds was stalking back and forth impatiently on its chain. It growled and stopped long enough to wrinkle its rat's face at Janacek and bare a row of yellowed canines. "He is a liar," Lorimaar high-Braith said. "Even our dogs smell out his lies. They do not like him."

"A mockman," added his *teyn.*

Garse Janacek turned his head very slightly. The shifting firelight woke red highlights in his beard as he smiled his thin and threatening smile. "Saanel Braith," he said, "your *teyn* is wounded and thus insults me with impunity, knowing I cannot call on him to make his choices. You enjoy no such safety."

"For the moment he *does,*" Roseph said harshly. "That is a trick we do not allow you, Ironjade. You will not duel us, one by one, and save your outbond *teyn.*"

"I have sworn that I have no wish to save him. I have no *teyn*. You cannot strip me of my rights under the code."

Small, shriveled Roseph—the smallest of the Kavalars by half a meter—stared at Janacek and refused to flinch. "We are on Worlorn," he said. "And we do what we will." Several of the others muttered agreement.

"You are Kavalars," Janacek insisted, but a flicker of doubt passed across his face. "You are Braiths and highbonds of Braith, bound to your holdfast and your council and its ways."

"In years past," Pyr said with a smile, "I have seen many of my *kethi* and even more the men of other holdfasts abandon the old wisdoms. 'This and this and this are wrong,' the mincing Ironjades would say. 'We will not follow them.' And the sheep of Redsteel would echo them, and the womanly men of Shanagate, and sadly many Braiths. Are my memories false? You stand and preach code at us, but do I not recall the Ironjades in my youth telling me that I may hunt mockmen no longer? Am I misremembering the soft Kavalars who were sent to Avalon to learn spaceships and weaponry and other useful things, who returned full of lies about how we must change this way, and that way, how so much of our old code was a thing of shame, when it had been so long a pride to us? Tell me, Ironjade, *am* I wrong?"

Garse said nothing. He folded his arms tightly against his chest.

"Jaan Vikary, once high-Ironjade, was the greatest of the changers, the liars. You were not far behind," Lorimaar said.

"I have never been to Avalon," Janacek said simply.

"Answer me," Pyr said. "Did you and Vikary not seek to change old ways? Did you not laugh at the parts of the code you disliked?"

"I have never broken code," Janacek said. "Jaan . . . Jaan would sometimes . . ." He faltered.

"He admits it," fat Saanel said.

"We have talked among ourselves," Roseph said in a calm voice. "If highbonds can kill outside the code, if the things we know as truth can be changed and disregarded, then we too can make changes, and shun false wisdoms we do not care for. We are bound by Braith no longer, Ironjade. It is the best of holdfasts, but that is not good enough. Our old *kethi* had taken too many soft lies to their hearts. We will be twisted and toyed with no more. We will return to the old true things, to the creed that was ancient before Bronzefist fell, even to the days when the highbonds of Ironjade and Taal and the Deep Coal Dwellings fought together against demons in the Lameraan Hills."

"You see, Ironjade," Pyr said, "you call us false names."

"I did not know," Janacek said, a bit slowly.

"Call us truly. We are no Braiths."

The Ironjade's eyes seemed dark and hooded. His arms were still crossed. He looked at Lorimaar. "You have made a new holdfast," he said.

"There is precedent," Roseph said. "Redsteel was birthed by those who broke from Glowstone Mountain, and Braith itself grew out of Bronzefist."

"I am Lorimaar Reln Winterfox high-*Larteyn* Arkellor," Lorimaar said in his hard, pain-filled voice.

"Honor to your holdfast," Janacek answered, holding himself stiffly, "honor to your *teyn.*"

"We are all Larteyns," Roseph said.

Pyr laughed. "We are the highbond council of Larteyn, and we keep the old codes," he said.

In the silence that followed, Janacek's eyes went from one face to the next. Dirk, still helpless and kneeling in the sand, watched his head move, turning from one to the other. "You have named yourself Larteyns," Janacek said at last, "and so you are Larteyns. All the old wisdoms agree on that much. Yet I remind you that all the things you speak of, the men and teachings and the holdfasts you invoke, all these things are dead. Bronzefist and Taal were destroyed in highwars before any of you were born, and the Deep Coal Dwellings were flooded and empty even during the Time of Fire and Demons."

"Their wisdoms live in Larteyn," Saanel said.

"You are only six," Janacek said, "and Worlorn is dying."

"Under us it will thrive again," Roseph said. "News will go back to High Kavalaan and others will come. Our sons will be born here, to hunt these choker-woods."

"As you will," said Janacek. "It is no matter to me. Ironjade has no grievance with Larteyn. I come to you openly and ask to join your hunt." His hand dropped to Dirk's shoulder. "And I bring you a blood-gift."

"Truth," Pyr said and was silent for a moment. Then, to the others: "I say let him come."

"No," said Lorimaar. "I do not trust him. He is too eager."

"For a reason, Lorimaar high-Larteyn," Janacek said. "A great shame has been put on my holdfast and my name. I seek to wipe it clean."

"A man must keep his pride, no matter the pain," Roseph said, nodding. "That is truth enough for any-one."

"Let him hunt," Roseph's *teyn* said. "We are six and he is alone. How can he harm us?"

"He is a liar!" Lorimaar insisted. "How did he come to us here? Ask yourselves that! And look!" He pointed at Janacek's right arm, where glowstones burned like red eyes in their settings. Only a handful were missing.

Janacek put his left hand on his knife and slid it smoothly from its sheath. Then he held out his right hand to Pyr. "Help me hold my arm steady," he said in a calm conversational tone, "and I will cast away Jaan Vikary's false fires."

Pyr did as he was asked. No one spoke. Janacek's hand was sure and quick. When he was finished, glow-stones lay in the sand like coals from a scattered fire.

He bent and picked one up, tossed it lightly into the air and caught it again, as if he were testing its weight, smiling all the while. Then he drew back his arm and threw; the stone sailed up and off a long way before it began to fall. At the far end of its arc, sinking, it looked a bit like a shooting star. Dirk almost expected it to hiss when it sank into the lake's dark waters. But there was no sound at all, not even a splash at this distance.

Janacek picked up all of the glowstones in turn, rolled them in his palm briefly, and gave them to the lake.

When the last of them was gone, he turned back to the hunters and held out his right arm. "Empty iron," he said. "Look. My *teyn* is dead."

After that there was no more trouble.

"Dawn is near upon us," Pyr said. "Set my prey to running."

So the hunters turned their attention to Dirk, and it went much as he had been told it would go. They cut him free of his bonds and let him rub his wrists and ankles a bit to get his blood moving once again. Then he was pushed back against an aircar, and Roseph and fat Saanel held him still while Pyr himself cut his clothes away. The bald hunter handled his little knife as deftly as he did his baton, but he was not gentle; he left a long cut down the inside of Dirk's thigh, and a shorter deeper one on his chest.

Dirk winced when Pyr slashed him, but made no effort to resist. Until he was finally naked, and beginning to shiver in the wind, his back pressed too hard against the cold metal flank of the aircar.

Pyr frowned suddenly. "What's this?" he said, and his small white hand wrapped around the whisper-jewel where it hung against Dirk's chest.

"No," Dirk said.

Pyr yanked hard and twisted. The fine silver chain dug painfully into Dirk's throat; the jewel popped free of its improvised clip.

"No!" Dirk shouted. He threw himself forward suddenly and began to struggle. Roseph stumbled and lost his grip on Dirk's right arm and went down. Saanel hung on grimly. Dirk punched him hard in his bull-thick neck, just beneath his chin. The fat man let go with an oath, and Dirk swung around at Pyr.

Pyr had picked up his baton. He was smiling. Dirk took a single quick step toward him and stopped.

That was enough of a hesitation. Saanel slid a thick arm around his head from behind and began applying a headlock that gradually turned into a choke.

Pyr watched with disinterest. He thrust his baton into the sand and held the whisperjewel between thumb and forefinger. "Mockman jewelry," he said disdainfully. It meant nothing to him; there was no resonance in his mind with the patterns esper-etched into the gemstone. Perhaps he noticed how cold the little teardrop was to his touch, perhaps not—but he heard no whispers. He called to his *teyn,* who was kicking sand onto the fire. "Would you like a gift from t'Larien?"

Saying nothing, the man came over and took the jewel and held it briefly, then put it into a pocket of his jacket. He turned away unsmiling and began to walk around the perimeter of the Braith camp, extinguishing the ring of electric hand torches planted in the sand. As the lights went out, Dirk saw that the first blush of dawn was on the eastern horizon.

Pyr waved his baton at Saanel. "Release him," he ordered, and the fat man undid his chokehold and stepped away. Dirk stood free again. His neck ached, and the dry sand beneath his feet was coarse and cold. He felt very vulnerable. Without the whisperjewel, he was now very much afraid. He looked around for Garse Janacek, but the Ironjade was off on the other side of the camp talking intently to Lorimaar.

"Dawn is already here," Pyr said. "I can come after you at once, mockman. Run."

Dirk glanced over his shoulder. Roseph was frowning and massaging his shoulder; he had fallen hard when Dirk yanked loose. Saanel, smirking, was lean-ing back against the aircar. Dirk took a few hesitant steps away from them, toward the forest.

"Come, t'Larien, I am certain you can run faster than that," Pyr called out to him. "Run fast enough, and you may live. I will be on foot as well, and my *teyn,* and our hounds." He took out his sidearm and tossed it through the air, spinning, toward Saanel, who caught it and smothered it in two massive slab-fingered hands. "I will carry no laser, t'Larien," Pyr continued. "This will be a pure clean hunt, of the oldest sort. A hunter with his knife and his throwing-blade, a naked prey. Run, t'Larien, run!" His bony black-haired companion had come over to join him. "My *teyn,*" Pyr said to him, "unchain our hounds."

Dirk spun and began sprinting for the edge of the wood.

It was a run out of nightmare.

They had taken his boots; no sooner had he gone three meters into the trees than he cut his foot on a sharp rock in the dark and began to limp. There were other rocks. Running, he seemed to find them all.

They had taken his clothes; it was better in the shelter of the trees, where the wind was not so bad, but he was still cold. Very cold. He had gooseflesh for a time, then it passed. Other pains came, and the cold seemed less important.

The outworld wilderness was too dark and too light. Too dark to see where he was going. He stumbled over roots, skinned his knees and palms badly, ran into holes. But it was too light as well. Dawn was com-ing too fast, too fast, the light spreading agonizingly through the trees. He was losing his beacon. He looked up at it every time he reached a clear space, every time he could see between the dense overhang-ing foliage, looked up and found it. A single bright red star, High Kavalaan's own star aflame in Wor-lorn's sky. Garse had pointed it out to him, and told him to follow it if he lost his way. It would lead him through the woods to his laser and his jacket. But dawn was coming, coming too quickly; the Braiths had delayed too long in cutting him loose. And every time he looked up again and tried to go the right way— the forest was thick and confusing, the chokers formed impenetrable walls at points and forced him to take detours, all directions looked the same, it was easy to go astray—every time he searched for his beacon, it was fainter, more washed out. The eastern light had taken on a reddish tinge; Fat Satan was rising somewhere, and soon his homing star would be washed from a mock-twilight sky. He tried to run faster.

It was less than a kilometer to run, less than a kilometer. But a kilometer is a long way to go through a wilderness, naked, close to lost. He had been running ten minutes when he heard the Braith hounds baying wildly behind him.

After that, he neither thought nor worried. He ran.

He ran in animal panic, breathing hard, bleeding, his whole body trembling and aching. The run became an endless thing, a thing outside of time, a fever dream of frantic pumping feet and snatches of vivid sensation and the noises behind him of the hounds, growing ever closer—or so it seemed. He ran and ran, and got nowhere, and ran and ran, and did not move. He crashed through a thick wall of firebriars, and the red-tipped thorns cut his flesh in a hundred places, and he did not cry; he ran, he ran. He reached an area of smooth gray slate and tried to scramble over it quickly and fell and smashed his chin with a crack against the stone and his mouth was full of blood and he spat it out. Blood on the rock, as well, no wonder he had fallen; his blood, all of it, from the cuts on his feet.

He crawled over the smooth stone and reached the trees again and ran some more, wild, until he remembered that he was not looking for his beacon. And when he found it again, it was back behind him and to the side, very faint, a small shining dot in a scarlet sky, and he turned and went to it and across the stone once more, tripping over unseen roots, tearing the foliage away with wild hands, running, running. He ran into a low branch, sat down hard, got up holding his head, ran on. He tripped on a slimy bed of moss, black, smelling of rot, rose covered with the slime and the smell, ran on, ran on. He looked for his beacon star, and it was gone. He kept going. It had to be the right way, it had to. The hounds were behind him, baying. It was only a kilometer, it was less than a kilometer. He was freezing. He was on fire. His chest was full of knives. He kept running, staggered and tripped and fell, got up, kept running. The hounds were behind him, close, close, the hounds were behind him.

And then suddenly—he did not know when, he did not know how long he had been running, he did not know how far he had come, the star was gone—he thought he caught the faint odor of smoke on the forest wind. He ran toward it, and came out from among the trees into a small clearing, and ran toward the other side of the barren open space, and stopped.

The hounds were in front of him.

One of them, at least. It came slinking out of the trees snarling, its little eyes deadly, its hairless snout drawn back to flash its ugly fangs. He tried to run around it and it was on him, knocking him over, slashing at him and rolling with him, then jumping up. Dirk struggled to his knees; the hound circled him and snapped savagely whenever he tried to rise to his feet. It had bitten his left arm and drawn more blood. But it had not killed him, had not torn out his throat. Trained, he thought, it was trained. It circled him, circled, its eyes never leaving him. Pyr had sent it out ahead and was coming behind with his *teyn* and his other dogs. This one would keep him trapped here until they arrived.

He jumped to his feet suddenly, lunged toward the trees. The dog leaped, knocked him over again, wrestled him to the ground, and almost tore loose his arm. This time he did not get up. The hound backed off again, stood waiting, poised, its mouth wet with blood and slaver. Dirk tried to push himself up with his good arm. He crawled a half-meter. The hound growled. The others were near. He heard the baying.

Then, from above, he heard something else. He looked up weakly into the small slice of cloud-streaked sky, dim with the dawning rays of the Hell-eye and its attendants. The Braith hound, backing off from him a meter, was looking up too. And the *sound* came again. It was a wail and a war yell, a lingering ululating shriek, a death hoot that was almost musical in its intensity. Dirk wondered if he were dying and hearing the sounds of Kryne Lamiya in his mind. But the hound heard it too. It was squatting, paralyzed, looking up.

A dark shape dropped from the sky.

Dirk saw it fall. It was huge, very black, pitch almost, and its underside was puckered with a thousand small red mouths, and they were all open, all singing, all sounding that terrible shuddering wail. It had no head that he could see; it was triangular, a wide dark sail, a wind-borne manta ray, a leather cloak someone had cast loose in the sky. A leather cloak with mouths, though, and a long thin tail.

He saw the tail whip around once, suddenly, and snap at the Braith hound's face. The dog blinked and stepped back. The flying creature hovered for an instant, beating its vast wings with exquisite rippling slowness, then settled down over the hound and wrapped itself around it. Both animals were silent. The hound—the huge muscular rat-faced dog that stood as tall as a man—the hound was gone. The other covered it completely, and lay in the grass and the dirt like a black leather sausage of immense proportions.

Everything was silent. The hunter's wail had stilled the entire forest. He did not hear the other hounds.

Carefully he rose to his feet and walked, limping,

around the torpid killer-cloak. It scarcely seemed to stir. In the dawn half-light, it might have been a big misshapen log.

In his mind, Dirk saw it still as it had looked in the sky: a black shape, howling, falling, all wing and mouth. For an instant, glimpsing only the silhouette, he had thought that Jaan Vikary had come to rescue him, flying the gray manta aircar.

The far side of the clearing was a choker tangle, thick and yellow-brown and very dense. But the smoke came from beyond it. Wearily Dirk dodged and squeezed and pushed the waxy limbs aside, breaking them when he had to, and forced his way through.

The wreck had ceased to burn, but a thin pall of smoke still hung above it. One wing had scraped along the ground, tearing a great gouge in the earth and felling several trees before snapping; the other jabbed up into the air, its bat shape distorted by fused runnels of frozen metal and holes punched through it by a laser cannon. The cabin was black and shapeless, open to the outside through a wide jagged hole.

Dirk found his laser rifle nearby. He also found bones: two skeletons twisted around each other in a death's embrace, the bones dark and wet, still brown with blood and bits of clinging meat. One skeleton was human, or had been. All the arms and legs were broken, and most of the ribs shattered and gone, but Dirk recognized the triple-pronged metal claw that ended one twice-broken arm. Mingled with it, and just as dead, were the remains of whatever creature had dragged the carcass from the smoking aircar out into the open—some scavenger whose bones were black-veined and rubbery-looking, curved and very big. The banshee had caught it feeding. No wonder it had been so close.

There was no trace of the leather and fur jacket that he and Garse had dropped here. Dirk dragged himself over to the cold hulk of the aircar and climbed into its shadowed maw. He cut himself on a sharp metal surface going in, but hardly noticed it;

what was one more cut now? He settled down to wait, sheltered from the wind, and hoping he was hidden from banshee and Braiths both. Most of his wounds seemed to have clotted, he noted dully. At least he was only bleeding fitfully, here and there. But the brown scabs that had formed were all crusted with dirt, and he wondered if he should do something to fight infection. It did not seem to matter, though; he pushed the thought aside and held his laser a bit more tightly, hoping the hunters would get here soon.

What had slowed them down? Perhaps they were afraid of disturbing the banshee; that made a certain amount of sense. He lay down in the cold ashes, resting his head on his arm, and tried not to think, not to feel. His feet were bundles of raw agony. Awkwardly he tried to lift them in the air, so they would not touch anything. That helped a little, but he did not have the strength to hold them up for long. His arm was throbbing where the Braith hound had bitten him. For a time he wished fervently that he could stop hurting, that his head would stop spinning so badly. Then he changed his mind. The pain, he thought, was probably the only thing that was keeping him conscious. And if he fell asleep now, somehow he did not think it likely that he would ever wake up again.

He saw Fat Satan hanging over the forest, its bloody disc half obscured by a screen of blue-black branches. Nearby a single yellow sun burned very brightly, a small spark in the firmament. He blinked at them. They were old friends.

The sound of Braith hounds brought him back to attention. Ten meters away, the hunters came eagerly out of the foliage. Not as close as he had expected them. Of course, he thought, they had gone around the chokers instead of fighting through them. Pyr Braith was almost invisible, blue-black like the tree he stood against, but Dirk saw his motion, and the baton he carried in one hand, and the bright silvery shaft taller than he that he held in the other. His *teyn* was a few steps ahead of him, holding two hounds on short chains; the dogs were barking wildly and pulling him forward almost at a trot. A third hound ran free at his side, and began bounding toward the downed aircar as soon as it was out of the underbrush.

Dirk, lying on his stomach amid the ashes and the shattered instruments of the wreck, suddenly found it all immensely funny. Pyr hefted his silver shaft above his head and began to run; he was sure he had his prey at last. But he had no laser, and Dirk did. Giggling and giddy, Dirk raised the rifle and took careful aim.

As he fired, a memory came back to him, as sudden and stabbing as the pulse of light that flashed from his laser. Janacek, just a short time ago, stern-faced, shrugging: *Your life may depend on how fast and straight you can run, and how accurately you can fire your rifle,* he had said. And Dirk had added; *And whether I can kill.* It had seemed terribly important, the killing; how much more difficult it would be than simple running.

He giggled again. The running had been very difficult. The killing was just something he did, and it was almost easy.

The bright burning knife of the laser hung in the air for a long second, impaling Pyr square in his broad gut as he ran toward the hulk. The Braith stumbled and fell to his knees. His mouth hung open absurdly for a second before he collapsed on his face and was lost to Dirk's sight. The long silver blade he had carried remained stuck in the torn ground, swaying back and forth as the wind whipped at it.

Pyr's black-haired companion let go of the chain he was holding and seemed to freeze when his *teyn* went down. Dirk moved the laser slightly and fired once more, but nothing happened; the weapon was still in its fifteen-second recycle. That made the hunting a *sport,* he remembered; it gave the game a chance to get away if you missed. He found himself giggling again.

The hunter woke up and threw himself flat, rolling over the ground into the long gully ripped by the aircar's wing. Down in the trenches looking for his laser, Dirk thought, but he won't find it.

The hounds had surrounded the aircar, barking at him whenever he shifted his position or raised his head. None of them tried to come in for the kill. That was the hunter's business. Dirk took careful aim and shot the nearest one through the throat. It dropped like dead meat, and the other two backed off. Pulling himself to his knees, Dirk crawled out of his shelter. He tried to stand, steadying himself with one hand on the twisted wing. The world was spinning. Savage stabbing pains ran up his legs, and he found he could no longer feel his feet at all. But somehow he kept himself erect.

A shout rang out, something in Old Kavalar; Dirk did not know the word. The huge hounds charged, one right after the other, wet red mouths agape, snarling. And in the corner of his eye he saw the hunter emerging, two meters away, his knife out already. One of his long thin arms flicked it around in a sideways sort of motion, and it clattered off the aircar wing Dirk was leaning against. Already the man had turned and was running, and the nearest hound was there, in the air. Dirk let himself fall and brought up the rifle. The canines snapped, missed, but the beast's body smashed into him, knocking him spinning, and then it was on top of him in the dust. Somehow he found the trigger. There was a brief light and the smell of wet hair burning and an awful whine. The hound snapped again, feebly, choking on its own blood. Dirk pushed the carcass off and struggled to one knee. The Braith had reached Pyr's body and was lifting the long silver blade. The other hound had caught its loose chain on a jagged edge of the wreck. When Dirk rose, it yelped and lunged, and the whole great burned hulk of the aircar seemed to shake a little and move, but still the beast was caught.

The black-haired hunter had the silver thing. Dirk

aimed his laser and fired; the beam burned wide, but a second is long enough, and Dirk swung the rifle sharply, right to left, left to right.

The man fell even as he released his weapon. It sailed a few meters, slid off the twisted wing, and stuck in the ground, where it moved back and forth in the wind. Dirk was still swinging his laser, left right left right left right, long after the hunter had fallen and the light had gone out. Finally it recycled and pulsed again for a second, burning nothing but a row of chokers, and Dirk, startled, released his hold on the trigger and dropped the weapon.

The hound, still caught, was snarling and lunging. Dirk looked at it, open-mouthed, almost uncomprehending. Then he giggled. He got down on his knees, found the laser, and began to crawl toward the Kavalars. It took an awfully long time. His feet hurt. His arm as well, where he had been bitten. The hound finally fell silent, but there was no quiet. Dirk could hear crying, a continuous low whimper.

He dragged himself through the dirt and the ashes, over the burned-out trunk of a choker, to where the hunters had fallen. They were lying side by side. The gaunt one, the one whose name he had never learned, who had tried to kill him with his knife and his dogs and his silver blade, that one was still, and his mouth was full of blood. Pyr, lying face down, was the source of the whimpers. Dirk knelt by him, shoved his hands beneath him, laboriously turned him over. His face was covered with ashes and blood; he had smashed his nose when he fell, and a thin red trickle still ran from one nostril, leaving a bright trail across his soot-smeared cheeks. His face was old. He kept whimpering and did not seem to see Dirk at all, and his hands were clutching his stomach. Dirk stared at him for a long time. He touched one of his hands—it was strangely soft and small, clean except for a single black slash that ran across the palm, almost a child's hand that ought not to belong to that old bald face —and lifted it away and did the same with the other hand and looked at the hole he had burned in Pyr's gut. A big gut and a small dark hole; it ought not to have hurt him so much. No blood, either, except from his nose. That was almost funny, but Dirk discovered that he had no more giggles left in him.

Pyr opened his mouth then, and Dirk wondered if the man was trying to tell him something, some last words perhaps, some plea for forgiveness. But the Braith only made a thick choking sound, and then resumed his low whimpers.

His baton was lying nearby. Dirk took it up and wrapped his hands around the hardwood knob at one end and placed the small blade over Pyr's chest where his heart ought to be and leaned all his weight forward and down, thinking to give the other release. The hunter's heavy body thrashed horribly for an instant, and Dirk withdrew the blade and thrust it in again, and yet again, but Pyr would not keep still. The little blade was too short, Dirk decided after a time, so he used it differently, found an artery in Pyr's fleshy throat, held the baton very tightly right up by the knife end and pressed it in through the pale fatty skin. There was a terrible lot of blood then, a spurting stream that caught Dirk right in the face until he let go of the baton and pushed himself away. Pyr thrashed again and his neck continued to spurt where Dirk had cut him, and Dirk watched, but each spurt was a little feebler than the one before, and after a time the fountain was only a trickle and after another time it seemed to stop. The ashes and the dirt drank up a lot of the blood, but there was still a great deal of it around, a regular little pool of it between the two of them, and Dirk had never known that a man had enough blood in him to form a real pool of blood. He felt very sick. But at least Pyr was still, and the whimpering had stopped.

He sat alone, resting, in the wan red light. He was very hot and very cold all at once, and he knew he should take some clothing from the corpses and cover himself, but he could not find the strength. His feet hurt horribly, and his arm had swollen to twice its normal size. He did not sleep, but he was barely conscious. He watched Fat Satan rise higher and higher in the sky, approaching noon, with the bright yellow suns shining painfully around it. He heard the Braith hound howling several times, and once he listened to the eerie hunting wail of the banshee and wondered if the creature would come back to eat him and the men he had killed. But the cry seemed a long way off, and perhaps it was only his fever, and perhaps it was only the wind.

When the sticky wet film on his face had dried to a brown crust and the little pool of blood that lay in the dust was finally gone, Dirk knew that he must move again, or he would die here. He considered dying for a long time; it seemed like a very good idea, somehow, but he could not bring himself to do it. He remembered Gwen. He crawled over to where the body of Pyr's *teyn* was lying, ignoring his pain as best he could, and went through the man's pockets. He found the whisperjewel.

Ice in his fist, ice in his mind, memories of promises, lies, love. Jenny. My Guinevere, and he was Lancelot. He could not fail her. He could not. He crushed the cold teardrop hard in his hand and took the ice into his soul. He made himself stand up.

After that it was easier. Slowly he stripped the dead man of his clothing and dressed, though everything was too long for him and the shirt and the chameleon cloth jacket had been slash-burned across the front and the man had fouled his pants. Dirk pulled off the corpse's boots as well, but they were too narrow for his bloodied, scab-crusted feet, and he was forced to use Pyr's. Pyr had huge feet.

Using his laser rifle and Pyr's baton as canes, he struggled toward the wild. A few meters into the trees he stopped and looked back briefly. The huge hound was barking and howling and fighting to yank free, and the aircar gave a metallic shudder every time it lunged. He could see the naked body in the dirt, and beyond it the tall silvery thing, still swaying in the wind. Pyr he could hardly see at all. Beneath the bloodstains, the hunter's suit had gone to a mottled black and brown, and here and there a dull red, so he blended with the ground he had died on.

Dirk left the hound chained and barking, and limped off through the tangled chokers.

chapter **13**

The run from the hunters' camp to the wrecked aircar had covered less than a kilometer, and it had seemed to Dirk to take forever. The walk back took twice as long. He was certain, afterwards, that he was not entirely conscious as he walked. What memories he retained were only pieces. Stumbling and falling, tearing his pants open at the knee. A swift-running cold stream where he stopped and washed the crusted blood from his face and took off his boots and plunged his feet into the icy rushing water until they had gone numb on him. Climbing over the tilted ridge of slate where he had fallen previously. A dark cave mouth staring at him, a promise of sleep and rest he did not heed. Losing his way, searching for the sun, finding it and following it, losing his way again. Tree-spooks flitting from branch to branch among the chokers, chittering in little voices. Dead white husks peering down at him from waxy limbs. Far off, the banshee wail, lingering, haunting. Stumbling again, half in clumsiness and half in fear. The baton rolling away from him, down a short sharp incline, lost among thick bushes that he did not bother to search. Walking, walking, putting one foot in front of the other, leaning on the baton and on the laser after the baton was gone, his feet aching, aching. The banshee again, closer, almost overhead. Looking up through a tapestry of branches into the gloomy sky, trying to spot it, failing. Walking, hurting. He remembered all those things, and knew that surely there were other things between them, connecting them one with the other, but those he did not remember. Perhaps he slept as he walked. But he did not stop walking.

It was late afternoon when he reached the small sandy area near the green lake. The aircars were still there, one twisted and lying deep in the water, the other three on the sand. The camp was deserted.

One of the cars—Lorimaar's huge domed vehicle—had a hound guarding it, bound to the door on a long black chain. The creature was lying down, but it rose at Dirk's approach and bared its teeth and growled at him. He found himself laughing wildly, insanely. He had walked all this long way, walked and walked and walked, and here was a dog chained to an aircar growling at him. He could have had that without ever moving half a meter.

He detoured carefully around the perimeter of the dog's chain and went to Janacek's car and climbed in and sealed the heavy door behind him. The cabin was dark and stuffy and cramped. After freezing for so long, he felt almost uncomfortably hot. He wanted to lie down, to sleep. But first he made himself search the supply locker, and he found a medical kit and pulled it out and opened it. It was full of pills and bandages and sprays. He wished he had thought to tell Janacek to drop the kit near the wreck, along with his laser. He knew that he should go outside and wash methodically in the lake and clean all the filth out of his wounds before trying to bandage them up, but the massive armored door looked too heavy to move again just now.

He pulled off his boots and stripped away his jacket and shirt and sprayed his swollen feet and his left arm with a powder that was supposed to prevent infection, or fight it, or something. He was too tired to read the instructions all the way through. Then he looked at the pills. He took two fever pills and four painkillers and two antibiotics, swallowing them dry because he had no water on hand.

Afterwards he lay down on the metal floorplates between the seats. Sleep came instantly.

He woke dry-mouthed and trembling and very nervous, some aftereffect of the pills. But he was thinking again, and his brow was cool (though covered with a clammy sweat) when he touched it with the back of his hand, and his feet were less painful than before. The swelling in his arm had subsided a bit also, although it was still bigger than normal and quite stiff. He put on his burned, blood-crusted shirt again and his jacket over it, gathered up the medkit, and went outside.

It was dusk; the western sky was all red and orange, and two small yellow suns burned intensely against the clouds of sunset. The Braiths had not returned. Jaan Vikary, armed and clothed and experienced, clearly knew how to run a good deal better than Dirk.

He walked across the sand to the lake. The water was frigid, but he got used to it soon enough, and the mud squished soothingly between his toes. He stripped and ducked his head and washed, then took out the medkit and did everything he should have done earlier, cleaning and bandaging his feet before slipping back into Pyr's boots, scrubbing out the worst of his wounds with disinfectant, dabbing at the inflamed bite marks on his arm with a salve that claimed to minimize allergic reactions. He swallowed another handful of painkillers as well, this time washing them down with fresh water scooped from the lake.

Night was settling quickly by the time he was dressed again. The Braith hound was lying by Lorimaar's aircar, gnawing at a chunk of meat, but there was no sign of its masters. Dirk walked carefully around the beast to the third aircar, the one belonging to Pyr and his *teyn*. He had decided that he could help himself to their supplies with relative impunity; the other Braiths, returning to an empty camp, would never know that anything had been taken.

Inside he found a whole rack of weapons: four laser rifles emblazoned with the familiar white wolf's head, a brace of dueling swords, knives, a silver throwing-blade two and a half meters long and an empty bracket beside it. And two pistols thrown carelessly onto a seat. He also found a locker of fresh clothing, and changed eagerly, stuffing his torn garments out of sight. The clothes fit badly, but felt very good. He helped himself to a mesh-steel belt, one of the side-arms, and a knee-length chameleon cloth greatcoat.

When he lifted the coat from where it had been hanging, it revealed another storage locker. Dirk yanked it open. Inside were four familiar boots and Gwen's sky-scoots. Pyr and his *teyn* had seemingly claimed them as booty.

Dirk smiled. He had never intended to take an air-car; the chances were too good that the hunters would see him at once, particularly if he overtook them by day. But he had not been thrilled by the prospect of walking, either. The scoots were the perfect answer. He wasted no time changing into the larger pair of boots, though he had to leave them unlaced after he got his bandaged feet inside.

Food was stored in the same locker as the scoots; protein bars, sticks of dried meat, a small chunk of crusty cheese. Dirk ate the cheese and shoved the rest into a backpack along with the second sky-scoot. He strapped a compass around his right wrist, slung the pack between his shoulder blades, and climbed outside to spread the silver-metal tissue on the sand.

It was full dark. His beacon of the night before, High Kavalaar's star, burned bright and red and lonely above the forest. Dirk saw it and smiled. Tonight it

would be no guidepost; he had guessed that Jaan
Vikary would make straight for Kryne Lamiya, in the
opposite direction. But the star still seemed a friend.

He took up a fresh-charged laser rifle and touched
the wafer in his palm and lifted. Behind him the Braith
hound stood and set to howling.

He flew all night, keeping several meters above the
treetops, consulting his compass from time to time and
studying the stars. There was very little to see. Beneath
him the forest rolled unending, black and hidden, with
no fires or lights to break its darkness. At times it
seemed that he was standing still, and he was reminded of his last trip by sky-scoot, through Worlorn's
abandoned subways.

The wind was his constant companion; it came from
behind him, strong to his back, and he gratefully accepted the extra speed it lent him. It whipped the tail
of his coat between his legs as he flew, and pushed his
long hair time and time again into his eyes, and he
heard it moving in the forest beneath him, making the
more pliant trees bend and rustle, shaking the sterner
ones with cold savage hands until their last leaves fell
away. Only the chokers seemed impervious, but there
were a lot of chokers. The wind made a thin wild
sound as it fought through those tangled limbs. The
sound fit; this was the wind of Kryne Lamiya, Dirk
knew, born within the mountains and controlled by
the Darkdawn weather machines, moving toward its
destiny. Ahead the white towers were waiting, and the
frozen hands beckoned it onward.

There were other noises as well: bounding movements in the woods below, the hoots of nocturnal
hunters, the rushing of a small thin river, the thunder
of a rapids. Several times Dirk heard the high
squeaking chitters of tree-spooks and saw small forms
darting from limb to limb. His eyes and his ears became strangely sensitive. He passed over a wide lake
and heard something splashing in the black waters,
then several somethings. Far off, on the shore, a short

honking bellow rattled the night. And behind him an answering challenge; a long, ululating wail. The banshee.

That noise chilled him, the first time he heard it. But the fear soon passed. When he was naked in the forest, the banshee was a terrible threat, death incarnate on the wing. Now he had a rifle and a sidearm, and the creature was scarcely any threat at all. In fact, he reflected, perhaps it was an ally. It had saved his life once. Perhaps it would do so again.

The second time the banshee wailed its shuddering wail—still behind him, but higher now, gaining altitude—Dirk only smiled. He climbed, to keep the beast below him, and did one slow loop to try to glimpse the creature. But it was still far away, and black as his own chameleon cloth, and all he saw was a vague ripple of motion against the forest, perhaps nothing but branches moving in the wind.

Keeping high, he consulted his compass again and circled to resume his flight toward Kryne Lamiya. Twice more that night he thought he heard the banshee crying out to him, but the sounds were far apart and faint and he could not be sure.

The eastern sky had just begun to lighten when he first heard drifting music, scattered snatches of despair, too familiar for his liking. The Darkdawn city was near at hand.

He slowed and hovered, scowling. He had flown the course he thought Jaan Vikary would run; he had seen nothing. Possibly his guess had been dead wrong. Possibly Vikary had led his hunters in some other direction entirely. But Dirk did not think so. More likely he had passed over them, unseeing and unseen, in the dark of night.

He began to retrace his course, flying into the wind now, feeling the cold ghostly fingers of Lamiya-Bailis on his cheeks. In the light his task would be easier, he hoped.

The Helleye rose, and one by one the Trojan Suns. Thin wisps of gray-white cloud scuttled across a forlorn sky while morning mists moved on the forest floor. The woods beneath him turned from black to yellow-brown; chokers everywhere entwined like awkward lovers, and red light gleamed dimly from their waxy limbs. Dirk climbed and his horizons expanded. He saw rivers, the flash of sun on water. And overgrown lakes with no flash at all, dark, covered by a floating greenish film. And snowfall, or what looked like snowfall until he was above it and saw that it was an area of dirty white fungus blanketing the wild.

He saw a fault line, a rocky slash running through the woods north to south, as straight as if it had been drawn with a ruler. And mud flats, black and brown and smelly, on either side of a wide slow waterway. And a cliff of weathered gray stone that rose unexpected from the forest, chokers sloping right up to its foot and chokers leaning out at crazy angles from its crown, but nothing on the vertical rock face itself but a few white lichens and the carcass of some large bird dead in its nest.

He saw nothing of Jaan Vikary or the hunters who pursued him.

By midmorning Dirk's muscles ached with fatigue, his arm had begun to throb again, and his hope was fading. The wild went on forever, kilometer after kilometer, a vast yellow carpet which he was searching for a mite, a silent world shrouded by twilight. He turned back toward Kryne Lamiya again, convinced that he had come too far. He began to wander, covering the route in a drifting sine wave instead of a straight line, searching, always searching He was very tired. Near noon he decided to fly in circles over the most likely area, spiraling in to try to cover it all.

And he heard the banshee screaming.

He saw it this time as well. It was flying low, near tree level, far beneath him. It seemed impossibly slow and still. The black triangular body scarcely seemed to move; the wings were held very rigidly, and the creature appeared to float on the Darkdawn wind.

When it wanted to turn it caught an updraft and wheeled about in a wide circle before descending again. Dirk, having nothing better to do, found himself following it.

It screamed again. The sound lingered.

And then he heard an answer.

He touched the wafer in the palm of his hand and began to descend rapidly, listening, suddenly alert again. The sound had been faint but unmistakable: a pack of Braith hounds, barking wildly in anger and fear. He lost sight of the banshee—no matter now—and chased the fast-fading sound. It had come from the north, he thought. He flew north.

Somewhere close, a hound let loose a howl.

Dirk grew briefly alarmed. It was possible that if he flew too low the hounds would start barking at him instead of the banshee. It was a dangerous situation in any event. His coat was doing its best to take on the colors of Worlorn's sky, but the silver of the sky-scoot could flash brilliantly if anyone chanced to look up. And with a banshee in the vicinity they *would* look up.

But if he were to help Jaan Vikary and his Jenny, no real choices remained to him. He gripped his weapon tightly and continued to descend. Below him, cutting through the forest like a knife, was a swift-running blue-green river. He looped toward it, his eyes scanning back and forth restlessly. He heard the sound of rapids, traced the sound, found them. They looked fast and dangerous from above. Naked rocks strung out like rotten teeth, brown and misshapen, the water boiling white and angry around them, the chokers pressing close on either side. Downstream the river widened and grew more gentle. He glanced that way briefly, then back at the rapids. He crossed the water, circled, recrossed.

A dog barked loudly. Others took up the sound.

His attention jerked back downstream. Black dots in the water, wading in where the flow looked reasonable. He flew toward it.

The dots grew, taking on shape and human form. A square little man in yellow-brown, fighting the current to wade across. Another man nearby on the shore, with six of the huge hounds.

The man in the water retreated. He had a rifle in his hand, Dirk saw. He was a very wide little man. A pale face, a thick torso, heavy arms and legs—Saanel Larteyn, Lorimaar's fat *teyn*. And Lorimaar on the shore, holding the pack. Neither of them was looking up. Dirk slowed to keep his distance.

Saanel climbed out of the water. He was on the wrong side of the river still, the side with Lorimaar, the side away from Kryne Lamiya. He was trying to cross, though. But not here. Now the two hunters began to move away, heading farther downstream, moving clumsily among the weeds and rocks and chokers that lined the riverbank.

Dirk did not follow. He had the sky-scoot and he knew where they were going; he could always find them later, if he had to. But where were the others? Roseph and his *teyn*? Garse Janacek? He turned and went back upstream, feeling a bit more confident. If the hunting party had broken up, they would be easier for him to deal with. He flew low above the river, quickly, the water churning two meters below his feet while his eyes raked the banks for another group trying to cross.

About two kilometers northeast of the rapids—the channel was narrow and swift here—he found Janacek standing above the water with a puzzled expression on his face.

He seemed to be alone. Dirk yelled at him. Janacek looked up startled, and then waved.

Dirk came down beside him. It was a bad landing. The hump of rock Janacek was standing on was covered with a slick green moss, and the underside of Dirk's sky-scoot slid right across it, and he almost went pitching into the river. Janacek caught him by the arm.

Dirk killed his gravity grid. "Thank you," he muttered. "It doesn't look like easy swimming down there."

"That was precisely the thought that I was thinking as I stood here," Janacek replied. He looked haggard. His face and clothes were dirty, and the red beard was damp with sweat. A long strand of hair hung down across his forehead, limp and greasy. "I was attempting to decide if I should risk this sort of current or waste time by continuing upstream, in the vague hopes of finding a place I could safely ford." A weak smile broke across his face. "But you have solved that problem with Gwen's toy. Where—?"

"Pyr," Dirk said. He started to tell Janacek about his flight to the wrecked aircar.

"You are alive," the Ironjade said quickly. "I can do without the tedious details, t'Larien. Much has happened since yesterday dawn. Did you see the Braiths?"

"Lorimaar and his *teyn* were going downstream," said Dirk.

"I know that," Janacek snapped. "Had they crossed?"

"No, not yet."

"Good. Jaan is very close now, perhaps only a half-hour ahead of us. They must not reach him first." His eyes swept the far bank of the river, and he sighed. "Do you have the other scoot, or must I take yours?"

Dirk set down his rifle on the rock and began to unsling his backpack. "I've got the other," he said. "Where is Roseph? What's going on?"

"Jaan has run magnificently," Janacek said. "No one could have expected him to cover so much ground so fast. The Braiths did not, in truth. And he has done more than simply run. He has set traps." He brushed back his fallen hair with the back of his hand. "He camped last night. He was far enough ahead of us. We found the ashes of his fire. Roseph stepped into a concealed pit and impaled his foot on a buried stake." Janacek smiled. "He has turned back, his *teyn* helping him. And you say Pyr and Arris are dead?"

Dirk nodded. He had pulled the boots and the second scoot from his pack.

Janacek accepted them without comment. "The hunters grow few. I think we have won, t'Larien. Jaan Vikary will be weary. He has run without sleep for a day and two nights. Yet we know he is not hurt, and he is armed, and he is of Ironjade. Lorimaar and that slug he keeps as *teyn* will find no easy prey."

He knelt and began to unlace his boots, talking all the while. "Their mad conceit of a new holdfast here will be stillborn. Lorimaar is berserk to even dream of it. I think his mind snapped loose of its anchor when Jaan's laser burned him back in Challenge." He pulled off one boot. "Do you know why Chell and Bretan were not among them, t'Larien? Because that pair had too much sanity for this high-Larteyn scheme! Roseph told me all about it as we hunted. The truth, he said, is this: Lorimaar announced the madness when the Braiths returned to Larteyn after Myrik had been killed. The six we encountered in the woods were there, plus old Raymaar. Bretan Braith Lantry and Chell fre-Braith were not. They had tried to pursue you and Jaantony, and later passed through some of the cities where they thought it likely you had taken refuge. So Lorimaar was essentially without opposition. He has always cowed the others, except perhaps for Pyr, and Pyr was never interested in anything save the taking of mockman heads."

Janacek was having difficulty fitting into Gwen's narrow boots. He scowled and yanked hard, forcing his foot in where it did not want to go. "When Chell returned, he was furious. He would not go along. He would not even listen. Bretan tried to calm him, Roseph claimed, but to no avail. Old Chell is a Braith, and Lorimaar's new holdfast was treason to him. He issued a challenge. Lorimaar was immune to challenge, in truth, since he was wounded, but he accepted nonetheless. Chell was very old. As challenged, Lorimaar made the first of the four choices, the choice of numbers."

Janacek stood up, and stamped down hard on the slick rock to jam his foot into the boot more tightly. "Need I tell you that he chose to fight single? It would have been quite a different duel had Bretan Braith confronted him as well as Chell Empty-Arms. Lorimaar, even wounded, disposed of the old man rather easily. It was death-square, and blades. Chell took many cuts, too many perhaps. Roseph believes he lies dying back in Larteyn. Bretan Braith remains with him and, more important still, remains Bretan Braith." Janacek spread out his sky-scoot.

"Did you find out anything about Ruark?" Dirk asked him.

The Kavalar shrugged. "It is all much as we suspected. Ruark contacted Lorimaar high-Braith by viewscreen—no one seems to know where the Kimdissi is presently—and offered to reveal where Jaan was hiding if Lorimaar would name him *korariel* and thus grant him protection. This Lorimaar did willingly. Jaan was fortunate in that he was within his aircar when they came. He simply took off and ran. They pursued him and finally Raymaar overtook him just beyond the mountains, but he was yet another old man and not nearly the flyer that Jaan Vikary is." There was a note of gleeful pride in Janacek's voice, like a parent boasting of a child. "The Braith went down in combat, but Jaan's car was damaged as well, so he was forced to land and run. He was already gone when the high-bonds of Larteyn found where he had crashed. They had wasted time trying to assist Raymaar." He waved an impatient hand.

"Why did you split from Lorimaar?" Dirk asked.

"Why do you think? Jaan is close now. I must reach him first, before they do. Saanel insisted the crossing would be easier downstream, and I took the chance to disagree. Lorimaar is too tired to be suspicious now. He thinks only of his kill. His burn is still on fire, t'Larien! I think he sees Jaan Vikary lying bloody before him and forgets who it is he chases. So I went away from them, upstream, and for a time I feared I had made a mistake. The crossing *was* easier downstream, was it not?"

Dirk nodded again.

Janacek grinned. "Then your arrival is a luck, in truth."

"You are going to need more luck to find Jaan," Dirk warned. "The Braiths have probably crossed the river by now, and they have their hounds."

"It does not concern me overmuch," Janacek said. "Jaan runs straight now, and I know something Lorimaar does not. I know what he runs for. A cave, t'Larien! My *teyn* has always been intrigued by caves. When we were boys together in Ironjade, often he would take me exploring beneath the earth. He took me into more abandoned mines than I ever wished to see, and several times we went under the old cities, the demon-haunted ruins." He smiled. "Blasted holdfasts, too, hearths blackened in ancient highwars and still teeming with restless ghosts. Jaan Vikary knew all such places. He would guide me through them and recite history to me, unendingly, tales of Aryn high-Glowstone and Jamis-Lion Taal and the cannibals of the Deep Coal Dwellings. He was ever a storyteller. He could make those old heroes live again, and the horrors as well."

Dirk found himself smiling. "Did he scare you, Garse?"

The other laughed. "Scare me? Yes! He terrified me, but I became tempered in time. We were both young, t'Larien. Later, much later, it was in the caverns under the Lameraan Hills that he and I pledged iron-and-fire."

"All right," Dirk said. "So Jaan likes caves—"

"One system opens very near to Kryne Lamiya," Janacek said, returning to the issue at hand, "with a second entrance close to where we stand. The three of us explored it during the first year we came to Worlorn. Now, I think that Jaan will complete his run underground, if he can. Thus we can intercept him." He scooped up his rifle.

Dirk lifted his own weapon. "You'll never find him in the forest," he said. "The chokers provide too much cover."

"*I* would find him," Janacek said, his voice a little ragged and more than a little wild. "Remember our bond, t'Larien. Iron-and-fire."

"Empty iron now," Dirk said, glancing pointedly at Janacek's right wrist.

The Ironjade grinned his hard distinctive grin. "No," he said. His hand went into his pocket, came out, opened. In his palm the glowstone rested. A single jewel, round and rough-faceted, about twice the size of Dirk's whisperjewel, black and nearly opaque in the full ruddy light of the morning.

Dirk stared, then touched it lightly with a finger, so that it moved slightly in Janacek's palm. "It feels . . . cold," he said.

Janacek frowned. "No," he said. "It burns, rather, as fire always does." The glowstone vanished back into his pocket. "There are stories, t'Larien, poems in Old Kavalar, tales they tell the children in the holdfast creche. Even the *eyn-kethi* know the stories. They tell them in their women's voices, but Jaan Vikary tells them better. Ask him sometime. Of the things *teyn* has done for *teyn*. He will answer you with great magics and greater heroisms, the old impossible glories. I am no storyteller or I would tell you myself. Perhaps then you could understand a bit of what it means, to stand *teyn* to a man and wear an iron bond."

"Perhaps I already do," Dirk said.

A long silence came between them as they stood on the slick mossy rock a bare half-meter apart, their eyes locked, Janacek smiling just a bit as he looked down on Dirk. Below them the river rushed by untiring, the sounds of its waters urging them to haste.

"You are not so terribly bad a man, t'Larien," Janacek said at last. "You are weak, I know, but no one has ever called you strong."

At first that sounded like an insult, but the Kavalar seemed to intend something else. Dirk stopped to puzzle it out and found a second meaning. "Give a thing a name?" he said, smiling.

Janacek nodded. "Listen to me, Dirk. I will not tell you twice. I remember when I was a boy in Ironjade, the first time I was warned of mockmen. A woman, an *eyn-kethi*—you would call her my mother, though such distinctions have no weight on my world —this woman told me the legend. Yet she told it differently. The mockmen she cautioned me against were not the demons I would learn of later from highbond lips. They were only men, she said, not alien pawns, no kin to weres or soulsucks. Yet they were shape-changers, in a sense, because they had no true shapes. They were men who could not be trusted, men who had forgotten their codes, men without bonds. They were not real; they were all illusion of humanity without the substance. Do you understand? The *substance* of humanity—it is a name, a bond, a promise. It is inside, and yet we wear it on our arms. So she told me. This is why Kavalars take *teyns,* she said, and go abroad in pairs—because . . . because illusion can harden into fact if you bind it in iron."

"A fine speech, Garse," Dirk said when the other had finished. "But what effect does silver have on the soul of a mockman?"

Anger passed quickly across Janacek's face, like the shadow of a drifting stormcloud. Then he grinned. "I had forgotten your Kimdissi wit," he said. "Another thing I learned in youth was never to argue with a manipulator." He laughed and reached out and clasped Dirk's hand briefly and tightly in his own. "Enough," he said. "We will never meet as one, yet I can still be *friend* if you can still be *keth.*"

Dirk shrugged, feeling strangely moved. "All right," he said.

But Garse was already off. He had let go of Dirk's arm and touched his finger to his palm, and he rose straight up a meter and then lurched out over the water, moving quickly, leaning forward, somehow fleet and graceful in the air. Sunlight shone on his long red hair, and his clothes seemed to shift and flicker, changing colors. Halfway across the surging river he threw his head back and shouted something to Dirk, but the rush and tumble of the current swept his words away, and Dirk caught only the tone—a bloody, laughing exultation.

He watched until Janacek had reached the far side of the stream, somehow too tired to take to the air at once. His free hand slid into his jacket pocket and touched the whisperjewel. It did not seem quite so cold as before, and the promises—oh, Jenny!—came but faintly.

Janacek was soaring up above the yellow trees, up into a gray and crimson sky, his figure receding rapidly.

Wearily Dirk followed.

Janacek might disparage the sky-scoots as "toys," but for all that he knew how to fly one. He was soon racing far ahead of Dirk, climbing up the steady wind until he flew some twenty meters above the forest. The distance between the two of them seemed to widen steadily; unlike Gwen, Janacek was not inclined to stop and wait for Dirk to catch up.

Dirk contented himself with the role of pursuit. The Ironjade was easy enough to see—they were alone in the gloomy sky—so there was no danger of getting lost. He rode the Darkling winds again, accepting their steady push against his back while he abandoned himself to aimless musings. He dreamed strange waking dreams of Jaan and Garse, of iron bonds and whisperjewels, of Guinevere and Lancelot, who had—he realized suddenly—been pledge-breakers both.

The river vanished. The quiet lakes came and went, and the patch of white fungus that lay like a scab upon the forest. He heard the baying of Lorimaar's pack once, far behind him, the thin noises carried to him on the wind. He was not worried.

They angled south. Janacek was a small dot, black, flashing silver when a shaft of sun caught the raft on which he rode. Smaller and smaller. Dirk came after, a limp bird. Finally Janacek began to spiral down to treetop level.

It was a wild region. Rockier than most, with a few rolling hills and outcroppings of black rock streaked with silver-gold. Chokers were everywhere, chokers and only chokers. Dirk's eyes cast this way and that searching for a single tall silverwood, for a blue widower or a gaunt dark ghost tree. A maze of yellow stretched away unbroken to both horizons. Dirk heard the frantic noises of the tree-spooks and saw them under his feet flying short flights on tiny wings.

The air around him shuddered to the sound of a banshee wail, and a cold tingle brushed Dirk's spine for no reason he could name. He looked up quickly, into the distance, and saw a pulse of light.

Brief, throbbing against his weary eyes, and too intense, this sudden finger of brightness did not belong, not here, not in this gray dusk world. It did not belong, but it was there. Stabbing up once from below, a savage thin fire soon lost in the sky.

Janacek was a small rag doll ahead of him, near the light. The slender thread of scarlet brushed him, touched the silver sled he stood on, slightly, quickly. The image lingered in Dirk's eyes. Absurdly Janacek began to tumble, flailing his arms. A black stick went spinning from his grasp and he disappeared down among the chokers, crashing through their interlocking branches.

Noises. Dirk heard noises. Music on this endless winter's wind. Wood snapping, followed by screams of pain and rage, animal and human, human and animal, both and neither. The towers of Kryne Lamiya shimmered above the horizon, smokelike and transparent, and sang to him a song of endings.

The screaming ceased suddenly; the white towers melted, and the gale that swept him forward blew away the shards. Dirk swung down and raised his laser.

There was a dark hole in the high foliage where Garse Janacek had fallen through: yellow limbs twisted down and broken, a gap big enough for a man's body.

Dark. Dirk hovered above it and could not see Janacek or the forest floor, so thick were the shadows. But on the topmost limb he saw a torn strip of cloth flapping in the wind and changing colors. Above it a little ghost stood solemn guard.

"Garse!" he shouted, not caring about the enemy below, the man with the laser. The tree-spooks answered in a chorus of chittering.

He heard crashing under the trees; the laser light flamed again, brightly. Not up this time, but horizontal, a shaft of impossible sun in the gloom below. Dirk hovered indecisive. A tree-spook appeared on the limb just below him, oddly fearless, liquid eyes gazing up, wings spread apart and thrumming in the wind. Dirk pointed his laser and fired, until the little beast was nothing but a soot stain on the yellow bark.

Then he moved again, circling out in a spiral until he saw a slanting gap among the chokers, wide enough for him to descend. The forest floor was murky; the chokers, joining overhead, screened out nine-tenths of the Helleye's meager light. Huge trunks loomed all around him, gnarled yellow fingers twisting every which way, stiff and arthritic. He bent—the moss along the ground was decomposing—and pulled his boots free of the silver grid, so the metal went limp. Then the shadows parted between the chokers, and Jaan Vikary came out to stand above him. Dirk looked up.

Jaan's face was lined and empty. He was covered with blood, and in his arms was a mangled red thing that he carried the way a mother might carry a sick child. Garse had one eye closed and one eye missing, torn from his face. Only half of his face was there at all. His head lay gently against Jaan's chest.

"Jaan—"

Vikary flinched. "I shot him," he said. Trembling, he dropped the body.

chapter 14

There was no sound in the wilderness but Vikary's labored breathing and the faint skittering noises of the tree-spooks.

Dirk went to Janacek and rolled him over. Bits of moss clung to the body, soaking up the blood like sponges. The tree-spooks had torn out his throat, so Garse's head lolled obscenely when Dirk moved him. His heavy clothing had been no protection; they had bitten through everywhere, leaving the chameleon cloth in wet red tatters. Janacek's legs, still joined together by the useless silver-metal square of the sky-scoot, had been cracked in the fall; jagged bone fragments protruded from both calves, almost identical compound fractures. The face was the worst—gnawed. The right eye was gone. The socket welled with blood that dripped slowly down his cheek into the ground.

There was nothing to be done. Dirk stared helplessly. He slipped a quiet hand into a pocket of Janacek's battered jacket and took the glowstone in his fist, then rose to face Vikary again. "You said—"

"That I could never fire at him," Vikary finished. "I know what I said, Dirk t'Larien. And I know what I did." He spoke very slowly; each word dropped from his lips with a leaden thud. "I did not intend this. Never. I sought only to stop him, to knock out the sky-scoot. He fell into a tree-spook nest. A tree-spook nest."

Dirk's fist was clenched tightly around the glowstone. He said nothing.

Vikary shook; his voice took on animation, and there was a desperate edge in his tone. "He was hunting me. Arkin Ruark warned me when I spoke to him by viewscreen in Larteyn. He said that Garse had joined the Braiths, had sworn to bring me down. I did not believe." He trembled. *"I did not believe!* Yet it was truth. He came after me, came hunting with them, just as Ruark said he would. Ruark . . . Ruark is not with me . . . we never . . . the Braiths came instead. I do not know if he . . . Ruark . . . perhaps they have slain him. I do not know."

He seemed weary and confused. "I had to stop Garse, t'Larien. He knew of the cave. Gwen to think of too. Ruark said that Garse in his madness had promised to hand her over to Lorimaar, and I called him a liar until I glimpsed Garse behind me. Gwen is my *betheyn,* and you are *korariel.* My responsibility. I had to live. Do you understand? I never meant to do this. I went to him, burned my way through . . . The grubs in the nest-heart were all over him, white things, the adults too . . . burned them, I burned them, brought him out."

Vikary's body shook with dry sobs, but no tears came; he would not permit it. "Look. He was wearing empty iron. He came hunting me. I loved him and he came hunting me!"

The glowstone was a hard nugget of indecision within Dirk's fist. He looked down once more at Garse Jana-cek, whose garments had faded to the colors of old blood and rotting moss, and then up at Jaan Vikary, so very close to breaking, who stood pale-faced with his massive shoulders twitching. Give a thing a name, Dirk thought; and now he must give a name to Jaantony high-Ironjade.

He slid his fist into the darkness of his pocket. "You had to do it," he lied. "He would have killed you, and Gwen later. He said so. I'm glad that Arkin got to you with a warning."

The words seemed to steady Vikary. He nodded wordlessly.

"I came looking for you," Dirk continued, "when you didn't return in time. Gwen was concerned. I was going to help you. Garse caught me and disarmed me and delivered me to Lorimaar and Pyr. He said I was a blood-gift."

"A blood-gift," Vikary repeated. "He was insane, t'Larien. It is truth. Garse Ironjade Janacek was not like that; he was no Braith, no giver of blood-gifts. You must believe that."

"Yes," Dirk said. "He was deranged. You're right. I could tell from the way he talked. Yes." He felt very close to tears and wondered if it showed. It was as if he had taken all of Jaan's fear and anguish into himself; the Ironjade seemed stronger and more resolute with every passing second, while grief came unbidden to Dirk's eyes.

Vikary looked down at the still body sprawled beneath the trees. "I would mourn for him, for the things that he was and the things that we had, but there is no time. The hunters come after us with their hounds. We must press on." He knelt by Janacek's corpse for an instant and held a limp bloody hand within his own. Then he kissed the ruin of the dead man's face, full on the lips, and with his free hand stroked the matted hair.

But when he rose again, he had a black iron bracelet in his grasp, and Dirk saw that Janacek's arm was naked and felt a sudden pain. Vikary put the empty iron into his pocket. Dirk held back his tears and his tongue, saying nothing.

"We must go."

"Are we just going to leave him here?" Dirk asked.

"Leave him?" Vikary frowned. "Ah, I see. Burial is no Kavalar custom, t'Larien. We abandon our dead in the wild, traditionally, and if the beasts consume what we leave, we do not feel shame. Life should nourish life. Is it not more fitting that his strong flesh should give strength to some swift clean predator rather than a mass of vile maggots and graveyard worms?"

So they left him where Vikary had dropped the body, in a little open space amid the endless yellow-brown thicket, and they set off through the dim undergrowth toward Kryne Lamiya. Dirk carried his skyscoot with him, and struggled to match Vikary's rapid pace. They had been walking for only a few moments when they came upon a high steep ridge of twisted black rock.

When Dirk reached the barrier, Jaan was already halfway to the top. Janacek's blood had dried to a brown crust on Jaan's clothing, and Dirk could see patches of it clearly from below. Otherwise the Kavalar's clothes had turned black. He climbed smoothly, his rifle strapped to his back, his strong hands moving with assurance from one handhold to another.

Dirk spread the silver tissue of his sky-scoot and flew to the crest of the ridge.

He had just ascended past the topmost boughs of the chokers when he heard the banshee cry out briefly, not so far away. His eyes swept about, searching for the great predator. The small clearing where they had left Janacek was easily visible from above, a patch of twilight close at hand. But Dirk could not see the body; the center of the clearing was a living mass of struggling yellow bodies. As he watched, other tiny shapes flitted from the nearby woods to join the feast in progress.

The banshee came out of nowhere and hung motionless above the fight, wailing its terrible long wail, but the tree-spooks continued their mad scramble, paying no mind to the noise, chittering and clawing at each other. The banshee fell. Its shadow covered them, its great wings rippled and folded, and it dropped; and then it was alone, spooks and corpse alike wrapped within its hungry grasp. Dirk felt strangely heartened.

But only for an instant. While the banshee lay inert, a sharp squeak sounded suddenly, and Dirk saw a quick small blur dart down and land atop it. Another followed. And another. And a dozen, all at once. He blinked and it seemed as if the spooks had doubled. The banshee unfolded its vast triangular wings again, and they fluttered weakly, feebly, but it did not lift. The pests were all over it, biting at it, clawing at it, weighing it down and tearing it apart. Pinned to the earth, it could not even sound its anguished cry. It died silently, its meal still trapped beneath it.

By the time Dirk climbed off of his sky-scoot at the top of the ridge, the clearing was a mass of heaving yellow once again, just as he had first glimpsed it, and there was no sign that the banshee had ever been there at all. The forest was very silent. He waited for Jaan Vikary to join him. Together they resumed their wordless trek.

The cave was cold and dark and infinitely still. Hours passed beneath the earth as Dirk followed the small wavering light of Jaan Vikary's hand torch. The light led him through twisting subterranean galleries, through echoing chambers where the blackness went on forever, through claustrophobic little passages where they squirmed on hands and knees. The light was his universe; Dirk lost all sense of time and space. They had nothing to say to each other, he and Jaan, so they said nothing; the only sounds were the scrape of their boots over dusty rock and the infrequent booming echoes. Vikary knew his cave well. He never hesitated or lost his way. They limped and crawled through the secret soul of Worlorn.

And emerged on a sloping hillside among chokers to a night full of fire and music.

Kryne Lamiya was burning. The bone towers screamed a shattered song of anguish.

Flames were loose everywhere in the pale necropolis, bright sentinels wandering up and down the streets. The city shimmered like some strange illusion in the waves of heat and light; it seemed an insubstantial orange wraith. As they watched, one of the slender looping bridges crumbled and collapsed; its blackened center fell apart first, down into the conflagration, and the rest of the stone span followed. The fire consumed it and rose higher, crackling and shrieking, unsatiated. A nearby building coughed dully and imploded, falling in a great cloud of smoke and flame.

Three hundred meters from the hill on which they stood, looming high over the choker-woods, a chalk-white hand-tower remained yet untouched by the blaze. But, outlined in the terrible brightness, it seemed to move like a thing alive, writhing and grasping in pain.

Above the roar of the fire Dirk could hear the faint music of Lamiya-Bailis. The Darkdawn symphony had been broken and transformed; towers were gone, notes missing, so the song was full of eerie silences, and the crackle of the flames gave a pounding counterpoint to the wails and whistles and moans. The Darkling winds that came endlessly from the mountains to make the Siren City sing, those same winds were fanning the great fires that ate at Kryne Lamiya, that darkened its death mask with ashes and soot and ultimately bid it quiet.

Jaan Vikary unslung his laser rifle. His face was blank and strange, washed by the reflections of the great burning. "How—?"

"The wolf-car," Gwen said.

She was standing a few meters away, downslope from them. They looked at her without surprise. Behind her, beneath the shadow of a drooping blue widower at the base of the hill, Dirk glimpsed Ruark's little yellow aircar.

"Bretan Braith," Vikary said.

Gwen joined them near the entrance to the cave and nodded. "Yes. The car has passed back and forth over the city a number of times, firing its lasers."

"Chell is dead," Vikary said.

"But you're alive," Gwen replied. "I was beginning to wonder."

"We are alive," he acknowledged. He let his rifle slide from limp fingers. "Gwen," he said, "I have killed my *teyn*."

"Garse?" she said, startled. She frowned.

"He turned me over to the Braiths," Dirk said quickly. His eyes touched Gwen's. "And he was hunting Jaan, running at Lorimaar's side. It had to be done."

She glanced from Dirk back to Jaan. "This is the truth? Arkin told me something of the sort. I didn't believe him."

"It is the truth," Vikary said.

"Arkin is here?" Dirk said.

Gwen nodded. "Inside the aircar. He flew from Larteyn. You must have told him where I was. He tried some new lies on me. I knocked him out. He's helpless now."

"Gwen," Dirk said, "we've misjudged Arkin badly." The back of his throat was thick with bile. "Don't you understand, Gwen? Arkin warned Jaan that Garse was going to betray him. Without that warning, Jaan would never have known. He might have trusted Janacek, might not have shot him down. He would have been taken, killed." His voice was hoarse and urgent. "Don't you understand? Arkin . . ."

The fire put cold reflections in her eyes as she watched Dirk. "I understand," she said in a thick, wavering voice. She turned back to Vikary. "Oh, Jaan," she said. She held out her arms to him.

And he came to her and rested his head on her shoulder and wrapped his own arms tightly around her. And then he began to cry.

Dirk left them and walked down to the aircar.

Arkin Ruark was tightly bound to one of the seats. He was dressed in heavy field clothes, and his head was slumped down so his chin rested against his chest. When Dirk entered he looked up, with an effort. The whole right side of his face was a swollen purplish bruise. "Dirk," he said weakly.

Dirk took off his cumbersome backpack and lowered it to the floor. He leaned up against the instrument panel. "Arkin," he said evenly.

"Help me," Ruark said.

"Janacek is dead," Dirk told him. "Jaan lasered him and he fell into a tree-spook nest."

"Garsey," Ruark said, with some difficulty. His lips were swollen and bloody, and his voice trembled. "He would have killed you all. Utter truth, utter. Warned Jaan, I did, warned him. Believe me, Dirk."

"Oh, I believe you," Dirk said, nodding.

"Tried to help, yes. Gwen, she's gone wild. I saw the Braiths take Jaan, I'd just come to join him, they were there first. Was afraid for her, I was. Came to help. She beat me, said I was a liar, tied me up and flew us here. She's wild, Dirk, friend Dirk, all wild, Kavalar wild. Like Garse almost, not like sweet Gwen at all. I think she means to kill me. You too, maybe, I don't know. She is going to go back to Jaan, I know it. Help me, you have to help me. Stop her." He whimpered.

"She's not going to kill anyone," Dirk said. "Jaan is here now, and me. You're safe, Arkin, don't worry. We'll set things right. We've got a lot to thank you for, don't we? Jaan especially. Without your warning, there's no telling what might have happened."

"Yes," Ruark said. He smiled. "Yes, truth, utter truth."

Gwen appeared suddenly, framed in the door. "Dirk," she said, ignoring Ruark.

He turned to her. "Yes?"

"I made Jaan lie down for a while. He's very tired. Come outside where we can talk."

"Wait," Ruark said. "Untie me first, eh? Do that thing. My arms, Dirk, my arms . . ."

Dirk went outside. Jaan lay nearby, his head up against a tree, staring blindly off at the distant fire. They walked away from him, into the darkness of the chokers. Finally Gwen paused and swung around to face him. "Jaan must never know," she said. She brushed a loose strand of hair back from her forehead with her right hand.

Dirk stared. "Your arm," he said.

Around her right forearm Gwen wore iron, black and empty. Her arm froze at Dirk's words. "Yes," she said. "The glowstones will come later."

"I see," Dirk said. *"Teyn* and *betheyn,* both."

Gwen nodded. She reached out and took Dirk's hands in her own. Her skin was cool and dry. "Be happy for me, Dirk," she said in a small sad voice. "Please."

He squeezed her hands, trying to be reassuring. "I am," he said, without much conviction. Between them lay a long silence and a great bitterness.

"You look like hell," Gwen said at last, forcing a little grin. "Scratched all over like that. The way you hold your arm. The way you walk. Are you all right?"

He shrugged. "The Braiths aren't gentle playmates," he said. "I'll survive." He let go of her hands then and reached into his pocket. "Gwen, I have something for you."

Within his fist: two gems. The glowstone round and rough-faceted, lit faintly from within, smoldering in the hollow of his hand. And the whisperjewel, smaller, darker; dead and cold.

Gwen took them wordlessly. She rolled them in her hand for a moment, frowning. Then she pocketed the glowstone and gave the whisperjewel back to Dirk.

He accepted it. "The last I have of Jenny," he said as his hand closed around the echoing ice-drop and it vanished once again into his clothing.

"I know," she said. "Thank you for offering. But if truth be known, it doesn't talk to me anymore. I guess I've changed too much. I haven't heard a whisper in years."

"Yeah," he said. "I suspected something like that. But I had to offer it to you—it and the promise. The promise is still yours, Gwen, if you ever need it. Call it my iron-and-fire. You don't want to turn me into a mockman, do you?"

"No," she replied. "The other one . . ."

"Garse saved it, when he tossed the rest away. I thought maybe you'd want to have it reset, with the new ones. Jaan will never know the difference."

Gwen sighed. "All right," she said. Then: "I find that I'm sorry about Garse, after all. Isn't that curious? All the years we passed together, there was scarcely a day when we weren't at each other's throats, with poor Jaan trapped in between, loving us both. There were times when I was almost certain that the only thing that stood between me and happiness was Garse Ironjade Janacek. Only now he's gone, and I find that very hard to believe. I keep expecting him to turn up in his aircar, armed to the teeth and grinning, ready to snap at me and put me in my place. I think that maybe when I really come to know it's true, then maybe I'll cry. Don't you think that's curious?"

"No," said Dirk. "No."

"I could almost cry for Arkin too," she said. "Do you know what he said? When he came to me in Kryne Lamiya? After I called him a liar and hit him and broke him down—do you know what he said?"

Dirk shook his head, waiting.

"He said he loved me," Gwen said, smiling grimly. "He said that he had always loved me, from the moment we met on Avalon. I can't swear that he was telling the truth. Garse always said the manipulators were clever, and Arkin didn't need to be a genius to see how his revelation affected me. I almost set him free when he told me that. He seemed so small and pitiful, and he was sobbing. Instead— You saw his face?" She hesitated.

"I saw," Dirk said. "Ugly."

"Instead I did that to him," Gwen said. "But I think I believe him now. In a sick sort of way, he did love me. And he saw what I was doing to myself; and he knew that, left to my own devices, I would never leave Jaan, so he decided to use you—use all the things I told him, trusted him with—and get me away from Jaan that way. I suppose he figured that you and I would lose each other again the way we did on Avalon, and then I'd turn to him. Or maybe he knew better. I don't know. He claimed that he was only thinking of me, of my happiness, that he couldn't stand seeing me in jade-and-silver. That he had no thought for himself. He says he's my friend." She sighed hopelessly. "My friend," she repeated.

"Don't feel too sorry for him, Gwen," Dirk warned. "He would have sent me to my death, and Jaan too, without a moment's hesitation. Garse Janacek is dead, and several of the Braiths, and innocent Emereli in Challenge—and you can lay it all on friend Arkin. Can't you?"

"Now you're the one that sounds like Garse," she said. "What did you tell me? That I had jade eyes? Look at your own, Dirk! But I suppose you're right."

"What do we do with him now?"

"Free him," she said. "For the present. Jaan must never suspect the truth of what he did. It would destroy him, Dirk. So Arkin Ruark has to be our friend again. You see?"

"Yes," he said. The roar of the fire had diminished to a gentle crackling, Dirk noticed; it was almost quiet. Glancing back in the direction of the aircar, he saw that the inferno was guttering out. A few scattered fires still flickered weakly among the rubble, casting a shifting light over the ruined, smoking city. Most of the slim towers had fallen, and those that remained had grown entirely silent. The wind was only a wind.

"Dawn will be here soon," Gwen said. "We should be going."

"Going?"

"Back to Larteyn, if Bretan hasn't destroyed that as well."

"He has a violent way of mourning," Dirk agreed. "But is Larteyn safe?"

"The time for run-and-hide is over," Gwen said to him. "I'm not unconscious now, and I'm not a helpless *betheyn* who needs to be protected." She raised her right arm; distant fires illuminated the dull iron. "I'm *teyn* to Jaan Vikary, blooded even, and I've got my weapon. And you—you've changed too, Dirk. You're not *korariel* anymore, you know. You're a *keth.*

"We're together, for the moment. We're young and we're strong, and we know who are our enemies are and how to find them. And none of us can ever be Ironjades again—I'm a woman and Jaan's an out-bonder and you're a mockman. Garse was the last Ironjade. Garse is dead. The rights and wrongs of High Kavalaan and the Ironjade Gathering died with him, I think, for this world at the least. There are no codes on Worlorn, remember? No Braiths and no Ironjades, only animals trying to kill each other."

"What are you saying?" Dirk said, though he thought he knew.

"I'm saying that I'm tired of being hunted and hounded and threatened," Gwen said. Her shadowed face was black iron; her eyes burned hot and feral. "I'm saying that it's time *we* became the hunters!"

Dirk regarded her in silence for a long time. She was very beautiful, he thought, beautiful in the way that Garse Janacek had been beautiful. She was a little like the banshee, he decided, and he grieved a private grief for his Jenny, his Guinevere who never was. "You're right," he said heavily.

She stepped closer to him, wrapped him within the circle of her arms before he could react, and hugged him with all of her strength. His own hands came up slowly; he hugged her back, and they stood together for a good ten minutes, crushed against each other, her smooth cool cheek against his stubble. When she finally broke from him, she looked up, expecting him to kiss her, so he did. He closed his eyes; her lips felt dry and hard.

The Firefort was cold at dawn. The wind swirled around it in hammering gusts; the sky above was gray and cloudy.

On the roof of their building they found a corpse. Jaan Vikary climbed out carefully, his laser rifle in hand, while Gwen and Dirk covered him from the relative safety of the aircar. Ruark sat silently in the back seat, terrified. They had freed him before leaving the vicinity of Kryne Lamiya, and all the way back he had been alternately sullen and ebullient, not knowing what to think.

Vikary inspected the body, which lay sprawled in front of the tubes, then returned to the car. "Roseph high-Braith Kelcek," he said curtly.

"High-Larteyn," Dirk reminded him.

"In truth," he acknowledged, frowning. "High-Larteyn. He has been dead several hours, I would estimate. Approximately half of his chest has been blown away by a projectile weapon. His own sidearm is holstered."

"A projectile weapon?" Dirk said.

Vikary nodded. "Bretan Braith Lantry has been known to use such a weapon in duel. He is a noted duelist, but I believe he has chosen his projectile gun only twice, rare times when he was not content to win by wounding. A dueling laser is a clean precise instrument. Not so this sidearm of Bretan Braith's. Such a weapon is designed to kill, even with a near miss. It is a great sloppy savage thing, and it makes for short deadly duels."

Gwen was staring out to where Roseph lay like a pile of rags. His clothing had the dirty dust color of the roof, and it flapped erratically in the wind. "This was no duel," she said.

"No," Vikary agreed.

"But *why?*" Dirk asked. "Roseph was no threat to Bretan Braith, was he? Besides, the code duello—

Bretan is still a Braith, isn't he? So isn't he still bound?"

"Bretan is indeed yet a Braith, and *that* is your 'why' for you, Dirk t'Larien," Vikary said. "This is no duel. This is highwar, Braith against Larteyn. There are very few rules in highwar; any adult male of the enemy holdfast is fair prey, until a peace comes."

"A crusade," Gwen said, chuckling. "That doesn't sound much like Bretan, Jaan."

"It sounds a great deal like old Chell, however," Vikary replied. "I suspect that his *teyn* swore him to this course as he lay dying. If this is truth, Bretan kills under a pledge, not simply in grief. He will have very little mercy."

In the back seat, Arkin Ruark leaned forward eagerly. "But this is all to the best!" he exclaimed. "Yes, listen to me, this is fine. Gwen, Dirk, Jaan my friend, listen. Bretan will kill them all for us, will he not? Kill them one and all, yes. He is enemy of our enemies, best hope we have, utter truth."

"Your Kimdissi proverb is misleading in this case," Vikary said. "The highwar between Bretan Braith and the Larteyns makes him no friend of ours, except by chance. Blood and high grievance are not forgotten so easily, Arkin."

"Yes," Gwen added. "It wasn't Lorimaar that he suspected of hiding in Kryne Lamiya, you know. He burned that city in an effort to get *us*."

"A guess, a mere guess," Ruark muttered. "Perhaps he had other reasons, his own, who can know? Perhaps he was mad, crazed with grief, yes."

"Tell you what, Arkin," Dirk said. "We'll drop you off in the open, and if Bretan comes along, you can ask him."

The Kimdissi flinched and looked at him strangely. "No," he said. "No, safer to stay with you, my friends, you will protect me."

"We will protect you," Jaan Vikary said. "You have done as much for us." Dirk and Gwen exchanged glances.

Vikary threw their aircar into sudden motion. They

rose and flitted away from the roof over the dawn-dim streets of Larteyn.

"Where . . . ?" Dirk asked.

"Roseph is dead," Vikary said. "Yet he was not the only hunter. We shall take a census, friends, we shall take a census."

The building that Roseph high-Braith Kelcek had shared with his *teyn* was located not too far from the Ironjade residence and very close to the undertubes. It was a large square structure with a domed metallic roof and a portico supported by black iron columns. They landed nearby and approached it stealthily.

Two Braith hounds had been chained to the pillars in front of the house. Both of them were dead. Vikary looked them over. "Their throats were burned out with a hunting laser fired from some distance," he reported. "A safe, silent kill."

He remained outside, laser rifle in hand, wary, standing guard. Ruark stayed close at his side. Gwen and Dirk were sent in to search the building.

They found numerous empty chambers, and a small trophy room with four heads in it; three of them were old and dried, the skin tight and leathery, the features almost bestial. The fourth, Gwen said, was a Blackwiner jelly child, fresh-taken, from its look. Dirk touched the leather coverings on some of the furniture suspiciously, but Gwen shook her head no.

Another room, close by, was full of miniature figurines: banshees and wolf packs, soldiers struggling with knife and sword, men facing grotesque monsters in strange combat. All of the scenes were finely executed in iron and copper and bronze. "Roseph's work," Gwen said tersely when Dirk paused despite himself and lifted one figure for inspection. She beckoned him to move on.

Roseph's *teyn* had been eating. They found him in the dining chamber. His meal—a thick stew of meat and vegetables in a bloody broth, with hunks of black bread on the side—was cold and half consumed. A pewter mug full of brown beer stood next to it on the long wooden table. The Kavalar's body was almost a meter away, still in its chair, but the chair lay flat on the floor and there was a dark stain on the wall behind it. The man no longer had a face.

Gwen stood over him frowning, her rifle slung casually beneath one arm and pointing at the floor. She picked up his beer and took a sip before passing it to Dirk. It was tepid and stale, its head long gone.

"Lorimaar and Saanel?" Gwen asked when they stood outside again, under the iron pillars.

"I doubt that they have returned from the forest yet," Vikary said. "Perhaps Bretan Braith is somewhere in Larteyn waiting for them. No doubt he saw Roseph and Chaalyn fly in yesterday. Perhaps he is lurking somewhere close at hand, hoping to pick off his enemies one by one as they return to the city. Yes I think not."

"Why?" That was Dirk.

"Remember, t'Larien, *we* flew in at dawn, and in an unarmored aircar. He did not attack. Either he was sleeping, or he is no longer about."

"Where do you think he is?"

"In the wild, hunting our hunters," Vikary said. "Only two of the Larteyns remain alive to face him, but Bretan Braith has no way of knowing that. At his last knowledge, Pyr and Arris and even ancient Raymaar One-Hand were all living, and forces to be reckoned with. I would guess that he has flown off to take them by surprise, perhaps in the fear that otherwise they might return to the city in a group, discover their *kethi* slain, and thus be warned of his intentions."

"We should run then, yes, before he gets back," Arkin Ruark said. "Go somewhere safe, away from this Kavalar madness. Twelfth Dream, yes, to Twelfth Dream. Or Musquel, or Challenge, anywhere. There will be a ship soon, then we will be safe. What do you say?"

"I say no," Dirk replied. "Bretan would find us. Remember the almost supernatural way he found Gwen and me in Challenge?" He looked pointedly at Ruark. To his credit, the Kimdissi remained admirably blank-faced.

"We will stay in Larteyn," Vikary said decisively. "Bretan Braith Lantry is one man. We are four, and three of us are armed. If we stay together, we are safe. We will post guards. We will be ready."

· Gwen nodded and slipped her arm through Jaan's. "I agree," she said. "Bretan may not even survive Lorimaar."

"No," the Kavalar said to her. "No, Gwen. I think you are wrong. Bretan Braith will outlive Lorimaar. That much I am sure of."

At Vikary's insistence they searched the great sub-terranean garage before leaving the vicinity of Roseph's residence. His guess paid off. With their own aircar stolen in Challenge and subsequently destroyed, Roseph and his *teyn* had borrowed Pyr's flyer to return from the hunt in the wilderness; it was parked below. Jaan appropriated it. While it was not Janacek's massive olive-green war relic by any means, it was still a good deal more formidable than Ruark's little car.

Afterwards they found quarters. Along the city walls of Larteyn, overlooking the steep sheer cliff that frowned down on the distant Common, were a series of guard towers with slit-windowed sentry posts above and living quarters below, within the walls themselves. The towers, each with a great stone gargoyle roosting on top, were strictly ornamental, a flourish to make the Festival city truly Kavalar. But they were easily defensible and gave an excellent overview of the city. Gwen selected one at random and they moved in, raiding their former apartment for personal effects and food and the records of the almost-forgotten (by Dirk, anyway) ecological researches that she and Ruark had conducted in the wilds of Worlorn.

Once secure, they settled in to wait.

It was, Dirk decided later, the worst thing they could have done. Under the pressure of their inactivity, all the cracks began to show.

They set up a system of overlapping shifts, so two people were up in the guard tower at all times, armed with lasers and Gwen's field binoculars. Larteyn was gray and empty and desolate. There was little for the watchers to do except study the slow ebb and flow of light in the glowstone streets, and talk. Mostly they talked.

Arkin Ruark did his shifts along with the rest of them, and he accepted the laser rifle that Vikary forced on him, although with some reluctance. Over and over he insisted that he was unsuited to violence, that he could never fire the laser no matter what. But he consented to hold it, because Jaan Vikary asked him to. His relationships with all of them had changed radically. He stayed close to Jaan as often as he could, recognizing that the Kavalar was his real protector now. He was cordial to Gwen. She had asked him to forgive her for Kryne Lamiya, claiming that fear and pain had temporarily pushed her over into paranoia. But she was no longer "sweet Gwen" for Ruark; the bitterness between them came more to the surface every day. Toward Dirk, the Kimdissi maintained an uneasy, suspicious attitude, alternately smothering him in good fellowship and drawing back into formality when it became clear that Dirk was not warming. Ruark's comments during the first watch they stood together indicated to Dirk that the chubby ecologist was waiting desperately for the Fringe shuttle *Teric neDahlir,* due to land the following week. He seemed to want nothing more than to remain safely in hiding and get offworld as soon as possible.

Gwen Delvano waited for something entirely different, Dirk thought. While Ruark scanned the horizons with apprehension, Gwen was tense with anticipation. He remembered the words she had spoken when they talked together in the shadows of fire-wracked Kryne Lamiya. "It's time *we* became the hunters," she had said. She still meant it. When she and Dirk shared a watch, Gwen did all the work. She sat by the tall narrow window with an almost infinite patience, her binoculars hanging down between her breasts, her arms resting on the windowsill, jade-and-silver next to empty iron. She talked to Dirk without ever looking at him; all her attention was directed outside. Except for trips to the bathroom, Gwen refused to leave the window. Every once in a while she would lift her binoculars and study some distant building where she had glimpsed motion, and less frequently she would ask Dirk for a brush and begin to stroke her long black hair, which was constantly being disarrayed by the wind.

"I hope that Jaan is wrong," she said once while she sat brushing her hair. "I would rather see Lorimaar and his *teyn* come back than Bretan." Dirk had mumbled some sort of agreement, on the grounds that Lorimaar —much older and wounded too—would be far less dangerous than the one-eyed duelist who hunted him. But when he said it, Gwen only set down her brush and gazed at him curiously. "No," she said, "no, that isn't the reason at all."

As for Jaantony Riv Wolf high-Ironjade Vikary, the waiting seemed to wound him worst of all. As long as he had been kept in action, as long as things had been required of him, he had remained the old Jaan Vikary —strong, decisive, a leader. Idle he was a different man. He had no role to play then; instead he had unlimited time to brood. It was no good. Though Garse Janacek was mentioned seldom in those last days, it was clear that Jaan was haunted by the specter of his red-bearded *teyn*. Vikary was too often grim, and he began to fall into sullen silences that would sometimes last for hours.

He had earlier insisted that all of them should remain inside at all times; now Jaan himself began to take long walks at dawn and dusk when he was not on watch. During his hours in the guard tower most of his conversations were filled with rambling recollections of his boyhood in the holdfasts of the Ironjade Gathering,

and tales taken from history, of martyred heroes like
Vikor high-Redsteel and Aryn high-Glowstone. He
never spoke of the future, and only rarely of their present circumstances. Watching him, Dirk felt he could almost see the man's inner turmoil. In a matter of a few
days, Vikary had lost everything: his *teyn,* his homeworld and his people, even the code that he had lived
by. He was fighting it—already he had taken Gwen as
teyn, accepting her with a fullness and a total depend-
ence that he had never shown toward either her or
Garse individually. And it seemed to Dirk that Jaan
was trying to keep his code as well, clinging tightly to
whatever pieces of Kavalar honor had been left to
him. It was *Gwen,* not Jaan, who spoke of hunting
the hunters, of animals killing each other now that all
codes were gone. She worded things as if she spoke
for her *teyn* as well as herself, but Dirk did not think
that was so. Vikary, when he spoke of their impending
struggles, always seemed to imply that he would be dueling Bretan Braith. On his long walks through the city
he would drill with both rifle and sidearm. "If I am to
face Bretan, I must be ready," he would say, and like
an automaton he would take his daily practice, usually
within sight of the tower, preparing himself for each
Kavalar dueling mode in turn. One day he would run
through death-square and ten-paces, burning down his
phantom antagonists, and the next day it would be
free-style and walk-the-line, and then single-shot and
death-square again. Those on watch above would cover
him and pray that no enemy saw the insistent throbs of
light. Dirk was afraid. Jaan was their strength, and he
was lost in his martial delusion, his half-spoken as-
sumption that Bretan Braith would return and grant
him the courtesies of code, despite everything. Despite
all of Vikary's vaunted prowess in duel, despite his
daily ritual of drill, it seemed to Dirk increasingly unlikely that the Ironjade could triumph over Bretan in
single combat.

Dirk's own sleep was plagued by recurrent nightmares of the half-faced Braith: Bretan with his strange

voice and his glowing eye and his grotesque twitch, Bretan slim and smooth-cheeked and innocent, Bretan the destroyer of cities. Dirk woke from those dreams sweaty and exhausted, twisted in his bed clothes, remembering Gwen's screams (high shrill laments like the towers of Kryne Lamiya) and the way Bretan looked at him. To banish these visions he had only Jaan, and Jaan had a weary fatalism about him now, though he might still go through the motions.

It was Janacek's death, Dirk told himself—and more, the circumstances of that death. Had Garse died more normally, Vikary would be an avenger more angry and impassioned and invincible than Myrik and Bretan combined. As it was, however, Jaan was convinced that his *teyn* had betrayed him, had hunted him like a beast or a mockman, and the conviction was destroying him. More than once, sitting with the Ironjade in the small watchroom, Dirk felt the urge to tell him the truth, to rush up to him and shout *No, no! Garse was innocent, Garse loved you, Garse would have died for you!* Yet he said nothing. If Vikary was dying this way, consumed by his melancholy and his sense of betrayal and his ultimate loss of faith, then how much quicker would the truth kill him.

So the days passed and the cracks grew and Dirk watched his three companions with growing apprehension. While Ruark waited for escape, and Gwen for revenge, and Jaan Vikary for death.

chapter 15

On the first day of vigil it rained most of the afternoon. The clouds had been piling up in the east all morning, growing thicker and more threatening, obscuring Fat Satan and his children so the day was even gloomier than usual. Near noon the storm broke. It was a howler. The winds whistled by outside so loudly that the guard tower seemed to shake, and rivers of brown water ran wildly through the streets and down glowstone gutters. When the suns broke through at last—they were already close to setting—Larteyn glistened, its walls and buildings shining wetly and looking cleaner than Dirk had ever seen them. The Firefort seemed almost hopeful. But that was the first day of vigil.

On the second day things were back to normal. The Helleye rode a slow red path across the sky, Larteyn glowered dim and black below, and the wind brought back the dust of the Common that yesterday's rains had washed away. At dusk Dirk spied an aircar. It materialized high above the mountains, a black dot, and swept out over the Common before turning back to descend on them. Dirk watched it carefully through the binoculars, his elbows resting on the stone sill of the narrow window. It was no car he knew—a dead black thing, a small stylized bat with wide wings and enormous headlamp-eyes. Vikary was sharing that watch with him. Dirk called him over to the window, and Jaan looked with disinterest. "Yes, I know that craft," Jaan said. "It is no matter to us, t'Larien, only the hunters from the Shanagate Holding. Gwen reported seeing them leave this morning." The aircar had vanished by then, lost among the buildings of Larteyn, and Vikary went back to his seat, leaving Dirk to reflect.

In the days that followed, he saw the Shanagates several times, and they never ceased to seem unreal to him. How odd it was to think of them coming and going, untouched by all that had happened, living their lives as if Larteyn was still the peaceful dying city it seemed, as if no one had perished. They were so close to it all, and yet so distant and uninvolved; he could imagine them returning to their holdfast on High Kavalaan and reporting on how dull and uneventful life was on Worlorn. For them nothing had changed; Kryne Lamiya still sang its wailing dirge, and Challenge was still fervent with light and life and promise. He envied them.

On the third day Dirk woke from a particularly virulent nightmare in which he was fighting off Bretan alone, and he was unable to get back to sleep afterwards. Gwen, off watch, was pacing back and forth in the kitchen. Dirk poured himself a mug of Vikary's beer and listened to her for a while. "They should be here," she kept complaining. "I can't believe that they're still searching for Jaan. Surely they must realize by now what's happened! Why aren't they here?" Dirk only shrugged at her and expressed hope that no one ever showed up; the *Teric neDahlir* was due soon. When he said that, she spun on him angrily. "I don't care!" she snapped; and then, ashamed, she flushed red and came to the table and sat down. Beneath a wide green headband her eyes were haggard. She held his hand and told him haltingly that Vikary had not touched her since Janacek's death. Dirk told her that it would be better for them once the starship came, once they were safely off Worlorn, and Gwen smiled and agreed with him, and after a time she wept. When she finally left him, Dirk went back and found his whisperjewel and held it in his fist, remembering.

On the fourth day, while Vikary was out on one of his dangerous dawn walks, Gwen and Arkin Ruark quarreled during a watch, and she hit him with the butt of her laser rifle, hard across his bruised face where the swelling had only recently responded to ice packs and ointments. Ruark came down the ladder from the tower muttering that she was mad again, trying to kill him. Dirk, awakened from a sound sleep, was standing in the common room, and the Kimdissi stopped dead when he saw him. Neither of them said anything, but after that Ruark lost weight rapidly, and Dirk was certain that Arkin *knew* what he had only suspected previously.

On the morning of the sixth day, Ruark and Dirk were sharing a wordless watch when the short man, in a fit of pique, suddenly threw his laser across the room. "Filthy thing!" he exclaimed. "Braiths, Ironjades, I don't care, Kavalar animals is what they are, yes. And you, fine man from Avalon, eh? Ha! You are no better, no better at all, look at you. I should have let you duel, kill or be killed, like you wanted. That would have made you happy, yes? No doubt, no doubt. Loved sweet Gwen and made you a friend, and where is my gratitude, where, where?" His fat cheeks were growing hollow and sunken; his pale eyes shifted restlessly.

Dirk ignored him, and Ruark soon fell silent. But later on that same morning, after he had picked up his laser and sat for a few hours staring at the wall, the Kimdissi turned to Dirk once again. "I was her lover too, you know," he said. "She didn't tell you that, I know, I know, but it is the truth, the utter truth. On

Avalon, long before she ever met Jaantony and took her damn jade-and-silver, the night you sent her that whisperjewel. She was so drunk, you know. We talked and we talked, and she drank, and later on she took me to bed, and the next day she didn't even remember, you know that, she didn't even remember. But that doesn't matter, it is the truth, I was her lover too." He trembled. "I never told her, t'Larien, or tried to make it come again. I am not such a fool like you are, and I know what I am, and it was only a thing of that moment. Yet it existed, that moment, and I taught her a lot and I was her friend, and I am *very* good at my work, yes I am." He stopped and caught his breath and then silently left the tower, although there was still an hour to go before Gwen was scheduled to relieve him.

When she finally came up, the first thing she did was ask Dirk what he had said to Arkin. "Nothing," he replied truthfully. Then he asked her why, and she told him that Ruark had wakened her, crying, and telling her over and over that no matter what happened she should make sure their work was published, and that his name belonged on it, no matter what he had done, his name belonged on it too. Dirk nodded and gave up his binoculars and his post by the window to Gwen, and very soon they were talking of other things.

On the seventh day the late-night watch fell to Dirk and Jaan Vikary. The Kavalar city wore its dull nighttime glow, the glowstone boulevards like sheets of black crystal beneath which red fires burned dimly, dimly. Near to midnight a light appeared over the mountains. Dirk studied it as it flew toward the city. "I don't know," he said, holding the binoculars. "It's dark, hard to make out. I think I can see the vague outline of a dome, though." He lowered his glasses. "Lorimaar?"

Vikary stood over him. The aircar grew closer. It slid silently above the city, and its silhouette was distinct. "It is his car," Jaan said.

They watched it veer out over the Common and circle back, heading for the cliff face and the entrance to the underground airlot. Vikary looked thoughtful. "I would not have believed it," he said. They went down to rouse the others.

The man emerged from the darkness of the undertubes to find himself facing two lasers. Gwen had her pistol trained on him, almost casually. Dirk, armed with one of the hunting rifles, had aimed at the tube doors and stood with the sight pressed against his cheek, ready to fire. Only Jaan Vikary did not have a weapon out; he held his rifle loosely in his hands, and his sidearm was holstered.

The tube doors slid shut behind him, and the man stood very still, understandably frightened. It was not Lorimaar. It was not anyone Dirk knew. He lowered his rifle.

The man's eyes touched each of them in turn and finally settled on Vikary. "High-Ironjade," he said in a low voice. "Why do you accost me?" He was a medium-sized man, horse-faced and bearded, with long blond hair and a scrawny build. He was dressed in chameleon cloth that was somber red-gray now, flushed and feverish like the glowstone blocks of the pavement.

Vikary reached over and gently pushed Gwen's pistol to the side. The act seemed to wake her. She frowned and holstered her weapon. "We were expecting Lorimaar high-Braith," she said.

"The truth," Vikary affirmed. "No insult was intended, Shanagate. Honor to your holdfast, honor to your *teyn*."

The horse-faced man nodded and looked relieved. "And to yours, high-Ironjade," he said. "No insult was taken." He plucked at his nose nervously.

"You fly Braith property, do you not?"

He nodded. "In truth, and ours by right of salvage. My *teyn* and I stumbled on it in the wild while we pursued an ironhorn in flight. The creature stopped to drink, and there the car was, abandoned by a lake."

"Abandoned? Are you quite certain of that?"

The man laughed. "I know Lorimaar high-Braith

and fat Saanel too well, and take no chance of initiating high grievance with such as they. No, we found their bodies also. Some enemy had been waiting at their camp, inside the aircar we do believe, and when they returned from hunting . . ." He gestured. "They will take no more heads, mockman or otherwise."

"Dead?" Gwen's mouth was tight.

"Entirely dead, each for several days," the Kavalar replied. "Scavengers had descended on the corpses, of course, yet there was still enough left to determine who they had been. We found another aircar close at hand, in the lake itself, in truth, wrecked and useless, and also marks in the sand that indicated other cars had come and departed. Lorimaar's vehicle was still functional, though full of dead Braith hounds. We cleaned it out and claimed it. My *teyn* is following me in our own car."

Vikary nodded.

"These are very unusual events," the man was saying. He regarded the three of them shrewdly, with unconcealed interest. His gaze lingered for an uncomfortably long time on Dirk, and then on Gwen's black iron bracelet, but he commented on neither. "Few Braiths seem to be about of late, fewer than normal, and now we find two of them slain."

"If you search hard enough you'll find some others," Gwen said.

"They're starting a new holdfast," Dirk added, "in hell."

When the man had gone on his way they began the slow walk back to the watchtower. No one spoke. Long shadows grew from their feet and followed them down the somber crimson streets. Gwen walked as if she were exhausted. Vikary was almost jumpy; he carried his rifle warily, ready to snap it up and fire should Bretan Braith suddenly take form in their path, and his eyes probed every alley and dark place along their route.

Back in the brightness of the common room, Gwen and Dirk slumped quickly to the floor, while Jaan stood for a moment just inside the door, his face thoughtful. Then he set down his weapons and broke out a bottle of wine, the same pungent vintage that he had shared with Garse and Dirk the night before the duel that never was. He poured three glasses and handed them around. "Drink," he said, raising his own glass in a toast. "Things draw to a close. Now there is only Bretan Braith left. Soon he shall be with his Chell, or I shall be with Garse, and in either case we will have peace." He drained his glass very quickly. The others sipped.

"Ruark should drink with us," Vikary announced abruptly as he refilled his glass. The Kimdissi had not accompanied them to their midnight rendezvous. His reluctance had not seemed to be from fear, however; at least Dirk did not think so at the time. Jaan had gotten him up, and Ruark had dressed with the rest of them, slipping into his finest silkeen suit and a little scarlet beret, but when Vikary had handed him a rifle at the door he had only looked at it with a curious smile and handed it back. Then he had said, "I have my own code, Jaantony, and you must respect it. Thank you, but I think I will stay here." He delivered the statement with quiet dignity; beneath his white-blond hair his eyes looked almost cheerful. Jaan told him to continue the watch from the guard tower, and Ruark consented to that.

"Arkin hates Kavalar wine," Gwen said wearily to Jaan's suggestion.

"That is of no matter," Jaan replied. "This is a bonding between *kethi,* not a party. He should drink with us." He set down his wine glass and went up the ladder to the tower with easy grace.

When he returned an instant later, he was less graceful. He dropped the last meter and stood staring at them. "Ruark will not drink with us," he declared. "Ruark has hanged himself."

On that particular dawn, the eighth of their vigil, it was Dirk who went walking.

He did not go into Larteyn itself. Instead he walked the city walls. They were three meters across, black stone covered over by thick slabs of glowstone, so there was no danger of falling. Dirk was alone on watch (Gwen had cut down Ruark's body, and afterwards she had taken Jaan to bed), staring out on those walls with his laser uselessly in hand and his binoculars around his neck, when the first of the yellow suns came up and the fires of night began to fade. The urge had come upon him suddenly. Bretan Braith would not be coming back to the city, he knew; the watch was a useless formality now. He left his rifle leaning against the wall, next to the window, as he dressed warmly and went outside.

He walked a long way. Other guard towers much like their own stood at regular intervals. He passed six of them, and estimated the distance from tower to tower to be roughly a third of a kilometer. Every tower had its gargoyle, and none of the gargoyles were quite alike, he noticed. Now, after everything, he suddenly recognized them. They were untraditional, those gargoyles, not Old Earth cast at all; they were the demons of Kavalar myth, grotesque mythologized versions of dactyloids and Hruun and *githyanki* soulsucks. All real, in a sense. Somewhere among the stars, each of those races still lived.

The stars. Dirk paused and looked up. The Helleye had begun to edge above the horizon; most of the stars were gone already. He saw only one, very faint, a tiny red pinpoint framed by wisps of gray clouds. Even as he watched, it vanished. High Kavalaan's star, he thought. Garse Janacek had shown it to him, a beacon for his run.

There were too few stars out here anyway. These were no places for men to live, these worlds like Worlorn and High Kavalaan and Darkdawn, these outworlds. The Great Black Sea was too close on one hand, and the Tempter's Veil screened off most of the galaxy, and the skies were bleak and empty. A sky ought to have stars.

A man ought to have a code too. A friend, a *teyn,* a cause—something beyond himself.

Dirk walked to the outer edge of the walls and stood staring down. It was a long, *long* drop. The first time he had sailed over the wall, on a sky-scoot, he'd lost his balance just from looking at it. The walls went down a ways, and below them the cliff went down forever, and way at the bottom a river ran through greenery and morning mists.

He stood with his hands in his pockets, the winds ruffling his hair, shivering a bit. He stood and he looked. Then he took out his whisperjewel. He rubbed it between thumb and forefinger, as if it were a good luck charm. *Jenny,* he thought. Where had she gone? Even the jewel did not summon her back to him.

Footsteps sounded nearby, then a voice. "Honor to your holdfast, honor to your *teyn.*"

Dirk turned, the whisperjewel still in his hand. An old man was standing next to him. Tall as Jaan and old as poor dead Chell. He was massive and leonine, with a head of wild snow-white hair that blended into an equally stormy beard to form one magnificent mane. Yet his face was tired and faded, as if he had worn it a few centuries too long. Only his eyes stood out—intensely, insanely blue eyes, eyes like Garse Janacek once had, burning with icy fevers beneath his bushy brows.

"I have no holdfast," Dirk said, "and I have no *teyn.*"

"I'm sorry," the man said. "An offworlder, eh?"

Dirk bowed.

The old man chuckled. "Well, you haunt the wrong city then, ghost."

"Ghost?"

"A ghost of the Festival," the old man said. "What else could you be? This is Worlorn, and the living men have all gone home." He was wearing a black woolen cape with huge pockets, over garments of faded blue. A heavy disc of stainless steel hung just beneath his beard, suspended on a leather thong. When he took his hands from the pockets of his cape, Dirk saw that one of his fingers was missing. He wore no bracelets.

"You have no *teyn*," Dirk said.

The old man grumbled. "Of course I had a *teyn*, ghost. I was a poet, not a priest. What sort of a question is that? Beware. I might take insult."

"You wear no iron-and-fire," Dirk pointed out.

"Truth enough, yet what of it? Ghosts need no jewelry. My *teyn* is thirty years dead, haunting some holdfast back in Redsteel, I imagine, and I'm here haunting Worlorn. Well, only Larteyn, if truth be known. Haunting an entire planet would be rather exhausting."

"Oh," Dirk said, smiling. "Then you're a ghost too?"

"Well, yes," the old man replied. "Here I stand, talking with you for lack of a good chain to rattle. What do you think I am?"

"I think," Dirk said, "I think you just might be Kirak Redsteel Cavis."

"Kirak Redsteel Cavis," the old man repeated in a gruff singsong manner. "I know him. A ghost if there ever was one. His particular fate is to haunt the corpse of Kavalar poetry. He goes about at night moaning, and reciting lines from the laments of Jamis-Lion Taal and some of the better sonnets of Erik high-Ironjade Devlin. During the full moon he sings Braith battle chanteys and sometimes the old cannibal dirge from the Deep Coal Dwellings. A ghost, in truth, and a most pathetic one. When he especially wants to torment one of his victims, he recites some of his own verse. I assure you that once you have heard Kirak Redsteel read, you *pray* for rattling chains."

"Yes?" Dirk said. "I don't see why being a poet is quite so ghostly, in and of itself."

"Kirak Redsteel writes Old Kavalar poetry," the man said with a frown. "And *that* is enough. It is a dying language. So who will read what he writes? In his own holdfast, men grow up speaking only standard star-talk. Perhaps they will translate his poetry, but it is really hardly worth the effort, you know. In translation it does not rhyme, and the meter limps along like a broken-backed mockman. *None* of it is any good in translation, not a bit. The rattling cadences of Galen Glowstone, the sweet hymns of Laaris-Blind high-Kenn, all those dreary little Shanagates exalting the iron-and-fire, even the songs of the *eyn-kethi,* those hardly count as poetry at all. All dead, every bit of it, surviving only in Kirak Redsteel. Yes, the man is a ghost. Why else did he come to Worlorn? This is a world for ghosts." The old man tugged at his beard and regarded Dirk. "You are the ghost of some tourist, I would venture. No doubt you got lost while looking for a bathroom, and you have been wandering ever since."

"No," Dirk said, "no. I was looking for something else." He smiled and held up his whisperjewel.

The old man studied it, squinting his hard blue eyes while the cold wind flapped his cape. "Whatever it is, it is probably dead," he said. Far below them, down near the river that ran sparkling through the Common, a sound came drifting up: the faint, far-off wail of a banshee. Dirk's head snapped around, and he looked to see where the sound had come from. There was nothing, nothing—only the two of them standing on the wall, and the wind pulling at them, and the Helleye high in a twilight sky. No banshee. The time for banshees had passed here. They were all extinct.

"Dead?" Dirk said.

"Worlorn is full of dead things," the old man said, "and people looking for dead things, and ghosts." He mumbled something in Old Kavalar, something Dirk did not quite catch, and he began to move off slowly.

Dirk watched him go. He glanced toward the distant horizon, obscured by a bank of blue-gray clouds. Somewhere in that direction was the spacefield, and—he was certain—Bretan Braith. "Ah, Jenny," he said, talking to the whisperjewel. He flicked it out away from him, as a boy might skip a stone, and it went far and far before it began to fall. He thought for a moment of Gwen and Jaan, and for several moments of Garse.

Then he turned back to the old man, and called out after his retreating figure. "Ghost!" he shouted. "Wait. A favor for me, one ghost to another!"

The old man stopped.

EPILOGUE

It was a flat grassy place in the center of the Common, not very far from the spacefield. Once, in the days of the Festival, games had been held there, and athletes from eleven of the fourteen outworlds had competed for crowns of crystalline iron.

Dirk and Kirak Redsteel were there long before the appointed time, waiting.

When the hour drew near, Dirk began to worry. He needn't have. The aircar with the snarling wolf's-head canopy appeared in the sky just as predicted. It swept by once with its pulse tubes shrieking, a low pass to make sure that they were really there, and then came down for a landing.

Bretan Braith walked toward them over the dead brown grass, his black boots trampling a host of faded flowers. It was nearly dusk. His eye was beginning to glow.

"I was told the truth, then," Bretan said to Dirk,

with a touch of wonder in his rasping voice, the same voice that Dirk had heard so often in his nightmares, a voice several octaves too low and far too twisted for one as slim and straight as Bretan. "You are really here." The Braith stood several meters away, looking at them, infinitely pure, dressed in white dueling finery with a purple wolf-mask embroidered above his heart. His black belt carried two sidearms: a laser on his left side and a massive machine-pistol of blue-gray metal heavy on his right. His iron armlet was empty of glow-stones. "I did not believe the ancient Redsteel, if truth be known," he was saying. "Yet I thought, This place is so close, a check will do no harm. I can return to the port quickly enough should it prove a lie."

Kirak Redsteel got down on his knees and began to chalk a square out in the grass.

"You presume that I will honor you in duel," Bretan said. "I have no cause to do so." He moved his right hand and suddenly Dirk was facing the barrel of his machine-pistol. "Why should I not kill you? Here and now?"

Dirk shrugged. "Kill me if you like," he said, "but answer some questions first."

Bretan stared and said nothing.

"If I had come to you in Challenge," Dirk said, "if I had come down into the basement, as you wanted, would you have dueled me then? Or killed me for a mockman?"

Bretan slid his weapon back into its holster. "I would have dueled you. In Larteyn, in Challenge, here—it makes no difference. I would have dueled you. I do not believe in mockmen, t'Larien. I have never be-lieved in mockmen. Only in Chell, who wore my bond and somehow did not care about my face."

"Yes," Dirk said. Kirak Redsteel had the death-square half complete. Dirk glanced up at the sky and wondered how much time was left. "And one other thing, Bretan Braith. How did you know to look for us in Challenge, in that one city out of all the others?"

Bretan shrugged his awkward shrug. "The Kimdissi

told me, for a price. All Kimdissi can be bought. He had planted a tracer in a coat he gave you. I believe he used such tracers in his work."

"What was the price?" Dirk asked. Three sides of the square were drawn, white lines on the grass.

"I gave my honor-bond that I would do no harm to Gwen Delvano, and would protect her against all the others." The last rays of sunlight were fading; the trailing yellow sun had joined the others below the mountains. "Now," Bretan continued, "I have a question for you, t'Larien. Why have you come to me?"

Dirk smiled. "Because I like you, Bretan Braith. You burned down Kryne Lamiya, didn't you?"

"In truth," Bretan said. "I hoped to burn you as well, and Jaantony high-Ironjade, the outbonder. Does he still live?"

Dirk did not answer that question.

Kirak Redsteel rose and brushed the chalk from his hands, the square complete. He brought out the matched blades; straight sabers of Kavalar steel, with glowstones and jade set in the ornate pommels. Bretan chose one and tested it—it moved through the air with a song and a shriek—then stepped back, satisfied, to one corner of the square. He was very still as he waited; for an instant he appeared almost serene, a slim black figure leaning ever so slightly on his sword. Like the bargeman, Dirk thought, and despite himself he glanced wildly at the wolf-car to make certain it had not been transformed into a low barge. His heart was beating hard.

He pushed the thought aside, took the other blade, and retreated in turn. Kirak Redsteel smiled at him. It will be easy, Dirk told himself. He tried to remember the advice that Garse Ironjade had given him so long ago. Take one blow and give one, that's all, he said to himself. He was very frightened.

Bretan tossed his sidearms on the ground outside the death-square and moved the saber back and forth again, unlimbering his arm. Even across the seven meters that separated them, Dirk could see the twitch of his face.

Above Bretan's right shoulder a star was rising. Blue-white and large and very close, creeping up the black velvet sky toward zenith. And beyond the zenith, Dirk thought, to Eshellin and ai-Emerel and the World of the Blackwine Ocean. He wished them luck.

Kirak Cavis stepped outside the death-square and said a word in Old Kavalar. Bretan started forward, moving gracefully, light on his feet, very white, his eye glowing.

Dirk grinned the way Garse would have grinned, tossed the hair back out of his eyes, and went to him. No starlight ran down his blade as he lifted it and reached out to touch Bretan's. The wind was blowing. It was very cold.

GLOSSARY

ai. After interregnum.

ai-Emerel. Human world on the Fringe, settled shortly after the interregnum (hence, *ai-*) by arcologites from Daronne. Emereli civilization is technologically advanced, cultured, pacifist, but static and somewhat regimented. Citizens live in kilometer-high tower-cities (arcologies) surrounded by farmland and wilderness, but most never leave the buildings they are born in. The discontented are allowed to serve in ai-Emerel's merchant starfleet, but may not return to their home towers.

Altered Men. Genetically altered humans of the world Prometheus. The Promethean surgeons experiment constantly; thus there are many varieties of Altered Men. In common parlance the term is often used to denote all Prometheans.

Avalon. Human world in the jambles, colonized by

Newholme during the first century of the Federal Empire. A sector capital during the Double War, Avalon never lost starflight and played a large role in ending the interregnum through its vigorous program of exploration, trade, and re-education. Afterwards it became a center of learning. The Academy of Human Knowledge and its many associated institutes are located on Avalon. Avalon is also an important commercial center, with the largest trading fleet in the jambles. Ships from Avalon often trade for knowledge as well as goods.

Bakkalon. Deity worshiped by the Steel Angels, often depicted as a naked human infant holding a black sword; also called *the pale child*.

Baldur. First-generation human colony settled directly from Earth in the earliest years of starflight. A sector capital during the Double War, now an important center of trade.

banshee. Also known as *black banshee;* an aerial predator native to High Kavalaan.

Bastion. Human world in the jambles, details of settlement unknown. Bastion was once a human colony, then taken by the Hrangans during the Double War, finally retaken by humans, and today ruled by the Steel Angels, who have made it their capital.

betheyn. Kavalar term for a woman bonded to a man and under his protection; literally, *heldwife*.

Blackwiner. Native of the World of the Blackwine Ocean.

Braith. One of the four modern holdfast-coalitions of of High Kavalaan. Braith is generally conceded to be the most traditional of the four. Also, any member of holdfast Braith.

Braque. Human world near the Tempter's Veil, on the the outermost edge of the jambles. Braque is primitive and superstitious, ruled by a priesthood that strictly controls technology.

Bronzefist. Extinct holdfast-coalition of High Kavalaan.

Challenge. Festival city built on Worlorn by ai-Emerel. Challenge is an automated computer-operated self-contained arcology.

chokers. Common species of Toberian tree.

City in the Starless Pool. Festival city built on Worlorn, beneath the waters of an artificial lake, by the World of the Blackwine Ocean.

collapse. The period in which the Federal Empire of Old Earth disintegrated and fell. Dates for the collapse are difficult to fix; war had made communications between worlds even more chaotic than usual, and each planet experienced the collapse in its own ways and in its own time. Most historians cite the revolt on Thor and the destruction of Wellington as the key events in the Federal Empire's fall, but point out that the Empire had been a thin fiction for centuries before that as far as the more distant colonies were concerned.

cro-betheyn. Kavalar term for a *betheyn*'s bond to her highbond's *teyn;* literally, *shared heldwife*.

dactyloids. Human term for a winged Hrangan slave-race employed as shock troops during the Double War, given to the creatures because of their vague likeness to pterodactyls of Old Earth pre-history. Dactyloids were savage, but small-brained and only semi-sentient.

Darkdawn. Human world in the Fringe, close to the edge of intergalactic space. After Darkdawn there is nothing; winter skies are empty but for the light of the distant galaxies. Darkdawn is thinly populated, solitary, and haven to a number of strange religious cults. Weather control has been perfected to a fine art, but otherwise technology is de-emphasized.

Darklings. Residents of Darkdawn.

Daronne. Human world of the jambles, close to the Tempter's Veil. Colonized at least three times by aliens and twice by humans, Daronne is a patchwork of esoteric cultures.

Deep Coal Dwellings. Mythological holdfast-coalition of High Kavalaan, said to exist in ancient times. The folk of the Deep Coal Dwellings were cannibals who preyed on the other holdfasts until destroyed in war. They were alleged to be half human, half demon.

Double War. Centuries-long conflict between the Federal Empire and two alien races, the Fyndii and the Hrangans. Also known as the *Great War,* the *Fyndiin War,* the *Hrangan Conflict,* the *Thousand-Years War,* or simply as *the War.* In many ways the Double War was in reality two conflicts; the enemies never had any contact with each other and were in no sense allies, though both were engaged in warfare against humanity. The Federal Empire occupied the space between the two enemies, and thus fought on two fronts; the Fyndii hordes were inward toward the Core, the so-called Hrangan Empire outward toward the galactic fringe. The war against the Fyndii began first, and was generally a shorter and cleaner conflict, finally resolved through negotiations and the intervention of a third alien race, the Damoosh. The Hrangans were considerably less understandable and much more inimicable to humanity. Hostilities never officially ended between Hranga and Earth; both civilizations collapsed. Humanity underwent the interregnum and recovered, although never again as a single political unit. The Hrangans suffered virtual genocide at the hands of their own slaveraces and human colonials.

Earth Imperials. Originally, administrators sent out from Earth during the heyday of the Federal Empire. After the interregnum, commonly used to refer to any human who lived during the Empire period.

Emereli. Natives of ai-Emerel.

Erikan. Human world named after the religious leader Erika Stormjones, settled by her followers and dedicated to the precepts she espoused, notably immortality through cloning.

Eshellin. Human world on the Fringe, settled by a migration from Daronne. Relatively primitive and sparsely populated.

Esvoch. Festival city built by Eshellin.

eyn-kethi. Kavalar term for the breeding women of a holdfast, who are sexually available to all men; literally, *bonded-to-the-holdfast-brothers*.

Fat Satan. Red supergiant located beyond the Tempter's Veil, notable for the six yellow suns that circle it in a Trojan relationship to each other; the entire system is called the Wheel of Fire. Some speculate that the Wheel was created by a race of vanished superbeings capable of moving suns. Fat Satan is also known as *the Helleye* and *the Hub*.

Federal Empire. Political unit that ruled human space during the early centuries of starflight, colonized most of the first- and second-generation worlds and some of the third, and conducted the Double War, during the course of which it finally collapsed. The term itself was a convenient misnomer; the so-called empire was more correctly a democratic-socialist-cybernetic bureaucracy. The ultimate decision maker was the Chief Administrator, who was elected by and responsible to a tricameral legislature meeting in Geneva, Old Earth, but most of the day-to-day administration on Earth itself was conducted by the Artificial Intelligences, vast computer constructs. In the waning years of the Double War, the Federal Empire grew increasingly repressive and lost touch with its own colonies and even with its military arms.

FTL. Faster than light.

Fyndii. Alien race, and the first star-traveling sentients to make contact with humanity. The Fyndii were one of the enemies the Federal Empire faced in the Double War. Fyndii seem to feel almost no race loyalty; their societies are made up of empathically linked "hordes," and each horde is a bitter rival of all the others. Mindmutes, incapable of linking, are friendless outcasts. The Fyndii rule approximately ninety worlds, generally inward from the worlds colonized by men.

githyanki. Hrangan slaverace, often termed *soulsucks* by humans. Barely sentient, malevolent, and potent telepaths, the *githyanki* were capable of bending and twisting human minds, sending false visions, hallucinations, and dreams, strengthening the animal side of man and warping judgment and reason, all for the end of turning brother against sister.

glowstone. Stone native to High Kavalaan, capable of storing light and emitting it in darkness. Glowstone is used for both building and jewelry, and is an important Kavalar export.

Glowstone Mountain. One of the greatest holdfast-coalitions in Kavalar history, finally defeated and destroyed by its enemies, now abandoned.

Great Black Sea. Outworld term for the space between the galaxies, where there are no stars.

Haapala's City. Festival city built by Wolfheim and named after Ingo Haapala, the Wolfman astronomer who first discovered that Worlorn would pass through the Wheel of Fire.

Hellcrown. One name of the six yellow stars (collectively) that circle the red supergiant sometimes called *the Helleye,* and together with it form the Wheel of Fire. Also known as *Satan's Children,* and *the Trojan Suns.* The six stars are virtually identical, and orbit in a Trojan relationship to each other.

Helleye. See Fat Satan.

High Kavalaan. Human world on the Fringe, colonized during the Double War by refugees and miners from Tara. Hrangan raids destroyed most of the original colony; survivors evolved modern Kavalar holdfast civilization. Kavalar society is regimented and individualistic at the same time; the culture places strong emphasis on both loyalty and personal honor. Close to barbaric when rediscovered by traders, the Kavalars are now industrializing rapidly, educating their young, and acquiring their own fleet of starships. High Kavalaan, which claims legal jurisdiction over the rogue planet Worlorn, was one of the driving forces in the Festival of the Fringe.

holdfast. Basic social unit of High Kavalaan; an underground chamber or series of chambers, easily defensible from attack, that provides shelter for anywhere from six to one hundred people. In ancient times each holdfast was an independent entity, a combination of family and nation. Soon, however, holdfasts began to make alliances and merge with other holdfasts, and even connect up underground; these were called holdfast-coalitions. In modern times the term *holdfast* is often used loosely to signify what might more properly be called a holdfast-coalition.

Hrangans. Humanity's great enemy during the Double War, the Hrangans were perhaps the most alien sentients ever encountered. Their social system was structured on the basis of a number of biological castes, most of whom seemed to belong to different species, so different were they. Of the Hrangan millions, only the so-called Minds were truly intelligent, and mankind never communicated successfully even with them. The Hrangans were bitterly xenophobic; prior to the Double War, they had enslaved a dozen less-advanced races, and there is evidence that they had exterminated others entirely. The war effectively destroyed the Hrangans, except on Old Hranga itself and a handful of their oldest colonies.

Hruun. Hrangan slaverace often used in combat during the Double War. The Hruun were more intelligent than most other Hrangan slaves. Their homeworld was a heavy-gravity planet by human standards, so the Hruun were warriors of immense strength. Among their other attributes was an ability to see well into the infrared that made them especially suited for nocturnal combat.

Hub. See Fat Satan.

interregnum. Historical period between the collapse and the resumption of starflight. By its very nature, the interregnum is difficult to date precisely. Some worlds experienced the collapse early, some late; some lost starflight for five years, some for fifty, some for five hundred; some—like Avalon, Baldur, Newholme, and Old Earth—were never really isolated from the rest of mankind, while others perhaps have still not been rediscovered. It is commonly said that the interregnum lasted a "generation"; this is workable enough as a rough approximation, if only the major human worlds are considered.

Ironjade Gathering. One of the four modern holdfast-coalitions of High Kavalaan. The Ironjade Gathering is one of the two most progressive Kavalar holdfasts.

jambles. Wolfman slang, now common parlance in the outworlds, for the area of space between the Fringe and the highly civilized worlds around Old Earth. The Hrangan Empire occupied a large portion of what is now called the jambles, and it was there that the most terrible actions of the Double War took place, leaving many planets ruined and many civilizations broken and "jumbled," from which word the term derived. Notable human worlds in the jambles include Avalon, Bastion, Prometheus, and Jamison's World.

Jamison's World. Human world in the jambles, settled chiefly from Old Poseidon. Jamies live on the planet's lush islands and archipelagoes; the one large continent is largely unexplored. Jamison's World is a regional center for industry and trade, and is a commercial rival of Avalon.

Kavalar. Native of High Kavalaan.

Kenn. Extinct Kavalar holdfast-coalition.

keth, kethi. Kavalar term for the males of any holdfast or holdfast coalition; literally, *holdfast-brother*(s).

Kimdiss. Human world of the Fringe, settled by a group of religious pacifists, now the major outworld commercial power. Kimdissi are traditionally nonviolent, and consequently hostile to the code duello of High Kavalaan.

Kimdissi. Natives of Kimdiss.

korariel. Kavalar term, literally *protected property*. Originally used by individuals and holdfasts to designate certain mockmen or groups of mockmen as private game; poachers were subject to challenge and duel. Later used by the more progressive holdfasts to protect primitives from extermination at the hands of traditional Kavalar hunters. Properly, the term cannot be applied to a real human, only to a mockman or animal.

Kryne Lamiya. Festival city built on Worlorn by Darkdawn. Often called the Siren City, Kryne Lamiya was designed so that its towers made music of the controlled mountain winds, thus playing over and over a symphony by Darkdawn's leading composer, the nihilist Lamiya-Bailis.

Larteyn. Festival city built into the mountainwall of Worlorn by High Kavalaan. Larteyn, literally, means *bonded-to-the-sky,* or *sky-teyn.* The city was fashioned to a great extent of glowstone, and thus was often called the Firefort.

Letheland. One common name for a primitive human colony in the Fringe. Also known as the *Forgotten Colony,* or the *Lost Colony*. All of these terms are offworld in origin; the Lostfolk themselves call their planet

Earth. Letheland is the oldest human world beyond the Tempter's Veil, so old that all details of its settlement have been lost, and only conjecture remains. Its people are largely fisherfolk, with no interest in any way of life besides their own.

Musquel-by-the-Sea. Festival city patterned on those of Letheland, erected on Worlorn by a coalition of outworlders for the Forgotten Colony, which did not have the technology to build it so quickly. A weathered port of multicolored brick and wood, Musquel proved one of the Festival's most popular attractions.

Newholme. First interstellar human colony; an urbanized, overcrowded, highly technological world only 4.3 light-years from Old Earth. Since the interregnum and the isolation of Old Earth, Newholme is commonly regarded as the most advanced human world, and the center of commercial traffic between the stars. Newholme is also the nominal capital of the so-called Union of Humanity, a political unit that claims jurisdiction over mankind everywhere. Only three worlds beyond Newholme acknowledge this authority, however, so the Union is essentially a fiction.

not-men. Human beings who have evolved or mutated so far that they are no longer interfertile with the rest of the race.

Old Earth. Homeworld of the human race, formerly the capital of the Federal Empire. During the interregnum, and after the revolt of sizable portions of its armed forces, Old Earth recalled the remainder of its military and sealed itself off from the rest of humanity. The embargo remains in effect, with only a few exceptions. There are many legends and much conjecture about life on Old Earth today, but few facts. Also known as *Earth, Terra, Home.*

Old Hranga. Homeworld of the Hrangan race, and one of the few places where Hrangan Minds survive in numbers.

Old Poseidon. Third-generation human world settled early in the Federal period. A planet of turbulent seas and untold riches, Old Poseidon soon became an important trading center and a sector capital. After less than a century, the Poseidonites themselves were building starships and exporting colonists; they settled more than twenty other planets, including Jamison's World.

outworlds. Collective term for all the worlds of the Fringe; i.e., those fourteen human colonies between the Tempter's Veil and the Great Black Sea. Natives of any of these planets were commonly called *outworlders* by humans within the Veil.

Prometheus. Human world in the jambles, colonized by a military arm of the Federal Empire called the Ecological Warfare Corps during the Double War. Located deep within the war zone and the Hrangan sphere of influence, Prometheus was the headquarters for the biowar ships that spread disease, insects, and plant and animal pests among the Hrangans. After the collapse, Prometheus recovered starflight quickly, and also retained and developed techniques of cloning and genetic manipulation that had been closely guarded secrets of the Federal Empire. One of the most powerful human worlds of the jambles, Prometheus is de facto ruler of its closest neighbors, Rhiannon and Thisrock, and strongly influential on a number of other planets. See also Altered Men.

Redsteel. One of the four modern holdfast-coalitions of High Kavalaan. Redsteel is considered one of the two most progressive of the four. Also, any member of holdfast Redsteel.

Rhiannon. Human world in the jambles, colonized by Deirdre during the middle period of the Federal Empire. A rich pastoral world, Rhiannon today is ruled by Prometheus in all but name, and has no starships of its own.

Rogue's Hope. Human world in the Celian cluster, formerly a sector capital.

Rommel. Cold heavy-gravity planet colonized directly from Earth very early in the Federal period. Rommel and Wellington, its sister planet in the same system, began as unpleasant prison planets for incorrigibles from Earth, but during the Double War the two became the so-called *War Worlds* from which the Earth Imperials drew most of their assault squads. War Worlders, as troopers from Rommel and Wellington were called collectively, lived all their lives under a rigid military discipline, and were given drugs and special reaction training to enhance their fighting prowess. Ultimately, genetic alterations turned the War Worlders into *not-men*, unable to interbreed with other humans. Rommel lost starflight during the collapse and has never regained it. Traders avoid the world; Rommelans are considered inhuman and dangerous.

Satan's Children. See Hellcrown.

Shanagate Holding. One of the four modern holdfast-coalitions of High Kavalaan.

Son of the Dreamer. Religious leader who lived on Deirdre in the middle Federal period. The Son of the Dreamer preached a creed of physical pacifism and psychological aggression, and told his followers to resist their enemies with wit instead of force. Today his teachings are influential on Kimdiss, Kayan, Tamber, and several other worlds.

soulsuck. See githyanki.

standard. Monetary unit widely used in interstellar commerce, and on almost all of the most important human worlds. Also the language of such commerce and most star-traveling humans, also called *Terran, Standard Terran, Earthic, Common.* Also used as an adjective to denote units of time corresponding with those of Old Earth. Thus, standard hour, standard day, standard year, etc.

Steel Angels. Popular nickname for members of a powerful and widespread military-religious movement that developed among Federal Empire soldiers during the Double War, and has persisted and grown since. The Steel Angels believe that only humans (the seed of Earth) have souls, that race survival is the ultimate imperative, that strength is the only true virtue. Today, from their capital on Bastion, the Angels rule a dozen planets and have colonies, missions, and footholds on hundreds more. The members of the cult call themselves the *Children of Bakkalon*. Exact origins of the movement are in dispute. The Angels have had two major schisms and have conducted numerous wars, chiefly against non-human sentients.

Stormjones. Primitive planet in the Celian cluster named after the religious leader Erika Stormjones. See also Erikan.

Taal. Extinct holdfast-coalition of High Kavalaan.

Tara. Human world near the Tempter's Veil, on the outermost edge of the jambles. Tara was colonized at least five times by migrations from quite disparate worlds, and was also raided repeatedly during the Double War, so today it is home to many strange splinter cultures. The dominant influences, however, are both rooted in the first settlement: the Irish-Roman Reformed Catholic Church, and the hereditary warrior-ruler called the Cuchulainn.

Tempter's Veil. Cloud of interstellar dust and gas near the top of the galactic lens that blocks the Wheel of Fire and other outworld stars from view; the boundary between the Fringe and the jambles.

teyn. Kavalar term for a man bonded to another man, usually for life, in a co-equal relationship; the closest possible relationship between Kavalars; literally, *my-bond* or *close-bond* or *holdclose*.

Thisrock. Artificial world between Prometheus and Rhiannon created by the Federal Empire for use as a naval strikebase during the Double War. Thisrock is located in deep space, orbits no star, and is quite small, in some ways more like a large stationary starship than a real world. Today dominated by Prometheus.

Tober-in-the-Veil. Human world on the outer edge of the Tempter's Veil, generally considered to be part of the Fringe. Tober was discovered and settled during the Collapse by the Avalon-based 17th Human Fleet, in rebellion against the Federal Empire. The Toberians are the most technologically advanced of the outworld cultures, and have developed energy shielding and pseudomatter past even Federal levels. Tober maintains a strong military arm, and is influential on several of the more primitive Fringe planets.

tree-spook. A small predatory rodent native to Kimdiss, so called because it sheds its skin several times before maturity, and leaves the transparent husk around its nest to frighten away enemies.

Trojan Suns. See Hellcrown.

Twelfth Dream. Festival city built on Worlorn by Kimdiss. Twelfth Dream was considered by sophisticates to be the most aesthetic of the fourteen cities erected for the Festival of the Fringe. Its name derives from Kimdissi religion; the universe and all that is in it is believed to have been created by the Dreamer, whose twelfth dream was Beauty Unsurpassed.

Wellington. Warm heavy-gravity world colonized directly from Earth early in the Federal period as a penal colony. Wellington and its sister planet, Rommel, later became the *War Worlds* that supplied the fierce assault squad troopers of the Federal Empire. See also Rommel. All life on Wellington was destroyed late in the Double War, when the 13th Human Fleet under Stephen Cobalt Northstar rebelled against the Federal Empire. The event is often cited as the beginning of the collapse.

Wheel of Fire. Collective name for the seven-sun multiple-star system located in the Fringe, behind the Tempter's Veil. The Wheel is considered by some to be an artificial monument to a vanished race of superbeings. See also Fat Satan, Hellcrown.

whisperjewel. A crystal that has been psionically "etched" to retain certain emotions or thoughts, which are thereafter perceptible when the crystal is held by "resonant" or sympathetic minds. Any type of crystal may be fashioned into a whisperjewel, but certain kinds of gemstones retain the patterns far better than others. The strength and clarity of a whisperjewel may also vary with time, and with the degree of skill of the etching esper. The whisperjewels of Avalon are highly esteemed; Avalon has both a suitable base-crystal and a number of potent Talents. Some less developed worlds are reputed to produce even finer whisperjewels, but their products seldom find their way onto the interstellar market.

Wolfheim. Human world in the Fringe, settled during the collapse by refugees from Fenris. Wolfheim culture is considered dynamic and volatile; the planet is a strong economic rival to Kimdiss, and militarily second only to Tober among the outworlds.

Wolfman. A native of Wolfheim.

World of the Blackwine Ocean. Human world on the Fringe, settled in ai-137 from Old Poseidon.

Worlorn. Rogue planet first discovered by Celia Marcyan; site of the Festival of the Fringe, ai-589 to ai-599, while passing near to the Wheel of Fire.